SPEAKING DAGGERS

Lloyd Rees

Print ISBN 9780957245976

Published by
Llyfrau Cambria Books, Wales, United Kingdom.
*Cambria Books is a division of
Cambria Publishing.*
Discover our other books at: www.cambriabooks.co.uk

For Jasper and Harri

About the Author

Lloyd Rees was educated at Sussex University, where he took a Masters degree in English, and Swansea University, where he took a Masters degree in Education. He taught English at secondary level and then at undergraduate level. He became the Head of English and initiated the Creative Writing programme at Swansea Metropolitan University. He has been shortlisted for a number of awards for his poetry and fiction.

1

A man is sitting on his haunches, a position aped by his cross-breed collie. They are both patient and used to the rain. The dog emits a low growl, a sort of canine murmur.

'Easy, Prince,' the man says. 'Don't worry, nothing to be afraid of. It's just a drunk going home.'

The dog growls again as a figure cuts a diagonal path across the heart of the city. He is no danger to the man and his dog, but he will bring heartache and terror to young women. At the moment, however, he is an invisible nobody. He slides down the Kingsway, an artery that slices through the city from the suburbs of the west to the heart of the city, like a spreading stain. He pauses for a moment and lowers his head as a taxi swooshes past through the rain. The cabbie will be interviewed in a few days' time and say that he saw a couple of people as he was going home at the end of a long slow shift. This was at about two o'clock. He would not be able to describe either in any detail. As the tail lights fade to a fuzzy red in the misty downpour, the man on foot crosses the dual carriageway and, head still lowered, walks more briskly now towards Lower Oxford Street. Though the maze of little side streets that lead off from there is known as The Sandfields, the beach is another hundred yards to the south and there have been no fields hereabouts for a couple of centuries. It is an area that is populated by old working-class couples. This is where people's grandparents live, in their honeycomb cell of two up, two down penury, but there are a few larger houses too. Some of these have attic conversions with box windows or even the occasional new Velux window. These houses have been split into flats and bedsits, and it is to one of these that the unnoticed figure is headed. The other tenants are fast asleep and do not hear the key in the Yale lock click or the door softly closing.

***

Gus Reid's arm flailed out across the pillow next to his head. If he had not been alone a partner would have been slapped full in the face. The sudden spasm roused him from deep sleep to a second of near wakefulness. He examined the green digits of his radio alarm – and alarm was the right word for it too because the siren it emitted was enough to panic the deepest sleeper – and was comforted. Only 6.53. It was not that awful sound that had woken him, but some night terror or bad dream, he supposed. He found he was waking up at odd times these days, though of course he was rational enough, boring enough, Adele had often claimed, to recognise that no number is odd in the sense of unusual, it was just a number.

For much of his life he had been the soundest of sleepers and regularly awoke at exactly seven twenty. He was almost proud of this fact, liked the exactness, and pleased with himself because he had managed to engineer it. He had come to know that he tended to wake a minute before his alarm went off, so he simply set the time for 7.21. These days, however, he found himself staring at the baleful green numbers at all sorts of random times – twenty past three, eight minutes past four – and he was always tired, but apparently not tired enough to sleep. The knowledge that things changed when you got older was unpleasant, like a vague ache in the abdomen. Not a pain, but a prefiguring of it.

It was still dark of course. Gus sighed and let one leg dangle out of the bed, almost as if testing what it would feel like on this new planet, Monday morning. His toe touched the thick carpet, a luxury he had permitted himself that was not in keeping with the Spartan tone of the rest of his flat, and the toe sent a signal to the rest of his body that it was safe to emerge. He unfolded himself from the bed, groaning as he did so, and made for the door. He did not put a light on till he got to the bathroom and the sudden brightness when he pulled the light cord there made him lose concentration as he urinated. He rolled off some toilet paper and dabbed at the wooden floor where he had missed, feeling a boyish guilt, though no one would ever know, of course.

Then it was time to study today's face in the shaving mirror. The stranger there stared back at him dolefully. He was getting older. He pushed at a fold of flesh under his chin. Maybe time to grow a goatee.

Grey beards were acceptable for men in their fifties, though not as dignifying for someone in his position perhaps. If he was a teacher or a tax inspector it would be part of the uniform but somehow people were more likely to be suspicious of police officers with facial hair. He tried to smile at his reflection. The stranger, or old acquaintance now, winced back. Then he started shaving, a task he had hated for nearly forty years. He used an old-fashioned razor, a chrome affair with a single blade, not one of the plastic handled throwaways that had two or even three blades. It rubbed rather than glided but this had the advantage of inducing a pinkish glow into his face. He was glad to see the sallowness that he had had to look at a few moments before fading to a more human complexion.

Breakfast had to be porridge. His friend Tony, whom he had known since he was at school a thousand years ago, insisted that porridge was essential and it didn't matter if you were pathetic and claimed you didn't like oats. It was healthy, got the metabolism going, it was one of the five fists of food you needed to function properly but not gain weight. Gus had been gaining weight over the last twenty years, a pound a year, which Robert de Niro had claimed in *Cape Fear* was the inevitable lot of men past thirty. Tony told him that that was just a film and he needed to stick with the porridge in the morning, preferably with some ground nuts and blueberries. Gus preferred a cup of coffee, and a sad reminiscence about the Lambert and Butler cigarettes he had finally given up two years ago. Back then he could smoke three or four cigarettes before work and then realise he was suddenly, and for no apparent reason, running late. Today, however, he had nothing but time on his hands, so he found a sachet of Quaker Oats in the kitchen cupboard, emptied it into a bowl, and microwaved it. He would not even have known where to shop for ground nuts or blueberries. Feeling stupid, he bent down to watch the bowl turning slowly around on its turntable behind the wire mesh of the screen on the door. It took an age to ping and then the bowl was too hot to remove. Gus growled at himself to pull himself together. He was a senior officer in the South Wales Constabulary; he would not let himself be baffled by a shaving mirror or bemused by a microwave oven.

But he was not as senior as he might have expected to be by this age. He located a tea towel in a kitchen drawer in order to remove the hot bowl of porridge from the microwave. He was an inspector, but he had held that position for over twenty years. At the age of thirty he had envisaged an inevitable rise to Chief Super at least, but somehow his career had stalled, probably because he was not silver tongued and well connected, like the graduates who overtook him on the greasy pole. But at least he was CID and spared the politics, and the PR. And the dress uniform. He looked down at the tea towel. It was ancient, a relic from his marriage, and was intended to be humorous. It bore the legend 'As one door closes, so does another.' Now it was just sad, faded, a bit like its owner. But Gus wasn't really sad. He was, in his view, sardonic about the turn his life had taken. His marriage had lasted twenty years, which was eight years longer than the national average. The last eight he had trudged through like a muddied infantryman 'for the sake of the kids'. Adele herself, who always alleged she was the grownup, had turned into a big Trumpian baby, with her lying and cheating and her screaming tantrums. But the kids didn't thank him for serving out the extra eight years. 'You should have got divorced years before,' Josie said. 'It would have been kinder to everybody.' Gus had claimed that he had always been afraid of losing touch with her and her brother. 'We're not in touch now, are we, hardly?' she'd said.

He looked out of the living room window to see if his car windscreen needed de-icing. It had been raining, but the morning looked like it would brighten into one of those crisp January days that he had started to appreciate in latter years. A robin was staring at him from the gatepost. Life wasn't so bad. There was an unopened pack of cigarettes in the glove compartment but it could stay there. He turned away from the window to look back at his living room. He surveyed the empty walls and remembered the watercolours of nature scenes that had festooned the walls of his marital home. He didn't miss those. He had never been lucky with plants, or so he had told himself, and he had no greenery to brighten the place. On a coffee table by the television set in one corner there was a photograph of Josie, taken when she was a goofy thirteen-year-old. On the opposite wall there was a bookcase with paperbacks arranged alphabetically. Douglas Adams at one end of the top shelf, Zola's *Thérèse Raquin* in

4

the bottom right-hand corner. Apart from a couple of red cushions on the settee the spines of the paperbacks offered the only colour in the room. The carpet, curtains and settee and chairs were all in shades of grey. That was alright though. Gus liked grey.

With any luck the weekend would have passed with no great mysteries to solve, just the normal couple of burglaries and the odd actual bodily harm. Stuff that Willis and the constables could take care of without need for any of his cajoling or shepherding. He still had that report to complete for the inquest on the code blue with police contact.

2

Hamlet is the sanest character I've ever come across. They think he's mad because he sees things in words, not pictures. I'm the same, in my own little way, and I'll show them. Hence my message.

They'll think that he's clinically insane of course, the man who could have done those things. To such a sweet young creature. I can see them trotting out the school photo where she's all eyes and hair and butter wouldn't melt. Oh, and the bleary-eyed relatives who just don't understand. They'll all be looking for motives. Oh, the clichés! What if they profile the perpetrator (huh!) and there's nothing rational there? Clearly a man, but just a motiveless malignity, as they say. The dishevelled detective with his eye for the tiny fragment of a note poking out from under the settee; the bluff young constable, no, sergeant probably, who has to have it explained to him. They have to deal in motives and opportunities, and what's the other one? Means, of course. Order and procedure, logic and deduction. Clues to be unravelled, like the sleeve of care. It's like they're walking through an art gallery and there's pictures everywhere, but only some of them are worth looking at. They have to decide which to dwell on, which to ignore. But they're only pictures. Hamlet knew. You have to listen to the words, their music, their syncopation, but they've forgotten to read and to hear. Language has been texted to death. But Plod and his mini-plod will be looking for sense. Motive. If it's random, where would we all be? Swirling around in an unplotted universe like goldfish. Mood movement for dentists' surgeries. They wouldn't like that much. I'll show them, I'll show them all.

Oh but she did look so small and frail as I laid her to rest. The bitch.

3

It was eight o'clock exactly as Gus walked into Swansea Central police station, a piece of brick and glass functional but unlovely architecture that had replaced the old fire station on Alexandra Road a couple of decades ago. His mobile phone was vibrating in his pocket but as he was reaching for it he saw Sergeant Ben Willis approaching him with his mobile to his ear. He had a serious face with a rather long nose and heavy eyebrows. He was not exactly handsome, but he was tall and erect and doubtless a catch for a young woman who desired to be looked after, to be respected, to be taken seriously. He also had the sort of pale blue eyes that Gus associated with aspiring actors' publicity shots. The younger man sighed and dropped his hand, pressing a button on the phone as he did so. The buzzing in Gus's pocket stopped and Gus was about to say something – the word 'serendipity' was on his lips, though he wasn't even quite certain what it meant – but he was prevented from speaking by Willis' expression.

'What's happened?' Gus said, his voice lowered in expectation of some awful family tragedy.

'We've had a call about a body. It just came in. I was ringing you.'

'I could see that, but I'm here standing in front of you. Tell me.'

'We'd better go into your office,' Willis said. Gus looked round and saw that two uniformed officers and a secretary were looking at them, all three of them paused from whatever it was they had been doing a moment before.

'Anybody done anything yet? Where's the body?' Gus was suddenly alive and alert, but he let himself be guided by the sergeant into his own office.

'It's a young woman,' Willis said. 'Marcia took the call five minutes ago. Less. She's been dumped in a rubbish bin off High Street. That's all we've got. I was going to the scene straight away and I wanted to head you off so you could go there before you came into work.'

'Who called it in?'

'A good Samaritan. Said he was passing and he noticed an arm sticking out of a big bin.'

Gus bit his lip. 'You said it was *off* High Street. Where exactly? Nobody passes by *off* High Street.'

Willis looked surprised. His view of detective work had been shaped not through studying for a degree in criminology, though that had been a course he had seriously considered for a while, and not through years of experience, for big cases were rare in South Wales and he had only been a detective for four years. Rather, he had a view that great detective work was the result of eagle-eyed observation of tiny clues; the splinter on the edge of the table or the splatter of blood on the stair. His boss's attention to verbal detail was not something he expected, but Gus Reid was sharper than he sometimes appeared.

'Right,' Gus said, 'get Marcia to contact the pathologist and sort out a crime scene manager. You come in my car, we'll get over there straight away. And get a patrol car there to secure the scene. Did the caller just say an alleyway? No more precise location?'

'Marcia thinks he said it was by a takeaway, but the guy was mumbling a bit. She told him to speak up, you know what she's like. Guess he was in shock though.'

'Look it up on your phone map thing. There's a few lanes running off High Street, but I guess it's the one by the fake Kentucky Fried Chicken.'

Willis looked surprised and a little hurt, as if he suddenly suspected he had been fooled into buying ersatz Colonel Sanders takeaways on some youthful drunken night out.

'Louisiana Chicken, it's probably called, or Kansas fried chicken or something. Come on, don't just stand there, get on to Marcia. I'll see you outside.'

A little under ten minutes later the two men were standing in King's Lane, a rather grandly named narrow alley that led down to the Strand. This street had once been a riverside walk like the Embankment but was now a rather dubious street where working girls had plied their trade before the rise of the massage parlour. A constable had already taped off both ends of the lane and was talking into his radio as they approached. He looked up and pulled his shoulders back, serious and reliable and with the appropriate deference for a senior officer. He was probably no more than twenty,

Gus thought.

'She hasn't been touched,' the constable said.

'I should hope not,' Willis put in. 'Have you ordered a tent yet?'

'Just about to do that, sir.'

Gus sighed. 'Let's have a look then.' He slipped on a pair of nitrile gloves, lifted the lid of the bin and gasped. Willis raised his eyebrows, but then as he looked inside the container himself, he understood how his superior had reacted with such shock. The victim's face was a messy pulp of blood and bone, scarcely recognisable as a face were it not for its halo of dark hair. Willis wondered if she had been pretty and then instantly chided himself. That scarcely mattered.

Gus Reid was on his mobile as Willis turned round. He listened attentively, for he hoped one day to be in charge of a dramatic investigation of his own, and hopefully in a big city force, not just the South Wales constabulary. The inspector was asking if a pathologist had been contacted yet. Willis knew from training that nothing much could be done until photographs and measurements had been taken. They could not even lift the poor girl out of her undignified coffin until the correct protocols had been observed. He shuddered, hoping that the cold gust of wind that blew up the lane was the only cause.

'Okay,' Gus pronounced. 'Nothing we can do for her yet. 'But you can check on the CCTV, Willis.'

Willis looked slightly blank. 'Go and see what cameras we've got on High Street, I'm saying. There's obviously none here.'

'Oh, yes sir, of course.'

While Willis was striding back up the lane Gus started to think about his last murder case, a poor kid beaten to death for his wallet and phone. The boy had been walking home from Mumbles after a night out. That was about seven years ago now. But the perpetrators had not thought to dump the body like this. And it had not been a difficult case to solve: the gang of youths responsible had been seen talking to their victim earlier in the evening; they had taken his cash card to an ATM and one of their number had been captured on camera. A girlfriend of one of the boys had told her parents that she knew who'd committed the murder. Very little detective work was required in the end. This case was very different. From his knowledge of criminal profiling, which was admittedly not extensive, the

9

murderer here must have felt disgust towards his victim, to discard her body in this way. At very first sight Gus knew that this was not the murder scene. There was not enough blood.

He went back to the bin and steeled himself to look in once more. The constable averted his gaze as Gus opened the lid wide. No, there was nothing like enough blood, just a smear or two on the side of a cardboard box that she was up against. Gus looked down at the tarmac around the bin. It had been raining, but there might be a shoe print, or a partial at least, in some mud or dust. He could not see any, but he noticed something that might be of interest. In a glutinous patch of what might have been curry, either spilled or expectorated, there was a sort of groove that looked like it might have been made by something being dragged through the spillage. He checked the underside of the bin and saw that it was on four castors. He tried moving the bin but it resisted; presumably the castors were brake-fitted. He gave up, because he knew it was better to wait for the forensics team. Even at his age and with his experience he felt like a kid when officious medicos and experts rebuked him for tampering with their precious crime scene.

But he did not have long to wait. Jenny Sarka, the duty pathologist, hailed him from the lower end of King's Lane, 'Inspector Reid,' she cried out, 'as I live and breathe! Haven't they pensioned you off yet?'

'No ageist policies in the South Wales Constabulary, Jenny. And I'd be grateful for no ageist comments either.'

She smiled, but only for a fleeting moment. She was about ten years younger than Gus, though she wore her years well. He'd never really been that attracted to her, despite her good looks but he understood that her school ma'am's forthrightness might appeal to certain of his junior colleagues. She looked particularly stern and serious in this morning light. What she had to investigate was not likely to bring much joy or levity to her expression either.

'What have we got then?' she said curtly.

Gus pulled his coat around him. 'Young female, twenty-one, twenty-two, I'd guess. You'll be telling me in a minute or so that this isn't the crime scene and that the damage to her face is post-mortem ...'

'I'll be the judge of such matters, if you don't mind, Inspector.'

10

'Of course, but it's evident that she's been dumped, and I think the murderer wanted to make it difficult for us to identify her. It doesn't look to me like the facial wounds are the cause of death.'

'We'll soon find out,' Sarka said.

Gus watched the pathologist as she examined the top of the girl's head, then moved it to one side to look at the throat. 'Marks here,' she murmured. 'OK, could you pass me my Dictaphone please? It's in the side pocket of my case there.'

He gave her the device and she began recording her initial observations. Even though she was talking quietly into her Dictaphone he could hear what she was saying: there were ligature marks on her throat. Gus was pleased to hear that his immediate first impressions were proved right; and there was a crumb of comfort in the confirmation that at least the damage to the girl's face was inflicted after she'd been killed. Why would a person do such a thing? He must have hated her, or perhaps it was true he wanted to destroy her identity. Either way, Gus was convinced that as soon as they could move the body they would find that she had no belongings with her. Establishing who the victim was would be the first priority.

Sarka looked round. 'Where's the rest of your team?' she said. 'We'll have to move her in a minute.' With something of a struggle she pulled a mobile phone from her coat pocket. 'Has anyone called for an ambulance even?' she added, her voice thick with despair at human wickedness.

'Should be on its way,' Gus replied. 'I'll get my sergeant to check now.' Willis was approaching from the North end of the lane.

'Nearest CCTV cameras are down the road by Argos and up by the railway station, sir.' Willis said. Gus got the feeling that Willis' very serious and conscientious tone was affected by Jenny Sarka's presence. She was looking at the young officer quizzically.

'Isn't there one just opposite here?' she said.

'There was,' Willis said stolidly. 'But it's hanging down loose.'

'Can we tell how long it's been like that?' Gus asked.

'It doesn't look like it's been recently damaged,' Willis responded. 'But we'll check with the operators.'

'OK,' Gus said.' Get on back to the station now and requisition all the surveillance you can. And chase up the ambulance. As soon as we can get her moved and clear up here the better. The ghouls will be gathering soon.'

The scene of crime officers and the ambulance turned up about ten minutes later and all Gus could do was watch as the white suited forensic team moved around the crime scene like ants, seemingly at random but evidently with their own purposes. The girl's body was removed and bagged, far too roughly for Gus's sensibilities, but these people were inured to the horrors of their duties, he supposed. He waited patiently while the ant swarm completed their inspection and collection of possibly evidential material.

'What's in those bags?' Gus asked.

The officer pulled open one of the bags and a stench of rotting vegetables assailed both men.

'That other one?'

The second bag contained potato peelings and stained polystyrene fried food containers. No sign of any personal possessions

'Is that everything?' Gus asked.

The man looked at him as if he'd asked a completely outlandish question, like did he know what water skis Shakespeare used. 'Feel free to check,' he said. 'We'll get these tested for prints and let you know if there's anything.'

Gus searched the bin again but of course there was nothing left in there. He dropped back onto his feet, having had to clamber up the side of the container to reach inside, and he felt the squelch of the spilt curry, or whatever it was, beneath his sole. He examined the groove that he was sure the bin's castor had made and tried swinging the bin round so that the wheel would follow the same parabola. The constable was watching him all the while, though his duty was to keep an eye on the top end of the lane and ward off any unwelcome rubberneckers.

A SOCO came over and bent down and released a little catch and the bin rolled easily further away. The constable was looking at the wall and Gus saw his face open with amazement. He saw the cause and suddenly it was as if he had been transported to a shabby Whitechapel street in 1888. Scrawled in chalk on the peeling black painted stucco was the legend 'We shall this day light such a candle.' Gus tried to recall the exact wording of the famous graffito at one of the murder scenes in the Jack the Ripper case; it was something about the Jews being blamed. He could easily check as soon as he got back to the station. This message made no reference to Jews plainly, but surely it pointed to a psychotic killer with copycat intentions? But only of course if it had been written by the killer. Was there any way you could accurately ascertain *when* something had been written if it was written in chalk? Gus considered the positioning of the writing. It had rained last night. Could the rain have got to the message or was it kept dry by the bin? He looked closely for any signs of smearing but could see none. The writing looked quite new, but Gus couldn't recall when he'd last seen anything written in chalk, apart from pub menus, which were deleted daily. He felt a thrill of excitement. Cops on television were invariably cast down at the prospect of their city being haunted by a demonic killer, but that was in New York or Los Angeles. Britain was different. Gus decided he would also make it one of his first tasks, or Sergeant Willis' anyway; to check how many serial killers there had been in Britain in the past few decades. He couldn't think of a single one in Wales, but of course there had been a few in London and up north. There was the Yorkshire Ripper of course, and Harold Shipman, though he was rather a special case, and Dennis Neilson. And the Suffolk Strangler. He stopped himself: there were lonely psychotics anywhere and it was suddenly actually depressing rather than thrilling to think that his complacent life might suddenly be turned upside down. He could end up as an incompetent latter-day Inspector Abeline, pilloried in the press if he got nowhere solving this case. And that, he knew, was very likely if this was a non-domestic murder.

'We'll get this tested,' the SOCO said. 'Get the results to you soon as we can.' He pushed the bin back and snapped the brake back into place. Easy. Or not something that someone furtively depositing a corpse would even think about perhaps. Gus scratched the back of his head and noticed the young constable looking at him again.

'What?' he muttered in exasperation.

'Do you think it's connected, sir?'

Gus smiled. 'I don't know, son. It would be if we were in a cheesy Hollywood movie, but the class of criminal we normally deal with wouldn't be able to spell this correctly, I fear.'

13

The constable smiled nervously, which caused Gus to wonder if the man's own spelling was all that reliable. He guessed not, if the standard of English in the reports by the constables on the code blue case he was currently collating was anything to go by.

4

Josie Reid had been up for about half an hour as her father was pondering spelling and punctuation. She was coincidentally thinking of something very similar, for she had a batch of undergraduate assignments to mark by the following day and she hadn't been able to face looking at them over the weekend. They would be riddled with errors, adolescent solecisms and youthspeak jargon. 'Hamlet does my head in' was one of the considered judgements she had read the previous time she had set an essay on Shakespeare's notions of selfhood.

She poured herself a cup of jasmine tea and looked round the small kitchen of her Uplands flat. It was dark and cold – gelid, James Joyce would say – and musty, because for weeks now the weather had not allowed her to open the small window that gave on to the grubby back courtyard. She suddenly wished she had a cat, a fellow creature to comfort or to offer comfort, a presence in the flat other than her own ghosts. She sniffed disconsolately and sat down at the kitchen table. It was a huge old farmhouse table that the previous tenant had left for her and she loved it, though it was far too big for someone who lived on their own. Its prior existence as the focus of joyous family meals rebuked her, but she positioned a slate coaster under her cup, recognising that the table had no right to be marked or abused while it was in her temporary care. She gave the waxed oak surface an affectionate stroke, which made her think again that she urgently needed a cat, or a boyfriend perhaps. She was getting older; she would be twenty-seven next September. And she still didn't have a full-time job. Alexander the Great, Lawrence of Arabia, Pitt the Younger, they'd all achieved lifetimes of things by her age, she mused. Jesus too. Though actually He didn't get particularly busy till He was in His thirties. Josie smiled to herself, for she could hear the capital letters even though she was just thinking the words. Still a few years to go before it got utterly panicky, she reasoned.

But at the moment there were no signs of a full-time lecturing job at City University. In fact, there was considerable pressure to recruit more students to keep the hours that she currently had, despite the research she was doing, which could one day bring such huge kudos to this anonymous provincial establishment. She was fooling herself. She was lucky to have her own office at university, as most part-timers shared office space, and they were actually paying her a modest salary to do what she had always wanted to do: delve into feminist theory and Renaissance literature. In return she was obliged to try and teach Shakespeare and the rudiments of the development of the English language for eight hours a week to people who really wanted to work in the sports management or tourist industries, but had to take a few English modules. Nobody suffered too greatly and her research was allowed to creep on at its petty pace from day to day.

Monday. Richard the Third and Kingship. At least most of her students would come in; they tended to miss Thursdays because of Student Night the night before, but they usually tried to drag themselves in for the beginning of the week. And it was the beginning of a new term, not long after the New Year. Perhaps some of them had made a resolution to take things more seriously and at least try and attend on a more regular basis. She rinsed out her cup and took a last look at herself in the hall mirror. She had decided on a paisley dress that she'd got from Stewart's Seconds in Oxford Street (unfortunately not the famous one but Swansea's more dilapidated shopping area) and a white cotton rib shrug from Monsoon. It was rather more fashionable than was actually required for a seminar at City University but she'd given the outfit a maverick twist by putting on her Soul Cal high top pumps. They were all about youth. She pulled on a beige duffel coat purely for protection against the cold and, wrapping an old scarf around her neck as a gesture that she really belonged in Oxford, not the backwater she found herself inhabiting, she headed off on foot to her Townhill campus. It was a long and tedious climb up the city's steepest hill but she normally enjoyed the walk for the time it gave her to think about important matters like the role of the handmaiden or the youngest daughter in sixteenth century England.

But she did no serious critical thinking today. Instead she found herself thinking about Simon, her occasional lover, who seemed to be

16

getting more and more occasional these last six months. Then images of Ella, the girl she had slept with at Sussex, intruded. Where was she now? Probably not still in America; someone would have surely said something if she had made it in the fashion industry there, wouldn't they? Josie wasn't a lesbian; she hadn't even considered herself one during her brief but passionate fling with Ella. But Ella was committed to her sexual preference. It had been Ella's preachiness that had brought the affair to an end. No one had the right to proselytise about sexuality, Josie felt. You simply pursued what you felt was right at the time, as long as you weren't hurting anybody. But that moral ambivalence also allowed you to be like Simon, a married man who was adamant that he was not hurting anybody because his wife knew nothing about his affairs. It never seemed to occur to him that Josie herself might be hurt by his utter casualness. But in truth she was not much affected by it; it had suited her for a while to have a 'gentleman caller', as he over-gallantly termed himself. She was too busy for a full blown relationship, or that was what she told herself. She needed to be busier though.

She started thinking about the article she had promised to help research for her Head of Department, George Wright. Rather foolishly she had exaggerated her interest in linguistics and he had seized upon the opportunity to suborn her into doing some work on an obscure nineteenth century poet. The man had written in a Devon dialect and if she could just do a short piece on the dialectal features she could get a co-author credit, he'd said, with a smile he'd clearly intended as a winning one, but which she found a tad smarmy. As long as she did all the work and he put his name to the article, he meant. But she couldn't face the poetic vernacular of William Barnes today. Her own research was somewhat stalled too. She quickly tried to think of something else, to banish the reflux of guilt that would rise if she admitted how badly it was stalled.

She tried to focus on her breathing as she pushed herself more quickly up the last stretch of Townhill Road. She was passing a row of smug bow windowed semi-detached houses, whose owners had sought to protect themselves from the rest of the world through the agency of privet and hawthorn. She needed to get to the gym again. Christmas always intervened, though she tried to convince herself that a break from work and a break from the gym could be viewed as a period of creative lassitude, rather than just shiftlessness. She had tried to write some poetry sitting alone in her flat on Christmas Day. It was not going to be maudlin soul baring or image packed stuff about snow and skeletal trees, it was going to be vibrant political invective. In the end she watched *Life is Beautiful* again, which had replaced *It's A Wonderful Life* as her all-time favourite film. She didn't like to tell anyone this fact because simply mention of the titles might suggest that all she wanted was childish affirmation that existence was just lovely. You could never think that if you'd seen the Roberto Benigni movie though. Filmmakers had moved on since the sentiment of the James Stewart weepie, and Josie's tastes had moved on too.

Her leg muscles beginning to ache from the exertion of the final hundred metres, she paused at the entrance to the university. Les Jenkins, the ex-SAS security guard, was watching her from the Reception building. Mysteriously he was often referred to as 'Shinks', which Josie couldn't help thinking was more like a verb than a proper noun. She gave him a little wave because he appeared to be smiling at her and walked on quickly. She was not teaching until ten o' clock but it was best always to walk quickly about the campus as if you were constantly urgently needed somewhere else. Ambling across the quad was for the gowned dons in *Morse* or *Lewis* or whatever; here you would be reviled for your turpitude if you weren't racing to your next class.

Once inside the main building the first person she saw was George Wright. He was a handsome man, and Jesus, did he know it. He was in his mid-forties, Josie guessed, and had been at the university for perhaps twenty years. During that time he had written two books, both on the same subject, and about five articles for reputable journals. Two of those were co-authored too, probably by young female postgrads. George was lazy. He smiled lazily at her as they approached each other on the academic corridor.

'Hiya,' he said. It was so typical that he would speak like a teenager, for some effect of which only he was aware. He was incredibly articulate, Josie knew. She had been in a committee meeting once, standing in for a colleague who was ill, or said she was ill, and she'd witnessed him floor his colleagues with a diatribe about the ineffectiveness of efficiency measures. The meeting had gone quiet and mooched on to the next agenda item like a dog going back to its basket. You couldn't help admire a man with the intellectual powers to do that, yet you wanted to shake him and say, 'Write something meaningful! Use that brain!'

'Good morning,' Josie nodded. 'I'm afraid I haven't been able to get much done on Barnes yet...'

'Oh, don't fret,' George oozed, 'he's been waiting for this article to be written about him for a hundred and fifty years or so. Another few weeks won't harm. And I guess *Critical Review* is in no real rush for it either.'

Josie gave a polite smile and started to move towards her study.

'You're looking in extraordinarily good health today, Miss Reid,' George said. 'You must tell me your fitness regime.'

'I can't afford a car, that's my regime.'

He laughed and Josie was slightly annoyed at his reaction. It wasn't a joke, though she knew that people sometimes laughed at things that weren't funny, for some reason known only to themselves. She saved her own chuckles for genuine wit and, despite her better instincts, her guffaws for animals getting into comical trouble on YouTube or TV clip shows. It occurred to her that George was merely trying to continue the conversation, but probably his comment was based on the red cheeks she had from powering up the hill to work. She strode on, leaving George to look rather wistfully after her.

Once in her room she slumped into her swivel chair, banished George from her mind and tried not to think about Simon either. She gazed at the cream walls and was suddenly depressed. It was a private space but it was also a cell. She referred to it as her office, though the older lecturers liked to call their rooms 'my study'. No one sat back in a leather chair sipping sherry though, pontificating about modernism to clever students; they spent their day staring at their computer screens, dolefully reading educational reports or responding venomously to colleagues' e-mails about committee meetings. She thought about Simon again. Perhaps she needed to find someone to go clubbing with, get a date, have a bit of fun. She got up to put on her kettle and looked out of the window. A young couple were kissing on the steps that led down to the staff car park. They'd probably only just got up from a night of sex and here they were at it again. They looked no more than five or six years younger than her. But there was a crucial difference: if they were casting for plays based on great literature the girl would be Juliet to this young man's Romeo. Josie was always going to be Anne Eliot. She smiled at her own little conceit. Simon wouldn't have known what she was talking about if she said something like that to him. He would probably have thought she meant some old school friend. George Wright would have laughed lugubriously and said something charming. Or Witty, like 'Anne Elliot? Indeed not, Miss Woodhouse!' Or he might immediately think she was flirting and made a move on her.

She poured herself coffee, instant, with Coffee Mate, for her resolutions to drink only saffron infusion and green tea were invariably short lived. Then she switched on her computer to check today's e-mails. A survey of student satisfaction was to be conducted, could all tutors remind their classes? Why didn't they ever do a staff satisfaction survey? There was a note from a student to say that 'family circumstances' prevented her attending classes this week. It briefly made Josie think of her parents: her mother who had shacked up with a psychopath after her divorce, and her father, who was too busy trying to arrest psychopaths to bother with his only daughter. But that wasn't exactly true. He had made an effort since Josie had grown up, now that she didn't have such a terrible need, but when she was sixteen and was desperate for at least one of her parents to recognise her needs, he was too busy breaking up with her mother, or too busy at work. He'd had one or two lady friends after the divorce but he'd never remarried. That should have meant that he would want to spend a lot more time with his daughter, for her brother Charlie had moved to Australia five years ago, but for a while he preferred to just text her occasionally. Birthdays and Christmases as a matter of strict form, and now and again to say they must get together soon. But they hardly ever did. And now they both seemed to find it too awkward to resume a normal relationship. She was partly to blame for that, she knew, because she was so angry with him about the break-up. She'd missed him terribly, though it had been her decision to go and live with her grandparents. That was two years before she went off to university, a time when you wanted to be with your friends anyway, not your stupid parents.

She had never felt close to her mother, who, to the woman's shame, had once said to her when Josie was only about eleven, 'We're not the same, you and me, I guess that's why we don't get on.' She'd come in from the garden holding a glass of white wine and looked over Josie's shoulder as she was sketching something for Art. Then she'd said those hurtful words. Josie didn't even look up as her mother went out to the garden again and started laughing at something with the next-door neighbour. The sound of that shrill, false even, machine gun rattle always made Josie uncomfortable.

She hadn't seen her for four years now. She hadn't even responded to her mother's last text: 'Happy Xmas, love,' Ridiculous woman. The last time she'd seen her father was just before Christmas, when they'd coyly exchanged gifts in a coffee shop which they'd both pretended was the most convenient place to meet up. They had not opened the presents in front of each other, and perhaps that was just as well: he'd bought her quite an expensive bracelet and she'd bought him a book voucher. He was a good man, but he seemed to have forgotten how to be properly alive, and Josie needed passion, not polite generosity. She could not know that in he was about to leap back into her life and need her as much as she needed him.

5

I am here in my cribb'd and cabin'd life ... but ha ha ... this island's mine! I can't wait till they find her and release their careful statement. 'A young woman has been found dead in Swansea. Police say there are suspicious circumstances'. Their circumlocutions and their euphemisms! They'll be seeking somebody 'to assist with their enquiries', as if it's all to be handled with the kiddest of kid gloves and all anybody wants is to enquire as to one's reasons for behaving slightly aberrantly. Whereas what they really want to do is to smash your head against the cell wall and kick you till their feet ache. Ha.

But I shall be patient. It won't be on TV because they won't tell the press anything yet. The Evening Post might get it tomorrow maybe. Inspector Joe Plod will be standing beside some Deputy Chief Constable in his full regalia when they do give it to the news and they'll 'appeal for witnesses.' Good luck with that. They'll tell the public to be extra vigilant, which is their code for don't go out at night. God, I'd love it if they misspelled it and told everyone to be extra vigilante. 'We want everyone to go out with their baseball bats and batter anyone suspicious,' Swansea police announce. After all, there was that time somewhere up in the valleys where a mob beat up a paediatrician because they thought that was the same word as paedophile.

But though I'm the hero of this story I have to be invisible, except in this diary of course. Though I'm afraid, dear diary, you're for the bonfire if the going gets a bit heavy. It shouldn't though. I am, as the good Lord put it, 'lying doggo'. Mum's the word, ay, there's the rub, how's yer father? Tight as Andronicus, to coin a phrase. Sheer unprintable poetry. I'm Dylan without the drink, Andrew Motionless. Wordsworthless. Jesus Christ, I'm so alive! And she is so utterly dead. And so pretty.

6

Gus Reid was at his office desk before ten o' clock. It would be a day or more before a full post-mortem examination report would be filed, but hopefully Jenny Sarka would e-mail him with an interim cause of death before too long. Willis was checking the missing persons file and two detective constables had started door-to-door enquiries, though since the dump site was in the centre of town Gus had no great hopes there. The shopkeepers would know nothing and there would be no householders to ask. CCTV for the whole of the town centre might yield some images of vans or cars stopping at suspicious times in the night, but that was a long shot too. Stephanie would collate the images when they all came in but that was a task that would take a couple of days. The first forty eight hours was a time of hanging around, not the super action-packed drama that television wanted people to think it was.

In order to try and give himself at least the impression that he wasn't just hanging around Gus keyed in 'serial killers UK' into the internet search bar. He looked up furtively through the glass door to his office to check that no one could see that he was consulting Wikipedia. No one was watching. He found to his surprise that there were actually over thirty serial killers currently incarcerated in prisons across England. The term was misleading though, for men who had killed twice over a long period of time were included, and spree killers were classified separately. With any luck the still unidentified girl was someone who knew her killer, not a random victim of a new Ripper. He looked away from his computer and sighed. He had to prepare some sort of briefing for the team that would hastily be put together and at the moment he had nothing much more to say than that a girl had been killed. He pictured himself in front of cameras for *Crimewatch*, buttoned up tight but trying to look relaxed, wooden nevertheless in his performance, exactly like all those other DIs who had nothing to go on but were praying for a relative to grass up the villain in question. It was vital to reassure the public that all was well and they were a crucial part of a system that would always win in its enduring battle against wrongdoers. The statistics said something different, however.

But there was something else. He looked again at his computer screen and tapped in the message that was chalked on the wall behind the buster bin. The first entry was, predictably enough, a Wikipedia item. It told him the words had been spoken in the sixteenth century by an Anglican called Hugh Latimer. His cryptic utterance was intended to encourage the man alongside him to be brave, for they were about to be burned at the stake as heretics. Gus nearly stopped reading at this point, for this was all too literary for a psychotic killer, or vengeful lover, but he decided to glance at the next item. This was a question: 'Why did Ray Bradbury decide to use the full quotation in his novel *Fahrenheit 451*?'

The answer revealed that one of Bradbury's characters had also died for her beliefs, this time in books, however, not religion. It wasn't any more helpful though. Perhaps he would be able to persuade his Superintendent to pay for a handwriting expert to come up with something, if the forensics people could say when the message had been written. But what could he do with a prognosis that suggested that the author was right handed, and of an introspective disposition? DCI Newlands would probably just tell him to concentrate on door-to-door enquiries; the budget wasn't for freeloading so-called experts to tell us things that don't help us catch criminals.

He stepped out of his office in order to look busy and saw his sergeant talking to a constable.

'Willis, a word please?'

Willis looked startled and hurried over. 'Sir?'

'What progress?'

'We haven't got anything much yet, I'm afraid, sir. The manager of the takeaway shop says he put some packaging in the bin at about five yesterday and obviously he didn't see anything. We're still trawling through the CCTV but there's nothing of any interest. A car stopped near the top of the lane at one' o clock but you can't see anyone getting out. It drives off again a few minutes later. Do we know when the body was actually dumped yet?'

'No. Almost certainly in the early hours though. Nobody would have risked it while there were still drunks around, or when workers on early shifts were likely to be up and about, so I'm guessing somewhere between three and five o' clock maybe. As soon as the PM results are in we'll know the time of death, but it won't help us if she was moved there post mortem.'

Willis nodded. 'The trouble is, there isn't any CCTV at the bottom of the lane. If he took her up from The Strand we'll have no images, just physical stuff perhaps. Footprints, I mean.'

'Yes, Willis, I do understand.'

'Sorry, sir.'

'This your first murder, Willis?'

'Yes sir.' The young man pushed his chest out slightly. The movement was almost imperceptible, but Gus recognised in it the pride and apprehension that he had felt in his own early cases.

'Let's hope it's the last for a bit, shall we?'

Willis smiled. 'I'll get back to the camera footage then, shall I? See how Steph's getting on.'

Gus sighed. 'Yes. We'll do a briefing as soon as I know what team we've got together. Probably not till this afternoon. Try and have something for then.' Briefing was not a task that he was relishing, given the absence of evidence, but hopefully Jenny Sarka would soon find something to establish the victim's identity at least. Something else he never relished was reporting upwards, but it was time to let his superiors know what was happening too. His chief superintendent's first response would inevitably concern the media, but since it would initially only be the local newspaper, Gus supposed it would be his own responsibility to deal with a press release. BBC Wales would probably pick up the item but it was all pretty standard stuff – the body of a young woman had been discovered in Swansea but her identity was not known at present. Police were looking for witnesses to help with their enquiry blah blah. Chief Superintendent Tim Gaston would be holding a press conference in the near future, or as soon as people like Gus pulled their finger out.

It was only an hour or so later that the first phone call came. It was *The Evening Post*. Willis put the call through with a whispered dramatic introduction: 'It's the Media, boss. Andrea Linney.' Gus had not met her, but colleagues told him she was quite sharp. Gus interpreted the word as intelligent, but they may have meant confrontational. He would soon find out. She was reputedly something of a looker too, though Gus never trusted his fellow officers' judgements on that score. She had only been at the paper for a couple of years but Gus had read a few of her stories. They were rather hyperbolic, he felt.

'Inspector Reid.'

'Andrea Linney here, from *The Evening Post*. I gather you've got a psycho on the loose. Can I have a quick word?'

Gus knew that she would want more than that because today's deadline had gone and she would be looking for a big front page splash for the Tuesday edition.

Instinct told him to be initially guarded. 'How did you hear that?'

'Grapevine, what do you think?'

He sighed. 'I can't say much yet. Young girl, well, young woman I mean, no name, no witnesses. Not even sure of cause of death at this point. You'll have to wait for the press conference.'

'When will you be conducting that?'

'Not sure it'll be me doing it,' Gus said, then immediately regretted it.

Andrea was quick to realise the implication. 'So, this isn't a domestic then? Who's in charge?'

Gus adopted his most formal tones. 'At present I am leading an enquiry into the circumstances of a young woman's unfortunate death. Other officers may become involved in due course, but I cannot confirm that that will be the case. I can say that the circumstances are to be regarded as suspicious. The girl's body was discovered early this morning after a report to us by a member of the public.'

'Report?'

'Phone call.'

'A man?'

'Yes.'

'Was it the killer?'

Gus almost laughed. 'No, we are confident that it was not the killer.'

'Why?'

'The nature of the call didn't indicate it.'

This time it was Andrea who audibly sighed. 'What does that mean?'

'It means we know who called, I can't say any more than that. Enquiries are ongoing.' He paused. 'Look, it was a postal worker but I don't want that reported, okay?'

'Why not?'

'Because we'll need to talk to this person at some stage and I don't want you hassling him in order to add something sensationalist to your reporting, understand?'

There was a brief silence before Andrea replied, this time in a more steely voice, 'No need to patronise me Inspector Reid, we're both professionals doing our jobs here.'

Gus looked up through the glass of his office and saw some other professionals laughing and joking by a coffee machine. 'Forgive me,' he said. 'Between you and me this is not going to be an easy case and we may both find ourselves superseded in the days to come. But that's completely off the record, obviously.'

Andrea gave a low tooth whistle. 'It's a big one, you're saying?'

'I am most definitely not saying that, but whatever conclusions you draw are not my direct responsibility.'

Andrea almost laughed. 'Do they teach you how to talk like this in Hendon, Inspector?'

Gus smiled to himself. 'It's something you learn as you go along, in order to protect yourself from journalists, Miss Linney.'

'You can call me Andrea. And I do understand ...'

She was waiting for him to reciprocate but he declined. 'You can call me Inspector Reid,' he said, but his voice had more warmth to it now.

'Okay,' she replied. 'I look forward to seeing you at the press conference then. When will you,' she paused dramatically to stress the next words, 'or one of your superior officers, be talking to us?'

'Okay, Andrea, call me Gus if you're talking to me like this, but I need to be addressed as Inspector in front of other officers, if you don't mind. Sometime later today. I guess. We'll let you know in plenty of time to grab your notepad.'

'Keep up, Gus,' she laughed. 'I-pad, you mean.'

'Whatever.'

He put down the receiver and felt better. She wasn't flirting with him, he knew, but it felt something like that and for such tiny pleasures he was grateful enough.

7

Now, gods, stand up for bastards! Only I mean it metaphorically of course. Some people are born bastards, some achieve it through their own devices, in the end everyone is a bastard in someone else's eyes, I suppose. It's all relative. Actually, I wish I had an elder brother I could despise, and that's a fact. I'll just have to make do with a feeble father and a degenerate of a mother. They could never understand me; I was always too strong for them.

I've been thinking about my little adventure. You always think that what you do is the right thing, as long as it's not completely spontaneous, of course. If you've thought about it, it must be right. Our faith in the rational, you might say. But I keep wondering if I omitted anything or blundered in any way. The gloves are fine, I know, because even if they ever found them, which they won't, the best they could come up with is that they came from Singleton hospital. Suppose:

(a) They did track them back to the hospital

(b) They looked at every inch of hospital CCTV for the last six months

(c) They found footage of someone palming a pair of Marigolds from a cleaner's trolley

(d) They claimed it was me who was on camera

I'd just say, 'I'm sorry, officers, it's not me.'

The message. Probably too obscure, but they must have moved the bin and found it by now. Be interesting to see what they say when it gets reported. I can imagine Plod and mini-plod discussing it now: 'It's a quotation, you idiot!' 'I realise that, but what does it mean?' 'It means we've got a heretic on the loose!' Ha ha.

The worst thing, though it may be the best thing really, was dragging the bin up that lane. There was only some old cardboard in it, plus the subject of course, but it was surprisingly heavy and hard to manoeuvre. My poor heart was racing, though I knew nobody would be around at that time. But who says anything to somebody dragging a bin up a side street? Just moving this, you'd say, and they'd shrug and disappear.

Of course I could have been seen pushing her into the garage. There was nobody on the street, but you can't rule out somebody looking out of a window somewhere, with binoculars, say. I confess I'm rather confident on that score though. There's no houses nearby, just the shops in the distance and the back of the UCI, which doesn't have windows. Very slim chance of a binoculared Jimmy Stewart in a wheelchair spotting my felonious monkey business. Ha! Felonious monkey! The jazz great who had a side-line in criminal misdeeds! I should be a writer!

So. Thus I clothe my naked villainy, as the crookback would have it. God, this is fun! It's like even more fun than perpetrating the act, this writing about it and thinking back on it. Perpetrating, lovely word. I wish I could have filmed the whole thing though. It will doubtless pale and fade, like a morning mist, and when the rozzers finally admit defeat and people stop talking about their shock and the terrible loss of such a promising life etcetera I may feel a slight post-coital sadness, I suspect. She had it coming, is what I have to say about that. And she couldn't have foreseen that ending!

But, revenir aux moutons, as I believe our French cousins say, what else should I or could I concern myself about?

I disposed of her phone before even disposing of her. I'm not sure what they can track and what they can't, because we're not exactly in Washington D.C., but that was the first thing I did. It's in three different places actually, the sim card down a drain, the front part in a bin in the toilets in Walkabout and the back part in a skip outside a house renovation. Apart from her shopping bags there was just that and her little shoulder bag with her purse and keys and a few girly things. There was only two ten pound notes and a few coppers in the purse so I spent the money on something special – a nice Pomerol. They'll probably find the purse where I slipped it behind the bag of clothes someone left in the doorway of a charity shop. But they may well not. Some old biddy will have opened the shop by now and will assume it's something she can sell. I haven't opened the wine yet because I didn't want to be too crass about this, enjoying my ill-gotten gains, as if robbery were my base intent. But at least it's not Chianti. Why would a debonair killer like Anthony Hopkins relish such a common wine? Not that my Spar sells fava beans. Imagine what the women there would make of it if you went in and asked for them! Those gross middle aged hags - Vera or Joyce I'm guessing, but I never look at their nametags in case they think I'm eying up their ample bosoms - they'd probably think Fava was a brand name for baked beans and direct me to the canned goods section. Needless to say, I didn't get the Pomerol from my local shop. If I'd asked for it there Nobil would probably have looked behind him at the paracetamol and ibuprofen shelf. They tend to focus their alcohol marketing on old drunks and students. Different if I'd wanted strong lager or cheap cider or own brand vodka.

30

I've still got the house keys, the credit cards and driving licence, plus her student ID of course, but I'm going to have to dispose of them. The keys can find their own way home, via a drain somewhere but I fancy I'll melt the cards over a candle, for dramatic effect. I like fire, as my dear old mum would attest if she were still with us. But she's not. But just melting them won't be enough, so it'll be a question of dumping the molten plastic. If they've got any technological expertise at all, though I doubt they have really, they might be able to read the chip in her bank card even after it's burnt. So it's down another drain, I think. I like the metaphor anyway. Where is she now? Down the drain. She was so meek and yielding, so animal-like in her pathetic trust that I meant her no harm. How could she be like that? She knew she meant me harm when she spoke about me the way she did.

And that's about all. If no one saw me, which I'm convinced is true, and there's no forensic evidence, because how could there be, and I don't lose my mind and start confessing, which I don't plan to do, how could anything go wrong? Ah, but who would have thought the young girl would have so much blood in her? I'm joking, of course. She hardly bled at all when I hit her, and strangling is hardly unseaming a body from the nave to the chaps, is it? Ho hum. Or Fe Fi Fo Fum, I should say, I don't smell the blood of an Englishman. I must stop with these puns though, they demean me.

8

Josie had to hurry to her seminar room, even though she had had
plenty of time to get there early. On the way she saw Ailsa Minors
crossing the car park. She was Head of Quality, a title she revelled in
for its prestige but also for its irony, for both students and staff at
City University spent most of their time avoiding being caught out,
rather than pursuing any scarcely apprehended notion of excellence
or probity. Ailsa was a huge woman who seemed to sail around the
campus rather than walk, perhaps because she always wore
voluminous skirts and invariably a cape or a shawl insouciantly draped
about her person. Josie recalled a line of poetry and mentally likened
her to some quinquereme of Nineveh from distant Ophir. Her cargo,
as far as Josie's dealings with her were concerned, seemed to be spite
and sarcasm. Less poetically, she was a modern Amazonian, a cross
between an oversized bluestocking frump and a scary traffic warden
from the nineteen seventies. Josie avoided her and hurried into a
dimly lit corridor where a handful of second year students were
waiting, leaning against the wall or crouched down on the thin carpet
texting. They did not seem overjoyed at her arrival.

'Morning,' she said, hoping that she sounded business-like and
breezy.

One or two of the young men grunted in response and Cheryl, a
stocky loudmouthed girl from somewhere in the Valleys, cried out,
''Appy New Year, Josie. You 'ave a good New Year's? I was 'ammered
myself.'

'Well,' Josie replied, unlocking the seminar room, 'It all seems such
a long time ago now, doesn't it? But, yes, I had an extremely pleasant
time.' It was completely untrue, but though Cheryl was an amiable
enough student, Josie had no interest in sharing details of her barren
life with the girl.

They all filed in, like prisoners, and as the rest of the class turned
up in sullen twos and threes Josie organised her handouts into little
stacks. When she looked up the room was quite full. It was her duty
to keep a register, though they weren't in school anymore and Josie
didn't want to behave like a form mistress, so she tried to tick off

names discreetly. There were two names left and she could not put faces to either of them. She looked at the class hopefully.

'Rhodri's got a dental appointment,' one of the lads chirped up. 'Said he'll try and make it for half time.'

Cheryl, who was sitting just in front of the boy, turned round and hissed, 'It's Shakespeare, mind, not a bloody football match.'

The boy shrugged and Josie seized the opportunity to impose herself on the class. 'It is Shakespeare, you're right Cheryl, and it's the complex web of ideas about kingship that we find in his History plays that we shall be addressing today.'

One or two of the more conscientious students began pulling out notepads from their bags but a few others were still looking into their laps, which Josie knew meant they were engrossed in what was on their mobile phone screens. One girl, sitting in the corner of the room on her own, had her head turned towards the windows, but she could not have been able to see out onto the quadrangle from that angle.

'Zoe?' Josie hesitated, 'Is it Zoe?'

'Yes miss, I mean, Josie ...'

'Are you alright?'

'I was wondering where Lauren is. She's definitely coming and she's not usually late.'

'Lauren?'

'Lauren Tracey. She sits here, next to me.'

Josie was able to summon up an image of a dark haired and rather attractive girl. Of course, Lauren was the other missing name on the register. She rarely said much, but somehow she seemed brighter than the others. It was probably a matter of body language, someone actually listening, rather than simply waiting for the two hour session to trundle past like a slow goods train carrying unfathomable ideas.

'Oh, well, we can give her a couple of minutes, I suppose. Though actually I think we should make a start. Time and tide and so forth. Now then, Alison, can you tell the group what you think are the key notions debated in *Richard the Third*, do you think?'

'Um,' a thin lank haired girl began. 'Um, I'm not quite sure ...'

'Okay, I'll start us off,' Josie said.

It was always thus, she was thinking.

9

Gus Reid was a tidy man. He liked order. This was abundantly apparent in his house, where shirts were hung according to a work/leisure and a Summer/Winter principle and cans were stacked in his larder in rows according to their food types: pulses down one side, soups down the other, tinned tomatoes and tuna in their own little aisles. When he had a garage, during his marriage to Adele, tools were hung on evenly spaced tool hangers. Neatness pleased him, but it was counter-productive to his efforts as a detective. As he was well aware, a more haphazard arrangement of evidence and clues allows greater breadth of interpretation.

He was looking at the notes he had made on a sheet of paper on his desk. He had resisted making a list and instead had attempted a spider diagram, with possible killer motives in one quadrant, details of the dump site in another, and the legend 'Forensic Evidence' in a third sector. The fourth quadrant was empty and he was resisting putting a label to that area because again it would be the initial design for his notes that would be dictating his thinking, rather than what really mattered. Indeed, why had he even predetermined four areas in his diagram, not five, or eight or ten?

He stood up, though he didn't know where he was going, or indeed if he was going anywhere, but his phone trilled and he collapsed back onto his seat. It was Jenny Sarka.

'I can't give you a full report yet, Gus, you'll understand that, but I thought I'd give you a buzz to indicate probable time and cause of death. The deceased was strangled, by ligature, I mean, not manually, so you won't get any prints. There's occlusion of the carotid artery, but she'd suffered a blow to the head ante-mortem, so she may well have been unconscious. I can't be very precise about time, but I'd be fairly confident that it was some time before she was discovered. Body temperature and absence of blow flies suggests between eighteen and twenty four hours, I might venture.'

'Really?' Gus said. 'Anything else?'

'She hadn't had sex recently, so I can't provide you with a nice DNA sample, I'm afraid. As far as establishing who she was goes, you'll have to go on her clothes and shoes, whatever help they may be. She was wearing a t-shirt from Top Shop, I know that's utterly unhelpful ...'

'Size?' Gus interrupted, 'Colour even?'

'Oh, um, it's a blue woven front affair. Size 10. They cost about twenty pounds. I know that because I bought my daughter one for Christmas. The trousers were chinos. I think the young folk call them ankle grazers. Cream, with a cream belt.'

'Any sign of what the killer used to strangle her?'

'Nothing she was wearing, if you're thinking tights or whatever. She wasn't wearing any. Well, she wouldn't underneath trousers, would she? No interfering with her, no redressing of the body. But her shoes were from Rowberrys, which might be slightly more interesting. They were smart, and expensive. You'd expect trainers or sling backs or something, with the other gear.'

'Well, thanks for that,' Gus said. 'I'm glad you're a woman ...'

'So am I, but what are you saying?'

'A male pathologist wouldn't always know the names of the places a victim had shopped, I'm saying.'

'That's sounds dangerously like misogyny. I think I'd prefer a compliment about my professionalism, but don't worry, I'm only ribbing you. I just thought it might help you identify her in some way, particularly since everything looks comparatively new.'

Gus sighed. 'I wasn't trying to belittle you, I am genuinely pleased you paid attention to those details.'

'Okay then. Get back to you with further and better particulars in due course.'

'Thanks, Jenny.'

Gus put down his phone and addressed his spider diagram once more. It was crucial to find out who the girl was; the rectangle in the middle of the web still had no name in it. If he had to wait for missing persons reports to come through it might yet be a couple of days, but if she had been held for any period of time before the murder there could be a lead already in the system. He put through an internal call to his sergeant. 'Do we have any names from Mispers yet?'

Willis said, 'Hang on, I'll be there with what we've come up with now.'

Now. Now in a minute. They really meant 'in an undefined period of time, but certainly not on the instant'. The inaccuracies of Welsh English. Nevertheless, it was only a short time before Willis bustled through the inspector's door.

'Here's what we've come up with.' He handed Gus a manila folder. 'I contacted Bridgend and they've put out requests for lists from neighbouring forces, but if she was a tourist, or an exchange student, say, we might not get anything for weeks.'

'I know. But she was wearing clothes from Top Shop and shoes from Rowberrys, so I'm hoping that means she's not from abroad. With any luck she's local and we'll get a hit sooner rather than later. We'll get plenty of suggestions from Joe Public as soon as we've held a press conference, of course, but we're going to need a mini police force on its own just to deal with all the shit they come up with.'

'How many lads will be on the team, do you think?'

Gus smiled ruefully. 'Lads and/or lasses, I think you mean. Sorry, I'll let you know as soon as I know myself. After I've spoken to Newlands, and perhaps Gaston, who'll have to consult his budget genie, I'll know for definite. We'll get two or three DCs surely, it's a big case for us. Plus plenty of uniforms for the public to be reassured, of course. And we'll be offered all the assistance we need from major crimes as long as we don't actually call on them to spend any real time doing anything of any use. Sorry to be cynical, Willis, I can tell this is very dramatic for you, but this is the way it tends to work.'

'Can't we do something while were waiting for Missing Persons?' The young officer threw his arms wide, palms upward. 'Since we know what she was wearing, as soon as we release details of that somebody's bound to recognise her, or have seen her recently at least.'

'And everyone will wonder why we aren't also releasing a picture of her. There'll immediately be speculation about why not, and before we know it we'll have a Ted Bundy on the rampage in Swansea, especially if the nationals pick it up before we've got any further in the investigation.'

'What happens if nobody's reported her missing?'

'They will, but there's no telling when. She didn't have the look of a runaway or a homeless person. She'll live with a boyfriend, or a flatmate, or a family, and only a couple of days would normally go by before someone thinks something isn't right. The pathologist reckons she died some time yesterday, so she'll have been missing from wherever she lives for two nights by tomorrow morning.' He stopped to think for a moment. 'Listen, if this is a stranger attack we may well have to wait till there's another incident, in order to try and start establishing pattern. That's the sad truth of it. If it's her boyfriend or a jealous ex-lover or whatever, somebody is going to come forward and say something as soon as we've got an ID. There are only two viable possibilities here. That's the way we're taught to look at it anyway. But you know what, Willis? I think we've got something different going on. The facial damage was so severe and so centred on her mouth. I don't think a stranger could have hated her so intensely.'

'But you don't think it's a boyfriend or lover either?'

'Nothing suggests a sex angle, neither the position she was in nor the fact that her clothes were left untouched.'

'What other motive are you considering then?'

'I don't know. But the message he left, if it was our perpetrator who left it of course, also suggests that he's more concerned with the nature of the crime itself, not the victim. Do you know what I mean?'

Willis looked down. 'Hmm, not sure, but to my mind that would take us back to a psychopath.'

'I hope I'm wrong, Willis.'

10

Andrea Linney was sitting in a pub on Oystermouth Road. She had taken the table by the window and she was gazing out at the sweep of Swansea Bay, though the beach directly opposite her was obscured from view by an old poll stone wall. Two seagulls were arguing over the remnants of an abandoned takeaway. Then a couple of female joggers in light blue tracksuits passed on the other side of the road, joking and urging each other on. They didn't look the type; they were too old and ungainly. One was chunky, at best, and the other was flabby. Andrea looked down. She belonged to a gym but had not been since before Christmas. She had no need to lose weight anyway. She exercised and stuck to a reasonably healthy diet for the most part, though this was more to do with conforming to the expectations of her peers than any genuine desire to live longer, avoid heart disease and maintain her weight at eight stone eight forever.

Her job was more important to her than anything. She had once wanted to be a pilot. Then the star of a West End musical. Somewhere along the line her career aspirations had subsided to more achievable ends: she thought she might train as a graphic designer or perhaps become a personal assistant to someone famous, though she never quite worked out how that might transpire. Then, almost without realising how it had come to pass, she had found herself in Bournemouth doing a degree in Media Studies. The course did not lead to a job at the BBC or the BFI. She couldn't find any work in Bournemouth and was not quite ready at this stage in her life to pack her things in a handkerchief on the end of a stick and head for London. So she had gone home to Tamworth, trying to put a brave face on it, ostensibly to stay with her parents for a couple of months while she sorted things out and decided on her true direction. And there she had stayed for far too long, initially only getting part time work in pubs and cafés, then the full-time hell of a call centre. She eventually got a job in admin in the housing department, but it was numbing work and she had felt that her life had stalled very badly.

She had pitched up in Swansea two years later because her then boyfriend had got a computing job at the Driver and Vehicle Licensing Directorate, though everyone called it the DVLA. This time she knew she could not simply do whatever work was available, for that would probably lead to a repetition of the cycle of awful jobs in catering and at best a promotion back to menial admin. Instead, she decided she would have to take charge of her destiny, so one of the first things she did was coerce the editor of the local newspaper to let her write occasional articles on women's issues, though he thought that meant fashion. She knew that her degree in Media Studies had stood her in some stead but she also knew that it was her forcefulness that had got her the work. The editor had been impressed enough to appoint her on a short-term contract. Not long after she had moved to this new city the boyfriend had moved on, but now so had she. She had been permanent for nearly three years and had been promoted from the basement of writing fillers, which were just truncated stories from the internet and the national newspapers, to the dizzy heights of going out and finding her own stories. She was in this pub at this early time, before noon, because she wanted to give herself some time and space to take stock of how this new murder story might develop, and how she could hang onto the reins if possible. There were a couple of senior journalists who would seize the story and relegate her back to interviewing neighbours if she couldn't stamp her authority straight away.

She took a sip of her Americano and ran through the facts as far as she knew them. A girl killed violently. Body found by a member of the public, a postal worker apparently. Gus Reid had tried to be cagey but he'd admitted it was a man not a woman. Therefore the body was somewhere on a street, not out in the countryside. What if this postman was taking a shortcut through a park or a woody area though and found the body there? She had caught the scent at nine thirty this morning; that meant the body had been found relatively shortly before that. Sadly, she had not been able to prise out any information about the location from Reid or her earlier source. She took out her phone and looked at the text message she'd received at 9.27. It was from Fran, a girl she'd made acquaintance with at the gym, and who perhaps was a little star struck that her new friend was a journalist, she being a mere hairdresser's assistant. It read *Poss story for U. Body found. Probly murder cos police evrwhere. Good hunting.* Fran worked in a salon that Andrea didn't frequent but she knew it was somewhere in LA, as Fran put it. LA was the local dialect term for Lower Hafod, or more accurately, Lower 'Afod. It was an area of terraced housing with a few one-man garages and pubs for local people only. She might have seen the police presence there, or she might have seen it somewhere else on her way to work. Andrea didn't know where Fran actually lived, however.

The best course of action was to stick close to the police, hope to get the jump on everybody else and ensure she was the first to get to the victim's family, friends and neighbours. She could gather material for an ongoing story that way. The clichés started to race through her mind and she put down her coffee cup and physically shook her head to get rid of these banalities. Families were always in shock and grief too deep to express in words. The victim was always a cheerful personable type who was looking forward to a bright future and they never had a single enemy in world. They were either the most popular and/or the most beautiful girl or handsome boy in the world. Did horrible, ugly, cheerless people never get attacked?

She replayed Gus Reid's words in her head. She had not written anything down, but she was confident she could remember it verbatim. He hadn't denied that it was a big case, a dramatic one. She'd used the word 'psycho' and he hadn't immediately rebuffed the assertion. He had definitely hinted it might be a case for someone further up the food chain. Higher than an inspector? It couldn't be a standard case of domestic violence that had escalated. What was it about the body that made Reid think that he could be too lowly to lead the enquiry? Rape and murder perhaps. Necrophilia? No, Reid wouldn't confirm the cause of death, so it might have more to do with the identity of the victim than the nature of the attack. Perhaps she was someone famous. Andrea tried to think if there were any celebrities of the right age – a young woman Reid had said – who could possibly have been in Swansea over the weekend. A pop star, or reality TV star? There hadn't been any big gigs and certainly no female sports events in the city. She would have known about anything like that. That still left girlfriends of rugby players and footballers. There had been a former soap actress engaged to a local footballing legend, but he'd been transferred to a bigger club a while back.

This idle speculation only wasted a few minutes.

She'd checked if any press statement had been released before calling Gus Reid. Thus far she was ahead of everyone else. It would not stay that way very long.

The moment Andrea had heard of the death of this poor, still nameless girl her mind had flown back twenty years to when she was in primary school and the headmistress had unexpectedly summoned the whole school into the hall for an announcement. Andrea had been working on an article for the school newspaper that her bright new teacher had initiated. It was about cruelty to animals and she vaguely remembered that she had been inspired to write the article after seeing television coverage of the BSE crisis a few weeks before. She never finished the piece because they were interrupted by a messenger with this news that everyone had to go to the hall. There was a strange stillness and all the teachers looked serious. The headmistress waited for the last few stragglers then cleared her voice. Even then she didn't say anything for a long time.

Eventually she spoke and the words came out tightly: 'I've asked you all to come here because I have some very sad news ...'

Andrea could remember those words but not the exact phrasing that followed, for her heart had tripped over and fallen in a sad heap at the news. Marie Sinclair was dead. Killed. The headmistress didn't say it was murder; that came out in the next few days. Marie wasn't even her friend. She wasn't really anybody's friend for she was a bit 'slow' and came from 'a rough family.' Thinking about it now Andrea was surprised how quickly society had moved on and changed the terminology of demonisation. If it had happened more recently poor Marie would have had certain specific learning disabilities and her family would have been in need of support. But the news of a fellow ten-year-old suddenly being removed from the planet irrevocably was both stunning and intensely saddening. The headmistress spoke for some time but all anyone really remembered was that Marie was dead and they were allowed to go home early that day.

The bright new teacher gave up on the idea of a school newspaper.

Now another girl was dead. It sounded like she was twenty or something. Reid had corrected himself when he said 'girl' and changed it to 'young woman.' So, not a girl, but someone scarcely out of her adolescence. Still learning, but to no point. At Bournemouth someone she didn't know very well had died of leukaemia in her second year and been awarded some sort of diploma of higher education. The university had a policy of awarding this interim type of qualification to any student who predeceased their graduation. For the parents' sake obviously. Andrea could not imagine what receiving that piece of paper would be like.

Nevertheless, it was vital to speak to the family, as soon as the dead girl was identified. It would make remarkable copy for a provincial title if Andrea could scoop that. As long as the family was local, of course. *The Evening Post* did not pay travel expenses. The police would release a photograph in due course, but there could be more heart-rending pictures if she could win over the parents and access a family album. Otherwise she would have to resort to accessing images from a Facebook page, and the danger there might be that they were too frivolous. Silly pictures with mates on nights out. Not nearly tasteful enough.

She decided to make a list of the questions she would ask of any family members she might be able to interview. Not a script exactly, but an *aide memoir* so that she could cover all the ground but still come across as spontaneous and empathetic.

For instance, what were her most cherished possessions and/or memories? What was she like as a teenager? Was she a good student at school? Andrea tutted at herself as she jotted down these notes. Something different was required, a unique selling point for the story. What was at the heart of the mystery of her death? If she could use her charms to get the father, say, talking about his daughter's prowess at gymnastics, or whatever it was that the girl thought she could succeed at in life, Andrea could make a real story. People might sit up and pay attention then.

But the girl might not be local. She might be someone who had landed in this far-flung outpost of civilisation by some fluke, as Andrea herself had done. She might not even be English, or Welsh, though January was not the tourist season. Still, there was a significant influx of European workers these days. Andrea hoped the girl hadn't been Polish, or worse, Albanian. Xenophobia increased in direct proportion to the economic exigencies of the time, and she suspected that readers of *The Evening Post* were not exactly Guardian reading liberals.

She flipped her notepad shut and finished her coffee. No one worried about where she was; it was just assumed that she was out and about gathering crucial details of bowls club meetings and Bring and Buy sales. But she needed to get back to the office to find out when Gus Reid would announce the press conference, and also to speak to Bill, her editor. She needed this story.

11

Gus had spoken to his chief inspector as soon as he heard that he was in his office. DCI Terry Newlands was a bluff, aggressive man who had managed to learn some people skills through management courses, but he had done so very reluctantly. His instinct was to bully those who were beneath him, be jocular and clubbable with his immediate superiors and fawn to his ultimate masters. He knew Gus was competent, however, and he refrained from speaking until Gus had finished his summary of what was known so far, which was precious little.

The Chief Inspector stroked his shining bald head and spoke in his deep Merthyr accent: 'So what'll you need? Do you want to go to the press straight away?'

Gus was prepared. 'With all the door-to-doors and the trace and eliminates we'll doubtless have to do, I'd suggest a team of eight to ten detectives. I'm thinking of telling *The Post* this afternoon, but not going national for a day or two if we can avoid it. It won't look good on us if we can't come up with an ID even.'

'Good try,' Newlands laughed. 'You can have Willis and two detective constables. If we get swamped with calls when it's on *Wales Today* I'll draft in a few more bodies, but let's try and get this solved quickly, eh?'

Gus wondered aloud if it would be best for him to pick his team members but Newlands saw this one coming too. 'Take Dai Webb, he's solid enough,' he said, 'in every sense, eh? And PC Lucy Cain could use some experience. Watch her carefully, she's likely to nip home and see her kid at the drop of a hat. She'll be useful if you point her in the right direction though.'

'I'll need someone who's a bit techy too,' Gus said. 'Shall I draft in a uniform who's clued up on all that stuff?' Gus was thinking of Stephanie Beddall, who was already working on the CCTV data and who looked like she might be rather more dynamic than Newlands' stodgy offerings.

'Yeah, okay,' Newlands grunted. 'Are you thinking of anybody in particular?'

'Stephanie Beddall has been looking at the CCTV for us. She seems keen.'

'She the black girl? The attractive one, looks a bit like Halle Berry?'

'She happens to be black,' Gus said primly, 'but she's also good with computer stuff. It was more those skills I was thinking of.'

'Oh alright, Gus, don't get all correct with me. Who are you planning to talk to at *The Post*?'

'A girl called Andrea Linney.'

'Oh, so be it. I happen to know the editor quite well, but you play it your way, Gus. Anything else?'

'You and the Chief Superintendent okay with me handling the press then?'

Newlands looked at Gus suspiciously, as if he was afraid he was being tricked somehow. 'It's only the local rag, man. No particular kudos for Gaston in that.'

'Or for you, clearly,' Gus thought. He was happy enough with a team of four officers working full time though. He'd asked for a horse in order to get a cat and they both knew it.

Back at his desk he looked at his A3 sheet of paper with his spider diagram and realised he had not put in the phrase he had seen chalked behind the bin. 'We shall this day light such a candle'; he said the words out loud as he wrote them down on one side of the paper. It read like a crossword clue as much as a quotation. Did 'such' refer to anything else? Did it simply mean a huge candle, or was it pointing to something else, some other candle that they simply hadn't observed yet? Or maybe light source rather than actual candle. He tried to think what other meaning the word 'candle' might possibly have but his mind stalled at Roman candle, which was pretty much still a candle anyway. He squinted at the words again. Why 'we'? This was surely the work of a single predator. Did the perpetrator want to include the investigation team in his project? He pushed the paper away. There was not even any real proof yet that the killer was responsible for chalking up the phrase. But the wheel marks from the bin were compelling. He tried writing down the letters of the phrase in random order, then lost track of how many vowels he had used. He occasionally watched *Countdown* and even more occasionally managed to work out the conundrum, but that was nine letters long. This was far too complicated. He threw down his pencil and sighed. That sort of stuff was for the old-fashioned British cop dramas, where the irascible but brilliant lone detective would decode the message in a contemptuous few seconds. Gus was more of a procedural animal; he would have to do it by the book, eliminating this and revisiting that as the evidence slowly came together. He knew he could see the pattern in a string of lies from a guilty party, but abstract word games were beyond him and therefore a waste of his time.

He got up and walked out to the central area, where people were talking on phones or staring at computer screens. Willis was standing a few feet away talking to a young female uniform who was surreptitiously hitching up her belt as she listened obediently. Gus found all the paraphernalia of batons, handcuffs, radios, notebooks unfetching on these younger officers. They looked like pack horses, to his way of thinking. He knew that the whiff of dominatrix was a heady enough musk for many of the male officers however. He caught Willis' eye and beckoned him over.

'Sir?'

Gus saw that the young woman was trying to look completely professional as she turned away to her duties but her eyes were bright and there was a faint blush on her cheek. Ben Willis was, Gus forced himself to realise, a well built, and somewhat prepossessing young man, despite the eyebrows and the serious expression. Gus smiled as he threw an arm round the young man's shoulder and led him away to one side of the room. 'I hope your mind is on the case and nothing but the case?'

Willis looked hurt. 'Of course, sir.'

'Of course it is. Pretty little thing though, eh?'

It was Willis' turn to redden slightly. 'I'm not sure I ...'

'Oh, don't fret. I'm playing. I do play sometimes, you know. But you're right, playtime's over. So, any news yet from the door-to-doors?'

'People aren't due back till two, though some of them will get here earlier on the pretence that they've got loads to write up. I just heard Marcia on the radio though, talking to Inspector Warren ...'

'What's he got to do with this?' Gus started to interrupt.

'I know, I know,' Willis said, 'He's working on some break-in, in Port Tennant.' Willis noted Gus's frown. 'Anyway, it looks like he's questioned somebody and they might know something about our case. Marcia told him to refer it to us as soon as possible.'

'Well why the hell hasn't he got in touch straight away? I would have thought a murder trumps a burglary any day! Get me his mobile number.'

Willis winced slightly.

'Never mind, I'll do it. Chase up whoever's checking the missing person files.'

Willis nodded, but Gus knew that he was merely repeating an order he had already given. With only an approximate age to work with and without even a photograph of their victim, whoever was ploughing through the records would not have an easy task. More than half the missing souls were female and inevitably almost everyone reported would be in the right age group. It wasn't only runaway girls that occasioned the public to panic, of course. Occasionally someone's grandfather would wander off because he had dementia, but they usually turned up within a few days, unless they died of hyperthermia of course.

Gus went back to his office and got Jim Warren's mobile number from a list in the top drawer of his desk. Warren answered curtly with his rank and surname.

'DI Reid here,' Gus said ponderously.

'Warren sounded annoyed. 'What do you want, Reid? I've got a customer with me.'

Gus did not know Jim Warren well, but everyone said he was a no nonsense type of guy. That was usually code for stupid, in Gus's book.

There was a pause as Warren hissed something at whoever he was with, then he continued: 'Actually I'm doing your job for you, as it happens. I can't talk now, but I'll get back to you when I've finished interviewing, if you'll just have the patience.'

'What do you mean?' Gus said. "We're all doing the same job here, aren't we?'

'I'm talking about the case that you were landed with this morning, but I'll call you back.' The line went dead.

Gus looked out of the small window that overlooked the yard at the back of the building. A uniform was stubbing out his cigarette on a wall, despite there being a disposal unit fixed to the same wall a few feet away. He felt a moment of despair at the futility of trying to get anybody to even obey basic courtesies, let alone the laws of the land. Luckily Willis interrupted the moment by breezing into the office again,

'Marcia just said that Warren's arrested our murderer.'

'Inspector Warren,' Gus said routinely.

'Sorry, sir, Inspector Warren.'

'How on earth has he done that?'

'The guy just coughed to it apparently. PC Clark is with Inspector Warren and he was radioed about something else. He told switch he couldn't respond because he was with a suspect in a murder case.'

'Marcia must have got it wrong,' Gus sighed. 'I was just talking to Warren.' He paused and sighed. 'He did sound extraordinarily smug though.'

It wasn't till later, half an hour after the briefing, that he learned that Warren had indeed arrested a man for murder but as soon as he discovered who it was he suspected that the case was far from over.

12

They fuck you up, your mum and dad. Oh deary deary deary me, how sad that parents get the blame for the sins of their progeny. Unless they deserve it, of course. Poor old mum, pathetically in hock to her sad belief that she must be doing the right thing if the Major said it was right. Major! I laugh at that now. He was never in the army, not the real one anyway, just the weekend one. The toy one. He used to dress up on a Friday night just to shout at spotty privates who didn't want to go to Afghanistan but wanted to hold a gun. Not a lot of danger in the Territorials. Ironic that he died as a result of enemy fire, if I may be excused the pun. I couldn't be around to see it, unfortunately, but it must have been a delicious sight, him staggering from his bed and choking from the fumes of a conflagration he'd started himself twenty years previously, if truth be told.

In some ways I was sorry that mum had to go too, but it's doubtful she could have made much of a fist of living on her own, without him to tell her what to watch on TV or what to wear when she went out. She never went anywhere anyway, except to the supermarket. Still, despite that useless life, I hope she didn't suffer too much. You'd have to be a monster to relish the thought of your mother screaming in pain as she burned alive, wouldn't you? I used to say (in a serious voice) they both perished in an accident. People always assume it's a traffic accident and they don't enquire too much further. Sorry for your loss, they'd say. I always want to laugh. What loss?

But they do fuck you up. Perhaps if I hadn't constantly been told that I would never amount to anything I might have tried harder in school. The teachers were shit though. They must be trained to expect nothing but mediocrity because they certainly didn't recognise the imagination and originality I had to offer. But who am I kidding? A lot of the stuff they spewed out just wasn't for me, if I'm honest. Throw physics to the dogs, and all that. Until I got into the sixth form anyway. Then they finally showed me Shakespeare and I realised what I'd wanted all along: words, words, words, as the Prince has it.

But they didn't want to hear ideas. Coles' Notes, they said, it's all you need for now. Don't go bothering your silly little head with half-baked ideas of your own, just highlight the good bits in the model answers and memorise them. Copy them out in your exams and hey presto! Three years of drinking and PlayStation and meeting people your own age at some fleapit university. You won't get a job after anyway, but if everyone else has got a degree you'd be a fool not to get one, wouldn't you? Notes for Lecture 1 when I get to be a motivational speaker: 'Don't do what everyone else does.'

Of course I had to go to university eventually. I say eventually, but I'm still only twenty six, aren't I? I'd like to tell myself I resigned, could no longer serve with honour, but technically I was thrown out. Or rusticated, as they said, their flabby mouths rolling over the word as if it was food. I couldn't have carried on; it was worse than school in terms of the mediocrity they fostered so carefully. But the complaints from those silly girls incited them to such unwonted anger and righteousness that they kicked me out before I could tell them what I thought of their flatulent so-called university and their pathetic tutors.

Ah me!

13

Jim Warren was a broad shouldered, narrow minded, failed rugby player who tackled problems in the same manner as he'd tackled opposing front row players, head down, head on, sophistication not part of the game plan. Not too long after their brief phone call he was sitting opposite Gus Reid in the canteen at Alexandra Road police station, alternately sipping hot tea and taking large bites out of a Boost chocolate bar.

'Darren and his brother Jugs did her,' Warren repeated. 'We haven't tracked down Jugs yet, but we will. He'll be by some bins somewhere in town, or down the beach sleeping off some drunken binge.' He gave out a long sigh, like a motor dying. 'Easy result for you though. No need for an MIT. *Gus Reid, Super Sleuth, Solves Swansea Slaying.* I can see *The Evening Post* headline now.'

'Tell me again how Darren Bunn came to admit he committed this crime,' Gus said quietly. It had been his first question, but Warren had just said that the feckless Bunn had stuck his hands up straightaway. *It was me wot done it guvnor, it's a fair cop.* Or a slightly more mumbled version of that anyway. Gus needed a little more clarity. 'You couldn't have accused him of the attack, could you? How could you even have been aware that a body had been found?'

'Well, I wasn't aware, was I? This was ten this morning. I was on my way into the station and I heard over the comms that there'd been a disturbance outside a café in Port Tennant. I was coming from Birchgrove so I dived down there. Darren was arguing with the owner, Italian feller, when I got there and he literally put his hands out for me to cuff him. "If you're here about the girl in town, it was me and Jugs done her," he said. He even laughed about it. This Italian bloke stormed back inside his café while I had it out with Darren. Made him tell me what he'd actually done. He said he was being falsely accused of trying to steal a bottle of coke from the fridge in the café. Then when I gave him one of my looks he came clean and said he'd battered a prostitute in High Street. Shoved her in a bin down a lane leading off it.'

'Who's this Jugs?'

'Oh, Darren's brother Jan.'

'Yan?'

'Yeah, spelled with a J though, as if he was a foreigner. Which he isn't. The Bunn brothers hail from somewhere near Llanelli. No fixed abode at the present time, or pretty much ever, since they were in their teens. Jan's called Jugs because of his ears. He doesn't mind that though. He's a bit simple.' Warren glanced around the canteen, which was fairly empty, just one uniformed officer sadly studying the drinks machine. 'Or whatever they call them these days,' he added conspiratorially.

'I'm sure it's *we* not just *they*,' Gus said. 'Learning difficulties.' Gus paused for a moment. 'Used to be Special Needs, but somehow 'special' didn't work out too well. But anyway, it's a long time since 'simple' was acceptable.'

'Well, both of them have severe learning difficulties. They're well known over East Side, always nicking from shops, trying to break and enter, but usually getting themselves caught in fencing or cutting themselves on the glass they've just smashed. Recidivists, they are.' He pronounced the word with relish, as if it was the first time he'd used it.

'So they've done time? How come I haven't heard of them before?'

'There's hardly ever need for an investigation. They fess up on the spot. Darren especially. They usually get a week or two of community service. Sometimes just a little tap on the back of the hand. I believe they've both done a few spells in prison though. Three months, six months, that sort of thing.'

'So why do you think it would suddenly escalate like this, DI Warren?'

'Pissed up, off their faces on something, wrong place, wrong time. Who knows?'

'Well, I guess it's up to us to know, don't you think? Where's Darren now?'

'Having a nice cup of tea in the East Side station,' Warren chuckled. 'He's being brought over here as we speak. He'll provide you with all the gory details, don't worry.'

Gus knocked back the dregs of his hot chocolate, which was too sticky and too sweet. 'Alright, but it sounds to me like you've rounded up a time waster who fancies a spell in the warm. It would be good if you could track down the brother, while I interrogate Darren.'

'Sure,' Warren said with a smile. 'I could do with a little drive round town. Keep in the warm, as you say.'

Gus went back to his office thinking about Warren's language. Fess up, come clean, stuck his hands up. How many crimes had he solved and what was the proportion to the number of ancient British crime shows he'd seen, Gus wondered. There was a blitheness about Warren that rankled against Gus's own fastidious nature. Still, if it was a random attack by a drugged up homeless man there would be no further attacks to worry about. Gus put down his pencil, which he'd been tapping unthinkingly on his desk. Darren and his brother Jan? When did *two* perpetrators commit such a brutal attack? He turned his attention to the section of his spider diagram that he'd marked off as 'Motive'. He'd written in a tiny but legible hand the words 'Revenge', 'Sex', 'Money', 'Religious Fanaticism' and 'Power'. The victim had no bag or purse with her so it might be robbery. But it was hard to believe that she'd been killed by someone who'd then crossed town and tried to steal a bottle of Coca Cola from a café. Warren had given no indication that The Bunn brothers were known for sex crimes or religious fervour. Revenge? Possibly. Power? What sort? Gus would soon find out, whatever. If he'd been so anxious to confess his crime to DI Warren, he would doubtless be happy to talk to Gus.

And it was within the first five minutes of talking to Darren Bunn that Gus knew that he did not have the culprit before him. Darren had come shuffling into the interview room, pushed inside by a young constable. That would be Robbie Clark, Gus thought. Bunn was tall but incredibly thin, his face haggard though he was probably still in his twenties. He had a prominent nose and two deep blue eyes that looked like they'd been hollowed out of some unearthly material. He sat down opposite Gus and placed his bony hands on the table in a gesture of frank acceptance of his circumstances.

'Okay if I call you Darren, Mr Bunn?' Gus asked.

'Absolutely, buddy. Darren from Trimsaran, that's me. Oh, and before you start crucifying me, I was confused when I told the other feller that Jugs was in on it, what I done, I mean. It was just me.'

'Other fellow?'

'The big man. Mr Warren.'

'Detective Inspector Warren,' Gus routinely corrected. 'Now, DI Warren tells me that you wish to confess to a crime, Darren.'

'That's right. The girl in the bin.'

'And what did you do to this girl?'

'Smacked her one, didn't? Over the head. Then I bunged her in this big black bin they got by the chicken takeaway.'

'Two questions, Darren. Was she alive when you put her there? And what time did this attack take place?'

The suspect turned his head, as if to shield his answer from the constable standing near the doorway. 'Definitely a goner. Early hours. Hard to say exactly when.'

'Why is that hard to say, Darren?'

'Well, I don't wear a watch, do I? He looked round the room again. 'Say, about one, two. After the pubs shut anyway.'

'How many times did you strike this poor girl, Mr Bunn?

Bunn's head shot up. 'Once! I'm not a pervert.'

'And what did you hit her with? Did you use some kind of weapon? Or implement, should I say?'

Bunn thought about this. 'A bottle. I saw this bottle on the floor, so I picked it up and let her have it. With the bottle.' He sat back in his chair, satisfied with his adroit handling of this difficult interrogation.

'And what did you do with bottle then?' Both men knew there was no bottle on the ground near the buster bin, or in the bin.

'I disposed of it.' The young man looked pleased with his own choice of term. It sounded like the sort of word you'd use in an interview room.

'Where, Darren?'

'I just chucked it. Can't remember prezactly where.'

So much for the technical language, Gus thought, but he allowed no shadow of a smile to cross his expression. 'Well, we would need to know where, you see, for us to conduct the appropriate forensic analysis.'

54

Darren Bunn nodded. Yes, he understood something about that. His lips pursed. Perhaps not the exact details, his face said.

'Just trying to get this clear in my mind now, Darren. 'You haven't been charged with anything as yet, you're just helping with our enquiries on a completely voluntary basis. How many times did you hit this young woman? Just the once, I think you said?'

'Yep.' He looked directly into his interlocutor's eyes, to try and find the correct answer. 'Or twice, maybe. It could have been twice because it was late, and dark, and I can get confused about things sometimes.'

'Mm hmm. And what would you say was your motive … er … why did you want to hurt her, Darren?'

'Dunno. Sometimes I just does things without really knowing why, I spose.'

'Was your brother with you during this incident?'

'Ah! Yes, that's the thing. I thought he was. That's why I told your mate we both done it. But he wadn't. He was down The Slip. Well, that's where I left him earlier on. We was drinking with a bloke we knows down there. I must have been thinking that Jugs come up High Street with me but he never.' He looked down at his shoes, seemingly surprised that he was wearing any. Then he looked steadfastly back at Gus. 'I didn't touch her. I wouldn't do anything like that.'

'You mean you didn't do anything of a sexual nature? Nothing inappropriate?'

'That's right. I'm not one of them.'

Clearly murder did not fall into Darren Bunn's personal classification of inappropriate actions, but Gus knew it wasn't worth the cheap shot. He was clearly innocent. There was no weapon, his account of the attack was completely inaccurate, and the timing was all wrong. He somehow knew that the victim had been in the buster bin at some point in the night, however, and therefore he might be able to supply some useful information. Gus pressed on patiently. 'I need to know exactly when you found her, Darren. Help me here, please.'

Bunn looked at his wrist as if there might be a watch there that had magically stopped at the right moment. 'Like I said, I'm a bit hazy about time. Though hang on, I did see that it was two o' clock when

I walked past The Guildhall. That's about half an hour's walk to High Street, I'd say. So, about half two.'

The Slip, a small stretch of beach on the bay near the law courts and The Guildhall, was a ten minute stroll away from where the girl had been found. Perhaps it would take an inebriated Darren Bunn longer, but this was relatively unimportant. He had not even noticed that Gus had used the word 'found' rather than 'met' or 'attacked'. Somewhere between two o' clock and three fitted his earlier prognosis for when the body had been disposed, so at least the time frame was somewhat narrower now.

'Okay. We may need to talk to you again in due course but you're free to go about your business now, Darren.'

'Oh, don't I get a cup of tea and a biscuit or nothing then?' he looked downcast for a second then his face brightened again, 'Business, that's a good one. Right you are then, I'll get back to my business. I spose my chauffeur's waiting for me outside He'll usually *show for* me. Geddit?'

'Thank you for your time, Mr Bunn. We may have to get in touch again. You remain a person of interest.' Gus rose and held the door open for his guest. There was a particularly fetid odour to the man which nearly made Gus gag, but he managed to compose himself in front of Constable Clark.

'Person of interest?' Darren turned to say.' Good one. Not many people say that about me.'

***

An hour later Gus was tapping his pencil again, this time on the front desk of the meeting room. Four officers had filed in: DS Ben Willis, PC Lucy Cain, PC Dai Webb and PC Stephanie Beddall. Willis had tracked down photographs of the Bunn brothers and he handed them now to Gus, along with a new pack of whiteboard markers. Gus stuck the photographs to the whiteboard with blu-tack then drew a horizontal line across the board, marking off three points on the line in red.

'Right everyone. Some of you won't have worked a murder case before so I'll start with the absolute basics. We've got a female victim, unidentified as yet, looks to be in her late teens, early twenties. We don't know where she was killed but she was found in the disposal site, a large black bin in King's Lane, which is a narrow alley off High Street, at seven thirty or so this morning.' He wrote in the time on the right hand point of his timeline. 'The discovery was phoned in by a postie out on his morning round. I don't know why he was walking down King's Lane but we'll find out. It's very unlikely he's the perpetrator. We'll put out an appeal for witnesses obviously. The victim was strangled, but there aren't any fingerprints because a ligature was used. No sign of that yet. She also had her face smashed in, particularly around the mouth area. I'm not even sure if we'll be able to get any dental evidence to identify her at this point. She did not appear to have been sexually assaulted. Our pathologist, Jenny Sarka, will get us full details by tomorrow at the latest, and hopefully by later on today.'

Stephanie Beddall, a serious looking young detective quite new to the force, was looking uncomfortable, Gus noted. 'It's a pretty gruesome case, I know.'

'It's not that sir, I thought we'd already apprehended the perpetrator?'

'Ah,' Gus sighed. 'Now we may have been rather hasty there. DI Warren brought in a suspect who claimed he'd committed the murder, but the man has been released for the moment, pending further investigation, as we like to say.' He turned round to the whiteboard and pointed to one of the photographs with his red marker. 'This is the guy who confessed. Darren Bunn. That's his brother Jan next to him. Darren initially claimed they were both responsible, then subsequently retracted that statement and claimed sole responsibility. The thing is, he's a serial confessor and there are huge holes in his story. It seems certain that he saw the body, perhaps at about two thirty this morning, which at least makes it fairly certain that she was dumped there shortly before.' He turned again to tap the next point on his timeline and scribble in the numbers. 'That helps us quite a bit actually. But he claims he hit her with a bottle, which is nowhere to be seen at the site, and anyway Jenny Sarka is pretty convinced that the girl wasn't killed in King's Lane. So it doesn't make any sense. Also, Darren Bunn says he hit her twice at most, which doesn't correlate to the massive injuries to the poor girl's face. If we needed any further evidence, Bunn doesn't appear to have any motive and the profile so far suggests a murderer with strong personal motivation, not just a bit of drunken savagery. Sarka has also provisionally said that the murder took place some time the previous day. Bunn wouldn't have known that, naturally.' Gus paused again and sighed. 'And he said he'd killed a prostitute. She may have been working, of course, but her clothing doesn't suggest it. She had little or no makeup either. Sorry, ladies, if I'm stereotyping here, but prostitutes don't usually go for the demure look, in my personal experience.'

There was a snort from Dai Webb at this point.

'I mean professional experience, DC Webb.' Gus was not offended, realised in fact that it was a moment of comic relief from the awfulness of what they were dealing with. 'Anyway,' he continued, 'Bunn probably just assumed she was a working girl because from his point of view she was a young woman out on her own late at night. He's not the most imaginative of souls, our Darren.'

'Sorry sir,' Stephanie interrupted. Gus was half-pleased, half-wary that she was so keen. 'Are you saying she didn't have anything to identify her, if all we have is the body? Wouldn't it be likely to be a mugging, because girls always have a handbag, or a phone and wallet at least?'

Willis answered for Gus this time. 'She was killed elsewhere. Muggers don't kill somebody and then cart them off to a dump site, it's not in the job spec.'

'Alright, Willis,' Gus interposed. 'You're perfectly right, but let's try and keep this serious, shall we?' He looked at Stephanie again. She was bright eyed, and, as Newlands had noted, extremely attractive. Her hair was scraped up into a thick dark curly bun. Gus had a sudden fancy that she was like a cockapoodle waiting for a stick to be thrown. 'We'll go through the usual identification procedures,' he said.

'Missing persons, public appeal, fingerprints, do you mean, sir? I've already started on the mispers but there's nothing much yet.'

Willis helped out again, this time more solemnly: 'We're not sure a public appeal is appropriate just yet because we can't release a photo of such a damaged face without causing a lot of alarm.' He faced Gus again. 'I believe you were thinking about her clothing, sir?'

'Thanks, Ben. Yes, she was wearing some quite recently acquired items, reasonably distinctive too, so we'll pursue that avenue initially. She was wearing shoes from Rowberry, for instance, and they may have sale records that could help. Would you like to check that one out, PC Cain?' He was addressing the other female detective, a stocky ginger haired thirty something whom he had worked with once or twice and knew to be a plodder, but thorough enough. 'I'm not being sexist here; I just think the shop would respond to a woman detective better perhaps.' There were so many dangers these days, Gus felt, but Lucy Cain did not register anything in the way of resentment at the menial task. It was marginally better than door-to-doors.

'Now,' Gus said, 'I haven't put a number at this end of the timeline because we still don't have a TOD, but it's likely to have been somewhere between eight o'clock yesterday morning and two in the afternoon. Now she could have been killed anywhere so we need to first check any suspicious cars that may have brought the body to King's Lane at about two o'clock this morning. We've started on that already. But since it seems most probable that she was killed in daylight, and if she wasn't dumped from a vehicle, then it's also possible that the actual crime scene could be quite close by. It would have to be indoors somewhere but there aren't any houses around there. If we're to assume she was carried there, or pushed there in a trolley or something, we need to be checking nearby buildings for likely scenes of crime. Any warehouses or garages, outbuildings of some sort. PC Webb, can you get onto that?'

The three constables did not look particularly happy at their tasks, but at least they had tasks. Willis gave Gus a thin smile, suggesting perhaps that he knew too that today was going to be long and probably unproductive.

'Off you go then,' Gus said. 'Ben, can we have a word?'

The two men went back to Gus's office. As he closed the door Willis spoke,' I was wondering why you didn't mention the chalk message, sir.'

'I thought about it,' Gus replied. 'But the urgency is to identify Jane Doe and locate the crime scene. We can get down to the job of finding her nemesis and whatever crazy motivation he had in due course. And I'm not even certain that the message has anything to do with anything at the moment.'

'Not being obtuse, sir, but it's bound to have something to do with something, isn't it?'

'I'm afraid you're probably right there. Tell me, what's your instinct about it?'

'What was the exact wording again?'

Gus checked his notes. *'We shall this day light such a candle.* I checked to see if it was a famous quotation, and it is. Something one of the Guy Fawkes conspirators said just before he was executed, apparently.

'Phew. That doesn't sound very helpful. He didn't burn the body in any way, did he?'

'I don't think it's that literal.' Gus stroked his chin, then promptly stopped himself. He was no Sherlock Holmes. 'It's something Ray Bradbury quoted in *Farenheit 451* as well, if that helps.'

'Farenheit 451?'

'It's a book about people burning books.'

'I see,' Willis said. He plainly didn't, but in all honesty neither did his superior officer.

14

I'd seen her going into Lidl three times on Sundays, always about ten o'clock in the morning, just after they opened. That's what gave me the idea to scout out somewhere close by to do the dastardly deed. The place is a bit of a wasteland at this time on the Sabbath (I know!) but I knew it would have to be somewhere secluded. There's a sort of courtyard affair behind the cinema just over the road where they keep the bins and I considered that, but someone might have been working inside, a cleaner or caretaker or something, and they could have come out just at the right (or wrong) moment. I hadn't quite settled on how I was going to persuade her to take a little stroll with me but I was fairly certain that she wouldn't have willingly gone in there anyway. But I did spot something that looked more promising. There's a small building about fifty yards away where retired nuns live. Do nuns retire? Isn't being a nun a sort of whole life profession? Anyway, it's a home for Catholic women that no one wants to see any more, I think. Next to it is a garage, or outside storeroom, more like. I didn't imagine these ex-nuns do a lot of driving so I had a shufti through a side window and it looked absolutely perfect. The right sort of place for me to sit someone down and explain a few things, maybe ask a question or two, like, what did they think about humiliating someone in front of everybody and then just smirking about it? Not that I envisaged her being able to speak, with a very tight gag in her mouth.

There was, of course, a bit of a problem. A big thick steel problem. I studied this problem carefully and came up with a ruse I'm rather proud of, I have to say. First off, I angled the padlock a bit so that I could come back periodically and see if anyone had unlocked the doors to use the place. They'd never put the padlock back in the precise same position, would they?

I went down there half a dozen times and it hadn't been touched. Stage one satisfactorily completed. Then I took a photograph of the damn thing and went to B&Q to see if I could get one that looked exactly the same. Roughly the same would have done in all likelihood, but I got lucky. They had the same model. Except of course it was newer and shinier. I went to a small DIY shop in Sketty for the junior hacksaw because I didn't want any CCTV of me buying these two items at the same time. I'd bought some other stuff in B&Q, a hasp, or whatever it's called, and a pack of screws. Some hardware for the shed in my dad's allotment was what was running through my head, just in case anybody was ever going to give me a grilling about these purchases. I threw the screws and the hasp in the nearest bin, needless to say. Not me guvnor!

Now I had the problem of getting the padlock to look like it had a bit of wear. I soaked it in tea, but that just wiped off straight away. Galvanised metal, who needs it, eh? But after I'd given it a couple of whacks with a hammer – not too much, it had to open easily – and rubbed a handful of soil over it, it didn't look brand new. If plod ever locates the 'crime scene' (hah!) I'm sure the nuns wouldn't be able to say that it was a different padlock. Of course I knew I'd have to leave it open when we left because the coppers would ask for the key to open it and they'd discover it was a different one.

The next thing was to do the swop. I practised sawing through metal at home, but not so much that I'd blunt the hacksaw. It was hard work. I've seen people on TV shows snapping right through half an inch of steel with huge bolt cutters but I couldn't risk being stopped ambling through town with a giant pair of bolt cutters under my mac, could I? Also, even the dumbest of till monkeys would remember someone like me buying such a monstrous tool and naturally I choose not to be noticed. So, a couple of hours sawing with a junior hacksaw in the middle of the night was the only real way to go.

I cut through the padlock on Christmas morning. Nary a soul to be seen anywhere on the streets and, as I imagine, the nuns tucking into their mince pies while they listened to a carol service from Kings on TV. It didn't take as long as I thought either. I slipped the lock into my pocket and replaced it with my non tea-stained but rather grubby new padlock and made my way gaily back here, enjoying the satisfying clunk of the broken padlock as it banged against my side. At least until it met its watery end down a drain on St Helen's Road. I slipped it through the grille as I bent to tie an imaginary shoelace. Wearing my trench coat as I was, I felt like I was in East Berlin in the late sixties! I decided to keep the hacksaw though. It might come in handy one day, and it was a nice memento of a successful covert operation.

15

Josie had ground her way diligently but uninspiringly through *Richard III*, playfully diverting into *Henry IV Part One* at one stage, though that diversion turned out to be a dead end, and by one minute past eleven she was sitting in her study again. The lad who'd had a dental appointment, or who had at least claimed to have had one, did turn up. Not at half time, however, but ten minutes before the end of the session, really only in time to collect the handouts. Of the girl Lauren, there had been no sign. Not too bad an attendance then, Josie congratulated herself. She had another seminar at half past two but this was not on her mind right now. It did not need much preparation since the topic was regional dialectal differences and she had already put together a slide show and worksheets. The students would have plenty of anecdotal examples of their own, if last year's session was anything to go by, and they would probably respond well. Other people's language was funny. For now she could trawl through her emails again or perhaps look over some further examples for the seminar but neither task appealed much. Feeling a trifle guilty at the prospect of a listless couple of hours she picked up a copy of William Barnes' poetry but she could not face that either. She put it down again and looked at her phone. Nothing save for a few marketing emails.

She stood up to look out of the window. The wind was up again; branches swaying in the clump of trees beyond the tennis courts across the way, crisp packets swirling in a corner by two low brick walls. Beyond the roofs of the houses below campus was the midpoint of the crescent of the bay which stretched from the Marina at one end to the lighthouse at the other end. The sea was gunmetal grey, the waves crashing when normally they crept up the beach. She could not see anyone at this distance, but you could have drawn a straight line down from her office window to the beach and a point along that line about a mile distant was the seat where Andrea Linney had recently been sitting in the Sea Beach Tavern.

Josie was still thinking about the seven ages of man speech, trying to recall the description of the justice – something about severe eyes and a well cut beard – when her attention was caught by a figure tacking across the yard below. It was George Wright again, slightly less dignified and composed now as he battled against the gusting wind. He was trying ineffectually to pat down his fine head of hair. Josie was tempted to open the window and shout something down. 'Avast, me hearties', or something along those lines, for she was suddenly unaccountably feeling playful. But she resisted the impulse. It would let a blast of cold air into her study. Then George looked up, straight at her, as if he had been able to tell what she was thinking. He gave a little wave, then veered off into the doorway of the library building. Josie stood back from the window, feeling a little abashed.

Then less than ten minutes later her office phone rang. It was George. Was she free for twenty minutes? Did she fancy a coffee in the cafeteria? Couple of things he wanted to run by her. She pretended to flick through a desk diary and said brightly, 'Yes, coffee would be good. I've not long ago had one, but it was homemade, with Nescafe and powdered milk. I need some real coffee to get rid of the taste.'

She put down the phone and winced. She heard again the light, bright tone of her voice and thought it had sounded too coquettish. She put on her serious face and set off for the cafeteria, which was at the far end of the campus, through a number of corridors, open spaces and covered walkways where sneering colleagues could be loitering, waiting for something to gossip about.

She took a seat near the entrance because she had arrived before George and she was definitely not going to treat him to a coffee. She took out a paperback from her bag and opened at a random page. It was *The Goldfinch*, actually Donna Tartt's third novel but for most reviewers the long awaited follow up to *The Secret History*. She hadn't made it all the way through that book, though everyone said it was excellent. She had read the first page of this one but somehow doubted she'd make it any further than that. It did make a good prop, however, because it was the sort of book people would expect her to be reading. She didn't have to finish the paragraph she'd started cursorily reading before George was standing in front of her.

'I believe the title refers to a painting from the Dutch golden age,' he said urbanely, nodding at the book as she put it down.

'I haven't got into it yet,' Josie said.

'Nor me actually. But I find it expedient to have a snippet or two of information about a range of literature. The odd quote. Tends to stop people in their tracks when they're just about to try and tell you stuff you're not interested in, I find.'

'That's cynical of you George.' Despite herself, Josie had appreciated this tip. Too often she had spent an inordinate amount of time ploughing through one of the 'great works' of literature when perhaps she could have skimmed it and got the gist. It had seemed rude not to finish a book once you had committed to it, but life was short. And getting shorter by the day perforce.

'Well,' George sighed. 'Call me an Autolycus, if you will. I am no Hamlet, nor was meant to be.' He did something that was almost like a wink but he turned his head toward the cafeteria counter before Josie could be sure. 'I'll get us some coffee. Americano? Latte?'

'Americano, with cold milk,' Josie smiled. She thought about his throwaway line. Autolycus, Shakespeare's snapper-up of unconsidered trifles, and the reference to Alfred J. Prufrock. Two snippets in a single sentence. He had to practise these things, surely?

When he returned with the drinks Josie was determined to waste no further time on pleasant banter. 'So what do you want to run by me, George? Couple of things, I think you said.'

'Yes. Well, actually one academic thing and one rather more social thing.'

'The academic matter?'

'Yes. Well, I know you get on particularly well with our Second Years. They speak highly of your Shakespeare seminars you know.'

Josie interrupted him, because this looked like it was heading towards him asking her another favour. 'I don't know if that's all that true. If I were to judge by last year's evaluations, apparently I may be 'doing their heads in'.

'That was the bard, not you. I read the evaluation forms, Josie.' There was suddenly this much sharper tone to him. Josie had to remind herself that George Wright was a charmer, a ladies' man, but he also had a keen mind.

65

'So what were you thinking then?'

He smiled his most winsome smile. 'I was wondering whether you'd like to think about organising a trip for them up to Stratford-on-Avon. I used to do an overnight thing, see a play in the evening, take in Warwick Castle the following morning. I haven't done it for a couple of years now though. It's good for bonding, and if you pick a good production it can help with their interest in Shakespeare. See it as actual drama, not just as line after line of impenetrable blank verse, you know?'

'Were you thinking of this as a joint effort?'

George glanced down at his coffee. 'Are you suggesting I'd need to hold your hand?'

'Not at all. But you do have something of a reputation, you know. You do know that, don't you?'

He was not offended but he didn't react as Josie thought he might either. He simply looked rueful. 'I'm sure you know, as a Shakespeare buff, that reputation is an idle and most false imposition. Oft got without merit.'

Josie racked her mind for the source for this.

'Iago says it to Cassio in Act Two.'

'Yes, yes. I was just trying to place it,' Josie said. 'You are indeed a snapper-up of trifles, aren't you?'

'Bit early for trifle. I was thinking about a cookie to go with this coffee though.'

Josie had to smile. Obscure lines from Shakespeare and T. S. Eliot one minute, bad puns the next. 'I'll have a look at what's on at the RSC when I get back to my study,' she said. She inwardly tutted at her use of 'study' for 'office' but it was too late to correct herself. 'Okay, that's the academic matter. What was the other thing?'

'In light of your response to my Stratford suggestion I think maybe I ought to keep that matter for another occasion.'

'You were going to ask me out?' She knitted her brows, but only facetiously. 'George, aren't you married?'

'How single would I have to be?'

'A bit more than actually married, I'd say.'

'Oh, don't be like that. I was just thinking of an early evening drink. Just a chat, you know.'

Josie smiled. She had the upper hand in this conversation for the first time. 'I would consider an early evening drink as a friend. That sounds perfectly acceptable. Not tonight though. I've got plans.'

'Of course. Whenever you are free, naturally. Would you like to talk about William Barnes now?'

'Not really. Is that what you'd like to do?'

'Definitely not. Shall we just trade secrets and malicious gossip about our colleagues for a bit?'

'I'm happy to listen to a few secrets,' Josie said. 'I'm not sure I've got much to trade though.'

They both took a sip of their coffee and they both let their eyes wander over the heads of the people at the nearby tables.

She was not telling the truth about her plans for the evening, of course. It was true that today she had considered getting in touch with Simon but she was not yet a desperate single woman. Just an attractive young woman who happened to be single at the moment. The 'attractive' epithet she'd inserted into her disjointed interior monologue because of George Wright's obvious interest in her.

Back in her office she took out the mirror she kept in the bottom drawer of her filing cabinet and rested it against a couple of thick tomes of university regulations and procedures on top of the cabinet. Her cheeks were a little too red, but her eyes were brighter than usual perhaps and her hair looked good in this wind-tousled and interesting state. She would pass. But she definitely needed to read *Othello* again. Maybe they were doing it this season at the main stage in Stratford. Or even at The Swan, which was a more intimate venue. She opened her laptop and typed 'RSC' into the search bar.

***

When Andrea Linney left The Sea Beach Inn she was immediately buffeted by the wind and had to pull up the hood of her anorak. Nevertheless, she decided to cross the road to look over the wall at the tide, which was full in now. Salt spray flicked against her cheeks and lips and she relished the moment of communion with rough nature. There was only one person in sight on the beach, a dog walker with a big black Labrador bouncing alongside him. She wondered who it was that could walk their dogs at lunchtime. Didn't everyone work, or if they didn't work, stay in bed all day? Fran had texted at just before 9.30. That would have been almost certainly immediately after seeing the police at the crime scene. If Fran started work at 9.30 the body could not be too far from there, but in which direction? Even if she located the place where the body had been found there wouldn't be much point trying to squeeze any details out of a young constable guarding the scene. The scene might well not be in play now anyway. She breathed a last gulp of sea air and headed back to her newspaper office. She was annoyed with herself for wasting her time drinking coffee and imagining her punchy account of the tragedy and the follow up interviews with friends and relatives. It was time to do some proper investigating.

She decided she still wouldn't speak to her editor. Instead, it would be good to face him armed with as much detail as possible. She walked briskly along the seafront and then up past The Cross Keys, apparently Swansea's oldest pub, and then cutting through Castle Gardens she reached High Street. The *Evening Post* building was now housed in what planners called The Urban Village, a collection of offices and cafes that suggested new life was being breathed into the moribund city. She walked through the foyer, giving Dawn on Reception a brief wave, and made her way up to the area where archived reports were stored. She strode over to the bank of carrels on one side of the archive and plonked herself down. She pulled off her anorak, blew a stray hair from her eye line and began her search for 'murders in Swansea since 1994' though she didn't quite know why she had selected this date. Twenty years was surely a big enough time frame though. There were only nine cases, the earliest dating back to 1996 and the most recent in 2012. This was a gruesome murder by a man called Grabham, who had killed his wife of only a few months and put her mutilated body in a suitcase, then thrown the suitcase out of his car. The 1999 quadruple murder was an infamous case widely known as the Clydach Murders. Reams had been written about what had happened and at least one TV documentary had questioned the verdict passed on David Morris. Andrea knew all about this. She also knew as much as she ever cared to know about the thoroughly disturbing murder of a teenager called Ben Bellamy, and the butchery of a young woman Called Joanne Tregembo, but she was surprised that she had not heard of the other five murders. One victim was an old cannabis fiend, another a Big Issue seller, a third was a case of infanticide in 2007. The remaining two killings were perhaps the strangest. One was a stabbing by a Richard Davies of his best friend Jason Williams in 2001. The other was a case of murder and necrophilia. In 2002 a man called Richard Cullen had strangled a poor 21-year-old girl and raped her dead body three times. Andrea did not know if she had the stomach to delve into that case, but it was the only one which bore any strong resemblance to what might have happened somewhere in the city earlier that day, or perhaps the previous evening. She pulled up the paper's archive for that year.

It was a lurid business involving cross dressing and Satanism as well as plentiful detail about the battering and throttling this madman had inflicted on the poor girl. Apparently, she had infuriated her killer by calling him a 'nonce' for fancying a female character in the episode of *Buffy the Vampire Slayer* they had been watching together. Andrea looked away from her screen. She wanted a big story, but she wanted it to be a story that she could investigate in detail without feeling total nausea. In this she would be disappointed.

16

Gus was sitting disconsolately by his desk. The door-to-door reports and the list of missing persons would not be available for a few hours in all likelihood, and he was not holding out much hope that Lucy Cain would get anything from her shopping expedition. PC Webb would wander around the shopping mall across the road from the bottom of King's Lane for a couple of hours probably. There was a Starbucks at one end that might detain him for a while. Gus opened a drawer in his desk and pulled out a folder. It contained the statements from the officers involved in the code blue episode from a fortnight ago.

He had read them already, of course, and had been depressed by the uniformity of them. Four officers, three constables and a PCSO, had all witnessed exactly the same thing and all described events in identical language. Couldn't they even have just changed a phrase or two? He re-read the first statement, signed by PC Luke Garrard:

'At 20.14 on Friday 19th December I was parked in a lay-by in my patrol vehicle CT63AVP with PC Steve Landers when we both observed a blue Astra, vehicle index CU60SRN, travelling East on Fabian Way, Swansea. The vehicle was being driven by a person known to both PC Landers and myself as a person involved in drug dealing, namely Sean McTigue. We both thought that he was probably exceeding the speed limit though we didn't have our radar gun operational at that time. We set off in pursuit because the road was clear and the weather conditions permitted it and I noticed that the Astra had slowed down, indicating that the driver had in fact been speeding and that he had become aware of our presence. We drew alongside him and I waved at him to indicate for him to pull over, which he duly did. When I approached the vehicle I felt certain that Mr McTigue had just concealed something beneath the driver's seat. I asked him to get out of his vehicle but initially he refused to do so. I reached for the keys in the ignition and he grabbed my arm. Then he slumped out of the door as if I'd assaulted him, which I did not.

By this time PC Landers was standing by the passenger door and he saw exactly what I did. Mr McTigue was groaning as I asked him to step out of his car but he did alight and then he promptly sat down on the road. I considered him to be in an extremely dangerous position here so I tried to get him to stand up and move to the back of the car. Before I could do this Officers Simpson and Denney arrived and they came over to help me move Mr McTigue. I proceeded to conduct a rudimentary search of the Astra, because I suspected that drugs had been placed beneath the driver's seat. Whilst I was doing this PCSO Denney secured the suspect to the rear of his car whilst we awaited the arrival of medical assistance. Mr McTigue was questioned about the possible drugs and asked where he was travelling to and where he had come from. He was not in a state to talk clearly so PC Landers called for an ambulance. A paramedic arrived about ten minutes later and said that Mr McTigue had probably suffered a massive heart attack and he pronounced him dead. He was then taken to Morriston hospital while PC Landers and myself ensured that the area was coned off as we waited for a rescue vehicle to remove the Astra.'

Landers' statement was identical in essence, though he could not mention the elusive drugs, of course. No drugs had subsequently been found in the car. The statements by Denney and Simpson contained no differences at all. They had been passing and seen the police car and the Astra and had stopped to offer assistance. Denney had 'helped' Mr McTigue to the rear of his vehicle and had secured him there because he was trying to break free. He thought it was safer for everyone involved that he do this, rather than help McTigue onto the grass bank a few yards away, because the man seemed to be unaware of his surroundings and could have run out onto the carriage way and been injured or killed. Simpson had observed all this and noted that Landers had called for an ambulance. He thought that was at about 20.35, but later learned that the call had been logged at 20.42. All four officers claimed to have acted with the safety of Mr McTigue and other road users uppermost in their minds.

'You fucking handcuffed the poor bastard,' Gus said aloud, as he flung the file back onto his desk. There would be an inquest, naturally. The inquest would report an open verdict at best. PCSO Denney had already handed his notice in and was apparently just about to emigrate to New Zealand, where his brother lived. Garrard and Landers were still traffic cops. Perhaps they were more circumspect in their dealings with drivers violating speed limits. Perhaps they just thought McTigue had taken too much of his own product and there was one less villain out and about on their patch.

Gus had been asked to look over the statements before Professional Standards got their teeth into them. The rubber heelers would doubtless notice that all four statements were remarkably consistent, but in the absence of witnesses there wouldn't be much they could do As long as the men stuck together, of course. He put the file away; he had done his duty, and would report that the statements were acceptable and apparently truthful, but it left an unpleasant taste in his mouth.

He took out his spider diagram from another drawer and examined it again. His eyes were drawn to the legend 'We shall light such a candle'. He pulled out his phone and looked at the photograph he had taken of the message. It had been inscribed carefully in block capitals, which suggested that it was not just a piece of graffiti but some sort of clue, but perhaps that was too fanciful. He would need to get a forensic analysis of the writing carried out. It wasn't a priority yet, however, it was just a loose thread. When the victim had been identified he could begin working on motives. Till then he had to just wait for more information. And then a trilling sound announced that he would not have to wait too long. It was Jenny Sarka.

'Inspector Reid? I've got something for you.'

Gus felt a surge of excitement. 'You've identified the victim? Better still, the murderer?'

'Easy, tiger,' she said. 'I'll leave the felon catching to you but I have got two things that may help with identifying your victim. One, she had a gold tooth. Lower left-hand molar. They don't hallmark them, you understand, but it could make it easier to track her down through dental records, if you get some likely candidates through a public appeal, or through missing persons.'

'I thought we used dentals to identify people when they were totally decomposed, or burnt to a cinder.' Gus heard his own words and thought they sounded a little insensitive, but Jenny Sarka did not

72

rebuke him.

'That's true. It's a ratification process, inevitably. We can't ask every dentist in the land, can we?'

'Or in every country,' Gus said. 'We know nothing about her as yet. She could be a foreign worker, or an exchange student.'

'Well, that's where the second thing may be more helpful. She's got a tattoo. A small bird at the base of her spine.'

Gus immediately wrote the words 'small bird tattoo' at the bottom of his diagram, though he was hardly likely to forget such an important detail.

'If it was done locally you'll get a hit in no time, I shouldn't wonder. I'm sending my report to you shortly but I thought you might like to look at an image of it straight away. I'll send it now.'

'Anything else,' Gus asked. 'Time of death, any other injuries, signs of sexual assault?'

'It's all in the report. I just thought you'd want to know about the tattoo and the gold tooth straight away.'

Gus thanked her and ended the call and waited impatiently for the image of the little bird to come through. Even before that happened there was another revelation. Sergeant Ben Willis knocked on his door and entered immediately.

'There's another message,' he said,

'What?'

'Another message.'

'Yes, I heard that. What's the message? Wait. Where was this message? Not at the King's Road site, surely?'

'I've got it here. The SOCOs found a slip of paper in the stuff they took from the bin. They thought it was a bit odd and I should look at it. I mean, we should look at it.' He passed Gus a piece of paper about the size of a rizla tobacco paper but evidently cut from ordinary typing bond. There were just three words on it: 'sticks and stones'.

'May break my bones,' Gus muttered.

'Sir?'

'Sticks and stones may break my bones but words will never hurt me.'

Willis looked blank.

'It's an old saying. Kids in schoolyards used to chant it back at bullies.' He looked at the paper again. 'This looks typed, not word processed.' He made a sucking noise with his teeth. 'Strange. Who uses a typewriter these days?'

'Perhaps it's not new,' Willis suggested. 'Could be an old piece of paper that just got thrown out. Nothing to do with anything.'

'Where did the SOCOS find it?'

'It was with the cardboard that they took out, to analyse the blood and that.'

Gus held up the paper to the light. With huge luck there might be a watermark, or part of one. There wasn't. 'It looks too clean to be old,' he mused. 'I think we've got someone who's anxious to communicate with us, Willis. If it was with that cardboard she was lying on it must have been placed there deliberately. For us to find, I mean.'

Willis looked impressed. This was more like the Sherlocking he craved.

'Good work, Ben. Now I've got something very important for you to do.'

'Sir?'

'Get yourself a list of all the tattoo parlours in Swansea, and you can go a bit further out too, if you like, but we'll focus on the ones in town first.' Gus picked up his phone, found the photograph of the tattoo that Jenny Sarka had sent him, and turned the screen to his sergeant. 'This is what you're looking for. Our Jane Doe had this on her back, round about the coccyx, I'm told.'

Willis waited for further instruction, or more probably, elucidation.

'Just above her arse, son.'

'Oh, okay. Will do, sir.' He remained standing in front of Gus's desk.

'Yes?'

'Could you forward me the image, sir?'

Gus tutted. 'Of course. Sorry.'

17

I was re-reading A Confederacy of Dunces *earlier today. 'I mingle with my peers or no one, and since I have no peers I mingle with no one.' Poor old dead John Kennedy O'Toole, he might have been writing about me! They used to talk about my 'peers' when they slagged me off in my reports at school. 'He finds some difficulty mixing with his peers', one of them wrote. I wish I'd read O'Toole back then, I could have set that fat useless form teacher right! Why would I have wanted to consort with those flatulent fools and mascara'd morons?*

I just noted that I used two exclamation marks in the paragraph above. Tut tut! An exclamation mark is a sign that you haven't used the right word, that pompous Creative Writing tutor said. But what do they know? If they knew anything about writing they'd be doing it and making a living out of doing it, not proselytising and banging on about 'show don't tell' and all the rest of the guff they pass off as wisdom. Maxims are for mini-minds. There, now that deserves an exclamation mark. Perhaps I'll be a creative writing tutor when I grow up. I certainly wouldn't allow my students to attack each other's output. Unless it was juvenile, feminine, romantic mush, of course!

It's a shame I'll have to destroy this book of gems, as I like to think it could be called. But plenty of great writers have destroyed their babies, haven't they? Or tried to get them destroyed. Gerard Manley Hopkins, for one, except his mate didn't burn his poetry after all. I think Kafka was prepared to dump all his work too, but I'd have to check on that. The revered John Kennedy O'Toole never saw his stuff in print. Revered by his mum anyway. And me, of course. One of the Bronte sisters off-loaded her poems, I believe, too. Not much loss there though. I'd like to write a book about my activities, that goes without saying, but I think it would be safest to keep my cards close to my chest (stupid metaphor, it's not a game!) for the time being.

I wonder if Camus entertained actually murdering anybody before writing L'Etranger. I love something he said somewhere – I guess it was in the book, but it might have been in an interview – that there are crimes of passion and crimes of logic. He claimed that the boundary between them is not clearly defined. I'd claim that as well. You don't hear many people in the dock offering that defence though. 'M'lord, it was only logical that I bludgeon her to death', or 'M'Lady, it was

75

logical for me to burn my parents, they just weren't fit for purpose.'

I'm thinking about my messages. 'Sticks and stones' was a bit puerile. I regret that now. But I'm proud of the Edmund quote. They're bound to find that, they couldn't possibly miss it, could they? You never know with plod though. Not great readers of the bard. I suspect. I painted that one in nail varnish because I didn't want to use chalk in case it rained before they ever got round to finding it. That was risky really. Took me several minutes and I couldn't possibly have explained what I was up to if I'd been seen. I would have liked to use her nail varnish but she wasn't carrying any so I had to steal some from Boots later that day. I went to the branch in Uplands because they've only got one camera in there, and it's not trained on the nail stuff. Got to keep ahead of the game, you see. Ooh, I can't wait to read what they put in the local rag. 'Would anyone who knows a genius with a taste for fine words please come forward and help the hapless police'. Ha ha.

18

Josie's 2.30 seminar was a more turgid affair than she'd expected but she managed to drag through the full ninety minutes without shouting 'Wake up, you dozy idiot!' at anyone. She'd heard tales in the staff common room of lecturers giving up after twenty minutes and sending students away 'to do further research'.

Once, a few weeks after starting her lecturing work at the university she had found herself sitting at the same cafeteria table as Professor Ivor Stonewall, Dean of Humanities. He had asked her how her teaching was going and she had modestly enough said that she thought it was proceeding satisfactorily enough, though the students did seem to find two hour seminars very tiring. He had looked up from his pasta bake in astonishment. 'You mean you try and keep them the whole two hours?' She'd nodded and looked down as he shook his head in disbelief. 'We used to have a Sociology guy here who was very good at his subject but not, how should I put it, entirely empathetic to his audience. I bumped into him coming out of his lecture one day and I asked him how it had gone. 'Brilliant,' he said, 'I lost them after fifteen minutes!' Stonewall chuckled wheezily. 'And he was one of our better guys. No, give them a break half way through. Let them wake up a bit, Save the best bits for the last half hour.' And this was the advice from the person who occupied the topmost echelon of the academic hierarchy that Josie had thus far encountered.

She recalled this advice now as she sat back in her office. Another time Stonewall had recounted an incident from his halcyon days, this time to a few of his common room cronies, but within Josie's earshot, when a fellow lecturer had had to be woken up to go to a lecture. 'He was fast asleep, in that chair over there, I remember,' Stonewall laughed, 'and I knew he was supposed to be giving a big lecture in the main Lecture Hall.' He snorted and pushed his glasses back up. 'Ten minutes later I came into the Senior Common Room again and there he was, ensconced in his chair again. "What happened?" I said. "Oh,

I gave them my lecture on freedom and authority," he said. "I have the authority and you have the freedom. Walked straight back out. They told me later it was probably my best lecture." The old days, eh, boys?'

Stonewall was the oldest of old school. George Wright was medium old school. What did this make Josie? Or did everyone lapse into a torpor after a certain number of years? City University had no dreaming spires but there were a few good minds knocking around. The Head Librarian was an absolute polymath, for example, but he'd never taught. He just knew things and kept the keys to all the knowledge. Actually, Peter the Porter, a minion who kept his own counsel but was usually to be found hanging around in the Reception Building, was a man of amazing knowledge too. He'd garnered it all from his experiences in the SAS, and the world travel attendant to that previous life profession, it was said, not from mere books. Josie sometimes wished she could engage either or both of these quiet solitary men in some meaningful conversation, but she could not begin to think how she could strike up a dialogue. She was to them, in all probability, a mere slip of a thing who would soon move on to more verdant pastures. Thinking about it, George Wright might hold a similar view, but Josie didn't think so. He seemed genuinely interested when she talked about Shakespeare or the Renaissance. She hoped she was not being entirely gullible in this regard. Perhaps she would go for that drink. Early evening drink. Nothing more. But best not be too forward. Tomorrow evening. She would find out at some point that she had to meet her friend in town at eight o'clock (what could her friend's name be? Betsy? Annabelle?), but she could be free for an hour or so before that. Would it be too promiscuous to email him this news now, rather than wait till tomorrow? She dithered at her keyboard. Then she picked up the William Barnes book instead. Maybe she would do a couple of hours here in her office and then email George later, after he'd left work. That way he would not read it till next morning and Betsy/Annabelle would have had time to call and arrange a Tuesday evening meet-up. They would probably be going to that Portuguese restaurant on The Kingsway.

She put Barnes and his idiotic vernacular down again. Yes, nothing wrong with that. She wasn't Anne Elliot; she was, well, Bridget Jones perhaps. No, nothing that flaky. She was someone who would be played by Natalie Portman in her own biopic, a strong independent young woman with a good education and a fine intellect, but still vibrant and passionate.

***

It was getting toward the end of the shift for Gus and the team he had assembled. At this early stage there was no real need to suggest overtime but when he heard from PC Lucy Cain that she had some positive news from her trip to Rowberrys he decided to clear it with his line manager.

'I'm thinking of a press conference at 5.30,' he said to DCI Newlands. 'I'd like to have the team with me as well. It'll involve a bit of overtime, but not much.'

Terry Newlands was an old hand at this game and immediately suspected lead swinging. 'If you make this investigation snappy I think we can allow the boys and girls a couple of hours, but no taking the piss, Reid. Naturally you'll not claim yourself, will you? Noblesse oblige and all that.' A pause. 'You don't happen to know what that actually means, by any chance, do you? It's what my old boss used to say to me. You get my drift though, I'm sure.'

This exchange was on the phone. As he put down the receiver Willis came through his door beaming. 'DC Cain's back and she says you'll want see her as soon she gets in, sir,' he said, trying to maintain some composure, though obviously he was finding this new level of detective work very exciting.

'What's she got? Show her in.'

She entered the room sighing, as if she'd been doing a lot more exercise than she was used to. Gus motioned her to sit down. Willis loitered with intent. 'Positive news, you texted. CCTV of our victim, by any chance?'

'Well, there is CCTV in Rowberrys but we can't use that yet, sir. The manager can't remember when she sold the shoes but she knows it was a cash transaction. We could analyse all the tapes for however many of those there were. I don't know how long that would take. But what she does remember is that the customer was young and tried

79

to get student discount. She showed her university ID. They don't offer such a discount, that's why she remembers the girl. Thinks it was about a month ago maybe.'

Gus nodded. 'Good work. This manager remember anything particular? Was it Swansea University or City University for instance?'

Lucy Cain bit her lip. 'I'm sorry, sir, I didn't think to ask that. I suppose you want me to give her a call?'

'In a minute.' Gus addressed his sergeant, 'Anything from the tattoo parlours, Willis?'

Willis shook his head. 'I've drawn up a list of them and rung the first few, tried to describe what we've got, but they need more information than that. Like when the tattoo was done. Apparently it's a pretty generic design and location on the body even. They may be a bit more help when I visit and show them the tattoo but it's a bit late today.'

'I've cleared it with the bosses for overtime, so let's not let minor problems get in the way of a major investigation, shall we?'

Willis smiled awkwardly.

'Don't worry, Ben, I'm not shouting. Tomorrow will be fine. For now, I'd like you both to get onto the university registrars and see if they know anything about missing students. Long shot, I know, but if she's been kept somewhere for a while before she was killed somebody might have noticed or said something.'

The two officers shuffled out of the room and Gus thought about it. It was like finding a straw in a haystack, or a needle in a pile of needles. Gus preferred the literal to rural similes, he decided. He gathered his thoughts for what would amount to a press release, though it would be rather grandly termed a press conference. Andrea Linney from *The Evening Post* would definitely attend, plus someone from *Wales Online* and *The Western Mail*, he assumed. Maybe someone from S4C. BBC and ITV would pick it up tomorrow. They might not even cover the murder. Ah well. The facts then.

There was a murder victim of indeterminate age, but probably about twenty, with dark hair but largely unknown facial features, wearing shoes that she had paid cash for and in possession of a fairly generic tattoo. She was thought to be a student but it was not certain which university she attended. Since it was the beginning of a new term it might be one of the two institutions in Swansea, but that was not certain either. She might have been visiting a friend.

Gus sighed. It might not even have been her own student card. She could have borrowed it, or stolen it in order to try and obtain discount. It all amounted to an appeal for a missing girl. A girl missing most of her face. And then, of course, there was the business of the message chalked on the wall and the typed message adjacent to the victim's body. That was something he was most definitely not going into. That way led to sensationalist reporting of a mad psychopath on the loose and there was no sure evidence that either message even related to the murder. Gus should have felt satisfied by this justification but somehow he wasn't. In fact, he was almost certain that the messages did relate to the killing and were taunts at whoever the investigating detective turned out to be. That in turn suggested that this would be the first in a series of horrific attacks. Gus looked up at the ceiling, as if somehow there were a hidden microphone there and the killer was listening to his thoughts. If you are a serial killer could you try to be a little less cryptic, please?

When it came to 5.30 only Sergeant Willis accompanied Gus to the room where the meeting with the press was being held.

'Did you get in touch with all the team?' Gus asked.

'Lucy had to get home for her childminder. Stephanie's still working on CCTV, I think. No response from Dai Webb, sir.'

Gus pushed open the door and was greeted by just two expectant faces. One belonged to a young man from Radio Wales, the other to a confident looking young woman. This would be Andrea Linney from *The Evening Post*. Good, this would be short and sweet.

He read out his prepared text and looked at the two journos plaintively. 'Doubtless you'll have questions, but I fear I won't have any answers at this point,' he said.

The young man spoke first. He was clearly new to this. 'Jonathon Stratton, Radio Wales.'

Gus gestured for him to proceed.

'Would you say this was something for the public to be anxious about? I mean, is it likely to be a stranger attack? Should young women be warned to stay indoors?'

'I certainly wouldn't want to alarm anybody at this stage,' Gus

81

soothed. 'We are at an extremely early stage of our inquiry and I feel it is best to simply report there has been an incident and that we are treating the young woman's death as suspicious. Well, you know the language to use. Seeing that we are still trying to identify the victim we need to take things stage by stage.'

Andrea Linney spoke up. 'Could you be a little clearer about the difficulties you are experiencing with the identification procedure, Inspector Reid?'

Gus looked at her to gauge how disingenuous she was being. Her dark blue eyes met his as she stared him down. He decided to plough on with his official line. 'No personal effects were discovered at the scene, and I'm afraid to say there was quite some violence inflicted on the poor woman. We are working hard and following a number of lines of enquiry, however, and we hope to be able to inform family members of her sad demise as soon as possible.'

'Are you saying she was burned?'

Gus was shocked by her bluntness and he almost stammered. 'No, no, she did not suffer that indignity.'

'Would you care to comment on the level of indignity she did suffer then?'

Gus took a breath. 'It's Andrea, isn't it?' She bowed her head once in mock formality. 'Listen, Andrea, I will talk to you, and to your colleagues in the media of course, as soon as there is anything I can say. We are still awaiting a post-mortem report, so it would be wrong of me to speculate on any matters regarding the nature of the attack, or the motive of the perpetrator, or, well, anything really. But I promise I will keep you up to date as best I can, moving forward.' He heard the dreaded management phrase a nanosecond after it had escaped his lips and he smiled wryly. 'Sorry I can't be more helpful, but we may need the help of the public on this one and you are vital in that regard. We'll have to leave it there for now.'

But it wouldn't be left there. The young man (Gus had already mislaid his name) had pricked up his ears at the mention of the need for help from the public. 'Are you suggesting that there could be further attacks, Inspector?' Then he asked the question Andrea had already formulated in her own mind; 'Do your enquiries suggest that the victim might have been a sex worker?'

Gus raised a hand. 'Not at all. I do not mean to suggest anything like that. To either of your questions.' He looked at Andrea once more and he knew that she was reading his body language. She said nothing but he knew she had sensed that he was fearful of precisely what he was trying to deny.

It was a few minutes before Willis joined Gus in his office. As he closed the door behind him he exhaled, rather too dramatically. 'That Andrea's a keen one, isn't she?'

'No flies anywhere near her, I'd say. You didn't tell her anything you shouldn't have, did you?'

'Of course not. She grabbed me as soon as you'd turned the corner. Wanted to know what you meant by lines of enquiry. Asked if it had anything to do with any physical peculiarities or something. I refused to comment. Funny thing though, she looked as if I'd admitted something. She wanted to know what our girl had been wearing too, but I said I couldn't comment on that. Well, I kind of intimated it wasn't anything too racy. That's alright, isn't it? Anyway, I thought the briefing went well, myself.'

'Are you being sarcastic, young man?'

'Not at all, sir.

'You should be. It went terribly. Miss Linney was watching me like a hawk and she knows she's on to a big case here.'

Ben Willis nodded wisely but did not comprehend. He turned to go, knowing that there was still quite a lot to learn about this detective business.

Gus sat in his office for another half hour before deciding to call it a day. He had the remaining half of a home-made shepherd's pie waiting for him in his flat, but he was considering a Chinese takeaway as he pulled on his overcoat. The car would decide; if it went straight home it was pie, if it suddenly turned off a few streets before he got there it meant sweet and sour chicken was his destiny.

83

19

Gus woke at 7.20 and was both surprised and gratified that normality had returned to his waking pattern. He shut off the imminent alarm with a firm hand, then endeavoured to pick out the granules of sleep mucus which increasingly gummed up his early morning vision. He yawned and groaned to himself. Uttering unsocial sounds was one of the small pleasures granted to those who lived alone. He was feeling a little bloated, but a vigorous brushing of his teeth and a good belt of coffee would doubtless make him feel better. He had, of course, had a Chinese takeaway the previous evening but only one glass of Shiraz. He had switched to instant coffee after that because he did not believe the myth that it kept you awake.

Last night he had tried to watch television, but he kept forgetting who was who as the residents of Coronation Street murmured or shouted their lines at each other. For once there wasn't a murderer prowling the cobbles of Wetherfield and Gus was glad. After that there had been some sort of consumer programme which he had muted in favour of a doleful dollop of Bob Dylan. A verse from one of the tracks he had been listening to was running through his head now, as he swung out of bed to face the trials of a new day. He mouthed the words to himself; he was going to have to keep on keeping on, but tangled up in grey rather than blue perhaps. Something about the axe falling too; hopefully it would not be his own head on the block.

He would round up his team when he got to the station; find out if PC Webb had located any likely places where the girl had met her end, get Lucy and Stephanie to help Willis with the tattoo parlours. Uniformed officers would have submitted their reports on door-to-door enquiries by now. He couldn't see that CCTV would have provided any meaningful images. It was fine for spotting a kid running out of a sweet shop, or an inexperienced burglar staring up at the camera with a TV under his arm but not a very effective tool if you didn't know what you were looking for, or where, or even when.

That left the university angle. Lucy Cain and Willis had been tasked with contacting the university registrars, but Gus doubted if anything would have come of that yet. He wasn't even sure what hours they worked, let alone if they had information about someone who'd been missing for such a short time. One day into the term? No way, squire. He smiled to himself and tried to imagine the sort of wording an academic might actually use. 'I'm afraid we wouldn't have that sort of information immediately to hand, officer, but I'll advise staff as to the nature of your concerns and get back to you in due course.' Something like that probably. To be followed by a letter, or maybe even an email, about three months later, 'to inform you that there was in fact a student registered on a course who had not attended lectures for several weeks. Hope this helps.'

He was sitting by his living room window looking out on the damp street. His battered but extremely reliable Mercedes was parked immediately outside. It was green, but not quite British Racing Green, a colour which might have added a touch of class perhaps. He had owned it for twelve years now, which meant it was just about to enter its third decade. It had been a fortunate purchase since its sole previous owner had been a retired tax man who used the vehicle very sparingly indeed. Just twenty thousand miles on the clock, the son-in-law handling the sale purred. The old man had sadly passed away, but he was also called Reid and he too had been an inspector, albeit of a different type, so there seemed an inevitability about Gus becoming the new owner. He had scarcely haggled when he agreed the purchase. It occurred to him now that the smooth-talking son-in-law might have been making it all up. He could check the registration document but equally he could decide not to bother. He hadn't been robbed. Gus had an image in his mind of the young uniformed officer looking askance at the vehicle yesterday morning. Was that only yesterday?

He had skipped the porridge today. Tony wasn't necessarily right just because he was adamant about this breakfast business. He opened the window and let a gust of cold air into the room. He found that he was thinking wistfully about cigarettes again and he had a sudden mental picture of himself standing in his back garden on a day like this many years ago. This called forth a different image: his daughter standing in the doorway frowning at him about his filthy habit. He should get in touch with Josie again. In fact, he could actually do that today by going up to the Townhill campus of City University himself, instead of relying on Lucy Cain and/or Ben Willis. Two birds with one stone. He heard the phrase in his own head. How was that possible in any literal sense? The birds would have to be lined up in a very precise position. Also, he'd watched his kettle this morning and, despite common belief to the contrary, it had boiled.

***

Zoe Delahaye was also ruminating over coffee at this moment in time. She was slumped in an uncomfortable armchair in the grubby flat in St Thomas that she shared with her friend Lauren Tracey. She hadn't seen Lauren since the previous Friday. Zoe had stayed the night with her boyfriend that night but had spent most of Saturday and Sunday in the flat, trying to get some reading done for the new term. It was odd that Lauren was away all weekend because she hadn't been to see her parents over the entire Christmas break and surely wouldn't have gone back to Swindon at this point, would she? Then she hadn't turned up for Josie Reid's lecture yesterday and usually she was even more conscientious than Zoe herself. Zoe didn't know if she should worry. No one had responded when she had tweeted her concern.

She had only known Lauren since late September because Lauren had dropped out after her first year and had only rejoined the course then after working in a call centre for nine months. 'Sheer hell' was all she had to say about that experience. They had teamed up via a noticeboard message because Zoe's plan to flat share with three other girls had been scuppered at the last minute and both she and Lauren were desperate for somewhere to live. Despite this sudden and random living arrangement, the two of them got on reasonably well. Lauren was serious, of course, and sometimes a tad depressed even, but she was considerate, thoughtful and anxious to ensure she played her part in preparing meals, tidying up and so forth. She was also clever and could be very sharp witted. Wanted to be a writer. 'Doesn't everyone?' Zoe said. 'I don't think so, no,' was Lauren's considered response. 'It's a lonely life, listening to yourself all the time. Half the time wondering what you're going to say next, the other half wishing it would be something a bit more interesting.'

Zoe wondered whether it was sensible to let anyone official know about her friend's disappearance. It was surely too early to panic and call the police. The first thing they would do was ask how old Lauren was and then they'd smile condescendingly and reassure her that twenty-one-year-olds did not always keep everyone constantly informed of their whereabouts. She could tell one of her lecturers but the response would be much the same. They tended to show some concern when people disappeared for a month or so, but that was because of something to do with some danger to university funding, it seemed. She knew that none of her classmates would be much help either; Lauren kept herself to herself and discouraged small talk. 'Up herself' was the verdict of the other girls in the Shakespeare seminar, and the boys seemed wary of her, despite the fact that they must have found her attractive. Zoe knew there was no point in getting in touch with Lauren's parents either. 'We don't get on' had been Lauren's terse statement when the topic had come up. Zoe had a good relationship with her own parents, despite the fact that they had very little awareness of what course she was doing, let alone what her emotional and social life were like. Her mother baked, a life plan that seemed to work for her, and her father stared into space. He didn't stare gloomily though, he just stared.

The next time she should expect to see Lauren in university was in a class they shared on Wednesday mornings. If she hadn't shown up before then she would say something, Zoe decided. But as it transpired, she did not have to wait another day.

20

I have cast down my rod and lo, what a serpent it is! Blood and revenge are hammering in my head, as the poor Moor would have it. Huh. If I'd mentioned Othello in that infested cesspit of ignorance and bigotry of theirs they would have gone 'Othello? Othello? Who the fuck's that fellow?' To the tune of 'Living Next Door to Alice' no doubt, the plebs.

I've had to jot down some of my fine phrases because I want them to be word for word and it's too easy to misquote or slip into paraphrase. 'To thy law', for instance. I nearly wrote it as 'To my law.' Freudian slip. What do you call your mother's petticoat? Freudian slip! Boom boom. Not that I harboured anything oedipussy about the dear old mater. She was a snaggle-toothed, anorexic pathetic bundle of rags, if ever there was one. Can't quite imagine what the Major was thinking when he hitched his tumbril to that old nag. Call me unsentimental, call me lacking in that sickening maudlin family feeling that people seem to display for their halt, lame and feeble parents, but I see no reason to go all gummy and gluey about a pair of old age mentioners who did nothing but blight my incipient genius and originality. When one of their palsied clan used to visit at Christmas or Easter or any of those other ridiculous occasions the Major would say, 'Oh, ignore the boy, he's a bit strange.' And the mater would just stare at me as if I'd only just appeared in her life, like a crack in the plasterwork or a bit of mould in the bathroom. Then they'd drink their tea and discuss wallpaper or motorways or the price of fish. It would have been handy if the whole tribe of them had been gathered in the house on the night of the conflagration, or tragedy, as I'm obliged to call it, but 'twas not to be.

I've got a few more choice offerings for Swansea's finest (Hah!) but I think it's best if I don't use them all up too quickly and confuse them too much. I'll have to do the one to Horatio because it says it all so succinctly, doesn't it? More things than are dreamed of in their paltry philosophy. I'd like to inscribe that one in stone, or on a tablet I should say, but it'll have to be slightly less permanent, I fear. On the whiteboard in the Lecture Theatre would be perfect but that's going to be a dangerous little escapade. Doable though, I should think. I like my old chum Holden Caulfield's line about phonies too: 'I'm surrounded by them ... they were coming in the goddam window.' Except they came in the normal way, of course, through the goddam door, clutching their notepads (strictly for doodling in) and their mobiles, which they casually dropped in their laps and then held squeezed between their hefty thighs. Nobody would get a reference to The Catcher in the Rye any more though. VERY twentieth century.

Maybe I belong in a different century. Nineteenth century even. I used to feel like Alice, except my red queen was that emaciated hag, my mother, and the rest of my group were either mice or mock turtles or mad hatters. I'd sit at the back, like Ulysses in his tent, and watch them all racing round in a circle just like Lewis Carroll's anthropomorphs. The caucus race. Or the caucasian chalk circle, come to think of it. Mmm. That's quite neat, because old Bertolt Brecht based it on a Chinese crime drama, I think I read. Wank dynasty, doubtless. Wow, I'm buzzing here! I think it's because I've struck a blow for the Josef Ks of this world, and I don't mean the Scottish punk band either! Oh, words, words, words, they're so intoxicating. Stream of consciousness is a wonderful thing. It nourishes the parched mind. I wasn't really into all that stuff till I read Hunger a couple of years ago. I'm beginning to wonder now if Knut Hamsun was related to the Prince of Denmark. I mean, Denmark, Norway, they're pretty much the same sort of place, aren't they? Hamsun, Hamlet's son. Ooh, I'm getting all overjoyed here! Stephen Deadloss had a theory that Shakespeare's son Hamnet was the ghost of his own father, or something. Phew. I'd better slow down. I'll fall down a rabbit hole of my own in a minute.

I've still got the brick I hit her with. I know it's only a brick and it wasn't actually the murder weapon, but traces of skin and blood and all that. I've put it in the alcove with the other bricks holding up my bookshelves, in plain sight, like Poe suggests. But I'd better get rid of it and put the original brick back. I threw that one in the garden but if someone decides to clean the garden up I'll be a brick short when I dispose of my incriminating one. 'He's a brick short of a full hod', they'll say. They won't say that of course. Too original. They'll say 'he's mad as a hatter'. And round we go again in our ever-increasing circles.

I'm awfully tempted to go up to Townhill. Do a bit of a recce. Some people used to come up the path from Uplands, that way you get onto the grounds without passing Reception, so you can avoid the sentries they have posted there. Shinks and his mate Peter the Porter always ogling the girls and scowling at the lads. Probably sneaking sips of the whisky they keep behind the counter 'to keep out the cold'. I always wanted to say to that Peter bloke, 'This place is too cold for hell. How can you devil-porter it any further?' Trouble is, it's very doubtful he's up on his Shakespeare, even in Coles' Notes form, and he'd stare icily at me and perhaps reach for his gun. How do they let him keep a gun on campus anyway? Somebody said it was to do with rabbits and I did believe that story that he'd shot a bird that got into an examination room once. He's got that Gary Cooper quiet determination about him. Or Clint Eastwood without the cheroot. But still, a gun. 'Tis a mystery indeed.

21

When Gus arrived at the station Stephanie Beddall and Ben Willis were hanging around at Reception, presumably waiting for him and all too keen to get on with the thrilling job of chasing a madman murderer. They were an interesting pair, Ben tall, not handsome but manly, and the much shorter, frailer on the outside Stephanie. Gus reckoned that Stephanie would be the more resolute of them in an emergency, however. There was something in her eyes: not steely exactly, but hard, strong.

'PC Webb here yet?' he asked them.

'He's in the canteen, sir. Lucy too,' Willis said.

'Round them up then. Let's have a quick briefing.'

Gus got himself a coffee, purely out of routine, and went to check his voicemail. Nothing there. Five minutes later the team was assembled.

'Right, PC Webb. Anything on any likely murder sites?'

Dai Webb ostentatiously referred to his notebook. 'There's no houses as such near to the bottom of King's Lane, except that refuge place or whatever it is, for the old nuns. I checked round the back of the UCI cinema, no blood or other obvious evidence. She could just have been attacked on the street, couldn't she, sir?'

'No,' Gus said patiently, 'The pathologist maintains she was killed some time before lunchtime on Saturday and dumped in the early hours of Sunday morning. He had to have kept the body indoors somewhere.' He paused. 'I suppose I should say he or she, but I'm finding it hard to imagine a woman committing this level of violence. Anyone disagree with that?'

All four shook their heads sagely.

'Or possibly she might have been kept in a vehicle of some description, but I haven't heard anything from our CCTV yet. Stephanie, is there more footage to scrutinise?'

'Not in that vicinity, sir' Stephanie said. 'We're still going through all the stuff from the city centre but there's hours of it to watch and nothing stands out so far.'

'Okay then,' Gus continued. 'I've been through Jenny Sarka's report. No signs of recent sexual activity. No material under the fingernails or anything like that. Our killer is either forensically aware or plain lucky. I'm wondering if Lauren knew her attacker; it seems strange that she didn't try to fight him off. Anyway, we've got to identify her as a matter of urgency. Willis, you and Lucy chase up the university registrars. Anybody reported missing or behaving strangely.' He smiled. 'More strangely than normal, I mean.' Gus realised he had called Lucy Cain by her first name rather than by rank and surname and for a moment he thought he might have to do the same for Dai Webb but he found he couldn't. 'PC Webb, you take the tattoo parlours. Sergeant Willis will send you the photograph we have.'

'There was one other thing, sir,' Webb said, consulting his notebook again. 'You did say garages and outbuildings, didn't you?' Gus indicted he had. 'Well, it's not really a garage as such, but there is a sort of attachment to the nuns' place. I mean, it might have been a garage in a previous life, but I think it's more of a storeroom for old furniture now. Or old nuns maybe.' He chuckled to himself. 'I had a peek through the side window and it looks like no one's used it for quite a while.' He shrugged. 'But some kid had graffitied something a bit strange just below the window.'

Gus felt his stomach lurch. He tried to appear composed. 'What did it say?'

'*To thy law my services are bound.* I would have thought it was some religious thing that the nuns have to swear to or something, but it wasn't like it was a notice or anything official. It was definitely a piece of graffiti.'

Gus shook his head. 'Was it done in chalk by any chance?'

Webb did not appear surprised by this question. His expression suggested that nothing his bosses said ever surprised him much. 'No sir. Paint. Glossy paint. Very glossy, as a matter of fact. Looked freshly done to me. I've got no idea what it means though.' He swiped a hand through his hair and inspected his palm as if there might be something unexpected there.

'Neither have I, Dai.' There, he'd managed to use his first name

92

this time. 'But it's definitely something we need to know. Let's see what the internet has to say about it.' He typed the quotation into his search engine and read the Sparks' Notes explanation.

It says it's from *King Lear* and it's a speech by a character called Edmund. He read out the last sentence: 'He invokes "nature" because only in the unregulated, anarchic scheme of the natural world can one of such low birth achieve his goals. He wants recognition more than anything else—perhaps, it is suggested later, because of the familial love that has been denied him—and he sets about getting that recognition by any means necessary.'

'You said our man is looking for recognition, sir.' Ben said.

'I did. But it's distinctly odd if he's telling us he is. I think there's more to it, you know.'

He turned to PC Stephanie Beddall. 'Leave the CCTV for the present. There's something else I'd like you to do. Ben, can you chase up the uniform statements from the door-to-doors. Lucy, just take care of Swansea University, speak to the Registrar there.'

Gus gave a sweeping hand gesture of his own to indicate that there were tasks to be undertaken and time was of the essence. Willis, Cain and Webb filed out of the room, but Gus motioned to Stephanie to hang back. She waited expectantly, brightly.

'Did you go to university Stephanie?'

She looked a little taken aback, as if she was going to be rebuked for choosing a police career too early in life.

'No? Okay then, time to put that right. You and I are going to ascend ... well, we're going to drive up to Townhill to City University and see someone who might know something about laws and abiding to them. And lighting candles too.'

Stephanie was now really perplexed. 'Sorry, PC Beddall. I'm being a little lightheaded. I've been puzzling over a piece of graffiti that was found near where our victim was dumped, and now it seems we have another message. They're both rather cryptic so we need an expert to decode them. Wikipedia will only take us so far. As it happens, I may know just the person.'

The young constable still looked bemused.

'My daughter. She's a researcher at City University. English literature. She's bound to recognise these phrases and she may be able

93

to shed a bit more light on the matter. I could go on my own, but I'd like it to seem a bit more official than her old dad popping in to see her, if that makes sense.'

It didn't make a lot of sense, but Stephanie was glad of the chance to get away from the CCTV footage, and even gladder that she was being offered the chance of a larger role in the investigation. 'I'll drive,' she said cheerfully.

They were waved through the gates at the entrance to the university campus by Les Jenkins, who smiled wryly at the pretty young girl driving a police car into his domain, and they parked just outside what looked like a side entrance to the main building. In fact, it was an original entrance for the young ladies who enrolled at the teacher training establishment that had been the first incarnation of this grand Victorian poll stone building. Gus stepped out and looked over the sweep of bay in the distance. The sea was pigeon grey and untroubled by wind this morning but there was still chill in the air. Stephanie was not appreciating the view; she was looking at the markings on the tarmac and was apparently troubled by the fact that she had parked in a bay reserved for the Assistant Dean of Humanities.

'I'm sure it'll be no problem,' Gus assured her. Her expression changed to one of composure and determination. Ah, youth, Gus thought. He paused and looked up to the mansard roof of the building before pushing open the heavy door. He was thinking about Victorian young ladies seated by those windows above him, clutching their primers and volumes of sentimental verse, dreaming of bringing all sorts of beauty and knowledge to their young pupils after they had matriculated. Different from the present generation of trainee teachers smoking dope in grubby flats and scouring the internet for last minute lesson plans. But Josie had not been like that, she had been conscientious and abstemious, to the best of his knowledge anyway, so it was wrong to generalise. He held open the door for his colleague, as a tiny gesture to a more civilised past.

There was a short stone staircase which led to the midpoint of a rather gloomy corridor. Gus decided to turn left and scan the signs on the doors on the left-hand side of the corridor. On the other side a row of sash windows gave out on to some enclosed gardens. It

94

didn't look like anyone used this area for languid study for it was laid out into beds of hardy annuals and small squares of lawn clearly not designed for relaxing on. Gus moved down the corridor, Stephanie Beddall following at a respectful distance, till they saw what looked like a secretary's office.

'Let's check who's in charge, shall we?' he said. Stephanie pulled her shoulders back a fraction and fiddled with her belt.

The room had a single occupant, a bespectacled grey-haired woman of some age between fifty and seventy.

'Yes?' she said sharply. Clearly it was mainly people with complaints who paid court here.

'I'm Inspector Gus Reid, this is PC Stephanie Beddall. We're here to talk to a member of the Humanities faculty, Miss Josephine Reid. Could you tell us if she's teaching at the moment? And if she's available could you tell her that we'd like to speak to her please?'

It had been a good idea to bring an officer in uniform; the woman repressed a customary impulse to sneer or snarl and immediately picked up her phone. She didn't even enquire about the nature of this visit. She conveyed the message and then looked up to say that Ms Reid would be down after her current tutorial had ended. 'In half an hour, she says. Would you like to wait here?'

'No, we'd also like to talk to your Registrar, if they're available.'

The woman noted the choice of pronoun and seemed to approve. 'The Registrar is a *Mr* Followes but his office is on our Mount Pleasant campus. Would you like me to call him?'

Gus shook his head. 'No that's alright. Don't disturb him at present, thank you. Would the Dean of Humanities be available, do you think? I take it he, or she, is based on this campus?'

'He lives next door,' the woman said, with an obvious lack of relish. 'I'll tell him you're here.'

She picked up her phone again and repeated their names. Gus thanked her and turned to go back out. Professor Stonewall had already come striding out of his office and was outside the secretary's door as Stephanie stepped into the corridor.

They made their introductions as the man ushered them into his office. It was bigger and more elegantly furnished, but still not as grand as Gus might have imagined, not that he knew what a Dean

95

really was, or did. They were invited to take a seat and Gus took those few seconds to appraise the professor. He didn't look anything like the slightly frazzled and unworldly representations of academics on television. He was a solid, but not burly, man of about Gus's age with curling whitish hair and a florid face. He was a drinker definitely. He was wearing a suit and tie, but they spoke more of a business ethos than the world of education. The suit was well cut, the shirt immaculately pressed and the tie stylish. Gus might have expected leather elbows and a fountain pen peeping out of the jacket top pocket, but clearly Ivor Stonewall was not a man who would resort to a pen. He smiled a big open grin.

'So how can I be of help, Inspector?'

'We are pursuing some enquiries into the unfortunate death of a young woman who was possibly one of your students, sir. We're not certain of that yet, but we do have to pursue a number of avenues, you'll appreciate.'

Stonewall was not smiling now but he did not look particularly troubled either. 'Do you have a name?' he said.

'I'm afraid we don't. And we don't have a photograph even. But we are treating the death as suspicious and it may be that she had friends here who have noticed that she has been missing for the last few days. I don't know what your policies are regarding lecturers reporting absenteeism, but I don't suppose anything has come to your attention this week? How long would it be before people were concerned about a student not having been seen in lectures, or on campus even?'

Stonewall turned to gaze out of his window as if he was looking for the girl in the car park. When he faced Gus again there was a rueful grin on his face. 'There's no real prescribed time except for the three week rule, I'm afraid. That's three weeks of absence from a particular lecturer's classes. They're supposed to get in touch with students who haven't turned up in that time.' His smile faded. 'Having said that, I know some lecturers have been allowed more time to slide if they've heard from fellow students that someone's lost a relative, gone home for a bit and so forth. Do you suspect this girl was living on campus? That would be a lot easier to check up on.'

'I'm afraid we don't know that either. We've got very little to go

96

on. As I say, she might not even be one of your students.'

The affable smile returned to Stonewall's face. The expression reminded Gus of the sort of grin that he'd seen on a number of villains he'd nabbed who relaxed in an interview room when they realised that Gus had nothing on them. 'I'll make what enquiries I can, of course, Inspector.'

'Thank you,' Gus said. 'There is something else that your staff may be able to help us with too. I've asked to speak to Josie Reid, she's my daughter actually, but she has a part time post here as a lecturer. I'd like to talk to her on a professional basis about something which may turn out to be a clue in what is a rather disturbing case, Professor Stonewall. I don't know if you know Josie at all?'

'Please, Ivor. Your daughter, eh? Yes, of course I know her. Miss Reid is one of our fine young prospects. You should be proud.'

'Of course.'

Stephanie was looking at him strangely and Gus realised he must be sounding extremely formal. But how could she know of the strained relationship he had with his daughter?

'I believe she'll be free at ten o' clock. We'll wait in your secretary's office, if you don't mind.'

'That's a bad idea,' Stonewall said forcefully.' You'll wait here if you don't want to be turned to stone by a mere glance. Our Miss Hawtrey is not accustomed to company, shall I say. She can bring us coffee though.' He pressed an intercom and demanded three coffees, white. 'I don't suppose you take sugar? No one seems to these days.' He said this as if it were a matter of some personal regret, then redirected his affable Rotary Club smile at his visitors.

Later, back in the car, Gus asked Stephanie what she had made of Mr Smiley. 'He likes the ladies, I'd say,' she responded promptly. 'But I was looking at the books on the shelf behind him. Did you clock the titles, sir?'

'No, I didn't actually. Makes me a poor sort of detective, I suppose. What was interesting about them?'

'Nothing to do with any educational subject, that's what I noticed. A couple on golf, one or two on management stuff, some magazines. Couldn't see the covers because they were stacked like records, you know, end on. There was a dictionary and a thesaurus. I was just wondering what he was a professor of, you know?'

Gus chuckled. 'I'll check with Josie next time,' he said.

Josie had duly appeared at Ivor Stonewall's door at ten o' clock and when asked to enter she had looked askance at Gus's uniformed colleague. Gus had to explain quickly that it was lovely to see her but he also wanted to ask her a few questions in her professional capacity. About literature, he added quickly. They agreed to move to the canteen, and they left Professor Stonewall to his gazing out at the car park, or his magazines and his golfing manuals.

'So, how are you?' Gus asked his daughter. Josie, perhaps a little unnerved by PC Beddall's awkward presence, said she was fine but wondered why her father had turned up like this without calling beforehand.

'I didn't want you worrying that something was wrong,' he explained. 'I've got a bit of a weird request, and it's probably something I could have got somebody else to look into, but I wanted to see you and I thought I could do this personally. It's about some quotations that have been daubed on walls that I think may have something to do with a case we're working on.'

'Daubed?'

'Yes, that's the thing. One was done in chalk and I suspect the other one was done in lipstick or nail varnish. Something glossy. It's not anything we normally see.'

They had been talking as they walked up to the canteen. Now Gus was standing at the counter with Josie, Stephanie having claimed a table near the window. 'Coffee?' Gus said. 'I've just had one with Professor Stonewall but another one won't hurt.' Josie smiled her thanks and Gus ordered three Americanos.

'Come on then,' Josie said. 'What did these daubings say exactly?'

'One is possibly from a Ray Bradbury novel, *Fahrenheit 451*. Have you read it?'

Josie indicated that she had, as they manoeuvred their way through a throng of undergraduates and sat down with the young constable.

'But it might be from something one of the Guy Fawkes conspirators said,' Gus continued. '"We shall light such a candle," it said. I checked it out on the internet. It's not a normal graffiti by any means, is it?'

98

Josie took a sip from her drink and deliberated a second. 'It means that he thought his act would spark some sort of revolution. Or possibly alert people to some iniquity he felt. I don't recognise it in the context you're talking about but I do know Bradbury was quoting from history. What sort of case is this you're working on?'

Stephanie went to speak but Gus motioned her not to. 'It's a rather serious case, but I'm not sure if these quotations are anything to do with it yet. So I don't want to go into too much detail.'

'Dad.' The single word was enough to melt Gus's permafrost.

'Sorry, love,' he said. 'This is all terribly formal, I know, but we're struggling here. A young woman has been killed and we don't even know who she is yet. Just some evidence that suggests she might be a student and possibly she was killed by someone with a taste for obscure literary references. The other one sounds old too. "To thy law my services are bound", I think that's the wording. I checked it on the internet of course, but you could perhaps enlighten me a bit more.'

Stephanie had flipped open her notebook and was writing, because this was new detail as far as she was concerned.

Josie pursed her lips before replying. 'I know that one. That's from *King Lear.*'

'So I gather, but what does it suggest to you?'

'Edmund says it; it's part of his first monologue.' Gus's blank face persuaded her to go on. 'Edmund is the bastard son of The Duke of Gloucester. He resents his legitimate brother and the laws of the time which mean he cannot be recognised. Edmund, I mean. So he addresses Nature, and says he will obey her, i.e. natural laws, instead of manmade laws. He's a pretty egregious character.'

'Egregious?'

'Sorry, dad, I slipped into teaching mode there for a minute. He's not very nice. He despises the people he sees around him, sees them all as ineffectual and nothing compared to him. They lack his virility and vitality. I think Shakespeare might have wanted us to have a touch of sympathy for him initially. He comes to a bad end though, of course.'

'He's a narcissist then?'

'Precisely. You should do an English degree.' There was a note of levity in Josie's tone now, after the initial reserve. 'But it's kind of ironic that he says he wants to be in the service of somebody, or some force actually, when he regards himself as such an individual. It's not all as straightforward as it seems at first. Pretty well true of everything in Shakespeare, as a matter of fact.'

Gus was thinking. Stephanie was looking at her boss's daughter with a mixture of admiration and horror. Gus spoke eventually: 'Would anyone without a university education know his Shakespeare this well? And his history of treason, come to that?'

'I don't know. Anybody who'd done *King Lear* at 'A' level would be able to quote from it. Well, they should be able to, but who knows these days? The Guy Fawkes thing, if it's that, could be found easily enough on the internet. If whoever wrote it was quoting Bradbury, that's a bit different. But it doesn't necessarily mean they read the book, they could be quoting from the film, couldn't they?'

'You should be a detective,' Gus said, smiling. Stephanie was smiling now too, for she had noticed the growing détente between father and daughter. She was not thinking the word 'détente', however.

'Hang on,' Gus said, as he reached into his pocket for his mobile. His companions had not heard it buzzing. He turned away and listened intently. Then, with a curt, 'Thanks, Dai, that's brilliant,' he put the phone down. He looked at an expectant Stephanie. 'I think we've got a lead as to the woman's identity.' He said quietly, as if the canteen was bugged. 'We need to go and see Student Services, or whoever it is that's got all the records of the student population.' He glanced at Josie. 'Where do we go to find out if someone is registered as a student here?'

Josie was shocked. 'Are you saying you think it's one of our students who's been killed?'

Gus hesitated. 'We think we've got a name. We don't know if she was a student here, or a student even, but she may well have been. She showed a student discount card when she bought the shoes she was wearing when we found her. Of course, she might not have bought them herself. They could have been a present from somebody. But people don't usually buy shoes for other people, do they?' He knew he sounded desperate. 'Doesn't everyone try them on

100

first?'

Stephanie spoke for the first time. 'What name did you get, sir? Was that PC Webb you were talking to?'

'Yes. From the tattooist on St Helen's Road. The guy recognised the design and remembered doing it a month ago. Probably because of where on her body she had it done, I imagine. She paid by credit card, luckily.'

'I don't think she was all that lucky, sir'

'Sorry, yes, lucky for us, I meant.' He looked at Josie again. 'If I say this name you can't tell anyone until I say, okay?' He paused again, then something committed him. 'Tracey, the name was Tracey.'

Stephanie scribbled the name in her book. 'Second name, sir?'

'No, that's it. Surname Tracey.'

Josie's fist flew towards her mouth. 'Not Lauren Tracey?' she gasped.

Gus's eyes widened. 'You knew her? She was one of *your* students?'

Josie sighed and looked down at her lap. She picked off a piece of lint that had unaccountably got there. 'I hardly knew her. She's in my Shakespeare seminar but she wasn't there yesterday. I couldn't even remember her name. It was her friend who had to remind me. I feel terrible.'

'We're going to need to talk to this friend as soon as we can, Josie. What's her name?'

'Zoe ...' Josie struggled for a second. 'Zoe Delahaye. Yes, Delahaye. Not a run of the mill name.'

'Anyone in this class of yours who had some sort of grudge against Lauren Tracey? Anyone else we need to talk to urgently?'

Josie looked surprised. 'I couldn't possibly say. I mean, they don't get to say very much really. It's usually just me banging on about renaissance ideals, divine right and so on. They do occasionally contribute, but no one ever picks a quarrel with anyone else, if that's what you're getting at. It's not the right environment, I guess.' She looked haplessly at Stephanie. 'You know, don't you? Girls sometimes look askance at someone who's wearing something they don't approve of, or perhaps sometimes they'll sneer if they think somebody is trying to be too clever. That sort of thing. No one's plotting murder in my Shakespeare class though. Apart from

Edmund, of course. And Hamlet. And a few others characters, needless to say.'

Gus smiled. 'Where do we go to get this Zoe's details?'

Josie brightened again. 'Old Dotty Hawtrey will have a list of Humanities students. The office next door to The Dean's, where you've just come from. She'll have their mobile numbers and addresses. You're best off calling this Zoe though, our records of students' addresses aren't always up to date. They move in with boyfriends or move flats without informing us. They're all grown up, you see.' Stephanie looked like she understood this feeling as she smiled wryly.

Gus scraped back his chair. 'Come on then Stephanie, back to the gorgon's lair.'

Josie stood up as well. 'Gorgon, good classical reference, dad. Did you know there were three of them? Bet you can't name them.'

'Medusa. And her two mates, Dotty and Hawtrey I think they were called.'

Josie gave an approving nod. 'Be sure to come back and visit me if you need their classical names.'

'We should have a meal soon, Gus said. 'And in a restaurant, not a canteen.'

'That would be nice. Perhaps when you've solved this case.'

'I think it'd be better to plan something in the near future, don't you? I don't know how long I'll be unravelling this particular mystery. Actually, are you free tonight? That would be good.'

Josie hesitated. Technically she would be free after eight o'clock, because she would be ostensibly meeting Betsy/Annabelle then. George had emailed first thing this morning to say that he would pick her up from her flat at 5.30 for their early evening drink, but she had replied that she would not be leaving work till that time. Couldn't they just go to The Vivs, the nearest pub to the Townhill campus? She would have to get away by sevenish because she was meeting friends at 8.00. Betsy and Annabelle had suddenly joined forces in Josie's efforts to keep everything with George completely casual.

'I can't tonight, dad. I'm meeting some people for dinner.' She wondered whether they had different names now, but decided to leave things vague for the present. 'Soon though, I promise.'

'Okay. Good. We've got a fair bit to catch up on, haven't we?'

Josie smiled. 'I'll ask a friend of mine about that Bradbury quote. See if he's got a theory about it.' George was very knowledgeable.

Stephanie was stuffing her notebook back in her pocket. This had been a fascinating hour or so, and she was delighted to be a small part of a team that might solve a big mystery. She was interested in the way Josie Reid had carefully worded the reference to 'a friend' too. But she could have done without all this literature and mythology stuff.

Having reasonably easily persuaded the gorgon to give phone details for Zoe Delahaye, Gus called her and arranged to meet forthwith at her flat in the St Thomas area. It was only a ten minute drive away.

The flat was the ground floor of a small terraced house on Sebastopol Street. It was one of a row of that had last had a makeover some time in the seventies. The uPVC windows looked the worse for wear now but the pebbledash was clean. Gus happened to know that it was called Staffordshire Pink because he had been brought up in a terrace like this, He was leaning on the wall feeling the gritty texture as Zoe Delahaye promptly answered Gus's knock on the small leadlight in the door. She was wearing an oversized pink jumper and torn jeans. Gus believed youngsters bought them pre-torn, which was a cause of some bemusement to him, but then a lot about casual apparel was.

'We called,' Gus said, but the sight of Stephanie's uniform had already been enough for the girl to usher them quickly indoors, though Gus was not aware of any prying neighbours for her to concern herself with.

'Is it about Lauren?' she said. She had sat down quickly, as if already preparing herself for grave news. She gestured to the officers to sit down opposite on the settee.

'Do you have reason to be concerned about her?' Stephanie asked. Very keen, and to the point, Gus thought.

'Well, she hasn't been home for a couple of days and term has just started. We're both at City University. It's not like her to just disappear like this.'

'Does Lauren have a tattoo, do you know?' Gus said.

103

Zoe closed her eyes for a moment and then pulled her arms around herself as if she was suddenly feeling a chill. 'I knew something had happened. Is she alright? Has she been in an accident?'

'Could you tell me something about the tattoo please? The design, and where it was on her body? Maybe when and where she had it done?'

'It was a bird of paradise. A small one, at the base of her spine. She decided to get it done before Christmas. Said it was an early present to herself. I'm not sure where she had it done. Somewhere in town, it had to be. She hasn't been anywhere since she started again at uni in September.'

'I'm sorry to say this,' Gus said, his voice modulated to a gentle professional tone, 'but we've discovered the remains of a young woman with such a tattoo. We have reason to believe it's Miss Tracey's remains. Do you know if your friend had a gold tooth? Sadly, it looks like she's been the victim of quite a vicious attack and we may need to check with her dental records. I know, this is shocking for you, Miss Delahaye, but we need to proceed as rapidly as possible with our investigation into this matter. I apologise again.'

Stephanie made to get up. 'Should I make a cup of tea or something?' she asked in almost a whisper.

'No, no,' Zoe said. 'Oh, sorry, I mean no, I don't want any. Yes, of course, I'll do it. I should have offered you something to drink'

Stephanie sat back down. 'We're okay if you're okay,' she said. Gus was glad of her presence now. He probably would not even have thought of tea.

'Do you have a photograph of Lauren, Miss Delahaye?' Gus asked.

'On my phone, yes, of course. I could forward you what I've got.'

Stephanie spoke on Gus's behalf: 'That would be perfect.'

She scrolled through her mobile and settled on a picture of herself with another girl of about her own age. Both girls were laughing and happy. The one on the left had the same length and colour hair as the dead girl. Formal identification that it was Lauren Tracey now lying in the mortuary would be just that, a sober formality for the parents, once they had been told of the tragedy.

Stephanie shared the image to her own phone.

'And could you tell us if Lauren had a boyfriend, Miss Delahaye?'

'She was seeing someone a few weeks ago,' Zoe answered, 'but I think that fizzled out. I never met him. I'm not even sure what his first name is. Finn, I think, or Flynn. He's got an unusual surname though. She made a joke out of it. She said she didn't know if he was going to be a sheep or a ram. That's it, it's Oram. I'd never heard the name before.'

There was not much else to say but Gus was aware that they could not leave the distraught flatmate and friend just yet. Eventually he spoke again: 'Is there anything we can do for you, Miss Delahaye? Call someone for you perhaps?'

Stephanie gave Gus a meaningful look. 'I can stay for a little while, if you'd like that. Can I call you Zoe?'

Gus nodded his appreciation of this gesture and stood up. 'Don't hesitate to ask for help if you need it. PC Beddall will make that cup of tea now, I think. But I'd better be off. Thank you again for your help.' He shuffled out of the room feeling quite inadequate. It was easier dealing with felons than friends of victims. And he had to get back to the station because he had noted a text from Chief Inspector Terry Newlands just as he was getting out of the car some ten minutes or so previously. He had been summoned.

22

After the Monday afternoon press briefing Andrea Linney had returned to the *Evening Post* offices and quickly written a piece about a young woman having been attacked and killed. Police had suggested that the attack was unlikely to have been a domestic incident, but had not commented further. They were pursuing a number of lines of enquiry but could not name the victim at present. That would be read as a matter of tact, not inability to identify the body, surely. Parents to be informed and so on. She read through the few lines of text. If it seemed that she was criticising Gus Reid he would be unlikely to be very helpful in future, but there was her duty to her readers. The phrase 'horrific injuries' was trying to force itself into the second paragraph, but she managed to fend it off, for the present anyway.

She had spent her evening reading up on stranger attacks in a variety of newspaper cutting archives online and now, at eleven thirty on Tuesday morning, she had managed to catch her editor free for a few minutes. She explained that she'd filed her story last night but would it be okay for her to do some follow up stuff, as soon as she could find out some more detail? 'I mean, material about the young woman's past, quotes from people who knew her, that sort of thing.'

Her editor, Max Powell, was a veteran of regional news and not a man to be flattered or flannelled. He was a wiry, fairly grizzled man in his early fifties with a no nonsense buzz cut and surprisingly tiny hands. He was wearing a dark blue suit, but Andrea could not imagine who would ever have bought it, or indeed when. He was not wearing a tie, but less out of a sense that he was a man of the people than that he had forgotten to put one on. He wore an expression of despair that looked as if he'd put that on at about the same time as the suit's first public airing.

'You can have your head until you cock anything up,' he said. 'Then I'll bring Tom in and you can do background for him. So don't cock up, write well and work fast. Not too many flourishes now, this isn't the *New York Times*. But if this is a runner you'll get your first front page. Well done.'

Now, back at her desk, it was time to rustle up some more detail from Inspector Gus Reid. He was unavailable of course, but Andrea was insistent and the woman who'd taken her call reluctantly said she'd try and contact him on his mobile. She drummed her fingers on her desk, as if she would receive his call immediately. The phone lay stubbornly silent and it wasn't till mid-afternoon, just as she was pushing back her chair to make herself yet another a cup of coffee, that her mobile sounded. She had reverted to a standard old fashioned telephone bell from the various ringtones she'd tried out in the past and the urgency of the sound sent her crashing back down in her seat.

'Andrea Linney, *Evening Post*?'

'Oh hi, Miss Linney. Andrea, I mean. It's Gus Reid. You were calling for an update?'

Andrea tried not to sound too anxious as she spoke. 'Well, I've been trying since this morning. This is a big story, Gus, there'll be a lot of interest, as you'll appreciate.'

She could almost hear Gus sighing. 'Yes, I do understand. I promised I'd speak to you as soon as I could, and we do have some news. The young woman who was killed has been identified but we can't reveal the name just yet. I'm sure you know the procedures; we have to inform the family first. I've also had it confirmed in the last couple of hours that the cause of death was strangulation. And before you ask me, she wasn't sexually assaulted, but there were some rather concerning injuries.'

Andrea heard him thinking as the line went quiet for a few moments. 'Look, I know you have your own urgencies,' he added, 'but I'd appreciate it if you could bear with us for just a while on this one. Don't go rushing in all guns blazing, sort of thing. The body was found in King's Lane, just off High Street, and I think I already told you, it was a member of the public who reported finding it. That was at about eight o'clock yesterday morning. Ten minutes before, to be exact. We've traced who the caller was and he's in the clear but when we're ready for you to go to press you should say we're appealing for any other members of the public who have information to come forward.'

Andrea butted in at this point. 'Yes, you told me it was a postman.'

'I'm sure I said postal worker actually.'

'Okay okay. Any more than that?' She wasn't hopeful of anything else but you could but hope.

'Not really. But can I say one more thing, Andrea?' Gus's voice sounded very serious. 'We don't want any suggestion that it's unsafe for people to be on High Street. There are some dubious types there at night, we all know, but there is no suggestion that this poor young woman was wandering there on her own, or hanging around there, looking for business, shall we say.'

'You're certain of that? How do you know?'

'The post-mortem has revealed she was killed earlier than Saturday evening. It's going to come out soon enough but it's pretty certain that she was a university student. You can't print that yet obviously, for the reasons I've just indicated.'

'Being a student doesn't preclude a woman from earning extra money, Gus. Surely you're aware of that?'

'Granted, but she was wearing what I'm told would be casual day wear, not stuff to go out in. And, as I think I just said, she was attacked on Sunday morning, when I would think potential customers would be in church. No, sorry, that sounds too flippant. They'd be in bed with a hangover, most likely.'

Andrea racked her brains for ways to get him to say more but it was apparent that Gus Reid was something of a wily old fox. 'So,' she said, 'when will you be issuing this appeal? Will there be another press call, or will you just let me know? I've got to file something today.'

'We're getting in touch with the parents as I speak. Doubtless they'll be here in a few hours. They don't live in Swansea, you see. As soon as the formal ID is done we'll release the name and some further details. I don't know if that will be in time for your deadline, but we have to do things in the right order. You'll understand that, won't you, with a sensitive case like this?'

Andrea indicated that she did indeed understand, though with something of a harrumph rather than anything more gracious, but she also understood that she was, for once, a girl on a mission, a news hound, albeit one barking in a small courtyard perhaps.

***

108

Gus had obeyed Newlands' magisterial summons an hour before his call to Andrea. He knocked on the office door and Newlands' gravelly Valleys voice immediately bade him enter. There, sitting on one side of the large desk was DI Jim Warren, one leg folded over the other as if he'd been taking his ease there for some while.

'Come in Reid, take a load off,' Newlands said. 'Jim here has been telling me that you've been playing fast and loose with our murder suspect. Let him go, did you? Any particular reason for this ...'

Gus sensed that his superior officer was searching for the correct term. 'Act of altruism, Terry?'

'Yes, precisely. Well?'

'Darren Bunn did not commit the murder. It was painfully obvious that he had no part in it. Simple as that. I told him we'd probably want to talk to him again and he looked rather hurt at the fact that I was letting him go.' He turned to Jim Warren. 'You know he's a frequent attender, don't you? I think that's the phrase they use in the medical world for attention seekers.'

Jim Warren uncrossed his legs and leaned forward. 'I know he's a lowlife with a criminal record.'

'For petty theft and B&E and then usually when the weather gets too cold for him, maybe. Murder is a bit beyond him and he gave me an account of his actions that in no way matched the facts of what happened. I guess he thought he might get a bed for the night in the cells. I'm not even sure he thought much past that.'

Newlands intervened. 'So what's the state of play here, Gus? We got a mad axeman on the loose? We're going to have to bring in MIT anyway because it's a murder case, but it would be nice if we could get some of the credit before they get their hands all over everything.'

Gus related what he knew, and some of what he was only guessing at for the present. This did not amount to much, apart from a suspicion that the killer probably knew his victim, and that possibly he was leaving cryptic messages for the investigation team. 'I'm going to check out a possible murder site as soon as I go out again. One of these messages is written on a wall of some sort of garage opposite the back of the UCI cinema. There was another message written on the wall behind the deposition site. That's in the lane off High Street.'

'Anything else? Have you at least got the girl's name yet?'

'We have, but we can't say for absolute certain till the parents have identified the body. They should be doing that in a couple of hours.'

'So what have you got altogether, a name, a body and some cryptic nonsense, is that it?'

'I know it's not much, but I've got someone working on the messages. It looks like they're quotations, by the way. We've already interviewed the flatmate. We're looking into her social life, if she had a boyfriend etcetera. If there was one, we'll be tracing him and interviewing him as soon as we can.'

Newlands looked fairly content with this news. It was invariably the boyfriend or the husband, so he was happy that his officers could get the jump on a major investigation team. 'Okay then,' he said. 'Jim, go and find Darren Bunn and see if we can't oblige him with a cell for the night. You said he was caught in the act of thieving, didn't you?'

Warren looked uncomfortable. He shrugged and stood up to leave.

'It'll be Chief Inspector Tessa Penry coming from Bridgend from MIT,' Newlands said. 'Watch your step, boys, she's a stickler. She's due tomorrow. See what you can get done in the meantime.'

Gus had heard the name but had not met the woman who would now become his supervising officer. In a way he was glad that she might turn out to be a stickler, as Newlands had put it. It would make a change from slapdash policing.

He was stopped by Ben Willis as he went back to his office. He thought it might be best to call Andrea Linney prior to going to the garage where the graffiti was inscribed. Try and persuade her to be circumspect till there was something more concrete. Willis was looking pleased, as if he had made some important discovery. Gus was about to tell him that there was no need to still try and contact the Registrar at Swansea University, for they had now identified the victim, but Willis spoke first. 'I was looking at the PM report,' he said. 'It says there was says what appears to be brick dust in the victim's hair, where she was struck on the back of the head. It's kind of like a murder weapon, isn't it? I mean, I know she was strangled, but if we find the brick we've found something that the killer used in the attack. There could be fingerprints maybe.'

110

'I was thinking about that myself,' Gus said.' But thanks for the reminder. Trouble is, it's going to be like looking for a brick in a …'

Willis was smiling. 'A brick in a wall?'

'You don't need no education, I see.'

'Sir?'

'Oh, I thought you were quoting something. It's a song. Before your time, I suppose.'

'Well, if we definitely locate the murder scene I would have thought we'd have a good chance of finding the weapon. Nobody goes round still carrying the brick they've just smashed somebody on the head with, do they?'

'I honestly don't know, Ben. We seem to have a particularly strange perpetrator on our hands here. He could be wandering around town at this very minute, stroking the brick, or half-brick perhaps, in the pocket of his mac, or trench coat.'

A thought occurred to Willis. 'D'you think it's a flasher thing then? A flasher thing gone wrong?'

'No, I don't. I was just being whimsical. I very much doubt he's wearing an overcoat. And flashers don't stop to write messages to the police, do they? And anyway, don't forget this guy has kept her somewhere for nearly a day before dumping her body. I don't really understand the psychology myself, but I'd guess the thrill of flashing is all about the sudden moment. Don't you think?'

Willis had clearly not undertaken much research in the psychology of self-exposure either.

'Okay,' Gus said. You're with me now. Let's go and see this garage of Dai Webb's. Oh, just a minute, would you mind just going and waiting in the car? I won't be long, I'm just going to get that newspaper reporter off my back.'

Willis was serious again. 'I'll go and pick up the door-to-door reports. We can look at those after. See you downstairs, sir.'

23

I went up to the ill-starred college of knowledge today. I told myself it would be best not to risk being seen up there for a while but, as I believe Emma Woodhouse says, I could not resist. Naturally, I avoided the sheriff of Rottingham and his gun-toting deputy and trekked up the hill and got onto campus the back way. Still, you're out in the open coming from that direction and visible to all the prying eyes that peer through the hallowed windows. Can you have hallowed windows? The offices up on the second and third floors I mean. Didn't see anybody peeking though.

I wanted to check out the lecture theatre, see if they've got a keypad nowadays, or whether they still lock it after them with a clanking bunch of warder's keys. It was empty of course, and locked of course – think of the dangers of leaving a room like that open! Somebody could make off with the rows of plastic seats or, my god, the whiteboard! But they have fitted a keypad. If I was Tom Cruise or Matt Damon I would have blown fingerprint powder on the keys and seen the tell-tale signs, but I'm not American, so I decided I'll just have to hang around when someone goes in there. It's not like an ATM, where people cup their hands round the pad. And most of the lecturers are geriatrics who'll stab out the numbers VERY SLOWLY so they don't get it wrong. I decided not to hang around today though. Saw Mr and Mrs Plod at the other end of the corridor. Now that was quick! I probably would have recognised the man as a detective anyway – scruffy, disillusioned, probably alcohol-sodden – but his sidekick was in full copper regalia. Radios, handcuffs, CS sprays, folding truncheons, three or four kilos of kit, I shouldn't wonder. Pretty little thing though. Pretty for a black girl. She had her hair done up in a bun though and I don't like that.

I exited stage left, unpursued by any bears or pigs, I'm happy to say, and came back here to have a little mull over things. I've been waiting for the news coverage, and I didn't even expect they'd identify her for a few days. Somebody must have rung them up and said 'Help! We're missing a student! What'll we do?' Today's local rag hadn't even come out and I thought they'd have a bit of trouble identifying her with her face smashed in. Actually, I only meant to knock out a few teeth, but to be fair, a brick isn't a very precise weapon. Served her right though. No open coffin, I'm afraid Miss.

112

It did occur to me that they'd recognised the quotes and immediately, as if this was an episode of Morse, headed straight for the nearest professor. Professor Plum, with a brick, in the garage. Ha ha. I'm almost tempted to post that, but that's too cheap. I've got to admit I toyed with 'sticks and stones and bricks' for the wheelie bin note but that was too silly. It's all about the judicious choice of words, isn't it? Or that's what they tried to teach me anyway. Trouble is, they weren't really trying to teach anything, they were content to trot out platitudes like 'Show don't tell', 'try to avoid the pathetic fallacy' and 'up the stakes'. Well, you losers, the stakes are upped considerably, wouldn't you say? And I've shown but not told. Well, I have told a bit, obviously, but they'll never work out a motive they could understand. They'll be looking for a lover with a grievance, somebody who's been denied his inheritance or a vengeful Ripper with a thing for prostitutes. Even if I left a blatant reference to Othello they'd overlook the motiveless malignity angle. What d'you think his motive could be, Inspector? I don't know, Sarge, it's a right puzzler, this one.'

Still, it was slightly unnerving coming so close to the law. When I first resolved to do all this I fully expected to be hunted in a very pedestrian fashion. Like an eagle being tracked by a tortoise. I'm kind of glad they've got going, to tell the truth. I half-expected the chase to be a drawn out affair over months, and then end up with nothing happening. A few articles in The Evening Post about the devastated parents and the grieving boyfriend, then on to the latest council house fire or the latest on the planned development of the city centre. This way I can keep myself busy with literary taunting and fend off the awful tedium of being an unrecognised genius.

I don't know if I'll have another go at the lecture theatre though. If I do the Horatio quote there they'll simply trawl through the names of anybody who's done a Shakespeare module and I might rather too obviously stand out as a disaffected former student. I'd kind of like to produce fliers and stick them up in bus stops or something but it seems too desperate. I could do some with spelling mistakes; that would be fun. But if they were too illiterate they'd begin to suspect their fellow officers, wouldn't they?

Anyway, I'll sleep on it. Time for a nap, methinks. But first some scran. Scran, funny word. I think it's Scottish. I should have a fried Mars bar in honour of its etymology. But I haven't got a Mars bar. Or a deep fat fryer, come to that. I could go and buy a Mars bar and shallow fry it, of course, but it seems a lot of effort for the sake of a lexical whim. Lex Whim, that could be my superhero villain name. But I'm not a villain, squire, I'm someone who has been wronged

113

and is just doing his best to set the universe back on its feet. If only. The universe is legless and footloose. Feckless. All the F words in fact. God, I need my nap. A pack of Monster Munch and a lie down it is then.

But I couldn't sleep. So here I am again at my notebook. Journal. Draft of a novel, in a perfect world. I don't know what to call you, dear diary. Kitty? No, that's been done. Actually, this is more a chapbook than a diary. Chat Book, even. Writing is like talking, only more interesting. 'Does he talk to himself, matron?' 'No, he writes to himself.' If any of those people wrote about themselves like this they'd have to call it a Chav Book. Boom boom.

I used to do a bit of photography. I've given up on that now though. My self-portraits – not selfies, that would be too crass – just didn't tell the truth. I'm glad I burned them all because everyone's doing it now, gurning for the phone held aloft, smiling and pouting at a world they imagine gives a toss. My self-portraits were at least artistic. They had a bit of narrative to them. Me sitting at my desk. Me holding a lit match. Me stretching a blue rubber glove over a slender hand. No, I'm lying now. That's not a photo I took, that's an image from my latest career. There was one good one: me sitting facing into the room with the window behind me, my head bowed over a drink. It reminded me of the patron in the Hopper painting with the hair like mine. Only she was a woman, of course. I don't look like a woman. And the melancholy air was me faking it for the camera. I was giggling inside, to be perfectly candid. Can he? Yes. Did he? Yes, he did. You see, judicious words. And not necessarily in the wrong order. All order is wrong though. Unless it's one issued by The Major. Then it's irrefutable. Or so he thought.

24

Gus and Ben Willis parked in the car park by the huge Homebase store in Parc Tawe and strolled over the road.

'That's Mothercare over there,' Willis said, 'Evie's going to get me in there soon enough, I imagine.'

'You married, Ben? I didn't know.'

'No. Not even engaged. And she's not pregnant. We've been talking about it though.'

'I always preferred Fathercare myself,' Gus sniffed. 'Or Bargain Booze, as it's also called.' He chuckled. He was in a good mood, probably because he had seen Josie and there hadn't been too much tension. It was all wrong that a man of his age should be worried about his relationship with his daughter, but he had emerged from a marriage that was all wrong, and things didn't automatically start to go right just because you got older.

'Do you have kids, sir?'

'Two. Grown up now. A son who's in Australia, which makes no sense to me at all. And a daughter. We kind of drifted after I got divorced. I'd like to blame my ex-wife but it's my fault too. Don't let this job disrupt your family life if you do marry Evie, Ben.' Gus left it there. This wasn't a confessional. 'My daughter's a part-time lecturer at City University. I went up there today as a matter of fact and asked her if she could shed any light on the graffiti we've been presented with by our mystery man. Or woman, tedious to have to say. It's obviously a man.'

'We should get a profiler in,' Willis said brightly.

'That's for TV, Ben. This is Swansea. The only profiling you'll get to see here is officers arresting people because they're from Townhill or Penlan. True, we don't indulge in racial profiling, but that's mainly because our ethnic population is largely made up of restaurateurs and chemistry students. And medics, needless to say.' Can't go pinning petty theft on the doctors now, can we? Not even when they're nicking drugs for themselves.'

'That's pretty cynical, if you don't mind me saying, sir.' Willis looked as if he'd had his comic confiscated.

'Yep. Call me Mr Grumpy. My other name is Mr Realist.'

As they rounded the bend into The Strand Gus pointed out an anomaly in the row of buildings opposite. This stretch of road was occupied by the backs of the industrial and commercial concerns up above on High Street but there, squatting uncomfortably between the high walls and dumping grounds of those buildings was a neat two story dwelling with a blue and white plaque.

'That's where the old nuns live, is it?' Willis asked.

'I don't think they actually live here,' Gus responded. As they reached the building he read the inscription on the plaque. 'Unless one of them is a sort of house mother. It's a refuge for homeless people, as far as I can gather.' He read out the sign. 'Missionary of Charities of Mother Theresa Trust, that's a bit of a mouthful, isn't it?'

Willis nodded, then pointed at the statuettes and ornaments on the windowsills. 'That's all Catholic stuff, isn't it? No wonder Dai Webb thought it was a convent, or whatever.'

Gus was thinking hard. He had dismissed Darren Bunn's confession because he was clearly someone homeless looking for somewhere warm to spend the night, Perhaps it was after all a random attack by a homeless man, even though they were supposed to be the victims of such attacks themselves for the most part. He walked over to inspect the garage attached to the refuge. On the side, invisible from the road but plain enough if you were looking for it, was the message that PC Webb had told them about. He was tempted to scrape off a flake or two but it wasn't worth the hefty rebuke he'd get from the SOCOS. Nevertheless, he was impatient to know what it was so he sniffed at it. It smelled like nail varnish and seemed to have the right consistency. It would have been oilier of it had been lipstick or some other cosmetic substance. It definitely wasn't paint. But why not paint?

Willis was staring at him with horror as he saw Gus thinking about examining the substance. 'Shouldn't we wait …' he began, but Gus shooshed him. 'We're not certain that this is a crime scene yet, are we? I'm just being a curious copper. If we establish that a murder did indeed take place here I'll be all plastic gloves and galoshes, don't worry. Now let's take a peek, shall we?'

The two men tried to peer through the dusty side window but it was dark inside and the window was heavily cobwebbed. All either of them could see was some furniture piled up and what looked like bookcases leaning against the far wall.

'Let's ask Mother Superior,' Gus said. 'Or housemother superior anyway.'

They knocked at the front door of the main building. There was no immediate response and they waited for a long minute before trying again. This time there was some motion inside and eventually a spry woman in her late seventies opened the door. She was wearing a blue pinafore dress but not the habit and wimple that Willis had been expecting.

'We're not open yet,' she said firmly.

'Gus smiled. 'We're from South Wales Constabulary. We're not looking for lodgings tonight. Can we come in, please?'

'What for?' The woman looked horrified, as if she had been caught in the act of preparing a spliff, or thinking heretical thoughts perhaps.

'It's in connection with an assault we're looking into, Madam,' Gus intoned. 'We'd like to take a look inside your garage, if you wouldn't mind'

The woman looked confused. 'Oh, the storeroom, you mean. We don't have an automobile, officer.'

'It's not to do with a road traffic accident actually. Could you get me the key to the padlock please?'

'Oh, yes, of course.' She did not invite them into any communal space, so they were obliged to wait in the narrow corridor until she returned from a room at the back.

'Gloomy old place, isn't it, sir?' Willis sighed.

'They wouldn't want it to be too comfortable, I guess. Strictly temporary accommodation, you know.'

The woman came back with a bunch of keys and laboriously removed the relevant key. 'Nobody's been in there for quite a while,' she said. 'And I don't think the light is working. Take care, officers.'

The padlock wouldn't open. Gus tried, took the key out and examined it, then tried again. 'She's given us the wrong key,' he said. He motioned his head for Willis to knock again at the front door. The

117

old woman reappeared, looking annoyed, but when she saw that they had not managed to unlock the door she came scampering out and tried the key in the padlock herself.

'I don't understand,' she complained, 'it's definitely the right key. We haven't got any others like this one.'

'Shall I try, sir?' Willis offered.

Gus shook his head and addressed the housemother again. 'How long have you had this padlock on here?'

The woman looked nonplussed. 'I don't know. It's always been there.'

Gus weighed the key in his hand. 'Perhaps this is the right key and that's the wrong lock.' He examined the padlock more closely, rubbing off some dirt from the copper part. 'This is very shiny for an old lock, wouldn't you say, Willis?'

Willis repeated Gus's action and peered at the lock. 'There's no oil or grease on it. Strange it's in such good condition, if it's been here for a long time.'

'That's what I was thinking. Go and fetch a tyre iron from the car.' He turned again to the woman. 'We're going to have to prise this door open, Madam. I'll make sure any damage we do will be put right as soon as we can after we've conducted our search, but it's important that we see what's in this store.'

'You must do as you wish, constable ...' Gus winced at the term but did not correct her. 'But please make sure you do what you have to do as quietly as possible.' With that she turned on her heel and went back inside the refuge,

The hasp of the lock came off easily, for the wooden double doors were not in very good condition. Gus and Willis opened them wide to allow the weak January light to do its best to illuminate what was before them. They stared at a jumble of furniture, old curtains, papers, cardboard boxes and rolls of damp wallpaper. A space had been cleared at the front that might have been big enough for a body to be laid out, but it didn't look like a murder scene. Willis' eyes roved over the dusty walls in search of blood spatter but there didn't appear to be anyway. Oddly, he was disappointed.

'She was strangled, Ben,' Gus said softly.

'What about the evidence of brick dust in her hair?'

'We'll get the SOCOs down here because if this is where he killed her there might be some blood transfer, even if he knocked her out somewhere else. There could be just tiny drops, I guess. I need to call Jenny Sarka and find out if our Lauren Tracey was wearing nail varnish, and if there's a colour match to the writing outside. That would be strong enough evidence. In fact, could you do that? Ask her to send you a photograph of the colour, if the girl was wearing any, so we can compare right now. The thing is, I can't see why he would write a message for us, if that's what he's doing, in this specific place. Unless it's a very deliberate pointer.'

Gus waited as Willis made the call, but there was no answer. Willis left a message for the pathologist to get back to him or Inspector Reid as soon as she could. 'Okay, we'll sort that out later,' Gus said. 'Let's have a shufti ourselves before the forensics guys get here. You never know.'

They moved gingerly around the boxes and chairs to inspect the back of the storeroom but there were just more bits of broken furniture and a couple of rolls of linoleum. A huge spider scuttled away as Willis reached out to prevent a box of electrical items slipping. He lurched backwards and nearly sent another box crashing to the floor.

'There's worse things than spiders, Ben,' Gus said.

'I know. It just took me by surprise.' Then to recover his composure, Willis said, 'Do you really think the murder took place here, sir? It looks to me like no one's been in here for years.'

'Which would have made it an ideal spot for a well organised killer, don't you think? You see, what's troubling me is that padlock. I can understand someone breaking in here. Somebody turned away by our housemother friend, for instance. They could well have decided to get off the streets and spend a night in here. But they wouldn't replace the padlock, would they? So if it is a new lock, that suggests that someone broke in here, then took the trouble not only to replace the lock but to try and make it look like the original one. Scruff it up a bit.'

'Also,' Ben said, his eyes flashing, 'it didn't take much effort to rip the lock off the door, did it? So, if they were determined to break in, why not just rip the doors open like we just did?'

'Exactly. Someone either picked the lock, or maybe even sawed through it, and then replaced it with something that looked the same, as near as damn it. All of that suggests somebody hell bent on some sort of mission, doesn't it?'

'And then they left a cryptic message on the outside? It doesn't make sense.'

'It doesn't make sense to us, Ben. But we're normal people.'

Just then Willis' phone trilled. 'It's a text from the pathologist, sir. There's an attachment. Look, a picture of the victim's nails. But it's a different colour, isn't it?'

They went back to the side of the garage and compared the writing to the image on the phone. 'It's definitely different,' Gus sighed. 'This is dark red, blood coloured. Okay, let's get scene of crime people down here. And let's find out who was staying here over the weekend.'

'We'll be out of here as soon as we can, madam,' Gus said when the old woman came once more to the door, 'but we need details of the people who've stayed here over the past few days. Names, if possible, but descriptions anyway. And, if you can, it would be very helpful if you could tell us where these people tend to hang out in the daytime.'

She reluctantly let them back indoors and this time they were allowed to proceed to her small office. 'We don't insist on names, I'm afraid, but we've only had three or four people staying lately and I do happen to know who they are. Well, I know their first names, I mean.'

Willis took out his notebook and began to write.

'There's Terry, he's ex-army. He's a big man, about sixty, I'd say. Wears a bobble hat. A green one. Never takes it off. It's quite off-putting actually, you can see his hair growing through the strands of wool.' She paused to allow the young officer to catch up in his note taking. 'Then there's Mary, she used to be a teacher. Her child died and she rather lost her way after. She drinks heavily but of course we don't allow that here. She always smells of it though. Let me see now, I think Gareth stayed on Sunday. He's younger, in his forties probably. He comes to Swansea every now and then, but he walks from town to town. "I'm a man of the road," he always tells me.' She paused to think. 'Oh, and a new gentleman stayed on Saturday and

Sunday. He didn't tell me his name but I think I heard Gareth calling him Stan. Yes, Stan. Or it might have been Dan. I hope this helps in some way, officers.'

'Very helpful,' Gus said, though he was not thinking quite that. Still, a first name would probably be all that was required when they came to interrogating any homeless characters they could locate. 'And would you know where they are likely to be at this time of day. On the off chance, I mean?'

She sniffed. 'I don't make it my business what they do when they're not staying here,' she said. 'I try to show them the way to God's love when they'll listen, but we're a charity, you know, we're not obliged to keep a track of their movements.'

'We could try the beach and the parks, sir,' Willis put in.

'Yes, I know that. I was just wondering if they have any sort of routine.'

'I'm not sure routine is something these unfortunate people have as their first priority, officer,' the woman said. 'Is there anything else I can help you with? I need to get on with preparations for meals, you see. Routine is a definite priority for me.'

Gus thanked her for her time and guided Willis back out.

'What now, sir?'

'Let's check whether Miss Tracey's parents have identified the body,' Gus said. 'And if we've got confirmation I need to get back to her flat and go through her possessions. She'll have a laptop at least. Maybe letters and photographs. We need to reconstruct her life and find out who she met last Sunday. You get back to the station and round up Cain and Webb, then see if you can't find some homeless people between the three of you. I think we can rule out the teacher, don't you? But you're looking for anyone who answers to the name of Terry, Gareth and either Stan or Dan. In the meantime I'll take the car and get over to Sebastopol Street. If you're out of luck and you can't find anybody, I'll meet you back at the station at about five o'clock. No need to drag the others back there though. We'll go through what we've got with PC Beddall then. You haven't got anything special planned for tonight, have you?'

Willis looked uncomfortable. 'Nothing that can't be re-arranged, sir.'

'Good man. Oh, and get that padlock to forensics. Doubtless it won't have any fingerprints on it, especially since we've touched it now, but we have to have it checked.'

25

Gus left the gruesome business of escorting Lauren Tracey's parents to the mortuary to Stephanie, though he was certain that she had not had to perform such a task before. She had, in his opinion, a good blend of calm efficiency and empathy, and she didn't baulk in the slightest at his phoned request. She called him as he was sitting in the café at Sainsbury's, just five minutes away from the flat Lauren had shared with Zoe Delahaye. The parents had been in too much shock to say much at all, but Gus knew he would have to interview them for information about Lauren's brief life. He had asked for them to wait for him to return to the station. He perhaps should have asked Willis to conduct the search at Sebastopol Street in order to talk to Mr and Mrs Tracey sooner, but he felt he might be armed with something that would aid that painful exchange if he found anything useful in Lauren's room.

Fortunately for Gus, Zoe had not gone into university. She was clearly not in a fit state to see anybody and, as she let him in, Gus could see that she was overwhelmed by what was happening. It didn't matter that Lauren had not been her lifelong friend, someone she had shared at least some intimacy with was suddenly dead. She had not changed out of the scruffy pink jumper and her eyes betrayed her recent tears. She slumped into the threadbare old settee as Gus explained that he needed to look through her flatmate's possessions.

'I'll try and be as quick as I can,' he said, but she hardly seemed to notice.

Lauren's bedroom was small and dark. It had once been perhaps what people referred to as 'the middle room', gloomy because the light that entered came from a sort of alley outside. There was a poster of a Paris street scene on one wall, something done in greys and dark browns with only a *Metropolitain* sign to distinguish the street from any other rainswept city street. Above the bed was a single shelf of books but there were other books piled in a corner of the room. Gus quickly took in the titles, quite a few by authors unknown to him but a Zadie

Smith that Josie had told him he should read and some collections of short stories by authors he had heard of. Lauren had been taking Josie's module on Shakespeare but he could not see any volumes of the plays. Perhaps they read the bard online these days. Perhaps they didn't read the plays, just talked about what the critics had made of them. When Gus had gone to comprehensive school teachers had largely abandoned the idea of wading through a whole Shakespeare play and instead gave out extracts of the best bits printed on that technological dinosaur, the banda machine. The paper was often warm with a delicious pungent smell, so it was more often a tactile experience than a literary one.

He was hoping to find a laptop but it was not immediately on show. He rifled through the papers on the side table she had used for a writing surface. Some credit card statements, a few fliers, a sheaf of photocopies of lecture notes. He looked at the handwriting and compared it to a To Do list that was blu-tacked to the mirror above the table. It seemed that she must have been in the habit of skipping lectures and photocopying other students' notes. Different students too, that was clear from the handwriting. Perhaps she did not have one close friend, but she was able to persuade her classmates to help her without difficulty. One of the perks of being beautiful, in all probability. Gus wouldn't know, he was not beautiful. He opened the table drawer, hoping to find a diary, or love letters, or photographs at least. There was one 4" x 6" of a young man in a white shirt and yellow shorts. It looked like it had been taken on a holiday but the background contained no clues as to where. There was no writing on the back either. Still, could be a brother or a boyfriend. Handsome chap, wavy dark brown hair, lean, fit body and an intelligent look about him. Gus pocketed the photo and resumed rummaging.

The laptop was not in the bottom of the wardrobe, which had been his next guess, but he continued his methodical circuit of the room. There was nothing remarkable about her wardrobe. A little black dress, which Gus had heard was *de rigeur* for any self-respecting young woman, or indeed perhaps any woman. Adele had had one, only it was a large black dress, in truth. There were several pairs of jeans and chinos, some dresses, some heavy duty winter skirts and a couple of lighter cotton affairs. On a shelf above the hanging space were some jumpers and cardigans and at the bottom a number of pairs of shoes. Two pairs of trainers, a pair of court shoes, as Gus believed they were called, though he couldn't think why. Also, a pair of Ugg boots and two pairs of knee length boots, one in brown and one in black. This could be Josie's wardrobe, he thought. Then he hoped that her life wasn't as meagre and insignificant as the small life that was on show in this poor room. Finally he looked under the bed. The laptop was there, together with a shoebox. He pulled them out and turned his attention to the box first. It contained a Rabbit and spare batteries. He sighed and pushed the box back. He wondered whether Zoe knew that Lauren kept her most intimate possessions under her bed like this. He could ask her if she happened to know Lauren's password but that would reveal that he had violated her privacy. It wasn't a problem; the laptop would go to technical support and Gus would find out soon enough what secrets, if any, it held.

He went back into the lounge. Zoe was still sitting in the same position on the settee. Gus showed her the photograph. 'Do you recognise this chap?' he said.

She shook her head miserably.

'Could it be her boyfriend?'

'I don't know. I told you I never saw him. I think she only went out with him a couple of times.'

'Well, is there anything you could tell us about him? Is he a student as well perhaps?'

'No. He works somewhere. He's a bit older than me and Lauren. I think it's a bakery, or a butcher's perhaps. He drives an Alfa Romeo though. I saw her getting into it once. I couldn't describe him though. That was a few weeks ago.'

'Notice the colour, or the registration? A lot to ask, I know.'

'Dark. Grey maybe. I didn't look at the number plate. I'm sorry.'

'No need to apologise. I'm glad you were able to recognise the type of car. People usually say hatchback, or estate car, or "all cars look the same to me, officer". We may well be able to trace an Alfa Romeo, if it's local.'

She went to get up to show him out but Gus told her it was not necessary. 'But I'll have to take this photograph. And this laptop of course,' he said. She shrugged and turned away to hide her sadness.

125

When he returned to Alexandra Road his first task was to meet the Traceys. They were sitting on opposite sides of a soft interview room staring straight ahead but silent. Gus wondered why the man was not sitting next to his wife comforting her. Grief isolates, he knew, but people usually tried to go through the accepted procedures. He had a fleeting mental image of the stultifying family home with solid but unemotional parents that Lauren must have felt she was escaping. He apologised for keeping them and politely wondered whether they intended returning to Swindon soon.

'We've booked into a B&B,' the father said flatly. 'We don't know what we're supposed to do. We can't just turn round and go home, can we?'

Gus asked if Lauren had any siblings but there was a sad shake of the head from Mrs Tracey. That ruled out the possibility that it was a brother in the photograph in his breast pocket. 'Well, it would be helpful if you could fill in some details about your daughter's friends, her interests, anything really. So that we can get a picture of where she'd been and where she was going when she was ...' What? Attacked, murdered, set upon? 'I mean, if we could know her habits, perhaps have an idea of someone she might have been meeting. That sort of thing.' Gus sounded lame, he knew, but they didn't look like the sort of people to start screaming at him to stop wasting time talking to them and just get out there and catch their daughter's murderer. Indeed, they looked like they didn't know how to utter any sound, let alone scream. Eventually Mrs Tracey put down the tissue she had been holding to her nose and spoke.

'We've been cut out of her daily life, Inspector. She rarely rings. She didn't come home at Christmas even. She wants to be independent. She gave up university after her first year and I thought then she'd come home and we could be a family but she stayed here in Swansea. Got a job. I thought she was giving up to be with some boy but it wasn't that. She lived on her own in a bedsit. She must have been so unhappy.'

Her husband decided to butt in. 'We don't know that, officer. She was always a bit of a loner. Said she needed her own space because she wanted to write.'

'I was hoping she was just going through a phase,' Mrs Tracey said, apparently ignoring her husband's comment. 'It looked like she was getting back on track, starting up at university again. She emailed that she thought she'd found a flat to share with another girl, but she never got back again after that. Three months and no word! Mark told me not to get het up about it, didn't you?' She was looking bitterly at her husband but he remained stony faced. 'Then she texted to say she was staying here in Swansea for the Christmas holiday ... vacation, whatever they call it ... because she had a lot of studying to do.' She dabbed at her nose with the tissue again. 'I didn't even see the text for two days because I don't really use my mobile phone that much.'

The Traceys were not much older than Gus himself but they seemed to belong to a different world. He would have said in a small grey town in the fifties, if pressed. He looked at Mr Tracey. 'You say she was interested in writing. Did she show you any of the things she wrote?' He was already anxious to see what there might be on her laptop but it might help to know what sort of things she wrote about, and if they were ever meant to be read, rather than merely functioning as a form of self-catharsis.

Tracey looked puzzled and his wife answered for him. 'Not since she was little.' Then to her husband: 'You're not being fair, calling her a loner, Mark. She was just self-contained.' She thought for a few seconds. 'She did have a poem published in a magazine when she was in school. Her teacher said it was very mature. I didn't get to read it though. I never found a copy of the magazine even.'

'She should have got a job in Swindon,' Mr Tracey said grimly. 'This would never have happened then.'

Gus knew that young women were attacked, murdered even, in any town, but he understood that the man had probably not been to university himself and had an idea that the business of higher education was fraught with much greater danger than a job in an office, say.

'We'll do everything in our power to apprehend the culprit, Mr and Mrs Tracey,' he said. 'If you could just give me the names of any close friends you do know of, and if she did have any interests she might have been pursuing, that might help too. Gym membership, swimming clubs, dance classes maybe, that sort of thing.'

The Traceys looked at each other across the desert of the room.

127

'She liked walking,' the mother said in a soft sort of despair.

'Can you think of a password she might have had. Name of a family pet, perhaps? We haven't managed to recover her mobile but we have got her personal computer. We'll obviously be looking at that.'

No pets, definitely no pool and not much of a phone. They were parents of means by no means. 'I have to ask this too, I'm afraid,' he said. 'Were there any money problems that you know of? Serious issues, I mean. I understand she was a student and therefore money would be pretty tight.'

Mrs Tracey looked up from her makeshift handkerchief. 'I think she saved while she was working, Inspector. She was probably a bit better off than her friends.'

Mark Tracey snorted. Gus took it to insinuate that he suspected that his faulty daughter had had few, if any friends. It made him resolve to get Josie to open up to him about the intricacies of her personal life, as far as it was possible anyway.

'Well, I'll give you a few minutes to see if you can recall any details of her friends, or anybody she was likely to be in touch with over the last few months. I'll ask a colleague to come in and give you a hand jotting down anything that comes to mind.' It was another task which required the empathy of PC Stephanie Beddall, Gus felt. As he reached the door he turned back, Colombo-style. 'I wonder, does the name Oram mean anything to you, Mr and Mrs Tracey?'

They both looked blankly at him.

'No? No matter. Just asking because someone mentioned the name.'

***

It was gone five o'clock when Ben and Stephanie joined Gus in his office.

'Cain and Webb reported back yet?' Gus asked.

Willis raised an eyebrow a fraction. 'Marcia said Dai radioed in to say they hadn't tracked down anybody who knew a Stan or a Dan. They'd have another go tomorrow, unless we decide to send a uniform down to the refuge tonight. I'm assuming Lucy's gone home too. She's not here in the station.'

'Not to worry. I've got a name for a former boyfriend, so he needs checking out first. Even if it's only for elimination purposes.' Gus took out the photograph and showed it to them. 'Doesn't look all that pathological, does he? Mind, we don't know if this is him or not. But we need to find the boyfriend sharpish. His name is Oram apparently, first name Finn, or Flynn. There can't be many of them in Swansea.' He took back the photograph and studied it again. 'How old do you think this guy is? Stephanie?'

'He looks early twenties, I'd say.'

Willis looked again. 'Do we know when this was taken?'

'Exactly, Ben,' Gus said. 'Zoe Delahaye said she thought Lauren's boyfriend was quite a bit older. I took that to be thirties at least. Maybe forty even. But Lauren doesn't have a brother. So this could be the man Zoe was talking about, if the photo's old. I just don't think it is though.' He took a deep inbreath. 'Anyway, Stephanie, what did the Traceys come up with? Anything useful at all?'

Stephanie opened her notebook. 'She had one close friend at school, but they thought there hadn't been any contact since then because the friend went off to Edinburgh to study medicine. A boyfriend for a few weeks when she was in the sixth form but that fizzled out. I've got his first name and his address, if we do need to follow up. They couldn't remember his surname. Actually, I got the feeling that they didn't know very much about their daughter at all.'

'I had that impression too,' Gus said.

'The father hesitated when I asked him what course Lauren was doing. Mrs Tracey had to help him out. Business Studies and English Studies. She started off doing straight honours Business Studies but quit after her first year. Came back this year to do a joint honours degree instead.'

'The father said she liked writing,' Gus said. 'He said it with a certain distaste, like she'd taken up a nasty habit.'

'Marcia said you found her laptop at her flat, sir,' Willis put in.' Perhaps there's stuff on that about who she might have been seeing, or generally about what she was getting up to. Also, we should check for any signs of any drug abuse. Did the pathologist find anything sir?'

'No. Nothing in her system and no sign of any gear at the flat. She wasn't a smoker even. But you're right about the laptop. I've asked the tech guys to download whatever they can find. I'm hoping for some pictures, but she may have had everything on her phone, of course. As for her writings, Mrs Tracey mentioned she'd had a poem published, but something more in the nature of a journal would be what I'm hoping for. Or a short story that's transparently about her own life, maybe.'

Stephanie wanted to speak. Gus paused and she took the opportunity. 'Perhaps the English department at the university would have copies of her creative writing assignments. Even if she'd wiped stuff off her laptop we'd still have some idea of what she was thinking about, wouldn't we?'

'Good,' Gus said. 'Okay, tasks for tomorrow. We need to get back up to Townhill; we need to track down this Mr Oram, and we also need to find the homeless men who stayed at the refuge on The Strand over the weekend. Oram drives an Alfa Romeo, so if we've got nothing on file we could at least look at dealerships that might service cars like that. All of this we need to get under way as soon as possible, before the MIT team stands us down and gets us back on traffic duty, or break-ins. There's a Chief Inspector Tessa Penry who's going to head up the investigation from tomorrow. Let's make it look like we've got it all in hand so she can be content with taking the credit. She is, according to Terry Newlands, a stickler. I think that means we'll have to write everything down in triplicate. Convene here at 8.00, okay?'

Willis and Stephanie both gave Gus their best determined, professional smile and Gus was left to consider again the question of the cryptic graffiti. He had a feeling DCI Penry would not be likely to give the messages much weight but they had very little else to go on at present.

26

George Wright rang Josie on her office phone at 5.20. 'Shall I come over now?' he said. His voice was deep and rich, just this side of oily, but Josie felt she was prepared for whatever charm offensive he was mounting.

'That's okay. I'll meet you in the car park. You are driving aren't you?'

'Yes, it's the dark red Porsche. Not really, it's a grey Saab. You'll probably see me struggling to open the door. Have you seen the gale brewing down there?'

He was indeed standing by the open door of his car when she stepped out into the cold January air. She hurried over and bundled herself in, hoping that her hair had not completely lost all shape over her fifty yard dash through the biting wind. 'Thanks,' she said, rather more abruptly than she'd meant it to sound.

'Keep your head down as we go past Shinks's sentry box,' George warned, 'He's a mine of misinformation and gossip. Not a bad soul though really.'

Josie did not duck down. Instead, she gave Les Jenkins a broad smile and a friendly wave as they slowed to negotiate the speed bump outside his office. He waved back vaguely. 'We're going for a quick drink after work,' Josie said. 'Not necessarily just us two either. What's he likely to say?'

'I was thinking about you, not me,' George said. 'Nothing too nefarious in an after work drink, as you point out. And it's not as if we're going for a drive in the country, The Vivs is our local, practically.'

'Quite right,' Josie said, with a primness that was partly jokey, partly a gentle warning, if George needed one.

They parked in a pay and display but George did not buy a ticket. He jumped out and beckoned impatiently for her to join him, as she was still sitting in the car waiting for him to go to the ticket machine. 'The wardens knock off about this time of day,' he said airily. Josie shrugged and joined him as he made a dash for the pub.

It was quiet in The Vivian Arms at this time of day. Two middle aged women were conspiring against their husbands at one table and a young man was looking sadly at the fruit machine as if imploring it to do something other than just flash and beep at him. There was nobody else in the main room, not even someone behind the bar. George asked her what she wanted to drink and she thought for a moment. 'White wine, I suppose,' she said. 'Preferably Chardonnay, but whatever they've got that's dry.' She sat down near the window and watched as litter danced past to the skirl of the wind outside. George waited at the bar for a minute or so, then rapped a coin on the counter for attention. A red-haired youngster who could only just be old enough to serve in a pub strode in from the other room. Josie expected him to speak in an Australian accent but he was evidently local. 'Aright mun, I was busy. What can I get you?'

George ordered and Josie noted that he had got himself Guinness. She hadn't thought about it but she might have expected him to drink malt whisky, or a gin and tonic perhaps. He came back already sipping at his foam. In his other hand was a large glass of chardonnay.

'So,' he said. 'Good day today?'

'No, not good at all. I don't mean workwise, I spent most of the day preparing for Thursday's lecture. And a tutorial with one of my third years this morning.' She took a small mouthful of wine. It was freezing cold but there was a delicious tang. 'I had some bad news, that's all. It's not anything I can talk about though.'

'Really? I'm a good listener. Well, I constantly tell people I am. Don't know how true it is actually because I do love to talk too. But I promise I'll just listen, if it's something you need to talk about.'

Josie looked rueful. 'It's not a personal thing, it's something I've been asked not to talk about.'

George indicated that he knew all about such matters. 'A friend in difficulty, eh?'

'Something like that.' Josie took another drink, to prevent herself saying anything else and to give herself time to pick a new topic of conversation. 'What about you? Busy day?'

'Well, there's busy and there's pretending to be busy, in case someone asks you to do something. Sometimes there's pretending to

132

yourself that you're busy. You know, when there's an important task but suddenly all your pencils need sharpening and the filing cabinet needs restructuring.'

'I haven't got much in my filing cabinet yet,' Josie admitted. 'In fact, there's still stuff in there from the person who last had my office. Psychometric tests, strange little articles about learning styles. I think it was a Psychology lecturer who was there before me. Must have retired and couldn't face looking at all his old papers, I guess.'

'Yes. It was old Ted Potts. He must have had a good mind at one time, I suppose, to get the job in the first place. Barking mad old duffer by the time I came across him though.'

'I thought you've been at City forever,' Josie said. 'Twenty years or something.'

'Thanks. How old do you think I am? I've been lecturing for fourteen years. I was a researcher before that. In Bristol.'

Josie gave a playful smile. 'I would have put you the wrong side of forty. I kind of assumed you'd have got your job straight after your doctorate.'

'There is no wrong side of forty,' George said, and there was a grin in his voice, if not on his face. 'Not for a man anyway.'

'Careful you don't stray into misogyny, George. I think even those two old biddies over there would object to anything non PC.'

'I'm always very prudent about straying. Josie. I'm a pussycat. House trained. Nothing feral here to see, officer.'

The word 'officer' jarred Josie back into her troubled thoughts about Lauren Tracey. 'That's good. Anyway, I've got a literary poser for you. Someone asked me today what connection there might be between two quotations that he'd come across. I recognised them both, which I was glad about, but I couldn't see any connection.'

'Try me,'

Josie repeated the phrases that her father had told her about that morning. George frowned. 'That first one's *King Lear* – Edmund in Act 2, I believe – but the other one isn't from anything in the literary canon, is it?'

'Well, I gather it's something one of the gunpowder plot conspirators said, but I recognised it from Bradbury, you know?'

'*Fahrenheit 451*? Mmm. Burning of the books. I suppose Edmund

133

is out to burn books in one sense, I mean, rejecting his father's authority. Does that make sense? Who was asking you anyway? 'Surely not your tutorial student?'

'No, it wasn't her. She's very nice and rather earnest but she mainly asks what adverbs are. It's a language tutorial and she struggles with the terminology, I'm afraid.'

'They all do. The metalanguage of their own language turns out to be a foreign language after all.'

The ease that George Wright displayed in turning a phrase like this was why Josie was here in the cosy warmth of a nearly empty pub on a weekday afternoon. She traced a circle in the condensation from her wine on the dark wood table. 'It's sort of a favour for someone I know, trying to understand the connection. I just thought you might be able to light a candle for me.'

'How very forward of you, Miss Reid,' George laughed loudly. 'I shall light a churchful of candles for you in the awful event of you meeting an untimely end. I will order a candle to be lit at a table in a discreet restaurant if you would do me the honour of dining with me one evening. I'll even hold a lighter up in a concert, if you should so bid me. But metaphorical candles, I'm afraid, I'm all out of.'

Josie could not stop herself. 'Oh, refrain, would you? You're a terrible flirt.'

'Terrible? Or ineffective?'

'Hmm,' Josie said. 'We'll have to see. But I warn you, I'm not a one glass of wine type of girl.'

'I wouldn't be here if you were,' George said. 'Though I am, perforce, a one pint of Guinness type of man. When I'm driving anyway.' He picked up her glass. 'But I also like ginger beer, so it's no problem. Same again?'

'You're too kind, kind sir.'

Josie decided to shelve the literary quotations problem for the time being and just enjoy a little elegant banter with her companion. He was well read but not too pedantic about it. He definitely wasn't one of those people who look aloft and said things like 'Wasn't it Nietzsche who declared …' He reminded her in some ways of his namesake in her favourite Austen novel *Emma*. An older man, a man of some means perhaps. Initially a little arch, maybe, but perhaps a

134

big old romantic at heart. She muttered 'George Knightley, meet George Wrightly' under her breath and it caused her to emit an unseemly giggle.

They spent much of the following hour relating how they had come to be at City University. George had been destined for the law, he told her, but after one term at LSE he had switched to an English degree. Much more thrilling, much more drama than tedious old tort, he said. Then a PhD at Warwick, a researcher's post at Bristol and a lecturing post in Swansea. Josie told him of her less steady path into academia. She was stuck in the middle of her PhD, which was a slightly dishonest way of saying she had partially lost interest in it, and had only done a little supply teaching at a further education college before coming to the university. 'They liked the sound of my interest in feminist re-readings of Shakespeare, I think,' she added. 'I'm not sure they'd ever want to read what I eventually produce, of course.'

'Do you know the average readership for a PhD thesis, Josie?'

'Not many, I'd guess.'

'Three. And two of those are you. The first time, when you're proofreading the damned thing, and the second time in utter disbelief a year or two later, when you ask yourself "Is that all I could come up with?" The other one is your supervisor, of course. Poor soul.' He laughed. 'Not *your* supervisor, I'm not downplaying the significance of feminist theory. Nothing so incorrect. I mean most people's supervisor.'

'My supervisor would be glad to read anything I've written. I haven't even spoken to her for the last two months.'

'Don't despair. *In lux tenebris* and all that. *Ordo ab chao*, come to that. That's what I found when I was completing my thesis.'

'Ordo ab what? Did you say KO?'

'Sorry,' George smiled. 'Chao.' He spelled it out. 'It's a similar sort of saying to the thing about light coming from darkness. It means order will come out of chaos. It's a Masonic phrase.' He looked serious again. 'That doesn't mean I belong to the dodgy trouser brigade, needless to say. No, god, no. Someone asked me if I wanted to become a freemason once. I said, when hell froze over I'd give it a glancing thought.'

Josie was pleased. George was plainly not a man to espouse

135

feminism because it was fashionable and neither was he a man to espouse anachronistic men's clubs for an easier life. She'd heard that the hierarchy at City University, nearly all male, were likely to be seen at their local lodge on a Thursday night. 'Any reason for that,' she asked innocently. 'Might it not be good for career advancement?'

'Ah, you've heard the rumours too, eh? I've got enough peccadilloes, I fear, without having to carry a little suitcase to cart around a few more.'

Talk eventually wheeled round to films and books, as it might do, Josie considered, if this had been a date. Delightfully, he named *Life is Beautiful* as one of his favourite films. But he also rated *Citizen Kane* highly, he said. Josie was always suspicious of people who agreed with universal opinion. She had merely nodded at his mention of the Benigni movie, but she wrinkled her nose a touch at the Orson Welles reference. 'Not a tad overrated, wouldn't you say?'

'I'm not sure of the exact measurement of a tad. Maybe. I like it for its monstrosity, do you know what I mean? I wouldn't want to watch it every day. I could watch a Marx Brothers every day though. I think I could anyway. More monsters of ego being deflated by snappy words and phrases, I suppose.'

'There's a literary article waiting to be written about that, I should think,' Josie said. '*Language and the Deflation of Ego in Marxist Artefacts*. Or something.'

'That's very witty.' George said. 'But I think there's just one ego you're trying to deflate here, isn't there?'

'Not at all. I'm having fun.' Josie looked at her watch. 'But I'll have to go soon. Meeting the girls. I promised I wouldn't be late.' The fellow diners had lost their names after two large white wines, she noted.

'Well, I'm having fun too,' George said, beaming. 'Shall we have another drink, another time, another place even?'

'Yes.' The word was out before she could even monitor what she was going to say. She girded her mouth as if it were her loins. 'We can have another pre-prandial libation at some time yet to be decided, venue to be announced, but I'll be paying on that putative occasion.'

'I'm not coming if you're going to throw big words at me. God save me from such periphrastic bombast, Miss Reid.'

'That's the second time you've taken the Lord's name in vain, sir. Do you take me for an atheistical bluestocking?'

'I just like the way you think, Josie. And the way you are unafraid of ill-founded reputations. Here be no dragons, I can assure you.'

'Oh, I'm not so sure about that,' Josie replied. But I can slay dragons if I need to. There's a bit of a George in me too.'

George did not react to the possibility of innuendo, which gratified Josie because anything like that would certainly have slain any chance he had to get to know her better. Instead, he touched her hand on the table. 'I look forward to our exchanges then,' he said.

Josie left the pub light headedly enough, but she was soon back to drab earth as she approached her meagre flat. It was a walk of about four hundred yards, but that was enough to sober a girl up and make her try to focus on the problem of her research into Elizabethan mores. It had refused to budge from its dormant state for far too long now. Perhaps the prospect of a dalliance with the charming Mr Wright would cattle prod her into some serious academic endeavour now. So she could have something to talk about, for one thing.

27

Andrea Linney read her piece in her local newsagents. She'd already seen it online of course, but it was more satisfying to see hard copy. She pretended to browse the paper on the counter but quickly turned to page five, where the paltry paragraph nestled alongside paras on the problems caused by roadworks in Morriston and a break-in in Clase. She had offered her own headline but the subber had replaced it with *Girl Found Dead*. She had been composing her follow up piece all day in her head but she had not yet written it down because it was hard to change what you'd written when it was committed to paper, or screen in her case. It would definitely contain the words 'murder' and 'mystery' but until she knew the victim's name it was hard to know how graphic, how sensational, or how sentimental her tone should be. If the girl did turn out to be a sex worker, despite what Gus Reid had said, it could be as sensational as she liked, with a heartfelt angle about the plight of such women. If it was somebody that had been killed by her boyfriend, the article needed to focus on issues of abuse. Reid had not called her back yet but surely they would have confirmed the girl's identity by now? She decided to phone him again and she did so as soon as she got back to her first floor flat in Mumbles.

He answered promptly and this time there was something she could work with. She had a name, an age, an occupation, if you could call being a student that, and confirmation that it was murder. No suspects, of course, but that could wait. She had dragged it out of the detective inspector that the family home was in Swindon, and also that Mr and Mrs Tracey were in Swansea for the unhappy task of identifying their daughter. He revealed that they were an elderly couple but he wouldn't say when they were going back. She guessed they might well stay overnight in Swansea. Probably in a guest house on the front. Perhaps even one of the places that she'd been sitting near yesterday when she'd had a coffee in The Sea Beach. But they might be the sort of people who always stayed in a chain hotel, like a

Holiday Inn. The only way she might possibly locate them would be to ring their house in Swindon and hope someone there might let slip where they would be tonight.

Her next task was easy. Track down their address and phone number. As soon as they were home again she could doorstep them for the quotes about how bright and happy and universally liked their daughter had been. Not so easy to get Max to let her go skipping off to Swindon, but he didn't need to know beforehand. She could reappear after speaking to the parents and present him with an eloquent profile of the tragic victim of Swansea's latest horror story. She opened her laptop and started searching. She knew she could find Lauren Tracey's address and phone number easily enough through 192.com but it would be good if she could approach the grieving family with a personal touch. If there was a news article mentioning a young Lauren Tracey's school sports day victory, or school orchestra's performance, she could lead with something more sensitive than 'I hear your daughter's been murdered, care to give us a quote?' She found the Swindon Advertiser's archive pages and began her trawl. A photograph would be the golden treasure, but anything would do.

An hour later she gave up. There were photos of groups of students taking part in a Swindon schools running event, a piece about the school prom at Ridgeway High. Wasn't that a series of books for adolescent girls? Other less photographic events. There were a lot of schools in Swindon, Andrea discovered. Too many. She was hungry and her coffee was cold. She had called the number listed for the Traceys but there was not even a voicemail prompt. She formed a picture of Lauren's parents in her mind. Old conservative voters who watched BBC news because they didn't trust ITV and wouldn't have Sky because it was too expensive, and they might be watching you through the TV screen. They would have no time for newspapers other than *The Daily Mail* or *The Daily Express*, although they might scan *The Advertiser* to see if any of their friends had died. Then the thought occurred to her that they had not answered the phone because they were still in Swansea. If they had arrived here mid-afternoon they might not go back until tomorrow. Too late for Wednesday's piece.

She had to eat. Stick the television on for an hour. She would write something and file it later tonight. It would be enough to tickle Max's fancy anyway. *Woman, 21, found murdered in Swansea street. Promising university student Lauren Tracey was discovered in the early hours of Monday morning. Her body callously slung into a waste disposal unit in King's Lane.* It was bound to be callous; equally self-evidently she had been a 'promising' student. You were always promising until life, or in this case death, found you out. She gingerly approached her fridge in case there was something that a callous junior reporter had dumped and left rotting in there.

She found a macaroni cheese ready meal that was only two days out of date and microwaved it for roughly the time it might need. Andrea understood that instructions were really only guidelines, in cookery as in her professional life. As she sat down before the *ITV News* she considered revising this mantra, however. The cheese was only slightly melted and the macaroni in the middle of the container was stone cold. But it sufficed, especially because it had only been intended as a sort of stomach lining for the bottle of Sauvignon Blanc she was now opening, if not exactly gleefully then with a certain self-congratulatory relish.

After only a single glass of wine she switched off the television and tried the Swindon phone number again. She'd formulated a plan. This time someone answered. Andrea had her opening line prepared but she still rather gabbled it. 'Oh hi,' she said, 'It's Family Liaison here, I'd like to speak to Mrs Tracey, if possible.' She was not exactly impersonating a police officer and she hadn't given her name. Nothing criminal here.

The woman who answered sounded elderly. 'She's not here at the moment, I'm afraid. She was called away suddenly.'

'Yes, I know,' Andrea said. 'I was just wondering when she might be back. I'll need to speak to her, you see.'

The woman fell for it. 'Well, they'll be catching the train tomorrow morning. I'm expecting them about midday. Can I ask who's calling again?'

'No worries,' Andrea said briskly. 'I'll call again tomorrow.' And she put down the receiver.

She opened her laptop once more. There were two trains that they might get, but she suspected it would be the 9.22 because that would get them to Swindon at about half past eleven. So, twelve o'clock back home. They probably wouldn't catch an earlier train because of the expense, Andrea reasoned. How many dazed elderly couples would there be catching eastbound trains then? It was the London train though. Still, if she was on the forecourt at nine, or even earlier, she had a chance of spotting them. Whether she could persuade them to talk to her would be a different matter of course.

She opened Word. Just a draft, she promised herself. She had till eleven o'clock to ensure she was in time for Wednesday's edition. Now, the keyboard millimetres away from her fingers, it was time to find the right words. She had been very good at writing stories at school, her imagination darting here and there like a beady eyed bird. Her journalism course had thrown its nets over that imagination, of course. You had to forget any big words you knew; had to learn to use sentences with a maximum of two clauses, above all remember the art of tripling. Readers were slippery as greased piglets, you had to hold them firmly or they would escape from the page and oink their way off to videos of cats or celebrities falling off wagons.

And there were newspaper words. You couldn't do anything with a glass of champagne other than sip it (a deb) or glug it (a pleb), If you reported a fire it had to rage, it couldn't just burn; temperatures couldn't just rise, they had to soar; similarly with costs going up, they had to soar too, or better still, skyrocket. You soon fell into step and reported that a 'troubled' youth had been arrested for some misdemeanour or other. He was probably a perfectly normal youth; male of course, but just daft and irresponsible like his mates. He was just the one that got caught. Andrea knew she would have to stop herself reporting on Lauren's Tracey's 'badly' decomposed body. Was there any good way you could decompose? But decomposing wouldn't be the word here anyway. It was a day or so between the death and the discovery of the body. Not minty fresh was all. She shivered at her own image. Sensitive and sensational was a difficult blend.

By ten thirty she had a well-honed piece. It was necessarily still quite short but it covered the five 'W's adequately and laid the ground for the human interest stuff which would follow in the next few days, as she dragged personal details out of the family and charmed some more gruesome stuff out of Inspector Gus Reid. She closed her laptop but allowed herself another twenty minutes off before checking it again, this time with as much of an objective critical eye as was possible. Then, pleased enough, she sent it singing through the ether to the sub editor's computer before the deadline and gave a last look around her living room before retiring to the bedroom.

Her flat was on the first floor of a semi-detached suburban villa in Mumbles, which was regarded as a 'good' area. She had been brought up in a small estate on the edge of Tamworth. Though the house was detached and in a cul-de-sac, and therefore deemed an ideal place for a child to grow up, she had always felt stifled by the sameness of the houses, the boring neighbours, the utter safeness of it all. University halls of residence were much more fun, of course, but there were wardens there too. She hadn't felt truly free and independent until she had come to Swansea and lived in a chalet with Richie, her DVLA boyfriend.

Unlike her present accommodation the chalet was tiny and quite dark, but it was in a field near one of the glorious Gower beaches and neighbours were free-spirited ex-hippies and musicians who gigged at organic food festivals. They didn't mock her Midlands accent, though Richie persistently mimicked it, and they didn't think she was a slave to The Man because she didn't weave her own clothes and she got a real job. But then Richie had left to find himself, and perhaps a less headstrong woman, and it was time to move into a proper flat of her own.

She'd been lucky. Someone at *The Evening Post* had mentioned that a friend who was looking for a tenant for his upper floor flat the year. Her landlord kept himself to himself and was frequently away on whatever mysterious business he was engaged in, so she had a spacious and quiet 'apartment' as she wanted to call it. The house was near Underhill Park, more of a playing field than a park, but she quite enjoyed hearing the cries of the schoolboy footballers as they drifted up on a Saturday afternoon. She also enjoyed sitting on the promenade and simply gazing across the bay at the steel factory in the distance while the lazy tide scraped on the shingle below. There was a Chinese takeaway a hundred metres away and a couple of wine bars further up the hill. There was also a newsagents but she rarely went there. She read newspapers online, like the rest of the world.

She couldn't get to sleep straight away. The thought of trying to arrange an interview with Lauren's parents and how to strategise such a meeting kept her mind buzzing for almost an hour before she eventually dozed off. The last thing she had been thinking was to offer to take them for lunch, she realised the following morning. Madness. She couldn't afford it anyway, but why on earth would two people almost certainly going through the worst experience of their lives think, 'Oh, great, that's exactly what we need right now, a lovely chat over a nice lasagne with some whippersnapper reporter eager to misquote us?

28

Despite her determination to start up again on her research, Josie could not face Elizabethan drama when she drew the curtains and settled down for the evening. She wished she hadn't come straight home. It would have been nice to meet up with friends and talk about her little liaison with George, but she did not have anybody like that. A woman who taught on the Primary Education course had invited her to join some colleagues one Friday last term but she had arranged to meet Simon that night. Josie said she'd like to join them but she couldn't make it on that occasion. The invitation was not repeated.

She had gone for a drink with Simon but he had insisted on driving to a village a few miles up the Swansea valley and he had been edgy and irritated the whole time. They'd sat in a small room at the back of a pub filled with grizzled locals and pestered their drinks for an hour or two but he hadn't been in a talkative mood. She presumed he was worried about some domestic concern but she didn't want to know about it. It was rather late in the day if he was starting to feel guilty and there was no way Josie could blame herself for making excessive demands of him. It was a casual thing, something that either of them could pick up or put down as they felt like. He had rung her once after that but he did not seem upset when she told him she was busy that night. Affairs need the constant stoking of furtive trysts or they fade like applause petering out when the actors don't come out for another curtain call.

She flicked through her onscreen TV guide. A British detective drama, all Lady Featheringtons and Jeeveses; an American cop show, all guns and cars and drug dealers, a movie she had already seen, but could possibly watch again, plus the usual melange of unreality shows and puerile quiz programmes. She found herself yearning for a serious play, something the BBC had excelled at producing in her father's days but all too rare nowadays. Where were today's Dennis Potters and Alan Bennetts? Probably writing commercials for comparison sites. Wasn't it Salman Rushdie who'd cut his authorial teeth with an advert for cream cakes? She put on *Sleepless in Seattle* and let Tom Hanks and Meg Ryan yearn for each other while she tried to excise the word 'yearning' from her own personal vocabulary.

But even as she alternately looked at the TV and rested her eyes she could not banish disturbing thoughts about Lauren Tracey. She could summon only a few mental images of her face, and only one exchange, apart from the odd 'good morning'. Josie had been talking about Regan and Goneril's rejection of their aged father, King Lear. She must have been looking down at her notes, or behind her at something on the whiteboard, for she recalled looking up as she was interrupted by a small voice coming from the back of the seminar room.

'Do you think they'd conspired about the cutting of his retinue, Miss?

It was the 'Miss' that had startled, and she'd been reminded of this unnecessarily formal address only yesterday when Zoe Delahaye had also used the term. But the question was also something rather more astute than she was used to in her Shakespeare seminar. She had always felt that the line 'What need one?' when Lear was arguing that he needed a number of followers was one of the most shocking lines in all of Shakespeare. It seemed that Lauren had reacted to the depth and poignancy of the line too. Thinking about that brief exchange one indistinct Monday morning made Josie contemplate what sort of life the poor dead girl had had. Josie knew that she had returned to university after some sort of sabbatical, but she did not know the details. It was sometimes illness, or drug related. More often it was boyfriend trouble. Josie was only in her second year of teaching but the patterns of student behaviour were becoming apparent.

She decided to ask George the following morning what he knew about the missing year, and in fact what he knew about Lauren. He must have taught her because he always took one first year module. 'To see what we're letting ourselves in for,' he claimed. To survey the talent would be a less charitable explanation, but perhaps George was not as bad as his detractors made out. The detractors were, Josie reasoned, starchy middle-aged women in the department who seemed to have grievances about everything. Male colleagues tended to be wary of his intellect but at the same time scornful about how few publications he had to his name.

She could arrange to meet him for coffee without seeming too keen because it would be for the purpose of finding out more about Lauren Tracey. Her father was the investigating officer in the case. And it would be a big case. It was completely natural that she should be seeking anything he might know in order to help her father with his enquiries. George would be bound to assume that she had a close relationship with her dad. And coffee was neutral. She was also feeling guilty that she had noticed so little about the girl herself. It was all too easy to teach to a point somewhere in the middle distance, about a foot above the heads of your class, and not even be aware of who was there in front of you. Unless they were visibly asleep or texting someone. Then you would pause for a moment until the culprit woke up, or slowly slid her phone into her bag. She knew these things about herself, because she had several times seen a student leaving at the end of the session and realised that she had not registered the face once for the last hour and a half. But she also knew from her experiences as a student that university lecturers frequently preferred to pontificate rather than communicate. From now on she would be a lot more interactive. It was so difficult though, when you were discussing the ideas of a man who had been dead for nearly four hundred years and who presented those ideas in iambic pentameter. It was the thees and the thous that got them.

29

Wednesday morning. 7.20, of course. Gus woke up and flailed at the alarm button. He didn't know what time the Chief Inspector from MIT would make her appearance, but he hoped he would have a little more than he had so far by way of tangible leads to present to her. With any luck he would have traced Finn Oram and either eliminated him or got him sitting down in an interview room to explain himself. Uniform patrols had been asked to talk to any vagrants they managed to stumble across overnight and an officer had been sent to the refuge on The Strand to check who had turned up there the previous evening. It wasn't a bad couple of days work, looked at in one way. In another way you could say they had got nowhere. A young woman had been strangled and dumped in the city centre. They had no suspects and no idea of motive and no witnesses. It had been a stroke of pure luck that he had found out her name just as he was talking to his daughter at the university she'd attended. Without the incredible coincidence of Josie mentioning Zoe Delahaye at that point they might be still struggling for an address, since it was clear that the Traceys had not even known where she'd been currently living. They were a bit blank about everything.

He dragged himself out of bed and hurriedly dressed. He'd showered the previous night. That would have to do. Over his first cup of coffee he called Willis, who answered on the first ring.

'Get a couple of copies of the post-mortem report printed, will you, Ben? DCI Penry will want to see that as soon as she arrives. I'm going to take up young Stephanie's idea about any creative writing Lauren may have done and get copies of whatever they've got at the university, so I won't come straight in. Get Cain and Webb to chase up the homeless leads, and they can collate any material on whatever we got from door-to-doors and CCTV. Also, could you ask Stephanie to check if we've got anything on this boyfriend character, Finn Oram? If he hasn't got a record she can start checking the electoral register and phone records. I'll find out if he was ever at City University, see if they met there.' Gus wondered if that covered everything. 'Did anyone check on that camera on The King's Arms? How long it's been out of action?'

Willis told him that had already been checked. It hadn't worked for three weeks. A dispute with the company that had installed it, so it hadn't been replaced. It wasn't hugely important. The camera had no direct view of the lane and would only have helped if the murderer had been on High Street.

Gus pondered whether it would be better to just call Josie or whether his request for any of Lauren Tracey's written work might be better made in person. If he phoned she would put it on her To Do list, or perhaps her To Don't list; if he called in again in person she might try to immediately find something. He didn't even know if he had the power to seize material like this. In any case a short story or some poetry would more than likely only tell him something about the girl's state of mind a few months before. It was merely the sort of evidence collecting that you did to prove that you were aware that evidence needed to be collected.

***

Josie was also drinking coffee, but not thinking about her father. The previous evening she had fallen asleep on the settee half way through *Sleepless in Seattle*. Irony, she mumbled to herself as she staggered into bed dishevelled and disorientated. She hadn't slept well and decided to get up at seven o'clock. The fierce winds of the last couple of days had died down at last and she surveyed the damage in her small courtyard at the back of her flat. There were only three outdoor potted plants and a raised bed where she had planted some bulbs. No sign of life yet there, of course, but she was hoping for a splash of yellow and white daffodils in a few weeks' time. The dwarf bay tree had tilted over but nothing was broken. A storm in a teacup sized garden.

She was wearing a dressing gown that had belonged to Simon, but not out of any sentimental attachment. He had stolen it from a hotel with pretensions above its true station when they'd stayed a night in

148

The Cotswolds. It was white, fluffy, and reminded her of the sort of thing Rock Hudson and Doris Day might have worn in one of their movies from the fifties. She had noticed him folding it up and putting it in his overnight bag so, while he was checking out the bathroom, she removed it and put it in her own case. He never mentioned misplacing it and she wondered anyway how he would have explained the acquisition of such an item to his wife. He was ostensibly on a business trip, but not to Stow-on-the-Wold, and there was a tiny label on the inside with the name of the hotel. Either he had seen the label and the purloining was an act of pure bravado or he hadn't noticed it and he was an idiot. She pulled the gown tighter round herself; it was cold and the central heating had only just kicked in. She didn't have to be at university till eleven that morning but at least she would be warmer in her office. She finished her coffee, got dressed and made ready for the enervating walk up Glanmor Road. She might find out what lectures Zoe Delahaye had today and seek her out. She felt miserable that Lauren Tracey had been killed, and somehow more miserable because no one had taken more care. She had been out on the blasted heath, albeit perhaps a heath of her own making, while everyone else was feasting in their castles, so to speak.

She took the shortcut up from Penlan Crescent, a sedate little enclave of bourgeois lives leading off Glanmor Road, and climbed the steep ascent to campus. As she was walking through the car park in front of the old building, George Wright's Saab came round the bend to park in a bay immediately outside the entrance. He was still standing by the driver's door as she approached.

'You're in early,' he said, with a smile that pleasingly creased his remarkable unblemished face.

'Same time as you,' she responded as brightly as she could, though she was still breathing heavily.

'Birds, worms, but, you know, as Roosevelt once said, we consider too much the luck of the early bird and not enough the bad luck of the early worm.'

'And where did you snap up that little gem, George? A management course perhaps?' Josie laughed.

'Oh, I've got a management early bird quote alright,' he said promptly. 'Something along the lines of "it's the early bird that gets the worm and the early fox that gets the bird". I think it was a course on how to succeed in the rapacious world of academic publishing. Or it might have been an article on how to maximise your sexual conquests. I find it difficult to distinguish between the two.'

Josie frowned. 'You're jesting, I know, but did you just invent that or have you actually read it? And it isn't great if you're saying you're the fox, you know.'

'I was joking, yes. But it is an actual quotation, more or less, I think it's from one of those self-help manuals that people write. You know, the people who like to self-help themselves to other people's money.'

Josie laughed. 'Are you busy right now?' she was emboldened to say. 'My turn to buy coffee if you're not straight off to a meeting.'

'I hate meetings. Well, meeting in board rooms type meetings. I'd love a coffee. I could be persuaded into a croissant too, I think. Are you one of those prudent people who makes breakfast before going to work, Josie? Or are you a devil may care type like me, who chances his arm in a canteen?'

'I live alone, George,' she replied. 'Making my own breakfast would be too sharp a reminder of that sad fact.'

'Now you're jesting with me.'

'It was my turn.'

'I like jests,' he said and he touched her elbow lightly before bidding her to go inside in front of him.

30

Andrea was standing outside High Street station at a half past eight. Old people left nothing to chance when it came to travel arrangements. They wouldn't roll up five minutes before their train departed. They'd probably have ordered a taxi at eight to pick them up no later than eight thirty. Then there'd be time for another cup of tea in the station buffet. She'd checked the platform as soon as she got to the station in case they'd already arrived but it was empty. She'd explained to the listless ticket collector that her grandmother had gone wandering off again and she tended to head for train stations. Dementia, sadly. He'd waved her through the barrier without a word and with scarcely a look, as if senile train spotters were a common occurrence.

Now, shivering in the cold wind that blew down High Street and swirled around the forecourt, she waited for her targets. Two potential couples passed, but they looked far too engrossed in other matters than personal grief. The first was a fat bald man with a wife who was struggling asthmatically but still smiling at something her partner had said. No way. An increasing flow of businessmen and backpacked teenagers passed by, then a very old couple appeared, but they were surely too old. Anyway, she heard an unmistakable Swansea accent as the man stumbled and swore to himself as he passed. Then at 8.40, a bitter faced woman and a blank faced man struggled out of a cab. They had just one overnight bag between them. It had to be the Traceys. Andrea approached them even before they got to the station entrance. They looked horrified as she went to speak but she was prepared for that.

'I'm dreadfully sorry for your loss, Mr and Mrs Tracey,' she began. The woman's face hardened a touch but the man still looked emptied of any thought or emotion. 'It is Mr and Mrs Tracey, isn't it? My name's Andrea Linney. I was wondering if we could have a quick word. Can I buy you a cup of tea? Or coffee perhaps? Are you catching the 9.22? We'll have time.'

They didn't say a word, but simply let themselves be guided to a table outside the small café opposite the booking desk.

'I'll have coffee,' the man said flatly. 'I've had enough tea already this morning.'

'I don't want coffee,' the woman said. 'Who are you anyway? They said they'd be in touch later, when we get home.'

'I'm not with the police, Mrs Tracey,' Andrea said softly. 'But I'd like to do whatever I can to help them with their enquiries. I work for *The South Wales Evening Post* and we'd like to appeal for people to come forward with what they know, so that whoever did this terrible thing to your daughter can be brought to justice.'

'It just doesn't make any sense.' The woman said. She was not as old as she had at first seemed, Andrea realised. She was probably only in her fifties, but she looked like she had made a decision some time ago to move into the last third of her life and accept that the decision involved walking more slowly, looking confused at everything and talking as if everyone was a foreigner.

'She should have stayed in Wiltshire,' the man said. He was older than his wife, but possibly only by four or five years. His face was drained of colour, as if he'd emerged from a mine, and he spoke slowly, as if he it was used to explaining things to people who found it hard to grasp his meaning. No one said anything, so he continued. 'She didn't make friends easily, you see.'

Andrea reached out to touch his hand on the table but he recoiled. 'I believe she was very intelligent,' she said, though this was not anything Gus Reid had told her.

'She was, she was,' Mrs Tracey said. 'And artistic. With words, I mean. She liked writing. Wanted to make a profession of it.'

'There's no money in it, Janice, don't kid yourself.'

Andrea sensed that they were in danger of wasting her precious few minutes with them in an old argument, so she quickly stepped in again. 'What sort of things did she like to write? Was she into romance fiction, or sci-fi or something?'

'Oh, nothing like that,' Mrs Tracey said. 'It was deep stuff. Poetry. And not just the rhyming stuff. You know, nothing soppy or tacky. Modern poetry about the world and all her ideas about it.'

'We'd better be getting to the platform, Janice.' Mr Tracey clearly

152

had little truck with metaphysics.

Andrea checked her watch. 'You've still got plenty of time. I'll make sure you don't miss your train. If you could just give me a few details about her hopes and ambitions it'd help readers form a bond, so to speak. Then they're more likely to come forward with useful information, we find.'

'She was an only child,' Janice Tracey, 58, declared. 'She won prizes at school for her poems. She was very popular, but she didn't throw herself into everything like some of the other girls. She was, what's the word, Mark?'

'Discerning,' the man grumbled.

'Yes, discerning. It's something people don't acquire till they're older usually. She was advanced, you see.'

Attractive but discerning loner, Lauren Tracey, 21, left her braindead parents for the bright lights of Swansea but was tragically taken from us. Andrea actually shook her head, to clear out the clichés, and pressed on. 'I believe she was highly regarded at university.'

'So highly regarded she failed her first year,'

'That's not true, Mark. She realised she was on the wrong course and decided to take a year out. That's what happened.'

Andrea had switched on a pocket tape recorder, though she had not asked their permission, fearing that such a formality might clam them up. She slipped her hand in her pocket to see if the button was still depressed. 'So what did she do in the year she took out, Mrs Tracey?'

'Got a job at the DVLA. It's a call centre they've got here.'

'Yes, I know that.' Boy, did Andrea know. No wonder she had decided to re-enrol at university. Lauren's artistic instincts would not have been in great demand in licence renewals.

'Was she happy as a youngster? When she was at Abbey Park. Was it Abbey Park, or Ridgeway?'

Mrs Tracey said it was Abbey Park. Lucky first guess. It was a bold question but sometimes directness like this paid off.

'She didn't complain about much,' the woman replied. 'She was the sort to just get on with whatever had to be done. She wasn't one to suffer fools gladly though, I will say that.' Her husband shuffled in

153

his seat again. 'Lauren and I got on well. And she never exactly rowed with you Mark, did she?'

'I wanted her to get a job after school. She wanted to go to university. We didn't see eye to eye on that one, but no, we didn't argue. She was a well-balanced girl. It's a tragedy. But we need to get a move on now. Make sure we get a decent seat on the train.'

'I understand. Mr Tracey,' Andrea said. 'Could I give you my card? If it's possible I might like to ask you a few more follow up questions, but we can do that on the phone, I'm sure. Once again, I'm so sorry for your loss. Let's hope the police can find whoever's responsible as quickly as possible. Take care now. Oh, I spoke to your house sitter last night. Neighbour perhaps?'

'Oh, you spoke to Marion, did you? She's my sister. We asked her to come over to watch the dog. She lives nearby.'

'Well, that must be a comfort for you.'

Mark Tracey gave a final snort and they got up to leave.

'Thank you for your time. I'll be as sensitive as I can in my article, you can be assured.'

It seemed that they had not even been aware that they were being interviewed for a newspaper article. They smiled wanly and left. They hadn't even asked how she had managed to be there at the station to waylay them, but they would probably work out that Marion had told them when they would be there.

It wasn't enough for a really good story, but as long as she stressed the words 'artistic' and 'independent' and avoided 'Billy No Mates' and 'sad loser' she could work something up. But before she started letting her own creative juices flow she determined to interview whoever it was who'd taught Lauren Creative Writing at City University. But first though, her old school. teachers loved talking; she might get some good quotes there.

She decided against going back to High Street to her desk. Her laptop was in her shoulder bag and she could make her calls and write her notes undisturbed with a decent cup of coffee in town. It would be better to have a solid draft, or at least the structure of her piece for tomorrow's edition, before she ran into Max Powell again.

The secretary at Abbey Park School was not massively impressed that a journalist was seeking to speak to the headteacher. How often

154

did this happen then, Andrea wondered. She had to be content with the promise that he, or one of his deputies, would get back to her in due course. She started making some notes for three or four paras on the teenage years of murder victim Lauren Tracey. Then her phone trilled.

'Rob Diamond, Deputy Head Pastoral, Abbey Park here. Could I speak to Miss Andrea Linney please?'

She tried to put on as much charm as possible, but Mr Diamond soon realised that he needed to choose his words carefully, when Andrea revealed that his former pupil had been killed. Nevertheless, he did let slip that Lauren had an unfortunate tendency to appear 'aloof' at times. When pressed on this he said that he was actually needed elsewhere but she should ring back later if there was anything else he could do. 'She will be sorely missed,' he said, to close down the conversation. No, she won't, Andrea knew, not if it was true that she had few friends and few to understand her. Next up, her tutor at university. Maybe whoever that turned out to be would be more forthcoming.

31

It was almost ten thirty when Gus got to Alexandra Road. He was given a warning look by Marcia on the switchboard and he accepted that DCI Penry was less than pleased at having to wait to see him. Marcia motioned in the direction of the Briefing Room and Gus reciprocated with a forced smile.

All eyes in the room turned to him as he entered. Tessa Penry was standing at the front leaning on a desk. Stephanie, Ben and Dai Webb were seated apart from each other. None of them looked very comfortable. There was no sign of Lucy Cain. She'd probably rung in sick. It was no great loss.

The new chief was a bony, sharp featured woman in her forties, Gus guessed. At the age when you have to decide whether to go grey or go blonde. At present her hair was a dark brown, not quite black. She had no signs of any makeup so the most striking thing about her was her dark eyes. They were blue, but a violet shade of blue rarely seen. Except for Elizabeth Taylor, Gus found himself thinking. Tessa Penry was not a beauty, however. There was not enough softness for that.

'Ah, the return of the wandering inspector,' were her first words. 'I'm Detective Chief Inspector Tessa Penry, MIT. I think you were supposed to be expecting me?'

'Of course,' Gus smiled. 'I've been chasing something up. Wanted to be as fully briefed as possible so we can get you off to a flying start.'

She mellowed a little. 'Okay, what have we got then? Is this open and shut, or do I need to draft in a whole team?'

'It's not going to be all that straightforward, I fear,' Gus said, perching on a table, 'but I'd like to be allowed to continue on the investigation, if you see fit. I'm sure Ben Willis here ...' He paused to check if everyone had introduced themselves, 'and PC Beddall would like to help too. PC Webb?'

'Always happy to lend a hand, sir. If required, of course.'

The look shared between Gus and Tessa Penry was greeted by a shrug by Dai Webb.

Gus asked what his new superior officer already knew and she told him to start from the beginning. She had read the PM report but that was all. He relayed the facts of the discovery of the body and the mysterious graffiti and outlined what they had discovered about Lauren Tracey's background. She nodded. 'You say there's a boyfriend? We need to TIE him straight away. What about the flatmate? Any signs of bad feeling between her and Ms Tracey? And the scene of the murder, has it been confirmed by forensics yet?'

Prompted by a confirmatory nod from Ben, Gus told her a team was currently at work there. He added that a technician was also working on the laptop Gus had retrieved from her flat. 'We'll get into her social media accounts as soon as possible. Tinder, if she was on it, but surely Facebook and Twitter. We'll soon find out if she had a stalker.'

'An online stalker anyway. What about this brick dust? Anybody got any ideas about where the offending brick might be?'

The fact that she was including everyone in her query suggested that she was not averse to his team continuing on the case, perhaps with the exception of the almost self-excluding Dai Webb. Gus had initially felt some trepidation about Tessa's intervention in the case, but he was now beginning to appreciate her clear and direct approach. He had perhaps been too caught up in thoughts about candles being lit and servants being bound to some unknown laws to focus properly on the physical evidence in the same hardnosed manner.

'The forensics team will find it if it's nearby,' Willis said. 'I'll give them a call and see what progress they're making.'

Stephanie took this as an opportunity to speak too. 'Should I get on with tracing Mr Oram, ma'am?'

Tessa Penry smiled, for the first time. 'Yes, good. Let me know as soon as you do. I'll set up in your office, DI Reid, if that's okay?'

'Of course,' Gus said. 'And you can call me by my first name if you like.' He stood up. 'I'll help you set up. Also, I think you should hear what I found out this morning when I was up at the university. Ben, can you source the reports on the homeless guys?'

'On it,' Ben said.

Gus sighed. 'Oh please, no. Not "on it". I can't stand those

Americanisms that suggest everything can be done at lightning speed. Can I suggest "Okay guv, or okay ma'am" as standard issue please? Let's try and do things like the army sappers used to, with alacrity but with dignity.'

Tessa looked at Gus oddly. 'Where did you get that expression from? You don't strike me as ex-army, Gus.'

'My father served in the war. He wasn't in the sappers though. He picked it up somewhere and must have said it to me when I was a kid. I liked the image of a lance corporal beating a hasty retreat from a minefield, but still conscious of the need to bear himself properly. I've kind of used it as a personal mantra too, actually.'

'Been in a lot of minefields then?'

'Not too many. Every day's a new battle though, isn't it?'

Tessa shrugged. 'Challenge, maybe. I don't know about full scale battle.'

Back in his office Gus pulled out a chair from a corner and offered his own chair, the more comfortable leather one behind the desk, to his new colleague. 'No, no,' she said. 'I like to pace. They say there's always one who sits and one who paces in a successful two man team. I obviously mean two person team when I say that, Gus. I think it's probably a metaphor but I like to take it literally. You sit down. I'll keep moving about, if that's not too distracting. So, what did you find out at the university?'

Gus related the substance of his visit to Townhill. He had bumped into Josie as she was walking from the canteen round the outside of the building down to the entrance by the car park. She was accompanied by a Dr George Wright, who was Head of English. It was Dr Wright who was of most use because he had taught Lauren Tracey in her first year. It was a module in creative writing. He'd also said he wasn't actually a practitioner himself, but he understood the principles. Lauren showed some real talent but unfortunately he didn't have any of her work since it was all returned to students. He'd explained that first year modules were all assessed internally and there was no need to keep material for external assessment or validation. There was one short story that he'd recalled because it was very powerful and some poems that had a lightness of touch and some 'felicitous phrases'.

'What did he make of our girl?' Tessa enquired.

'Very quiet. But not because she was shy, as you might expect, more that she liked to keep herself to herself. Like she didn't feel the need to make friends. He said it was something that he sometimes noticed amongst male students, and particularly male mature students, because they had a real life outside university, but it was comparatively rare in a young woman like Lauren Tracey.'

'I think I'd like to speak to this Dr Wright,' Tessa said. 'George, you say?'

'Mm hmm. Doubtless you'll find him very easy to talk to. He's got a certain way with words, some felicitous phrases of his own, you might say. There's definitely a charm about him. Not so much aimed at me, you understand, I think he reserves his best lines for the ladies.' He stopped for a moment, unsure if what he was about to say was in any way unfair to Josie. 'My daughter works at the university and it was because I'd gone there to ask a few more questions that I bumped into him. She looked a little star struck, if I'm honest. I'm sure he'll have no difficulty turning on the charm for your benefit.'

'And what about these 'messages' as you call them? Was he able to clarify what they might refer to?'

'Well, I've checked them myself, and one's from a book by a man called Ray Bradbury and the other's from *King Lear*. Shakespeare.'

'I know that, Gus. I'm not a numpty. I like the way you off-loaded PC Webb, by the way. Is he totally useless then?'

'Not totally. But I think there may be subtleties and nuances of crime investigation that could elude him from time to time perhaps.'

'Well, blow me down with a brass bedstead, it's all felicitous phrases today, isn't it?' Tessa said, with a surprising guffaw.

'I'm glad you didn't just dismiss us all straight off,' Gus said. 'I'd really like to get my teeth into this case and Ben's good. He's inexperienced but he's going to make a very good copper. Stephanie too, she's ever so keen and quite intuitive.'

'It's fine. I'm sure we'll get on. Sounds like we're going to need a bit of intuition on this one too. But first, the solid slog. Can you arrange for me to have all the reports we've got so far? I'll read through that lot while you chase up the homeless angle. You reckon there's no legs on that though?'

'It's the brutal nature of the crime. Brutal, but not sudden. Planned, almost certainly. That suggests a personal connection, doesn't it?'

'It does, yes. Luckily for us, most murderers are exceptionally stupid, however brilliantly they think they've planned their heinous acts.'

'Heinous, eh? And you mocked my 'nuances' a minute ago.'

'Just go and get the reports, Gus.'

'On it,'

Gus caught her smiling slightly as he left to get the paperwork. She was not quite the dragon that he'd feared after all.

He returned with the paperwork a few minutes later and noticed that Tessa was no longer pacing the room, but sitting at his desk, chewing the end of one of his pencils. He hovered for a moment. 'Just one other thing,' he said. 'Gorgeous George said something which I think may be of interest.'

Tessa removed the pencil and waited for him to elaborate.

'He said the reference to the candle being lit could be related to another Shakespeare play, rather than a quotation from the Bradbury book. I don't know the play but apparently there's a scene where The Porter makes reference to one of the gunpowder plot conspirators. It's just before they discover the old king has been killed by Macbeth. Wright said it could be that our killer was showing off his knowledge of Shakespearian tragedy. I don't know if it's all a bit far-fetched but it made me wonder. So I asked him if *Macbeth* and *King Lear* figured on the syllabus at Townhill. He said they did *Lear* in the first year but they didn't do *Macbeth*. But he did add that it was a pretty common text at GCSE and 'A' level. What do you think, ma'am?'

'There's no need for 'ma'am, at least when we're on our own.' She screwed up her eyes and put the pencil down. 'I did 'A' level English myself,' she said. 'Some decades ago admittedly. The exam boards change the texts every few years but we could get someone to find out when those plays were studied, I suppose. It wouldn't prove anything, but if we manage to find a suspect and we know that he studied the plays it might help in our interrogation. Get PC Beddall to find out which years it was on the syllabus, at 'A' level first. Remind her that there's a few different exam boards too.'

160

'What's your guess as to how old the killer might be?'

'If it's not the boyfriend, then it could be anybody couldn't it? So, eighteen to eighty. Well, perhaps not eighty. Eighteen to retirement age, say. Sorry, I'm being flippant. I know what you're getting at. You think it's someone adolescent, if they're trying to show off.'

That was what Gus was thinking. Especially if the slip of paper with 'Sticks and stones' on it was anything to do with the case. He added that there had been another message, though it was unclear if it was pertinent. It was found in the bin amongst the cardboard and the kitchen waste. He told her the wording.

'Mm, more pre-adolescent than adolescent. Sticks and stones may break my bones but words can never hurt me. You say her face was smashed in, particularly the mouth area?'

'Yes.'

'So she would have been incapable of speech, symbolically as well as literally?'

'Ah, I see what you're driving at,' Gus said. 'My first assumption was that he'd tried to disfigure her beyond recognition. There was no ID with the body. I thought it was an attempt to slow us down. I guessed he didn't know about her tattoo, and that she'd had it done recently. It could have taken us weeks to find out who she was. Until she matched a missing person report anyway.'

'If the killer really wanted to destroy her identity he would have burned the body.' Tessa sighed. 'Better still, buried it.' She picked up the pencil again and rapped it on the desk. 'No, whoever did this is more concerned with trying to prove how clever he is than with evading capture.'

'You think there'll be more snippets of Shakespeare, to hammer the point home, if you'll excuse the expression?'

'I don't know, but if he starts quoting from the complete works it would narrow down our field of suspects to a few university lecturers, wouldn't it? Your George Wright strike you as a homicidal maniac?'

'Not really. As I said, I think he may be partial to the ladies, perhaps to attractive young women like Lauren. I can't see him wielding a brick though.'

'What does your daughter teach?'

Gus's head reeled back, till he realised Tessa was teasing him.

'Actually, she does teach a module on Shakespeare, I believe. But she's going to be on our side if we do get any more messages. That I can guarantee. No maniacs in my family.' He paused. 'Well, if you don't include my ex-wife, that is.'

Tessa frowned. 'I'm sure your ex had many redeeming qualities, Gus. It's usually men that drive women mad. They rarely go mad on their own.'

'Moot, I'd say,' Gus said. 'But I mustn't stand here chatting, we have a homicidal maniac to hunt down. Possibly one with an 'A' level to his name. That is nothing set against the combined intellect of the South Wales Constabulary though.'

'And PC Webb, don't forget.'

It was Gus's turn to smile.

32

I keep going over the stuff they talked about in my Creative Writing module. Once, when one of the girls asked the tutor what he thought about the ridiculous nonsense she'd just read out, he smiled and said 'If it sounds like writing, rewrite it.' Smug bastard. It did make me look up though. I knew it must have been a quote from somewhere but luckily one of the girls asked him who'd said that. Elmore Leonard, he said smugly. Prior to that the quotes he'd come out with were from people like Alexander Pope and Voltaire and a bunch of other has-beens. I don't include Shakespeare in that, naturally. But perhaps he was a bit of a loser in real life too. I wonder what old Will would have been like to talk to? Presumably he wouldn't have actually spoken in blank verse, would he? He'd probably have moaned about his kids, or the bills, if you'd caught him having a swift half in Sheep Street or wherever. Why is everyone so mundane? We live in a banal republic with sheep on every street. So it's up to a lone wolf to extirpate the land. Extirpate, I wonder where that one came from. I mean, I know it's Latin, but where did it come from in my head?

Your head is a wonderful thing, just not a good place to live perhaps. But I don't mind. I wander through my detached dwelling place of a cranium and peek into all the rooms to see what mysteries abound. Now, that sounds like writing, so I'd better rewrite it. I suppose what I'm trying to say is, in words of no more than one letter, I, I, I. No, my one letter rule let me down there. What I'm saying is, we're made up of so much more than a name and some tag like 'pretty girl' or 'smug bastard' or 'strange one'. But to find out who you really are you have to do something, not promise that you'll do something, or pretend that you're doing something. Actually do it. Not talk about it. And today I did do something. I killed another person. I stabbed her through the heart.

Not really, of course. I just exchanged a few judicious words with her. She's not dead yet, but that doesn't mean she won't be, as soon as I deem it fitting to end her fatuous little existence. She thinks because she's the spawn of that piece of grotesquery, the ghastly gargantuan Minors woman, that she can swan around looking beautiful and delicate and everyone will fall at her feet. I didn't say much actually, just enough to pique her interest, I'd say. She's probably only about seventeen and if I'd gone at her like some thundering thesaurus she would have leaped away like a startled gazelle. I said, 'Hiya! It's Miranda, isn't it?' She was standing by the Gregg's in the bus station, for all the world looking like it was some sort of adventure, catching an omnibus, gadzooks. I don't know where she lives but it's probably somewhere out in Gower. Though that can't be right. She'd know about bus timetables if she lived out in the styx (as I think it should be spelled).

Whatever, she was staring up at the Departures board as if it was written in runes. I offered to help. 'Why, thank you, kind sir, I was all of a kerfuffle, what with me being middle class and not accustomed to the vagaries of public transport.' These were not her actual words, dear reader. She looked at me as if I'd asked her for a wank or something. 'It's Jeremy,' I said. I don't know why I picked that name. Just came to me. The pleasures of extemporising are not to be underestimated, though preparation is all if you're a true original. 'Don't you remember me from the Freshers' Ball? I extemporised. 'You've got me confused with somebody else,' she said. 'Oh, I'm terribly sorry,' says I, 'I thought you were Miranda Minors, Ailsa Minors' daughter.' That had her rattled. 'I've never been to a Freshers' Ball,' she says. 'I'm still at school.' 'I'm dreadfully sorry,' I rejoined, jolly as a jack tar, 'but I've definitely seen you at university, so I thought it must have been at Freshers.' She calmed down at that. 'My mother works at Townhill,' she said. 'Perhaps you saw me when I was picking her up from there with my dad.'

And that was enough for now. Ground broken, foundations dug, pillars of trust sunk into the all too yielding earth. Next time we accidentally run into each other we can chat about a range of topics. Like which bands we're into, ha ha. Or, is Burger King superior to McDonalds? All the shit that the callow mind boggles itself with. Though she's probably a bit smarter than that. I might try a sneaky reference to Emily Dickinson or Thomas Hardy. They like that sort of thing, the clever girlies. And when I say 'run into each other' I plainly mean when I accost her on her way out of school. She goes to Olchfa, a pleasant half hour stroll from chez moi. I know this because the last time I saw her she was in her uniform. Gift wrapped, you might say.

God, wouldn't she be horrified if I got her back here! 'OMG, why have you painted your walls this awful green,' she'd say. 'The ghastly pallid hue of a Hopper street scene?' I'd rejoin. 'Why, because it reminds me of a Chicago night in my youth when I lived in the windy city for the length of five long winters.' If there's anything to her at all, she'd half-hear a Wordsworthian echo and be mightily impressed. Plus, frightened witless, needless to say. But I'll never get her back here.

Best I'll manage is an empty park, I suppose. If I can make it Cwmdonkin Park at least there'll be a poetic resonance as she meets her untimely end at the hands of a solitary mister with hate in his heart and a brick in his paw.

It's good to have a new mission. But I must wait for a while, sadly. Just see what the police defectives have on me first. The great thing about the solitary life is that it doesn't need to be lived in any particular place. I could up sticks and go to France and paint lilies. How d'you know they're Lily's? Cos she was still wearing them! Boom boom. Or I could buy a hat and sit in Spain, smoke a cigar, drink sangria and occasionally watch matadors torturing bulls to the hysterical applause of the hoi polloi. Perhaps I could go Stateside and hire a Harley, head out on the highway, drop acid and screw waitresses. I don't know if I'd get a visa though, to be honest.

I also need to get some money. I've still got some from the insurance but it won't last forever. I've gone underground for over a year now since they stopped my student loan payments but I'm cheap to run so I don't need to panic just yet. I certainly don't plan to enter the job market, but the only other option is crime. I think selling drugs or stealing consignments of I-phones is a little out of my skill set though. That does leave kidnapping and blackmail of course, but that's extremely high risk stuff. I mean, I've got the mental and moral wherewithal for a quick kidnap but how do you collect ransom money these days? Gone are the simpler times when you get the police to leave a nice big bag of cash on a tray on a bridge and you just pull the tray down. And they mark the notes. I wonder if it works with £2 coins? Be a heavy bag then though.

I'll have to worry about such trivial matters another day. The Major said he didn't need money, just as long as he had enough for a bottle of scotch and forty fags a day. It was supposed to be some sort of joke, but no one ever laughed. I don't smoke or drink whisky, naturally. A Tesco ready meal and a glass or two of Adam's ale (or Pomerol, tee hee!) doesn't break the bank and Oxfam do a decent line in menswear for the undiscerning man about town. I would like more books though. I've found I've had to resort to free Kindle offerings lately. They're all utter rubbish of course, but reading rubbish helps refine the mind because it tells you what ordinary people think and feel and all you have to do is adjust your own mind to avoid thinking and feeling such platitudes.

Ah me. So it goes. I sometimes feel that I'm sub-letting my life. I don't quite know what I mean by it, but it sounds right. Bijou life to rent. Budget accommodation but extensive views. Admittedly a bit thin on conveniences. Suit single extraordinary person. If only the world would recognise its limitations, eh?

165

But they're all too busy with their body image and their online presence and their self-empowerment to realise what silly struggling ants they are, struggling to surmount the dunghill of their own making.

I was thinking of selling the car. It's not worth much though. But since I have resolved upon another adventure, this time with the gamine Miss Minors, I might need it. I might just happen to be passing the entrance to Olchfa school at letting out time and bob's your male relative. Well, hello again! Care for a spin in the Major's old MR5, young lady? Of course it's no trouble. Why don't we check out Cwmdonkin Park? Or the woods just up here?

33

Finn Oram was not a great deal older than Zoe and Lauren. He was thirty. A young man to Gus. Strange how perceptions of how old other people were changed as you floated or waded through life. Teachers had appeared old men when Gus was little. Then he'd meet them twenty years later and they were much the same age. Sometimes they actually looked younger than the men he remembered. Also, invariably a lot shorter.

Stephanie had traced Oram to a small bakery in Sketty. He was a master baker. Careful how you say that, she had joked, which was the first sign of levity she'd shown so far. She was settling in to the team comfortably. She had used her initiative and gone straight to the bakery on Eversley Road. Oram had had no objections to downing his rolling pin on the spot and coming into the station when he'd heard that Lauren was dead. Stephanie had asked if she could sit in on the interview and Gus decided to allow it.

She stood in the corner as Gus took a seat opposite Oram. He was lean and athletic though a remnant of childhood acne marred his otherwise quite striking features. He pushed his floppy hair back a few times but he didn't appear particularly nervous. Gus thought he probably had to wear a hairnet in work.

'As I think has been explained to you Mr Oram … do you mind if I call you Finn? … We're looking into the suspicious death of Lauren Tracey, whom I believe you knew quite well.' Gus had asked Stephanie to keep a close eye on his body language and had asked her to position herself behind him and slightly to his right. She was to watch what he did with his hands and check if there were any twitches or ticks as he was questioned. She was staring rather too obviously but Oram was looking directly at Gus and was probably unaware. 'Could I ask how well you knew Ms Tracey?'

'We went out a couple of times a few weeks ago.' Steady voice, direct gaze.

'And you were close?'

A shrug.

'Finn, were you in a sexual relationship with Lauren?'

'We had sex once. It wasn't anything spectacular. I'm sorry, I'm not trying to sound callous. We were both a bit drunk and it was more of a fumble.'

'And did the relationship continue after that?'

'Not relationship, no. We had a drink together once after but we didn't go there again.'

'When was the last time you were together? For this drink?'

'As I say, a few weeks ago. It would have been early December. It was a Friday night, so I could work out the date if you like.'

Gus looked up at a calendar on the wall behind Finn. 'Friday the sixth? Friday the thirteenth?'

This time Finn gave a slightly nervous laugh. 'No, not Friday the thirteenth. I would have remembered that. Must have been the sixth.'

'And you haven't seen her since?'

'No. Actually I've started seeing somebody, so no, definitely not.'

'I'm going to have to ask you where you were last Sunday between twelve o'clock and six in the evening. This is not an accusation, Finn, it's just something I'm obliged to ask.'

Finn visibly relaxed in his chair. 'Last Sunday? I was with Linzi. We went to Cardiff for the day.'

'Linzi?'

'She's the girl I've started seeing. We met at Christmas and we've been seeing each other practically every night since.'

'If you could write down her contact details,' Gus slid a piece of paper and a biro across the table. Finn wrote the name and phone number down in laboriously slow handwriting. It did not match the handwritten graffiti.

'You can check with the petrol station at Bridgend,' Finn said. He was not triumphant, as he might have been if he had forged himself an alibi. 'I stopped for petrol on the way up.'

'What car do you drive, Finn?'

To Gus's surprise it was a Honda, not an Alfa Romeo.

Gus knew that Tessa Penry was watching the interview on a screen in a nearby room and he wanted to make sure that he asked all the right questions, but there did not seem much point in carrying on. He

168

could try stalling till this Linzi girl had been contacted to confirm Oram's account of a trip to Cardiff but he was tempted to believe it anyway. If he was lying why would he offer the detail about the petrol stop, where there would be CCTV? He looked up at the discreet camera in the corner of the room and asked Finn if he minded waiting just a few moments while he checked something.

Tessa came out of the room where she'd been watching the interview and put her hand up in a gesture for him to stop before he even spoke. 'It's fine, let him go. He's nothing to do with this,' she said. Gus doubled back and beckoned to Stephanie as he held the door open.

'Thank you for your time, Finn. We won't keep you any longer. We will have to check what you've told us with your girlfriend, but don't worry, it's just a formality. Oh, in case you can think of anything which might help us in our enquiries, the names of any mutual friends etcetera, PC Beddall here will give you a number to call.'

When Finn had gone Gus told Stephanie to pay Linzi Stanton a visit. 'Find out exactly what time they set off,' he said. 'If there's any doubt we can always check the CCTV at the services they stopped in.'

She strode off, almost clicking her heels before doing so. Gus went back to his office to find Tessa waiting for him. She was pacing again. 'So who does this Alfa belong to then?' were her first words.

'I was wondering about that. When he told me it wasn't his I was thinking it might belong to this guy,' he said, He produced the photo that was still in his inside pocket. 'I was thinking this would be Oram but I'm not sure now. I mean, there is a resemblance there isn't there? But the hair's too dark.'

Tessa examined the photograph. 'Do you know when this was taken?' Gus shook his head. 'I don't think it's the same man, even if this is a couple of years old.' She screwed up her eyes and looked hard again. 'This guy's got nice skin.'

Gus took the image back and re-examined it himself. 'Yes, I think you're right. About the same age and he does look a bit like him, but if this isn't Finn Oram who is it? And why was it in a drawer, rather than on display in a frame? That would suggest it's somebody not very important, do you think? Or somebody she wouldn't want other people to know she knew perhaps?' If he'd been in an episode of a

169

TV cop drama, Gus was thinking, he would have found a vital clue. As it was he had a random photograph of somebody who probably had nothing to do with anything. He looked up again. 'Another thing. Zoe Delahaye said the Alfa Romeo driver was older, which I took to be not just a few years older. There's clearly another boyfriend, or gentleman caller, perhaps we ought to call him.'

'Who have you got looking into who the car belongs to?' Tessa said. 'Did Zoe see him outside their flat, or somewhere else?'

Gus had not thought to ask this, but he did not reveal his oversight to Tessa now. He would call Zoe as soon as he was on his own. He said he'd check if his sergeant had contacted the DVLA yet. 'You're still confident it was someone she was involved with in some way?'

'Just covering the bases, Gus. If we're looking for a complete stranger we're in deep faeces,' Tessa said.

'I'll get Ben to order some snorkels,' Gus said.

'And get him to order some extra strong Kevlar vests while you're at it. To protect us against the press, if they suspect we haven't got a clue about who's prowling about our manor killing girls. Female students at that. Though young Mr Oram did get your, hopefully unintended, reference to teen slasher movies.'

Gus looked confused.

'*Friday the Thirteenth*?' She said, with a 'Duh!' in her voice.

'Oh, that. Never seen it. Never wanted to. I think I may have been a bit put off by the fact that I was married to a female version of Freddie Krueger for a while.'

'That's A Nightmare on Elm Street, Gus. It was Jason in Friday the Thirteenth.'

'Aren't they all pretty much the same thing?' Gus asked innocently. 'And please, don't be talking about serial killers. This is little old Swansea. We have serial drunks and serial drug abusers but so far the place hasn't turned into a summer camp or a ...' He hesitated, 'A street with elms on it, I suppose.'

'Well, I haven't spotted any elm trees either, but it would appear that we have a killer with a taste for drama, if these Shakespeare quotes are anything to go by. So let's get busy before we need the stab-proof vests, eh?'

Gus left Tessa in the office and went to find Ben Willis. On his way he called Zoe. 'Hello Zoe, How are you doing? It's Inspector Reid. One other thing I need to ask you. Did you tell me you saw the man with the Alfa Romeo outside your house?'

'No. Did I say that? No, he picked her up outside Noah's Wine Bar in Uplands. We'd stopped off for a drink there on the way back from uni. She was going into town to meet Finn or Flynn, or whatever his name is, but he decided to pick her up instead.'

Gus thanked her and located Ben. Before he could even ask Ben said breathlessly, 'The Alfa belongs to a Rob Oram.'

Clearly Finn's father, or brother. 'How old is this Rob Oram?'

Ben consulted the piece of paper he was holding. 'Born June 20, 1978. So, hang on, thirty six. No, thirty five.'

Brother then. Zoe had seen Lauren getting into the car and presumably in the front. It had been his brother driving, or possibly his cousin, but it didn't matter which. Finn must have got into the back as a gesture to his girlfriend but Zoe had only noticed the person driving and hence had remarked on him seeming older. Gus hadn't thought to ask if there was someone in the back seat, but then why would he?

'Got the address for this Rob Oram?' Gus asked. Ben showed him the slip of paper he was holding. 'I suppose we could go and talk to him. Find out where they were going. Maybe he noticed some tension between Lauren and Finn. It's a blind alley though, Finn's got a secure alibi for Sunday.'

'Do you want me to contact him, sir?' Ben looked disappointed that his discovery had turned out to be of no great significance. Perhaps he was hoping that the brother would turn out to be a shifty character and that the case had been blown wide open.

'Yeah, might as well. Just ask him if he was dropping them off somewhere or whether they were together for the evening. Tell him we're just trying to trace Lauren's movements that day. It was Friday the sixth of December. But see if you can find out if Finn was telling us the truth about his relationship with Lauren. He said they were very casual and it petered out last month. If this Rob is offering Finn lifts he'll be close enough to him to have some idea, I guess.'

***

At five o'clock Tessa summoned Gus, Ben and Stephanie to the briefing room for an update.

Nobody said anything for a few seconds. Then Stephanie spoke up. 'The computer people got into Lauren's laptop. I've had a look through her photos but there's hardly anything there. All her recent stuff will be on her mobile, which we haven't got. She wasn't on Twitter or Tinder, as you thought she might be, boss. But she was on Facebook. Lots of the usual stuff, you know, pictures of distressed animals, memories of holidays, shares of people's outrage at what we're doing to our planet. Not so many pictures of all the brilliant meals she'd had, but she was a student, so I suppose she didn't think to photograph pot noodles and bowls of pasta.' Gus smiled and Stephanie looked pleased before she resumed her seriousness. 'The most important thing was that nobody appeared to be trolling her, which would have been the most useful thing to find, obviously. I'm thinking if there was anybody with a grudge against her he's either not very savvy or he's ultra-careful.'

'Okay,' Tessa said. 'Have Forensics reported on the crime scene? Was it definitely the garage?'

'They found a small amount of blood. Fresh blood, I mean. They've sent it off for testing but unless an animal's got trapped in there and injured itself it's bound to be from the head wound,' Ben said. 'We should know for definite in a few days.'

Gus was shocked. 'A few days! What do the lab people do with their time?'

'I think we're safe in assuming it's Lauren's blood,' Tessa said. 'At least, until we know any different we'll concentrate our efforts on The Strand and the surrounding area in terms of trying to track her movements. No CCTV down there, you say?'

'Nothing near the garage,' Ben answered. 'There's cameras on the shops in Parc Tawe but they won't be any use if she was taken there by car. You could come from either direction, up from the docks or down from Dyfatty, and not be spotted.'

'What about if she was walking from somewhere in the shopping mall? Does it make sense that she would have passed it on her way home?'

Gus intervened. 'Her flat is on the other side of the river. If she'd been shopping in Parc Tawe and was headed home she'd have been going the other way.'

'Not necessarily,' a newly emboldened Stephanie said. 'She might have been going up to High Street to buy something else. She might just have been going for a walk even.'

'Odd route to take for a Sunday walk,' Gus said. 'And she wasn't wearing jogging gear, so it probably wasn't an exercise thing.'

'We need to find out her weekend routine,' Tessa said firmly. 'Then we can rule things in or out.'

'Shall I speak to Zoe Delahaye again, sir?' Stephanie said. 'Sorry, I should be asking you that, ma'am.'

'Yes, do that. Students don't tend to be all that organised, but she may have been a creature of habit. It would be good for us if she was.' Tessa paused for thought. 'What about her bank account and credit cards? Did she have online banking? Have we been in touch with the relevant companies? I don't suppose the money trail is all that relevant if this is a crime of passion, but she may have bought something on card if she was shopping in this mall of yours. If she's using contactless no one will even have looked up and seen her but a transaction would place her somewhere specific at some point before the attack at least. Actually, thinking about crimes of passion, do we know if there's a religious dimension here?'

Ben and Gus both expressed surprise, but it was Stephanie who spoke first. 'The parents are both white. Do you mean she might have converted to Islam or something?'

Tessa looked at Gus, who was wincing at the casual racism implied in Stephanie's remark. 'Her flatmate would have mentioned it, wouldn't she, if that was a possibility? But let's not assume all hate crime is directed at Muslims. She might have been Jewish. Do you have any intelligence on neo-Nazi groups in Swansea?'

All three officers looked totally blank. 'No?' Tessa went on. 'I know, I know, we're shooting in the dark but you have to consider all possibilities when it comes to motive. There's no such thing as a murder without motive. Even the Yorkshire Ripper had a motive, and he was about as random as you get about his choice of victims.'

'Please don't be talking about random killings, Tessa.' Gus said. She gave him a stern look and he corrected himself. 'I mean, Ma'am.'

'Well, do the follow up on Finn Oram's brother,' she said. 'Will you do that, Sergeant Willis? I've got an appointment to see Dr Wright to see what he's got to say about Lauren's connections at university. PC Beddall, you can do some more checking on her internet stuff. Find out a bit more about these posts she's shared from action groups or whatever. And those financials. Even if we can't find any card transactions it's possible she owed money to somebody dodgy. Gus, will you handle the press? We'll do an appeal. We need to find out who saw her last Sunday morning. Where was she going? Where had she been? We may even have to do a reconstruction. Have you got anyone here at the station who looks a bit like Lauren?'

Gus and Ben both looked blank, then Gus remembered the young officer who'd been trying to flirt with Ben. 'I think we've got a uniform who'd fit the part,' he said.

'Would she be okay with doing it if we go ahead with something like that?'

'She'll be up for it,' Ben said confidently. Gus smiled. It was all so exciting when you were new to the job. Later on you just felt sickened at man's inhumanity.

34

The car won't start, so that's the kidnap plan off the table. But fear not, mes braves, something much less risky has popped up its cunning head. The stupid red MR5, a middle-aged major's rust-riddled erectile dysfunction substitute, has been sitting in the lock up for nearly two years so I knew the battery would be dead. I didn't know the tyres would be flatter than poor old mum's chest though. There's no way I could afford to get the thing going again without spending a king's ransom. Also, it would draw far too much attention from they who need to be avoided.

I don't know what I was thinking anyway. What teenage girl would get into a car with me, sports car or no sports car, these days? And even if she was that naïve all her Clueless mates would be offering a range of descriptions of the smiling man who'd picked her up to any jug-eared copper with a notebook and an IQ in double figures. It would be fascinating to see the identikit they'd do of me on the front page of the newspapers, of course, but I prefer the shadows. So, no cruising past Olchfa for yours truly. Actually though, now I think of it, Miss Miranda Minors and the MR5 would make an interesting arson art project. Can never happen, sadly.

But, as I say, all is not lost. I was checking for my media profile in the Post a little while ago and a new and much more intriguing cunning plan blossomed from the bud of serendipity. There was an article about an amateur theatre group, obviously a bunch of failed social workers and estate agents with dreams of provincial fame and accolades beyond the comprehension of their peers. And they're staging a production of The Tempest next week on the Friday and Saturday in the Dylan Thomas Theatre! This, in itself, would scarcely be of passing interest but young Miss Minors was actually holding a copy of the play at the bus station. Must be her A level set text. She wouldn't be reading the bard of her own accord now, would she? We're not all autodidacts. And you can be certain there'll be a school trip to the theatre if there's a production of a set text on offer. Teachers are inherently lazy. They'll show a film rather than do any work themselves. Even better if there's actors doing the words, amateur actors notwithstanding. (That was a favourite word of the Major's, when he was rebuking the mater. I am using it with my tongue coming out the other side of my cheek). I'm guessing they'd run a trip on Friday because they'd never do one on a Saturday. The kids wouldn't turn up, for one thing. 'What? Culture? On a Saturday night? You're havin' a larf, sir!' The teachers wouldn't want to take any time out of their precious weekend either anyway, would they? I'll book for Friday and Saturday night, just in case they're too lazy to organise a school trip. She might be going with her friends so that's bound to cover it. Nothing to lose, even if she doesn't go. I get all that poetry, not to mention casting of rods!

I haven't worked out how to get her on her own yet, but it'll be a simple matter to get chatting again in the foyer at half-time if she does go. 'Why, hello Miranda! Well met at midnight! Or (consults wristwatch) ten past nine, I see. What do you think of the actress playing your namesake tonight? That Caliban is a bit over the top though, isn't he?' In like Flynn.

I'll still have to separate her from the herd, so to speak, but I'll think of something. It would be tougher if it was a boyfriend, of course, but what healthy strapping young man would want to waste his Saturday boys' night out watching three hours of Shakespeare? Present company excepted. It's all a bit of a rigmarole but I doubt she goes to Lidl at a set time on the weekend. That was a gift, I have to admit. But she'll have some sort of routine, certes. An orchestra practice, a dance class, a pony trek. I'm guessing wildly here, naturally, but the chattering classes are pretty predictable when it comes to rearing their offspring. She'll probably be just at the rebellion stage though, when ponies and tutus and violins just don't do it for her anymore and she's determined to get off her face on vodka somewhere where there's a crowd of other bright young things. Can't see her on Wind Street though. She's rather skinny, and almost certainly without a bejewelled navel, so that'd rule her out of that Gomorrah. I can, however, picture her somewhere in Uplands. It's like a zoo there, or an aviary I should say, with all the birds of paradise let out for a good old squawk on a Friday and Saturday night. I wouldn't mind sneaking along with my bow and arrow. Figurative archery, dear reader! Yet another casual encounter, golly! With her having half a bottle of Smirnoff under her belt I'd be well in charge of events, I like to think.

Of course I have no proper revenge motive this time because she didn't recognise me from that time. She's actually going to be more of a symbolic sacrifice. Privilege and patronage, pleasantry and peasantry, the lieutenant before the ensign, it's always the same. Serf and toff, that's what's always on the menu. So, sorry Miranda, no brave new future for you, my girl. Caliban, Caliban, tally me bananas! As I'm writing this I'm realising the Horatio quote is not the thing at all. Far too corny. I'm going to have to come up with something more 'apposite',

176

as that old fart of a lecturer would say. I've been thinking hard about methodology too. Obviously I'd like something showy, an upside down crucifixion or a Jackson Pollock of blood and organs, for example. But simple is always best. The gloved hands in the shadows, subtler and sweeter than the axe and the gore. And I can't leave her in a bin like last time. That was a lot more effort than I expected, and much too dangerous, looking back on it. I need, as I think I wrote here before, a nice quiet park or tract of wasteland. That's why I was thinking about resurrecting the MR5, but as I say, that's not a goer. There's always dismemberment and suitcases but I'm not sure I've got the necessary mental vacuum for that. I did love the expression on the face of Steve Buscemi's mate in Fargo as he fed Mrs Lundegaard's body into the wood chipper, but give me credit, eh? Problems, problems.

If I can, I'll find out if she's one of the Uplands aviary. Then maybe I'll be able to discover where she roosts at night. If it's somewhere I can get to without having to take a cab I could simply pay her a home visit. The giantess and her husband must go out occasionally; they'll be birdwatchers or opera buffs or something. Miranda Minors-Bird must be on her own one dark evening. Then, by the pricking of my thumbs, Aaron Ferie this way comes. I could stagger up all stage-blood bloody and seek sanctuary or band aids. I could do the 'my car's broken down, could I borrow your phone' routine. I could claim I'd just witnessed her parents seriously injured in a bizarre birdwatching accident. Anything will do because she'll be so stunned at my presence on her doorstep that there'll be ample opportunity to wield my improvised cudgel – I'm thinking of the brick but that sets up a pattern and patterns are BAD – and bludgeon her into the desired state of passivity. A stone from the front garden would be ideal because it would suggest spontaneity and a thwarted burglar, but always be prepared. That's the Baden Powell watchword, isn't it? Dib dib dib, or in this case, club club club. Or stab stab stab indeed.

If she does, as I fear she may, live out in the Styx, I can't be catching buses, assuming that such things exist these days, so I'll have to think of another plan. There's a very promising back lane behind the bars on Uplands Crescent. There used to be a second-hand furniture shop tucked away there, run by a man called Keith Chugg. Chugg chugg chugg, could be the sound of the raven himself, hoarse with all his croaking of premonitions, if you're somewhat fanciful. And I have to say I am, if I am anything at all, a little fanciful. But seriously, how hard could it be to take a short cut through this lane with a drunk unbejewelled academic's daughter? Still the problem of being 'the last person seen with', however.

177

I have ample time to consider these matters. The play's the thing wherein I'll catch the girl that's thin. The rest is all supposition and chance really. I don't even have to do this one. I could go through my little courtship ritual and then decide to leave it there. I'd just be some clever, if rather strange, individual that Miranda met one time, and that's all she wrote. Can't help wanting it though. I like the idea that the police will be desperately struggling to find connections between these two awful events of early January, with only a brick and various fragments of Shakespeare to go on. Who's the bright spark with the Spark's Notes? That'll be what they're quizzing themselves over their paste sandwiches and slot machine coffee in their bright plastic canteen. 'Chief Inspector Dodo told The Evening Post "We're not ruling out an elderly dramatist" but enquiries are continuing.'

As to my next missive, or missile, to the supersleuths, I've been toying with Percy Bysshe's bon mots 'Look on my works, ye mighty, and despair!' but it's very glittery literary. Something sharper, less nineteenth century then. 'The wounded surgeon plies the steel that questions the distempered part' is good, but I'm not sure yet if I'll be stabbing, and it's a touch self-deprecating to call myself wounded, n'est-ce pas? I was trying to catch some silvery flashing phrases in my inter net this morning and I internetted a beauty. Pity I didn't use it on Miss Tracey. It's from Love's Labour's Lost, which I haven't read, but then who has? It was perfect for the one I chalked behind the bin: 'The tongues of mocking wenches are as keen/As is the razor's edge invisible.' The trouble is, it's been used as a title of a novel, like lots of memorable bits in old Shaky. Agatha Christie was a particularly virulent little tea leaf when it came to this sort of borrowing, I gather. I even saw a Star Trek episode the other day with a sneaky bit of bardolatry in the title. Not that your average Trekky would have recognised it. Makes you wonder who writes the scripts. There's an old joke about how you can tell a Trekky (geek, spotty, adolescent) from a Trekker (intelligent, well educated, ironic). One wonders what it would be like to make love to a Cyborg, or maybe it was a Klingon. The other wonders what it's like to make love. Not the sort of joke worth retelling and I'm boring myself writing it down now. I should delete this paragraph but I won't, because everything has a purpose, even junk. To the fertile mind, that is. Or the futile mind, perhaps I mean. Phew! Time for something else, I think. But this is FUN!

35

Andrea rang Gus at nine o'clock, as soon as she got to Adelaide Street. His phone went to voicemail. 'About the Lauren Tracey murder. I've got a piece in this afternoon's edition,' she said. 'I managed to talk to Mr and Mrs Tracey and they were kind enough to supply some background material, but I'd be grateful if you could give me an update as soon as you can. Please give me a call when you can.' She was hoping to bypass the normal press release. That was something her editor would see first. She knew the murder was likely to go viral any time now and there was no guarantee she could hang on to the story then. In the meantime she could try and get to see Lauren's tutor at university. Whoever that turned out to be might be slightly more forthcoming than the deputy head at Abbey Park.

She took a cab to the Townhill campus, rather than telephoning first, hoping to waylay her source before there was time to prepare the normal diplomatic responses to her questions. As she slid into the white Skoda and said where she was headed the driver didn't seem to register what she was saying. 'Oh,' he grunted, when she repeated her directions, 'the old training college, you mean.' Cabbies were set in their ways and refused to accept institutional name changes, it seemed. Luckily he was a taciturn type and did not regale her with conspiracy theories or racist remarks disguised as banter.

She was dropped outside a glass doored frontage that opened onto a foyer. There was no sign of a reception desk here so she turned into the canteen on her left and asked a smiling woman at the till if she knew the way to where English might be taught. It was not a very precise question but the woman was unfazed. 'Ask Mr Wright there,' she said. 'He's something to do with English.' Andrea turned round and saw a man getting up to put an empty cup on a trolley for used dishes. There was an unflappable quality about him and an air that suggested he knew he was always on show. He was flicking an imaginary crumb or piece of lint off the lapel of his fawn cord jacket

179

as she approached him.

'Excuse me,' she said. 'I'm looking for someone in the English department. I wonder if you could help?'

'You're probably looking for me,' George Wright said. 'I'm Head of English. Is it about an Open Day?' He spoke in a perfect Received Pronunciation accent that suggested he was not from South Wales, or indeed anywhere in particular.

'No, I'm afraid it's not about that. It's about one of your students. I'm Andrea Linney from *The Evening Post*. Lauren Tracey? She passed away a few days ago. I was wondering if she was somebody you taught.'

'Come with me,' George said, taking her lightly by the elbow. 'We'll go to my study.'

She was led down a short flight of stairs, round a series of corridors, then through a covered walkway into the old part of the building. There were more stairs, a series of double doors and a few more twists and turns before they eventually came to a lift. He ushered her in and they rode up to the next floor. Only when they got to his study door did he speak again. 'Come in, take a seat. What do you need to know?'

'I don't know if you read my paper,' Andrea began,' but there's a piece in today's edition about Lauren. Not so much about what tragically happened, more about her personal life. But readers will want some more detail about her time here at university. That's why I'd like to have a chat with you today.'

'Well, I did teach her, but that was two years ago. She took last year out, perhaps you already know, and I wasn't teaching her this year. I don't know how I can really help.'

'Could you tell me anything about any friends she may have had in her first year, do you think? I'm trying to build a picture, you see. I've spoken to her parents but they weren't able to help with regard to that.'

'I do recall some things about her, but not really any friendship groups, I fear. Perhaps you'd be better off talking to her colleagues at the place she was working last year. I gather she got a full-time job in Swansea.'

'I will do that. I'll have to check where that was first. You don't

180

happen to know, I suppose?'1

George Wright smiled. She was a callow reporter whose disingenuousness was all too transparent, his expression suggested. 'I believe it was the Driver and Vehicle Licensing Agency, Miss Linney.'

Andrea was not going to give up this easily. 'Was it a Creative Writing module that you taught, Dr Wright? Mrs Tracey said Lauren was interested in writing and I believe there is a module on that in the first year.' George confirmed that this was the case by a slight inclination of the head. 'Could you say what interested her in particular? Did she want to write in any particular genre, for instance?'

George glanced out of his window, perhaps trying to recall, or perhaps stalling so that he could find the right words. 'The module, at least as I taught it, involved a number of tasks, mainly involving experimenting with poetic forms and discussion of elements of the short story. Students could choose to write whatever they wanted to but they were encouraged to concentrate on economy and brevity.' He smiled. 'Not just to lighten the marking load, you understand. I did have genuine motives in getting them to keep their writing tight. I'm not sure how successful I was.' He thought for a moment. 'I also encouraged them to try and avoid graphic sex and graphic horror. They slip into all sorts of cliché far too quickly if you let them, you know. I suppose it's a sense of release after school. They can indulge their fantasies on paper, as well as in real life, I guess.'

Andrea seized on this. 'Would you say Lauren was a fantasist, in her writings anyway?'

George was letting his reserve go a little as he warmed to a potential discussion of literary concerns. 'I'd say the opposite. She was always aiming for some psychological insight. I don't think she was very interested in action scenes, chase scenes or drooling sex scenes, you know the usual derivative stuff.'

'That's very interesting,' Andrea said. George looked like a man who would respond well to a little flattery. 'What psychological insights did she have, do you think?'

'I can't really remember. But I do recall a particular occasion when she made her feelings very strongly felt about another's student's work. It was prurient stuff – a graphic sex scene involving S&M – and all the girls were finding it a bit too strong for their tastes. They have to read their work in progress out to the class in some sessions you see. It's more a workshop than a seminar then. Everyone's entitled to comment. They usually just say nice things, of course. No one likes a critic, do they?'

'What did Lauren say?'

'She stopped him as he was reading. Told him he couldn't write things like that. The other girls were all agreeing but I had to step in and referee.'

'Him? A male student then?'

'Yes, that year there was just one lad in the class. Well, I say lad, he was a mature student.'

'A man?'

'Well, they're mature students if they start university after twenty-one. I'd say he was in his early twenties. They can do an Access course if they haven't got the usual qualifications. Sometimes they're highly motivated and turn out to be the best students. Other times they find it all a bit much and they drop out.'

'Which type was this one?'

'The latter. Under a cloud too, if I recall. I'd have to check the detail on that.' He put on a more serious face. 'But this isn't anything to do with Lauren Tracey and you can't be quoting me on what's little more than gossip. You do understand that, I'm sure?'

'Of course,' Andrea said. She just had to get the name of this student that Lauren Tracey had lashed out at now. He would have plenty to say about the dead girl. A treasure trove of quotes for her next article, and maybe future pieces, if the case wasn't solved too soon. She smiled sweetly. 'Do you remember the young man's name, Dr Wright?'

'Why would you want to know that Miss Linney?'

'Oh please, call me Andrea. Andie, if you like.' George raised his eyebrow wryly. She pretended she hadn't noticed. 'I like to do as much research as I can. It doesn't seem like Lauren had many close friends and she had rather lost touch with her parents. She deserves to be written about with some sensitivity, I feel. Anything I can find out about her helps to paint a picture.'

'Hmm. Well, I do remember his first name. I can't quite summon up his surname at the moment but I could check that. He was called

Aaron. Strange young man. Short, with very red hair. Looked quite a bit older than he actually was, you know? Some people are cursed early in life with the face that they should eventually grow into.'

'You say he left under a cloud?'

'It wouldn't be appropriate for me to go into any sort of detail about that, Andrea.' He'd shifted from Miss Linney but was not so imprudent as to jump straight to Andie, she noted. 'Suffice to say, sometimes people leave; occasionally we sort of wonder aloud if they wouldn't be better off considering other career opportunities. Very occasionally we actually bid them leave the grounds, so to speak. I'm not going to say which happened in Aaron's case.'

'Could you say when he left then?'

'It was at the end of that year. The same time that Lauren decided not to continue, though she came back of course.'

When she felt that George Wright could not be coaxed into any further revelations she thanked him for his time and rose to place her card on his desk. He promised he would get in touch in due course with Aaron's surname and anything else he might recall but she knew he wouldn't do anything of the sort. She gave him her most alluring smile and sashayed out of his study. He would have watched her departure studiously and, she hoped, appreciatively.

Not feeling confident of the mazy route back up to the entrance she headed for the nearest exit. It brought her out into the staff car park with the crescent sweep of Swansea Bay as its dramatic backdrop. A stiff salty breeze was blowing in from the shore. As she took a strong lungful she noticed a woman getting out of a black Mazda. As the woman remotely locked the vehicle with a casual flick of the wrist Andrea sensed there was something official about her. She didn't look like a lecturer late for a class. She pulled out a black card holder as she was approached by a tall elderly man from the direction of the library. Andrea instantly knew, even from this distance, it was police identification. The woman was wearing a smart dark blue overcoat and good shoes and she looked very confident as she showed the man her ID. Plain clothes police meant it had to be something to do with the Lauren Tracey enquiry, but where was Gus Reid?

She didn't know if she dared approach this officer right now. Then

183

she was moving off with the man towards the library and the chance was gone. Andrea decided to call Gus to find out if he had been superseded or just chucked off the case. She had information for him anyway. There was somebody who might have borne a grudge against Lauren.

She phoned for a taxi but was told it would only pick her up outside the foyer at the North end of the campus. She walked round the side of the building and trudged up the steep slope towards Reception. A couple of workmen were standing outside a storage shed. One was smoking, the other leaning against the open door. Only a few years earlier they would have happily wolf whistled at her but those days were gone. She felt their eyes following her as she walked past. She was not sashaying this time. Sometimes you were happy to be the object of an admiring look, sometimes it was worse than being whistled at.

The cab came quite quickly and she tried Gus on her mobile as soon as she had given the driver his directions. This time Gus answered. At least he had put her number into his call list, because he addressed her by name immediately. 'I'll get in touch with you, Andrea, when I have something for you.' The words were curt but not the tone.

'Wait, Gus,' she said, anticipating being cut off, 'I've got something for you. Or I may have. Can we meet?'

Andrea knew he was pretending to consult a diary as there was a brief pause. 'What sort of thing? I'm pretty busy, you know, but I suppose I can spare half an hour. Do you want to come to the station?' he said, 'or would you prefer neutral ground?'

'Does Costa count as neutral, or are you a Starbucks fan?'

'I resent both as multinationals with dubious ethical practices but I do quite like their coffee. You choose, Miss Linney.'

'Why, Inspector Reid, you are a true gentleman!' This was in her best *Gone with the Wind* American accent, but it couldn't have been that impressive. Gus simply replied that he'd be at Costa in Uplands in twenty minutes.

He was there before her, though she got dropped straight off by her cab. 'Were you already in here when I called?' she said.

'Not far away,' he said cryptically. 'So, what have you got for me?

184

I am all ears.' He pronounced the word to rhyme with fears, rather than furze, as in the local accent. She had found it strange when she had first come to Swansea and heard the phrase 'I am all years'. It had been an elderly shopkeeper who had said it and she had wanted to console him, until she realised he was not talking about his advanced age.

'I was talking to Dr George Wright up at the university,' she began.

'Ah yes, he of the silver tongue,' Gus said wearily. 'We spoke to him yesterday.'

'Did he tell you about the row between Lauren and one of her classmates?'

Gus's eyes opened wider. 'He did not. And I am wondering why not now.'

'He couldn't or wouldn't give me the surname, but he said there was a student called Aaron who upset her with the stuff he'd written. He was reading it out in a workshop on their Creative Writing module and she told him to shut up apparently. Made me think that this guy might have nurtured some bad feeling towards her. He's not at university anymore. Left in circumstances that Wright didn't seem to want to get into. I don't know how you'd go about finding him.'

'You can leave that to us, Andrea, But well done for getting that information. It could be something, although this must have happened eighteen months ago. More perhaps. Not exactly quick revenge for a slight in a seminar.'

'Perhaps he thought it was a dish best served cold.' Andrea said.

'Or microwaved up the next day.'

'Don't mock, Gus. I'm trying to help out, you know.'

'Sorry. I am grateful for this titbit. And in return I'll see to it that you get whatever I can give you as promptly as I can.'

Andrea decided to pump him for anything else she might be able to use, though she suspected he would be guarded and not reveal much till the next press release. 'So,' she said. 'Any developments I should know about? From what I've gathered, Lauren Tracey was something of a loner. I take it you know where she was living and what she got up to in her spare time. Was she living on her own in a sad little bedsit?'

Gus looked at her with the stolid expression she had noted in the

185

press briefing two days earlier. Then he gave a wry half-smile. 'She shared a flat with another student. I don't know if that person would want you pestering her though. Okay, look, perhaps this Aaron thing may turn out to be a lead, so I'll tell you, but don't go all paparazzi on me, will you? Don't be sticking big camera lenses in her face.'

Andrea held up her hands in mock dismay.

'She lived in a downstairs flat over in St Thomas. Sebastopol Street, number 37. Her flatmate is a girl called Zoe Delahaye, but she's in deep shock so please be sensitive and discreet when you talk to her. And I didn't give you this information. You got it from university or something. Okay'

'Of course,' Andrea said. 'Anything else?'

'You are a greedy one, aren't you? Well, I'll tell you now, because you'll find out soon, There's a new Senior Investigating Officer from the major incident team. Her name is Tessa Penry. Detective Chief Inspector Penry to you. She'll probably want to do a reconstruction of Lauren's last movements, but that hasn't been finalised yet. Obviously, we'll let you know in time but there'll be TV crews attending as well. For the moment I'm still in charge of press liaison but that could change any time.'

'Is DCI Penry about forty-five with greying hair and does she wear a dark blue coat?'

'Are you telepathic? That's the more important question.'

She told him that she had seen Penry at Townhill just twenty minutes before. Gus remembered that Tessa had gone to interview Lauren's tutor.

'Well, we nearly bumped into each other. I was just coming from his office.'

'Swansea's a small place, Andrea. People bump into each other or just miss each other all the time.'

'Just one other thing,' Andrea said. 'You said there were no signs of a sexual assault. Are you absolutely confident that there was no sexual motive to the killing?'

'Why do you ask? I did tell you there wasn't, didn't I? There was no sign of any clothing being removed or replaced and the pathologist has confirmed there were no signs of assault. Some people would argue that there is a type of sexual release in the act of murder, of

186

course.'

'Yes, a power thing, I've heard. I'm asking because the business with this Aaron chap was over a story he'd written which was too demeaning to women, or too horribly sexually graphic. If she was a committed feminist or likely to overreact to something she thought was misogynistic she might have upset her killer. I was walking past a couple of workmen just now and I could feel their eyes almost penetrating me. They didn't say anything as it happens, but what if they had, and I'd reacted badly? Couldn't that lead to some type of physical confrontation?'

'This wasn't just a chance confrontation, I'm afraid. This was planned and executed carefully. We have evidence about that which I can't go into right now.'

'Oh please do.' Andrea was little girl pouting but she was semi-serious too.

'When and if the time is right, I will.' Gus was thinking that the time would only be right in the event of another attack, but that was definitely not for the papers at this point.

'I'm getting a sense that there could be wider implications, Gus. Do you think young women need to be warned that they could be in some sort of danger?'

'I didn't say that. At the moment we are not regarding this as a stranger attack, but you never know. We still have to trace and eliminate Lauren's friends and acquaintances. Somebody from her past could be involved, for all we know at the present time. Please don't start throwing assertions around about raving maniacs patrolling the highways and byways of our fine city now, will you?'

'Other than the ones we already know about, you're saying?'

Gus looked alarmed. 'What do you mean? I hope you're not casting aspersions on the displaced and the homeless.' Gus was thinking about Darren Bunn and wondering if Andrea had got wind of his interrogation. Surely not, he tried to convince himself. The last thing anyone needed was a delusional confessor talking to the press.

'Just joking,' Andrea said. 'Though this is scarcely the time or place for levity, sorry.'

'It's okay,' Gus reassured her. 'I'm prone to making light of things beyond my comprehension at times too.'

They both took a sip of their coffee, neither willing to admit that they were anxious to get away immediately and follow up on what they had just learned.

36

Gus went back to the station and summoned Ben to his office. 'News?' he asked.

'Rob Oram confirms that he picked his brother's girlfriend up at Noah's wine bar at seven on Friday the sixth.' Ben said. 'Took them into town and then went to his mate's house. He said Finn and Lauren were planning a night in Wind Street. Next time he saw Finn he asked how things were going with Lauren and was told that they weren't together any longer. He wasn't all that surprised, he said.'

Gus gave a questioning look.

'He said, and I'm quoting, "she was too up herself for my liking." Didn't you say Finn was a bit dismissive about her too?'

'Yes, but I wasn't sure if he was just trying to suggest that they were never very serious because he was afraid he was under suspicion. In other words he couldn't be anything to do with her being attacked because he didn't have very much to do with her.'

'Except for sleeping with her.'

'Young people today, eh, Ben? But it does seem she came across as a bit supercilious, doesn't it.'

'Yes, sir.'

Gus was unsure if Ben could have defined this word if put on the spot. 'You know, aloof,' he added.

Ben grunted. 'The other news is that Stephanie couldn't find any card transactions for last Sunday. Suggests she wasn't shopping anyway.'

'Some shops do accept cash,' Gus said sardonically. 'But what did she buy, and where is it now if she was shopping? We need to scour that whole area round The Strand. The forensics guys wouldn't have paid attention to a carrier bag in a nearby bin, necessarily.'

'The killer would have taken whatever she had with her along with her phone and purse, wouldn't he?'

'True. But if it was an item of clothing or makeup he'd have to get rid of it sharpish. She might have been nipping out for Tampax.'

Ben took this suggestion seriously. 'Not in Parc Tawe, sir. Unless she'd gone to Sainsbury's across the road from there, but then why would she be anywhere near the homeless place?'

Gus rubbed his nose with his thumb and forefinger. 'I've been thinking about the brick he must have used to subdue her. The SOCOS report any loose building materials anywhere near the scene?'

'I was wondering about that too, sir. No, nothing close by. Do you think he was carrying it around with him? If so, he must have had a bag of some sort. And why a brick, rather than a hammer?'

'It's a strange one indeed, Ben' Gus said. 'Well, we just need to find somebody who saw a man with a bag with a brick shaped bulge in it, possibly with a box of tampons in his hand and two phones and a ladies' purse in his pocket.'

'We need to find *anybody* who was in the area, sir. When are we doing a public appeal for witnesses? Maybe if nobody comes forward the reconstruction will jog someone's memory though, do you think?'

'We'll get the Darren Bunns of this world for certain. And a few people claiming their ex was involved. But what we need ideally is a nice little old lady with a good memory and very sharp eyesight. With the ability to tell a brick from a handsaw, or whatever the saying is.'

Ben didn't know of any such saying. He was one of today's young people.

***

Tessa came back to the station an hour later to report that there might have been someone in Lauren's past who had reason to wish her harm.

'I know,' Gus said. 'A student called Aaron Something.'

Tessa looked askance.' How do you know? I only just found out myself.'

'That young reporter from *The Post* interviewed George Wright just before you saw him. I assume that's where you've come from? She buttonholed me for more information but she let slip that Wright had told her about this fellow. He wouldn't give a surname though.'

'It's Ferie,' Tessa said. 'Aaron Ferie. Not a pleasant character by all accounts. But it does seem a bit of a long shot. Something happened

190

between him and Lauren in a seminar Wright was taking.'

'Andrea Linney - she's the local reporter - told me it was over a story he'd written. He was reading it out to the class and she told him to shut up. Hardly reason to kill somebody. Not in my book anyway.'

'Perhaps you're not reading the right type of books.' Tessa sat down. 'Can you get young PC Beddall to trace the other members of that class? Let's find out exactly what was said. See if anybody else turned on this Ferie, or on Lauren, come to that. Now, what else have we got? Anything new? How about the homeless people?'

'Willis collated the uniforms' reports,' Gus said. There were four people staying in the refuge last Saturday. An alcoholic called Mary, we're not too concerned about her, given the nature of the crime, and three men. One, a guy called Terry, was spoken to and had a perfect alibi. He was in casualty in Morriston hospital half the day, and certainly around lunchtime. Somebody else said that one of the others, a man called Gareth, was well on his way to Carmarthen by then. Seems he spends most of his days trudging up and down the A48, but I guess every man needs a hobby. The other one was the one we thought might be the most promising candidate. Name of Dan. The house mother couldn't remember if he was a Stan or a Dan but the gangs of drinkers that congregate in Castle Gardens said there was no Stan. Dan, yes, but he looks to be in the clear too. He's got Parkinson's and, according to his drinking pals, would never hurt a fly.'

'Did the uniformed officers interview him?'

'They will, but just to eliminate him, I'm certain.'

'Yeah,' Tessa sighed. 'My money wasn't on a homeless man anyway. This was way too planned. Still, wouldn't harm to locate the A48 guy, see if he's got anything to say for himself. Even if he's in the clear he may have seen something. Give the refuge a call and tell them to let us know as soon as he turns up again.'

'Will do,' Gus said.

'And that photograph of Lauren you've got. Have it blown up and get uniform to take copies round the shops in Parc Tawe, if you haven't done that yet.'

'There's a Sainsbury's nearby too, we should check that out. We might get a glimpse of her on their CCTV even if no one recalls seeing her. Ben suggested she could have gone there before going over to The Strand. If we strike lucky at least it would give us a better idea of timeline.'

Tessa looked up at this, as if to enquire what Gus could possibly be waiting for. He pushed a hand through his hair, exhaled and indicated he was 'on it', but he did not use those words.

37

Thinking about luring Miss Minors (I wonder if her dad's called Maurice, that would be cool) makes me realise I was remarkably fortunate in getting the Tracey girl to go up The Strand with me. I even offered to carry her bag of shopping! She gave me one of her trademark sneers when I said that, but they can't resist it when you offer them a chance to show their humanity, can they? All I said was, 'Hey, it's Lauren, isn't it? Can you give me a quick hand? There's an old man collapsed on the pavement just round there. I can't understand what he's trying to say. He's probably just drunk but he doesn't look in a very good way. The thing is, I haven't got my phone on me. I left it at home.' She just followed me. Only started getting suspicious when we were near the Missionary place and there was no old man in sight. Too late, my dear, and in the wrong reign. Went down like a sack of spuds before she had time to even turn round.

I got the brick from Homebase. Stroke of genius, though I say so myself. I just wandered in and strolled out to the gardening area outside. No cameras, no staff, no customers. Just yours truly slipping a nice new London facing brick into my satchel. I liked the irony of the name, I must say, seeing that it was destined for her face (I know, call me petty). I was studying the 'common' bricks but rejected them purely because of the name. I am uncommon, after all. Sentimental too. That was why I kept it, fibres and all! And it's part of the support system for my books, by Jove. Which are, of course, part of my own personal support system. Pffh! Support, my royal Irish arse, I hate that word. It's people trying to support each other all over the place that's causing us all to fall over IMHO.

'Twas but the work of a moment to get her into the garage. No sign of life from the missionaries. Too busy praying to their feathery father. I wanted her to wake up so I could give her a good talking to but I admit I was a little shaky and I couldn't really risk any undue bangings and scufflings. So I finished her off with a piece of rope without that pleasure and promptly went about my business disposing of the rope and her shopping and phone. Ah, the pathetic shopping! Three ready meals, a loaf of bread and a box of teabags. Is that all it comes to in the end?

I thought about eating the ready meals but they were all vegetarian nonsense. Pasta this and couscous that. I just don't get how people think mushrooms are any sort of replacement for good old-fashioned meat. They're fungus, for Pete's sake! (I was just about to write 'for fuck's sake' but I don't like the look of the word on the page. It looks too uncouth). Perhaps the people who write FFS feel the same way. Or that could just be laziness. Not just people my age either. Acronyms are a disease spreading everywhere like a new virus. (My IMHO above was meant as sarcasm, in case I start to accuse myself of hypocrisy when I re-read this). My pet hates at the moment are ATM (not the cash machine but lazy for 'currently') and WTF, which should stand for something about World Trade Fairs or something, but is just an acronym substitute for an exclamation mark, in my view.

Be that what it may, as The Major used to say. What does it even mean? Whatever, I've got a whole week before I can sidle up to Miranda in the theatre and put in place my potent plot. I have to amuse myself. Posting a little note in the lecture theatre at Townhill is still a possibility but should I court danger like this? Sometimes I am all wound with adders, as the half-man says, and want to run through briars and brambles to escape the noise of mediocre people drowning out the symphonies of my genius. Other times I get this insidious sneaking feeling that I may be, in fact, slightly off my rocker. Not in a bad way, just a little bit of faulty wiring. But who's got perfect wiring anyway? Anybody with any true substance is a bit off the wall. So many people on the wall, the special ones can't be blamed for falling off it. No, not falling, alighting, I want to say. It suggests choice, but with a pleasant pun on feeling light, or setting light to things too, of course!

But I'm straying from the issue. Miranda. Ah, Miranda, Miranda, whither shall I wander? Upstairs and downstairs and in my lady's chamber. Ooh, Missus! I can't remember it all now but there's something else about getting an old man by the leg and throwing him downstairs. Mmm, something for the message board perhaps? But it doesn't pay to be too literal, Plod will be checking everyone's staircase for an injured monoped. Tee hee!

OK. Stop fannying. Concentrate, Aaron! How many times have I had to tell you? (I don't know, mater. Seventy twelvety?) Right. Think. Say she doesn't just run as soon as she sees me at the theatre. I get a bit of conversation going about the play but then she moves off to talk to her friends. I could say, 'Are you guys going anywhere after Prospero buries his staff and drowns his book?' Well, I'd probably be better off just saying 'after the play', I suppose. Can't expect them to have read the sodding thing. Anyway, elicit some sort of response. I realise they're hardly likely to say, 'Yeah, we're going across the road to The Queen's to get smashed off our tits. D'you wanna come with?' But they may well let slip that

194

they're going to Wind Street or Uplands or something. If they do, then I'll have a good idea where she's likely to be on a Friday night. They don't stray far, these young ones.

It's all a bit nebulous though. I want things to be a bit more certain, like Tracey going to Lidl every Sunday morning. And plus, as they say these days (though I haven't heard 'but minus' yet, thank god) it's a long wait. A week tomorrow before I even get a chance, if she only goes out on the weekend. Plan B would be to do the home invasion gig. Just follow her and find out where she lives. I could do that by being outside Olchfa School at chucking out time any day, unless she gets picked up, of course. That would involve a boyfriend with a car presumably. But I'm still going to have to wait till she's home alone, when her parents go to their bridge night or whatever.

I'll have to mull my options. Can't be as off the cuff as dear old Iago. Now that was a desperately poor bit of plotting by the bard – a handkerchief – unbelievable! Imagine: 'Excuse me, Miranda, I think you may have dropped your snot rag and I can't help wondering if it could be a major contributing factor in me strangling you to death.'

I really want to toy with the defectives and leave literary breadcrumbs everywhere, but if I wind them up too much they may get all panicky and warn everybody to get off the streets and I'll be left wide-eyed and victimless. Either this evening or tomorrow though I'm definitely going to leave a message for the constabulary. I've typed out a few quotes as candidates, but I'm still thinking about using a new medium. Blood, of course, would be the perfect thing, but I've no intention of using my own, and pigs' blood isn't quite as easy to source as it seems to be in the telly programmes. Whenever someone daubs a message on the mirror, or on the wall behind the door, or behind the wallpaper (I saw that once!) they use the victim's blood. But I'm working ahead of myself and the victim is yet to bleed, so I need to be more original. There's always lipstick, but I don't want them thinking I'm some kind of pervert. Paint would be the unimaginative option. The other consideration is where to leave my little billet doux. Since abandoning the lecture theatre idea I've been a bit stumped, but I can't go back to that plan. They've got no way to connect me to Miss Tracey so I'd be mad to offer them that huge clue that we were once classmates. And O, sweet heaven, let me be not mad! Not mad! As if! I'm the sanest person I know.

38

It was five o'clock when Gus and Tessa met up again. They went to the briefing room, where Stephanie and Ben were due to report with the day's findings. They came in together, just after their senior officers, and were followed by PC Lucy Cain.

'You've missed the recent excitement, PC Cain,' Gus said.

'Yes, sir, sorry. Been off sick, I have.' She gave a sidelong glance at DCI Penry but it went unacknowledged.

Gus went to explain Tessa's status as senior investigating officer but Tessa brushed his intervention aside. 'Let's hear about today's findings,' she said. 'PC Beddall?'

Stephanie reported that she had -managed to trace three members of the Creative Writing class that Lauren Tracey and Aaron Ferie had taken. They were close friends and she'd managed to interview two of them together in the university canteen. She had the contact details for the third member of their group and was going to talk to her as soon as she could. She glanced at her notes and read out the names: Sharon Hopkins, Lynne Morcom and Jane Hawkes. She added that this Jane was always known as Trigger, on account of being a bit slow on the uptake. 'You know, like Trigger in *Only Fools and Horses.*'

'So she's not going to be a very reliable witness, I take it,' Tessa said impatiently.

'I wouldn't say that necessarily,' Stephanie replied. 'Academically she's supposed to be very bright. Three As at 'A' level. She's just not always as clued in to what's going on, they said. Bit of a dreamer, is what I thought they meant.'

Tessa exhaled. 'Go on anyway. What do they recall about this argument between Ferie and Lauren Tracey?'

Stephanie blew out her cheeks. 'Something and nothing, they said. This Ferie bloke was reading out a short story he'd written about a young girl being raped by a guy with some sort of super power. It was nasty stuff, they said, but badly written as well. Everyone in the room was feeling a bit uncomfortable, even the tutor, a Dr Wright. Then

Lauren, who was normally very quiet, told Ferie to shut up. Said she wouldn't listen to any more of this shit, or words to that effect.'

'Was that it? Nothing more than that?' This was from Gus.

'The tutor stepped in. Said that everyone had the right to have their material heard so they had to sit through the rest of his story. It wasn't very long. When he finished nobody said anything, except for Lauren Tracey muttering something under her breath. Then it was somebody else's turn to read out their stuff. That's what both Sharon and Lynne remember. As I say, I'll get this Trigger girl's version of events when I get hold of her. We'll see if it confirms their account. Can't see how it won't though.'

Tessa looked at Gus. 'Doesn't seem like a mountain, does it? But we don't know what type of molehill guy this Ferie may turn out to be. Let's locate him anyway, soon as we can, eh? Sergeant Willis, how about you? What have you got for us?'

Ben stood up.

'Easy, you're not in court,' Tessa said.

'Sorry, ma'am. I've got a bit of a breakthrough, I think. I was able to locate the itinerant we were looking for.'

'Itinerant?'

'The homeless man who walks back and fore between Swansea and Carmarthen. Name of Dan Whitlock. He doesn't know anything about Lauren's murder, but he said it was him who locked the padlock on the garage next to the refuge. He was leaving on Monday morning. Likes to get up early to get on the road, he says. Saw the padlock on the garage doors was open and thought he'd do the old biddy in the home a favour. His words, not mine.'

'Ah,' Gus said. 'That solves the puzzle of us trying to unlock it with the Missionary key. Seems like the killer hoped nobody would notice the doors were unlocked for some time. Nobody would twig it was a different lock then. He wasn't banking on us establishing the garage as the crime scene quite so quickly.'

'But that doesn't make sense,' Tessa objected. 'Why scrawl a cryptic message on the wall outside if he doesn't want anyone to know about the place?'

'He does and he doesn't. I think what we've got on our hands is a very narcissistic killer. He thinks he's clever but he's so arrogant he wants us to know how clever he is.'

'We need to establish who this Aaron Ferie is,' Tessa said firmly. We need to find out his university record straight away, see if he's got some intellectual superpower at least. Then track him down. You said the message on the garage wall was in handwriting? We can soon check that for a match if we can get hold of him.'

'The message behind the bin – the one in chalk – was in capitals,' Gus said. 'The nail varnish one on the side of the storeroom was handwritten but I don't know if that counts, if it's done with that little brush they have.' Gus said. 'It's different from holding a pen, I should think,' He looked at Stephanie, whose expression suggested that she knew nothing of such matters.

Tessa was looking at her hands, fingernails toward her as is women's wont, but she was thinking of something other than nail varnish. 'And has there been no CCTV turned up we can use?'

Ben replied. 'The only thing in all the CCTV we've looked at that's of any interest is a taxi very late on, driving down The Kingsway. I've checked with all the cab firms and we think we've got who the driver was down to one possibility. He's been asked to get in touch as soon as he starts his shift tonight. He might have seen somebody out on his own, or even with Lauren when he was moving her, if we're very lucky.'

'Right then,' Tessa said. 'Tomorrow Inspector Reid and I will interview George Wright again, see if we can get a better picture of our mystery misogynist. PC Beddall, you can go through our records for anything we've got on file on this Ferie character. Sergeant Willis, I'd like you to check on his personal history. See if we can get an address, bank and phone details etcetera. All clear?'

Lucy Cain waited expectantly till Tessa said to Gus, 'Inspector Reid, can you find PC Cain something to do? She looks like she's dying to catch up, mmm?'

Lucy grimaced, but only when Tessa had turned her back.

***

It wasn't till nearly eight that evening that Gus got home to find a single message on his house phone voicemail. He had not switched his mobile phone back on after his meeting with Terry Newlands. A meeting which had not gone well. He had started by telling Newlands that they had a promising lead, but when he had had to admit that they had not got an address or the address of any associates of the potential suspect Newlands' expression suggested that his own definition of 'promising' was rather different. He made it clear that he was disappointed that they had not seen fit to arrest Darren Bunn. An arrest, any arrest, would be good for our image, he'd implied. Gus said that DCI Penry was planning a crime reconstruction on Sunday. It was a fair bet that it would jog someone's memory and then they might well have a physical description of the killer to work with.

'There'll be TV coverage?' Newlands barked.

Gus assured him that there would definitely be a camera crew from S4C, and perhaps BBC Wales also. Also, *The Western Mail* and *The Evening Post* would give it plenty of coverage. 'Most importantly, *Wales Online* will give it plenty of air.' He said. That's where people are increasingly getting their news these days.' Newlands looked sceptical. He was not of an age or disposition to embrace newer technologies. Evidently cameras were a little new-fangled for him. The meeting had ended with a robust suggestion that Gus and 'this new woman' wrap up the case before next week.

He listened to his voicemail. It was from Josie and he felt a tiny thrill when he heard his daughter's voice. He was hoping she was calling to go ahead with a plan for them to meet for a meal. But it wasn't that type of message.

'Dad? I thought you ought to hear this as soon as possible. George, you know, my head of department, you met him on Tuesday? He discovered another message. A quotation. It was under his windscreen wiper and it was done in letters cut out of a newspaper, you know, like kidnappers used to do in the old films?'

Gus wanted to shout 'What did it say?' at the phone he was holding, for there was a long pause before Josie's voice continued. 'It was a line from *Richard III*,' she said. 'I do suspect I have done some offence that seems disgracious in the city's eyes'.

Gus wondered if he had heard correctly. Disgracious? No such word, surely. He put the phone down and rang Josie from his mobile.

'Say the quotation again,' he said, without even asking her how she was. She repeated the words slowly for him. 'And it was done in newsprint, you say?'

'Yes, all different sizes. The 'disgracious' was obviously cut up from two words but they were the same font, which made it even more weird. The 'suspect' was much bigger, like from a headline.'

'Where are you now?' Gus asked her. 'And when can I see this message?'

'I'm in The Westbourne on Brynymor Road. George is here and he's just shown it to me. I said you'd want to see it, so can you get here now? It's not far from you.'

'It's very nearly my local. It would be if I could ever manage to pass The Brynymor, but the beer's cheaper there. I'll come straight away.'

He slipped on a light weatherproof coat and hurried to the pub. It was often quite full at this time of night because there were a number of Indian restaurants nearby and couples and large parties would gather there for a drink before their meal. Tonight, however, there were only three or four couples. It was a damp Thursday evening, the sort of evening when you'd see the waiters at the Indian restaurants hanging around in the doorway smiling at passers-by or just furtively smoking and reflecting on their life choices. George and Josie were on opposite sides of a large circular table near one window. Gus pointed at their glasses but they both declined the implied offer of a drink. He noted that George Wright was nursing a J2O, which would indicate he had driven here. Surely he wouldn't be teetotal.

He ordered a pint of Abbott ale, noted from the accent that the barman was Russian, or more probably Latvian or Estonian, and sat down next to his daughter. Admonishing himself for paying such attention to insignificant details as the ethnicity of bar personnel, he put down his drink and waited for someone to speak. Then George Wright pulled out a neatly folded piece of paper from his inside pocket.

'I thought it was going to be a note from the porter when I saw it under my wiper blade,' he said. 'I mustn't park here on a Thursday or something. Then I saw the crazy lettering and I thought it must be a note from one of my colleagues. Like they'd borrowed a book and they were demanding ransom money for its return. Not that too many of my colleagues are that playful, I should add. Then, when I read it I knew it was a quote from Shakespeare. Couldn't quite place it at first but your daughter reminded me it was from *Richard the Third* when I told her.'

'What's the relevance, Josie?' Gus asked.

'Well, it's from your killer, as you think it must be, it means one of two things. He's a megalomaniac who thinks he deserves to be king or he's a twisted hunchback who hates everybody in general and women in particular.'

Oh,' Gus said, 'the hunchback. Is he the one with the kingdom but no horse? The one they found in a car park in Leicester last year, or the year before, was it?'

'That's Richard Plantagenet alright,' George said. 'Last king to die in battle. To celebrate the fact they built a council car park over him. Shakespeare wasn't a huge fan either. Depicted him as a vindictive, deformed and repulsive to women.'

Gus quickly took a drink to cover his startled expression. Then, recomposed, he told Wright that he and his senior investigating officer, DCI Penry, had been hoping to talk to him again about his former student Aaron Ferie. 'Did you not mention to her that he was an unprepossessing sort of fellow?'

'Ah, George said, 'you think Ferie left this note? That he identifies with a dead king?'

'Or a nasty little homunculus,' Josie said.

Gus didn't know the word. He looked appealingly at George. 'Very small creature in myths,' George explained. 'Bit like the Jewish golem, if you've come across that.'

Gus had a vague recollection of such a creature from standing outside a bookshop near the Pinkas cemetery in Prague. There was a clumsy primitive statue of the monster just by the shop door. He had no interest in dragging up any memory of that miserable weekend with Adele a lifetime ago, however. 'Aaron Ferie very short, by any chance?' he said.

George chuckled. 'Under average height, most assuredly. Lionel Messi sized, I'd say. But you're not saying Ferie's responsible for Lauren's death, are you? He was a loner, I'll grant you. Not much of a student either, to be perfectly honest. Hardly ever turned up and

201

just sulked and said nothing for the most part. But I can't believe he'd kill somebody.'

'That's what everybody says when they find out that they once knew someone who goes on to commit a terrible crime,' Gus said quietly. He looked at his daughter's face. She was deep in thought.

'I'm wondering if these quotations aren't meant to point us in a direction the killer wants us to look in. Away from himself and towards someone like this Aaron Ferie.' She looked up at Gus. 'Do people do that? Are murderers that clever in real life?'

Gus snorted. 'No. Very rare that we find a clever killer. But that doesn't mean there aren't some out there. There's plenty of stupid ones; we round them up easily enough, even if it does take a while sometimes. The really clever ones are never arrested because we never find out where they've hidden the bodies.'

'Until they start digging up a council car park anyway,' George said

'I wouldn't want us to have to wait that long. But I don't think we're talking about a criminal mastermind in this instance.'

Josie had been trying to remember something, it was obvious. Then her face brightened. 'Richard says at one point in the play that he's been cheated of feature by dissembling nature.'

'Meaning?'

'That he's ugly,' George explained. 'Though the portrait we've got of him doesn't suggest that exactly. He was no oil painting admittedly,' he stopped himself with a laugh. 'The picture we've got of him is an actual oil painting self-evidently, but you get my drift.'

Gus ignored all this frivolousness. 'And Ferie was ugly, true?'

'You wouldn't have wanted to come across him in a dark alley at night,' George admitted. 'Everything's subjective though, isn't it? Eye of the beholder sort of thing?'

'People don't often admit to themselves that they're ugly though, do they?' Josie said. 'I mean, whenever I've heard people talking about how attractive or unattractive they think they are they always say something like "I'm probably only a five or a six." Nobody says they're a one, or a zero.'

'In my experience most men think they're an eight or a nine and few women venture much beyond a seven,' George said. 'Peacocks

202

and peahens.'

Gus decided to put a stop to the hypothetical turn the conversation was taking. 'Have you got a photograph of Ferie at university?' he said. 'We're trying to get in touch with him so he can answer a few questions, that's all we're saying for the present. Dr Wright?'

George screwed up his eyes. 'I'm not sure we will have one actually. We take photocopies of their paperwork when they first enrol but you know, data protection and all that. I'm not sure we do keep photographs in the Humanities faculty. I'll find out for you tomorrow though.'

Gus made his excuses and left Josie and George together. He couldn't stop himself feeling a twinge of disapproval at the thought that there might be a relationship forming between them, but he tried to reason that it was only because of the age difference. It wasn't the simple fact that the man had spent a decade and a half more on the planet; it was the fact that Wright would have a history, surely. He might actually be married, but even if he wasn't he had to have had at least one serious relationship behind him. Josie was still so innocent. Gus stopped himself in his own tracks. She was twenty-six. He'd married Adele when she was twenty-three and he'd only been a couple of years older himself. Parents were such hypocrites. And Josie was sensible. She wouldn't let herself be swept off her feet by a man like Wright, would she? It was a problem for another time, however.

As soon as he got back to his flat in Bonville Terrace Gus rang Ben Willis to ask if the cab driver who had been out and about in the early hours of Monday morning had been contacted yet. What Ben had to say was scarcely a revelation but it was interesting. The cabbie, a man called Ismael, had driven his last fare from Wind Street to Mumbles at about one thirty. He had gone back into town but there was nobody about. He thought it was about two o'clock when he did one last circuit, which took him down Mumbles Road as far as the Guildhall, then back down St Helen's Road as far as Christina Street, where he turned left and went home via Walter Road and Sketty Road to his home in Cockett. In this time he had only seen two pedestrians, one a figure in dark clothing crossing The Kingsway and the other a drunk leaning against the railings by St James's Gardens. He thought

203

both were male. The one in the Kingsway did not appear to be drunk. He couldn't guess an age. The drunk was probably in his forties or fifties. Maybe grey hair. The reason he thought he was drunk? He tried to get up, took a few staggering steps then slumped back down against the railings. Did he normally notice details like dark clothing and grey hair? His job was to drive people around but he wasn't just a minicab driver; he drove a Hackney cab, and to be any good at that you paid attention, you had to be good at spotting likely fares.

The killer was no drunk staggering around near Uplands. But he could be the man crossing The Kingsway at about the right time. So where was he headed? The cabbie thought the man was heading west and he was clearly not interested in getting a taxi. That would suggest walking distance from home, if it was home he was headed for. Still, a whole warren of streets in The Sandfields and Brynmill. It didn't help much, but it would be interesting if Gus could find out where Aaron Ferie lived.

39

I stabbed her through the arras! I wish that was actually what I could write, but I'd prefer to write 'arris of course. Unseamed her from the buttocks to the chops, yer honour.

Actually it wasn't that tragedical. More of a rather undignified scuffle with far too many stabs, and none of them in the rear quarters. I got her in the ribs and (maybe) the liver but I think the coup de grace was the one in the back of the neck. But it wasn't anything like as satisfying as I'd imagined because they're surprisingly strong, these young fillies. I wanted it to be quick, naturally, considering where we were, but I also wanted to see the amazement in her eyes. The recognition of her own mortality and all that stuff. As it happened she turned to run back inside as soon as she saw me and I had to grab her from behind. She made it all the way out to the back door but I got to her on the patio. Then stab stab stab but she's still writhing and shouting. Had to plunge my trusty kitchen devil through to her trachea to stop the noise. No sign of nosey neighbours, no lights coming on or any curtain twitching from any Rear Window characters. Nevertheless, I'd planned to do her indoors so I was a bit rattled. Luckily they didn't have one of those motion floodlights but there was a pale glow from inside that bathed the scene in a macabre light. If anyone had seen me they would only have witnessed a black clad figure crouching over somebody who seemed to have fainted. All very amateur dramatics really. Or 1940s noir. But there was blood everywhere, much darker than you'd expect too, which wasn't what I'd planned at all. I thought it would be simple and elegant. Me as the unwounded surgeon plying the steel that questions the distempered part sort of thing. Now I'm standing over her with a bloodied knife clammy in my hand and she's lying in a crumple with her hair across her face and her legs white and bony in the feint light. And the front door was open all the while. Very messy, but that could work in my favour perhaps. Home invasion gone wrong. I could have just grabbed something from the hall on my way back out to make it more obvious it was a drug-crazed burglar but time is of the essence in circumstances like these.

It was all going so swimmingly. I was standing outside Noah's 'casing the joint' as they say and, lo and behold, the Amazonian Mrs Minors is cruising down Uplands Crescent on the other side of the road. The 'Cross Now' lights changed to the little green man just as I went to dart across to fall into step behind her. I knew she couldn't be going far because she's like an oil tanker in a dress and I imagine the only real walking she does is to the fridge and back. So I slope along behind her and she takes the turning into Eaton Crescent. At this point I didn't know if it was wise to follow, because there was no one else around, but she stops and goes into the fourth house along. I've discovered where Miranda's cave is without hardly trying! No hanging around outside her school, no clumsy chatting in the theatre. It was a gift! All I had to do now was establish some sort of routine for when she'd be home alone and the fair damsel (more of an auburn damsel in truth) was at my mercy. I even had my blade about my person. I love the serendipity of this.

When I was seventeen I was having a quiet drink in The Uplands Hotel and a guy standing next to me at the bar started talking to me. I wasn't interested of course but he kept on wittering and trying to engage me in some sort of conversation. Said his name was Alan, as if I cared. Then, I think he was trying to impress me, he pulled out a knife and said, 'I carry this around in case there's any trouble.' He was smiling inanely at me. I just legged it. He came running out after me shouting he didn't want to harm me, he just wanted me to look at it. I ran all the way into town. Bit embarrassing now, as I recall the incident. But the idea sort of stuck. So a bit later I decided to keep a blade in my jacket when I'm out and about.

Still, I didn't know how long I could hang about outside their house. Loitering, with or without intent is always a tad suspicious, and especially so when the street is filled with rich people terrified of burglars, drunks, junkies and other assorted people who aren't as rich as them. I thought I might walk slowly down towards the bend and then back up again, as if I was going somewhere but had forgotten something and turned back to get it. I could only do that once really so I had no great hopes. Then I reasoned that I could just wait at the top of the crescent, hang around by the corner where I could be waiting for my date or something. Date, date, you say? Did Iago go on dates? Who exactly was Caliban walking out with?

Then out she comes again, her husband like a little tug behind her. They're dressed for an evening out, as far as I could judge. This was seven thirty so they were probably headed for the cinema or a meal with their chums. 'Gorgeous boeuf bourgignon, Mavis, you must give me the recipe! Ooh, and this Chablis, it's to die for!'

No it's not, that's not what's to die for. Answering the door to your nemesis, that's what's to die for.

I had to give it ten minutes of course. Wouldn't want the old bloater returning because she's left something behind; her smirk, or her sneer perhaps. 'Twas a long ten minutes too. My breath vaporising in the winter air, my hands dug deep in my pockets, right hand round the handle of a 5" kitchen devil, my feet stamping like some old dray horse outside a pub cellar. I had a beanie on but it was so cold. Bit like my heart, the brief would say, smugly turning to twelve men good and true and stupid. Then all of a sudden a little tring on the doorbell, the slop slop of slippered feet on an expensive hall rug and a flurry of murderous action and I'm suddenly hotter than a nun in heat. And I've got blood all over my coat and trousers. And my shoes! I wasn't thinking of that. I knew I'd have to dispose of my outer garments of course, that's why I purloined the coat from an Oxfam when the little old lady went in the back. The trousers had had their best days anyway. But they were good shoes.

I have this belief that the forensics in this neck of the woods aren't anything like as thorough as they are in the TV programmes, but nevertheless, just a spot of her blood in the stitching of my lovely brogues and I'd be bang to rights. So I had to rush home, knowing there was tell-tale evidence on my very person. It was like when you're a kid and you're lying to your parents. Your ear muscles pull your ears back and your neck hair looks like a frightened cat as you swear blind it wasn't you. Nobody looks twice at a bloke in a beany hurrying home though. I changed into trainers and jeans and nipped back up to Walter Road to offload the incriminating footwear in a skip I'd spotted by the vet's. I didn't think I'd left a footprint but you never know. Better safe than sorry. Get a waif then worry.

I was thinking as I washed the blood off in the sink, 'Will all great Neptune's oceans wash this blood clean from my hand?' Yep. Drop of Fairy liquid and a quick rinse of the sink. No making the green one red at all. Anyway, it's not as if I've got an avocado green sink. Ha!

But it's not just blood, is it? I had to grab her hair. I don't think I left any DNA on her because I was wearing my Marigolds but they say you can shed hair follicles and skin flakes anyway. They've got nothing to compare with but I don't like the thought that I've left any bits of me, infinitesimally small or not, on the person of the young lady in question. Yuck!

I left my message up in Townhill a bit prematurely as it happens. I wanted to provoke them with a quote that gave a cryptic clue about Miranda but I went all Dick Three in my haste to jab Plod, or the media, in point of fact. They've been very slow and guarded in their reporting so far. I was able to use 'Suspect' from the Post's headline for that message but there wasn't much else of any worth. 'No

Leads on Murder Suspect' is bland fare, I'm afraid. The article was by someone called Andrea Linney. Cub reporter probably. Or should I say Brownie reporter? Nomenclature is so difficult these PC days. If a copper were to call me a wacko or a looney he'd be a non-PC PC, wouldn't he?

I didn't like the tone of her piece though. Got the sense that she was suggesting that it was some sort of sadistic maniac who'd done for Ms Tracey. Wonder what she'll make of a follow up attack. 'Looney strikes again'? Lock up your daughters, Mrs, there's a MAN about and it looks like he might mean harm! She may concentrate on the baffled police angle though. 'Coppers Completely Flummoxed as Literary Type Plays Cat and Mouse with the Law.' Probably not quite enough alliteration in that though. How about 'Coppers' Complete Cockup Concerning Crime Cause'?

I should be a writer. But that would exclude me from journalism.

The rest of the words I cut up were from photocopies I took of pages from books. I could have gone to the print shop on Brynymor Road because that would have been more convenient for me. But there's just one spotty loser working there and we don't want people remembering a man photocopying Dickens' novels, do we? So I had to walk down to the public library on the front. They've moved it from the lovely old building near the cop shop to just one room inside County Hall. It's like they're slowly trying to hide books from folk. Nobody looks at you in County Hall because they're all too ashamed that they've lost their parking permits or forgotten to pay their fines to look up from their own shoes. It didn't cost too much to copy a few pages and enlarge them for dramatic effect. As for the words themselves, 'Disgracious' was tricky but I knew where I could find the 'gracious' bit and I took the 'dis' prefix from 'disgust' because I thought that was apt. It would indeed have been tempting to cut each word from a different Shakespeare play but hey ho, life is short. I could have used The Complete Works of Shakespeare that the mater bought me 'because the boy likes to read' but I decided on Dickens. He pretty much used every word you can think of, plus a few he made up for himself. I had to use a couple of different texts though because it was too tedious dragging through The Old Curiosity Shop for all the right words. The result was a bit wavy, especially with the big SUSPECT in it obviously, but it didn't look quite as deranged as the ones you see in movies. I chose The Old Curiosity Shop for two reasons: (a) I had a copy of it and (b) old Dan Quilp, my halter ego, you might say. I kind of wanted 'the city's eyes' to be a phrase in itself somewhere but I couldn't find it on Google except in some book by an architect woman in America. I wasn't going to waste money buying some archaic rubbish by a feminist urban planner now, was I? Also, as I remarked earlier, time, essence etc. But every day in every way you learn more useless stuff. She had a crackpot theory about the eyes of ordinary people walking around being a sort of guarantee of public order. Something like that. Now that's precisely what I don't want. Prying eyes. I took 'offence' from Lolita because I wanted a word that Quilty uses. Again, two reasons, (a) he's an underrated literary genius and (b) his name is almost the same as Quilp's. See? It all works out, if you like literary puzzles, which I do. Plod? Not so much, I suspect.

Now, with the deed done in something of a hurry, I've got to think about a well-known phrase or saying (not too well known, of course!) apposite for a clue about Miranda. The obvious place to look is in The Tempest but I'm not sure I want it to be too obvious. Maybe some mad bit of Mercutio's Queen Mab speech. I can't quite face reading that right now though. More sleeping on it then? I think so. The joy of quoting is that there's no verbal patterns they can identify. I was reading up on the Derek Bentley case (because I love a loser!) and when he was eventually exonerated it was because the police accounts of his confession all used the same copper lingo. 'I then proceeded' etc. Apparently no one in the real world ever says 'I then'; it's always 'then I'. They teach stilted language on their police courses, I presume. Anyway, apropos of our dear departed Derek, I let her have it, didn't I?

40

Friday 10th January 2014

As soon as he got into the station, half an hour earlier than usual, Gus summoned Ben and Stephanie to his room to ask them what they had discovered about their chief suspect. It was not good news. Ben had checked with all the phone networks but there were no records of Ferie. Neither was there anything on the electoral role or the DVLA's car registrations.

'He can't be as stupid as DCI Penry thinks he is if he's managed to stay dark like this for however long it is,' Ben added.

Gus turned to Stephanie. 'Anything on file with us? A touch of larceny when he was a kid? Domestic disturbance?'

'The only mention I could find of anybody by the name of Ferie was an enquiry into a house fire in Killay in 2011. A couple by the name of Ferie died in the fire but there was no mention of an Aaron. They were the right sort of ages to be his parents. Fifty five and fifty four. I checked the newspaper records and there was some suspicion about whether the blaze might have been started by someone but in the end it was deemed to be an accident. I haven't been able to track down an insurance company yet to see if there was a pay out and who any beneficiary might have been.'

'And definitely no juvenile record?' Gus said.

'Nothing,' Stephanie repeated.

'Might he not have had a police record and then had it expunged?' Ben asked. His sergeant's exam revision was obviously still fresh in his mind.

'I think the point of expunging is to remove *all* traces,' Gus said drily. 'Anyway, even if he did get a ticking off for marijuana or urinating in a public place or whatever, he'd be long gone from any address he had at the time. We need to know if it was his parents who died in that fire, and find out where he went from there, if he was living with them at the time. How old do we reckon he is now?'

'He went to City University when he was at least twenty-one,' Ben

210

said. 'That was two years ago so he's got to be twenty-three or twenty-four. But that lecturer said he looked old, didn't he?'

'The years had not been kind, I think the gist was. If it was his parents who died in Killay they'd be in their late fifties now so he could be in his early thirties even. I suspect mid to late twenties for George Wright to make that comment though. If we go on the assumption that he left home at eighteen, say, where has he been for the last eight or nine years? Thoughts?'

The door flew open suddenly and Tessa Penry bustled in. She looked remarkably fresh, as if she had recently reapplied her makeup.

'We've been updating Inspector Reid about what we've found out about Ferie.' Ben said.

'Which amounts to very little, doesn't it?'

Gus gave a questioning look.

'Stephanie and I spoke earlier. We were both in before seven this morning, weren't we?'

Stephanie smiled sweetly. Boy, she was ambitious, Gus thought.

'I've been questioning Dr Wright again this morning. Why don't they keep proper records in those places?'

'They're terrified of flouting data protection,' Gus said gloomily.

'But aren't they required to keep student records for three years?' Ben said.

Tessa smiled. 'I asked Dr Wright about that. It would have been interesting if there'd been any signs of a budding serial killer in his essays, wouldn't it? The good doctor proceeded to explain very patiently that such personality traits were very rarely evident in First Year essays on Dickens and Shakespeare. He also added helpfully that he couldn't recall that Mr Ferie ever actually handed in any written work anyway. Seems like the only glimpse we have into his mind is hearsay about some lurid rape fantasy he wrote.'

'Ah yes,' Gus said. 'Did you get in touch with that other girl who was in that class? Trigger, I think you called her.'

'Yes, sir. She confirmed what the other two girls said. Though she did add that she thought Lauren had called Ferie an 'insidious pervert'. I had to look up 'insidious'. It seems to mean ...'

'Okay, okay, we know what it means, Stephanie,' Gus said, and then wished he hadn't, because the young officer looked crestfallen.

211

'When did she hear that? In the lesson?'

'Yes, the other girls just said that Lauren mumbled something, but Trigger must have been sitting closer to her because she remembers that was what it was. I told you, she's not as daft as her name suggests.'

The four officers looked at each other. It still didn't seem enough to strangle the poor girl and then smash her face in.

Gus broke the silence. 'Anyway, we were just talking about where Ferie's been for the last eight years or so. He's got no criminal record; he isn't on the electoral roll; he hasn't got a driving licence; he hasn't got a vehicle registered in his name, and he obviously uses a pay as you go phone. He's off the grid, or he would be if we were all in America. But he has to live somewhere, and he has to have money. I forgot to ask, did you check for bank records, Ben?'

Ben said he had, and it had been hard work getting through to most of them, but none of the major banks would say they had ever had a customer by the name of Aaron Ferie.

'Do you think he's staying with somebody, perhaps doing chores to pay for his food and rent?' Ben was trying to be creative but he was not convincing even himself.

'Could he be odd jobbing, or working on a farm or something?' This was from Stephanie.

'I'm inclined to rule that one out,' Tessa said. 'How would he get about if he hasn't got a car?'

'Hasn't got one registered in his name,' Gus said. 'Doesn't necessarily mean he hasn't got access to one. And people drive without licences, as we all know.' He placed a hand on the table before him and enumerated on his fingers the possibilities as he saw them. 'One, we need to find out if he was still living in the parental home in 2011. Perhaps neighbours can tell us something about him. Two, we need to find out where he was living in 2012, when he attended university. Three, and this is the hard one, we need to establish what he did and where he went when he was, what was that word again?'

Ben helped out. 'Rusticated.'

'What was that?' Tessa said. 'Rusticated?'

'Yeah, I'm told it's the posh university word for thrown out.' He studied his hand again, this time pointing to his ring finger. 'And four, where is he hanging his hat right now?' Gus looked ruefully at the

212

remaining finger, apparently regretting that there was not a number five.

'And it would be handy to know how he's managing to feed himself,' Tessa said.

There it was, number five. He tapped his little finger to emphasise that there always had been a fifth burning question.

'Just one other thing,' Stephanie said, emboldened by her sense of approval from her DCI, 'we should try and find out if there were any siblings. The report on the fire only mentions the man and wife, but if we're assuming Aaron is their son why aren't we assuming there might also be an older brother or sister who'd already moved out?'

'Everyone we've spoken to insists he was a loner, but you're right, Stephanie,' Tessa said. 'If we locate a sibling we'll have something more to go on. Can you get onto that straight away?'

But before she could leave a uniformed constable poked his head round the door. 'There's been another murder, sir. Ma'am.'

Tessa and Gus spoke at the same time, demanding time and location. The constable initially looked flustered but managed to give a measured response: '4 Eaton Crescent, in Uplands. A young girl's body was found in the back garden. She's been identified as Miranda Minors. Parents found her this morning, not ten minutes ago.'

'Who's attending?' Tessa demanded.

'Well, nobody yet,' the constable stammered. 'I thought you'd want to be the ones to examine the scene. I can get Inspector Warren to attend if you like.'

'Don't worry about that,' Gus said firmly. 'The DCI and I will go. Do we know cause of death yet?'

'She's been stabbed, sir. That's what the mother reported.'

Tessa gave Gus a look that might even have been one of disappointment. 'I know,' Gus said. 'But a different MO doesn't mean anything. Two in a week is highly unlikely to be coincidence. Let's get up there.' He turned to Stephanie and Ben. 'Not a word to anyone. Same goes for you, constable. Was it Marcia who took the call? Could you make sure she doesn't say anything yet either? We don't want the press getting hold of this until we've got a better picture of what's happened.'

The constable bowed out of the room, doubtless to tell everybody

213

there was another murder but no one was to tell anyone else about it.

***

When Gus and Tessa arrived at the Minors' home Ailsa and her husband Ieuan were sitting in their front parlour speechless with grief and incomprehension. They went through the kitchen out to the garden and saw in the early daylight the wretched and scrawny body of a seventeen-year-old girl splayed on the paving slabs. She did not appear to have been touched but they both understood that the sight of the blood on the girl's neck and round her head would have sent Ailsa Minors reeling back indoors. Tessa had rung from the car for the duty pathologist and ordered a Family Liaison Officer to be sent to the house as quickly as possible. The pathologist and the SOCOs would be glad that their scene had not been disturbed.

The FLO turned out to be PC Lucy Cain. She appeared only a few minutes after Gus and Tessa and showed that this line of work was more to her taste than the business of investigation by immediately setting about making tea and trying to comfort the bereaved parents. The bulky Ailsa Minors suddenly looked smaller as she accepted an arm round her shoulder. Gus wondered whether it had even occurred to the husband to offer this small token. He was sitting blankly on a leather sofa next to the chair where Mrs Minors was perched in an almost foetal crouching position. Despite this appearance of helplessness, he judged that it was she who was the major force in this household.

When she was finally able to speak, she recounted the terrible discovery she had made that morning, shortly after eight o'clock. 'We were out till quite late last night and we assumed Miranda had gone to bed. It's a school night and she's very conscientious, you see.' She sniffed miserably. 'Then I came down to make breakfast and I saw something outside on the patio. I didn't even register that it was Miranda for a moment. It looked like a pile of clothes had been dumped there. Like a washing line had broken. Oh god! Then I saw her hair and saw that it was Miranda. I still didn't quite take it in. I thought she'd got up early and gone outside for some reason. Get the cat in or something. And that she must have fainted. I rushed out of

214

course and that's when I saw the blood.' She broke down and sobbed. Her husband was useless. Struck dumb and overawed by the awful turn his life had taken. Perhaps guilty too that they hadn't checked on their daughter before going to bed. Lucy was watching, like a nurse at a bedside. 'Shall I get you something to eat, Mr Minors? Some toast perhaps?' It was inane but somehow right, for he looked up and smiled, indicating wordlessly that yes, toast might make some difference.

'She looked so white, so cold. Dreadfully cold,' Ailsa Minors said. 'She must have been out there all night, poor darling. Who would do such a thing? I just can't believe it. I wanted somebody to tell me I was imagining the blood and that she's been taken to hospital and she'll be alright as soon as she warms up.'

Ieuan Minors roused himself. 'There was no sign of a break-in, officers. Does that mean Miranda knew whoever did this, do you think? But it's not possible. She goes to a good school. She's in the orchestra!'

Gus could have said that violinists and woodwind players were not necessarily immune from brutal attack but he stayed silent, allowing Tessa to lead the questioning.

'We'll need details of all her friends and acquaintances, Mr Minors. Do you know if she had a boyfriend?'

Ailsa Minors answered. 'She had friends who were boys, but no, not an actual boyfriend. I would know if she had been seeing anybody, I can assure you.'

'We need to look at her social media,' Tessa said. 'Do you know where her phone is?'

'In her bedroom, I suppose,' Ailsa Minors said, her voice still cracked with pain.

'It's actually in the kitchen, on the island,' Ieuan Minors said. 'I noticed it when I came down and was surprised, because they always keep it on their person, don't they? I see the shape of it in her back pocket when she's wearing jeans. It's usually in her hand though. I put mine down when I'm not using it and then I can never remember where.'

'Oh stop gabbling, Ieuan!' Ailsa Minors shouted. 'We need to help these officers so they can find whoever did this.' She subsided again.

215

Lucy Cain had fetched the mobile and offered it to Tessa during this outburst.

'Do you know her code for unlocking this?' Tessa said.

'1997,' Ailsa Minors said authoritatively. 'The year Blair won the election.'

Tessa scrolled though the recent calls and harrumphed. 'We'll take this and go through it thoroughly at the station,' she said. She looked at the phone again and then quickly flourished a photograph she'd found in Gus's direction. She turned to show it to Ailsa Minors. 'Isn't this the Townhill campus of City University in the background?'

Mrs Minors shrugged. 'Yes, but why do you ask that? Miranda came to a graduation ceremony last summer. It's where I work. I'm Head of QA there.'

Tessa put the phone away. 'We're going to need a recent photograph of Miranda please. A head shot preferably. Now do you mind if we have a look at her room? Some scene of crime officers and the pathologist will be here presently so it's best if you're not here then. Are there any neighbours or friends you could stay with for a few hours?'

Ieuan Minors stood up and went over to his wife. 'Come on, old thing,' he said. 'Let's go and see if the Taylors can be prevailed upon.' He offered the unnecessary explanation that Mike Taylor was their GP and also their neighbour.

'We'll give you a call when our people have finished what they have to do here,' Tessa said.

Gus and Tessa went upstairs and peered into each of the three bedrooms on the first floor. One was clearly the marital bedroom, fussily decorated in Laura Ashley patterns; two others were made up in more neutral style as guest rooms. They trudged up to the second floor and found Miranda's room next to a surprisingly large second bathroom. The bedroom was rather gloomy because there was only a small sash window but when Gus pressed the switch near the door he noted that two standard lamps and a table lamp had been wired to the main switch, in the manner of an American movie. The room was bathed in a warm and welcoming light. The arrangement gave the place a serene atmosphere and not the sparse cold feel that the room might once have had as a serving maid's quarters. Gus imagined that

216

Miranda had spent a lot of her time up here, away from parents that she probably found all too overbearing and pompous. She had clearly been a meticulous young woman too. There was a small oak table with a computer monitor between two built in wardrobes on the wall facing the double bed. Labelled files for her schoolwork were stacked beneath the table. There was no clutter visible anywhere and even the wastepaper basket was empty. Leaving the files for the moment Gus began looking through the wardrobes, while Tessa took responsibility for a more intimate search of the drawers in the bedside table. There was no sign of a secret stash of letters or photographs but of course you wouldn't expect to find anything like that these days: personal material would all be on her mobile phone.

Tessa found nothing surprising or particularly interesting in the bedside table so she moved to the bathroom. Often the contents of the wall cabinet revealed key elements of a person's life. But Miranda had been healthy; there were no headache tablets, no insulin or asthma medication, definitely no pregnancy test material, just a modest range of cosmetics. There was nothing to suggest that she had been anything but a model daughter. She shrugged her shoulders as Gus joined her in the bathroom.

'There's nothing here, is there?' Gus said. 'The files are all just schoolwork, neatly organised. No doodles.'

'I doubt if she told her parents everything about her private life but if she was keeping any secrets, she didn't keep them here. They'll be in her computer or her phone. Or in the cloud, I guess.'

'Yes,' Gus sighed. 'Whatever that is.'

They agreed that there was not much else they could do but return to the station and await Jenny Sarka's verdict on cause and time of death. They held out little hope of the murder weapon being found, but SOCOs would undertake a thorough search of the grounds, neighbours' gardens and nearby bins and drains.

'Do you think this is Ferie again?' Gus asked Tessa.

'We don't know if it was Ferie last time yet, do we?' she responded.

'But yes, I do. It's not just that her mother works in Townhill either. At first my instinct told me this wasn't as well planned, or even with the same motivation. But you don't get two savage murders like this in such a short space of time without some connection.'

217

'It doesn't look like there was post-mortem damage to Miranda's face though.'

'Okay, slightly different savagery. I'm guessing here but I think the way Lauren's mouth and teeth were smashed in was symbolic, not an attempt to disguise her identity. That could be something to do with denying the victim her beauty, but we haven't picked up any sense yet that Lauren flaunted her looks, or relied on her physical appearance, have we? The opposite, in fact. She sounds to me like she might have felt a bit superior, but if she did it was probably more to do with her intellect. Maybe we'll find out that Miranda was some kind of brainiac too.'

'It's still different,' Gus mused aloud. 'Miranda Minors sounds to me like she was a pretty unassuming character. But she does have a connection to City University. If you were a trick cyclist you might be tempted to see this as a sort of proxy attack on Ailsa Minors.'

'We'll have to establish if her role in quality assurance means she was involved in the Ferie expulsion.'

'Rustication.'

'Whatever. On the other hand, there may even be something in the fact that her hair was covering her face. We could be dealing with someone who simply can't bear to look at attractive young women. You know, his mum was really pretty but locked him in a cupboard under the stairs for fourteen years scenario.'

'Well,' Gus said, 'Miranda was quite pretty, but so far she doesn't come across to me as an airhead whose main aim in life is to flaunt her looks. We'll see if that's true when we get into her phone album of course.'

'I don't expect any duck lip selfies there,' Tessa said. 'Maybe some shots of her with her orchestra mates.'

'Duck lip selfies?' Gus said, bemused.

Tessa turned to show Gus her profile, then turned three quarters to him and pouted her lips extravagantly.

'Oh, duck. I get it.'

'You're such a dinosaur, Gus.'

'Dangerous animal, the dinosaur.'

'Indeed. Come on then, you can be the velociraptor on the right. I'll take the left.'

'Velociraptor, eh? You do know, Miss Duck Expert, that they were only the size of a domestic turkey, don't you?'

'Not in *Jurassic Park*, they weren't.'

They looked at each other for a second or two, perhaps both aware that what they were really doing was trying to fend off their shock by being so flippant.

'If we're going to get our claws into somebody we need to identify our prey first.'

'I think we may have done that. But we still need to discover his lair.'

41

At twelve thirty, just as she was thinking of getting out of the *Evening Post* building and walking to Wind Street for a coffee in one of the many bars there, Andrea received a call on her mobile. It was from her switchboard. Did she want to give out her personal number to a caller who had important information on a big story? Of course she did! Any details on the mystery caller? None. Well, one. Male.

She recited her number, made the girl repeat it and hurried to No Sign Wine Bar, a very old, rather musty pub halfway down Wind Street. There she ordered a latte and sat in the dark area in the middle of the long bar waiting for a call. Although it styled itself as a wine bar there was nothing about this establishment that smacked of the wine bars of buzzing city life. Rather, it was a gloomy vault where in daytime lonely drinkers struggled to read a paper or a magazine in the dim light. At night it transmogrified into a useful venue for the young and reckless to indulge in a raucous session before heading to a club. As a creature of the daylight without any reading material about her person Andrea was reduced to a prolonged study of the dusty empty wine bottles on the shelves above her head as she waited for her call.

She thought it might be about a missing child, or a tip-off about a house burglary, but she was also feeling a spasm of excitement that it might be a vital breakthrough in the Lauren Tracey story. After forty minutes of stubborn silence she rang the switchboard. 'Did my caller leave a number at all?' she asked.

'No. But I can look up the number he called from if you like.'

Andrea thanked the receptionist and waited. When the receptionist called back with the number she entered it in her contacts list under the name Informant then rang it. She waited with trepidation, afraid that it would go to voicemail, but a voice answered at the third ring.

'Hello,' a male voice, hard to tell how old.

'This is Andrea Linney. I believe you were trying to get in touch with me?'

There was a brief silence. Then 'Ah yes, Miss Linney. Would you mind awfully if I were to call you Andrea? Don't want to sound too presumptuous, of course.'

'That's fine,' Andrea said quickly. 'How can I help you, Mr …?'

'I'd rather not reveal my name at the moment, Miss Linney. Andrea, I mean. But it's not a question of you helping me. It's the reverse. I wish to help you. You are covering the Lauren Tracey story, aren't you?'

Andrea's heart leaped but she managed to retain composure in her tone. 'That's right. Do you have some information that my paper could use? I should say that it's your duty to inform the police if you know something that would help with their enquiries, but our readers are anxious for the facts of the case too. Did you know Miss Tracey?'

'Not very well. But I do think I have something for you, Andrea. Probably not best to do this over the phone though. Would it be possible for us to meet, do you think?'

Andrea gave the offer a second's consideration. Whoever was on the line could be a stalker. He could be a madman. He could be a troll. It could be another journo playing a prank. He could even be the murderer himself. But it was essential to find out who the caller was. And if they were genuine, what they knew, or more likely, thought they knew.

'Yes, that would be good. Can you tell me first what sort of information you have? If you think you know who's responsible, I'd just have to hand that over to the authorities straight away. If it's a suspicion you have, you understand I won't be able to print anything libellous. But if it's background you can fill in for me, that'd be great. When and where would you like to meet?'

After a long pause the man spoke again: 'Perhaps we could meet this evening?'

'I'd prefer it if you could come into the office,' Andrea replied, really only testing to see if it was a hoaxer. Another long pause. 'But if that's not convenient, any time after six would suit me. Where would you like to meet up?' She had images of a government official in a trench coat with a fedora pulled down low over his eyebrows deep throating secrets in a murky underground garage or underpass. She wasn't going to say yes to anything that sounded too out of the

221

way, however. Somewhere bright and public would be fine.

'Do you know the church on the roundabout in Townhill? Our Lady of Lourdes, it's called.' The man said quietly. It was almost a whisper, but also too much like a hiss.

'Yes, I do,' Andrea said. 'But it would be more convenient for me if we met somewhere else. I'm not all that keen on churches, as it happens. Why don't I buy you a coffee, or a drink, somewhere in town? We can sit down somewhere comfortable and have a chat then.'

'Are you afraid of the dark, Andrea?'

There was definitely something creepy about his voice this time. She was on the verge of ending the call, deciding it was surely a hoax, when something stopped her. She put on a more authoritative voice. 'Look, if you're serious and you have something to tell me that's in the public interest we can meet tomorrow at two. I'll wait outside the school opposite the church. I'll only wait a couple of minutes, so make sure you're on time. And please, if this is a time-wasting exercise, tell me now. I have plenty of other things I need to get on with.'

'Oh Andrea,' the voice, more normal again now, assured, 'I wouldn't dream of wasting your time. Or indeed my own. I have very substantial information I am prepared to impart, but only to you. You see, I've been following your articles on the Tracey girl this week and I have to admit you're a very fine writer. It would be a shame to just do a press release and let the other media mangle it all, wouldn't it?'

Andrea did not rise to this. 'Okay, I'll see you in Townhill tomorrow at two. Don't be late. I'll be wearing a light brown mac.'

'Don't worry about that, Andrea. I know what you look like. Your photo's been in the paper. And I won't be late.'

Her photo had not been in the paper this week. Whoever this was had done some research. Andrea gave an involuntary shudder, but she told herself it was because of a gust of cold wind caused by someone who had just thrown open the door to the street. She pulled her coat round her and tucked her scarf in more tightly. She would not just sit around waiting till tomorrow though. She resolved on finding out more about Lauren Tracey's friends and acquaintances first.

First off was a trip across the bridge to Sebastopol Street. Despite Gus Reid's warning not to be too paparazzi she had decided to doorstep Zoe Delahaye. If the girl was as sensitive and in shock as he had suggested there was a good chance she would be at home, not at university. And so it proved. She answered the door after just a single knock and looked almost as if she was expecting this visit.

Andrea introduced herself and did her usual spiel that she was desperate to serve the public interest, but Zoe scarcely listened and did not appear at all suspicious of her motives. Some people clammed up immediately you revealed you were a journo; others couldn't wait to tell you their life story and the opportunity to list their many grievances. Zoe showed no emotion at all. She sat down in a large battered armchair and motioned for Andrea to sit on the settee. It was a black plastic affair partially covered in a yellow and black throw. Andrea perched herself on the edge.

'I'm sorry about your friend,' she began but Zoe dismissed the courtesy with a wave of her hand.

'We didn't know each other all that well. But I did sort of feel responsible for her, you know? She'd come back to university after a year out and her friends had moved on, formed new alliances, so to speak?'

The raised intonation that suggested a question when something was plainly a statement was something Andrea recognised as a nearly universal feature of younger people. It had shocked her when she first thought in these terms because somehow she was excluding herself from that happy band merely by being in her late twenties. 'I'd like to ask you about that,' she said. 'Did Lauren have any friends or classmates who might be able to shed any light on why she was attacked, do you think?'

'She started going out with a boy before Christmas but that ended quite quickly.' Zoe paused. 'We used to go to the pub sometimes. Um, I don't really know if she'd made any new friends this year actually. She was quite self-contained, if you know what I mean.'

'Really? Nobody I could talk to who knew her well?'

'There was one girl she mentioned a few times. I don't know if she still hung around with her. She's a third year at City. They call her Trigger but I think her name's Jane something.' She suddenly looked

223

round towards the kitchen door as if someone had entered or something had fallen over. 'Oh, I'm sorry, I didn't offer you anything to drink. Would you like a coffee, or a tea? I think there's teabags somewhere.'

Andrea smiled acceptance, but mainly to look round the room while Zoe was in the kitchen. Birds of a feather perhaps, she was thinking. Two sad lonely students who'd shacked up because all the good flatmates were taken. She saw Zoe's phone on the table by the window so she went over as if to look out of the window. She quickly found the album file and there was a photograph of Zoe and Lauren outside a shop doorway, taken by a third party. It was a sunny day. Presumably September then. Lauren had dark soft hair and was dressed in a navy sweatshirt and light coloured jeans. She had a quizzical expression on her face. Andrea closed the file and put the phone down just as Zoe returned with two mugs of liquid. It was not clear from colour or taste which of the options offered Zoe had gone for.

'I've remembered Trigger's surname,' Zoe said brightly. 'It was Hawkes. It was funny, I was reading a novel by John Hawkes. It's called *Second Skin*, do you know it?' Andrea shook her head. 'Well I was reading it when Lauren happened to mention her friend's name, and I said snap!'

'You wouldn't know where I could find this Jane Hawkes?'

'No. She may be back in Halls though. They keep the student accommodation for First Years but sometimes people coming up to Finals get them too. You could ask at Student Accommodation.'

'That's most helpful, Zoe, Thank you.' Andrea was anxious to get away but she pretended to sip at her tea/coffee for a further ten minutes, chatting about student life and asking the odd question about Lauren Tracey. Zoe seemed to know little about either topic.

Eventually, with a false show of reluctance, Andrea rose and excused herself. She expected Zoe to ask something about the exciting world of local journalism but she seemed to have slumped back into a torpor or some private misery. Andrea let herself out and closed the front door quietly behind her.

Though she was spending too much money on taxis these days she thought it would be best to get a cab to Townhill immediately.

She could simply have phoned Student Accommodation of course, but she knew that a friendly face usually achieved better results than a disembodied voice. With any luck she would find herself dealing with a young man, or young woman. It was an age thing not a sex thing. Older people were more suspicious. If this Jane girl had indeed moved back into halls she could try and locate her on the spot, or at least leave a message on her door.

She had to walk back across the bridge over the River Tawe to Sainsbury's to find a taxi but she didn't mind the exercise. She even considered walking further into town and possibly undertaking the long haul up Mount Pleasant (a real misnomer!) to Mayhill. From there it was a more leisurely stroll past some playing fields and an old water tower till you reached a roundabout with a tiny police station and a few local shops. The Townhill campus was a couple of hundred metres down the road from there. It was grand when you were up at that height looking down at the sweep of the bay and picking out the city's landmarks, but it was too long a trek, she decided. Maybe after she had found out what she could at the university she would take her ease on a bench on Pantycelyn Road, a narrow road that started behind the campus and circled round the city's steepest hill like a necklace. They said at night the streetlights directly below spelled out the word ELVIS but that was probably apocryphal.

There was a cab waiting in the car park of the supermarket and she was at the university within ten minutes. She asked the cabbie to stop at the main gate, for the reception building was just inside the grounds. Two men were watching her from inside as she approached. She pushed at the entrance door but it did not yield.

'Other door,' one of the men inside mouthed.

She went up to the counter a little abashed at her initial failure to negotiate something as simple as a door. She brightened. 'Hello, I wonder if you could help me?'

'Certainly try,' the older of the two said.

'I'd like to speak to a Student Accommodation officer if that's possible.'

The younger man ducked away to a room at the back and reappeared with a fresh-faced young man who was brushing away some pastry crumbs from his lips. 'Matt here is your man.'

'Andrea Linney, Evening Post.'

'Hi,' the young man said, still blushing, 'My name's Matt Eliot. Student Accommodation.'

Andrea could not help but wonder how he would ever exert any authority over maverick students, given his baby face and untidy snacking habits.

'Has someone complained about something?' he asked tentatively.

'No, that's not it. I'm looking for a third year student and I'm wondering if she's currently living on campus, that's all.'

He looked mightily relieved. 'Oh, good. We've got a small number of final year undergrads. Come on through to my office and I'll check for you.' He opened the counter flap and she squeezed past the two sentries, both of them grinning as if they knew something she didn't.

When she was ushered into Eliot's room she suspected that it was the grandiose word 'office' that had been the cause of their amusement. It was scarcely worthy of the name. It looked like it had once been a small storeroom and had been converted by the simple expedient of adding a desk, a chair and two filing cabinets. The young man pulled out a folder from the top drawer of one of these. 'What name were you looking for?'

'Jane Hawkes,' Andrea said.

It took him all of thirty seconds to locate the name. 'Yes, Miss Hawkes. Room 35. That's on the third floor of the building just across the way. I'm afraid the lift's not working at the moment. Would you like me to show you there? Sorry, could I ask what this is about? She hasn't been hurt or anything, has she?'

'No no. I just wanted to talk to her about someone she used to know.'

He gasped. 'Oh, is this about Lauren Tracey?'

Andrea would have preferred it if he had been slower on the uptake but fortunately he did not immediately adapt his manner and become official and obstructive. Andrea doubted he was fully capable of it anyway.

'It is, as a matter of fact,' she admitted. 'I just wanted a quick chat for some background on Miss Tracey. There's a great deal of interest in what's happened and my readers would appreciate some sympathetic picture of a life cut off so tragically.'

226

'Of course. I'll show you where Miss Hawkes' room is.'

They entered the building that faced the main entrance to the teaching block across the quadrangle and Andrea immediately smelled the smarting tang of bleach. The walls were painted a pale blue that had started to peel and, as she made her way up the stone stairs, she noted that the metal banister was also starting to rust. It felt like she had somehow been transported to East Germany circa 1984 and was entering a hospital or a women's prison. On the third floor Matt pointed down a long corridor and said, 'Number 35 is on the right at the far end.' He stood nervously till Andrea assured him she could take it from here.

She saw that there was a wooden frame for messages to be left on each of the depressing brown doors. This was lucky because it looked like the doors were too tightly fitted for a note to be slipped under. She had brought a notepad but she needn't have been concerned because Jane Hawkes answered immediately when Andrea rapped on her door.

'Come in,' she said gaily.

Andrea poked her head round the door and introduced herself. She was given a quizzical look. 'It's about Lauren Tracey,' she said quickly. 'It's terrible what's happened, isn't it? I gather you were friends. Can I call you Jane?'

'I go by Trigger actually. My mam even calls me that now. But Jane's fine, if you like. I've spoken to the police already so I don't know what help I can be. Hey, have a seat.' She sat down on the single bed and motioned towards the single chair in the room. Do you want something to drink? I could go and make a coffee. Or I've got a diet Coke?'

'I'm fine, thanks,' Andrea said. 'I've been chatting to Lauren's flatmate, Zoe, and she says Lauren was a bit solitary. But she did mention that you were good friends with her. Would you mind if I asked you some questions? You know, what she was like, who she hung around with, what she was into. Did she ever mention anybody she'd had a fight with? That sort of thing.' Andrea inwardly tutted at herself for possibly being too patronising in her tone but Trigger showed no sign that this was anything but normal talk, even for grownups.

227

'Well, as you say, she was a bit solitary. Didn't mix with people in our seminar groups particularly. But she got on with everybody really, you know, without being pushy. Well, everybody but that guy they threw off the course anyway.'

'Yes, someone mentioned there was an incident in a Creative Writing class, was it? Involving a lad called Ferie?'

'Creep of the first order,' Trigger said without hesitation. 'I think he fancied her but I can't imagine how he thought he'd have any sort of chance. God! I shouldn't speak ill of him really because I hardly knew him, but to tell you the truth he used to make me feel queasy when I even looked at him. Yes, ooh, I'd almost forgotten about him. He called himself Aaron, like that, rhyming with Darren, I mean. I always thought it was pronounced 'Air on' but it was 'Ah ron'. Lauren said once his name was probably originally Arrogant but he made the 'g' and the 't' silent. She was clever, Lauren was.'

Andrea wanted to tape the conversation but that might have made the girl more cautious. It was better to let her freewheel in this manner. To push her a little further she said, 'Did he overhear that, do you think?'

'Oh, she didn't say it in front of him. The only time she ever spoke to him, as far as I know, was the time when he read out his disgusting story and she called him a fricking pervert.'

'Did she say that?'

'I can't remember if she said frickin or the other word, you know, but she did call him a pervert. The room went dead quiet and George Wright, he was our lecturer, had to pull them apart, in a manner of speaking.'

'What does this Aaron Ferie look like?' Andrea said. 'I mean, was there something about him that was physically off-putting or something?'

Trigger guffawed. 'You ever seen *Lord of the Rings*? Imagine Gollum with bright red hair and bad teeth!'

'Ooh,' Andrea replied. 'I get the picture. 'But tell me, how did he speak? Anything distinctive about his voice at all?'

Trigger pondered this. 'Not so much, no. He was quite softly spoken actually. Normal accent.' She giggled. 'I mean normal for these parts. I don't mean your accent is funny or anything.'

'I'm from Tamworth,' Andrea smiled. 'People have commented on it. They think I'm a Brummie sometimes.'

'Nothing wrong with that,' Trigger said forcefully. 'I actually quite like it, oddly enough.'

Andrea let this slide. She was beginning to understand how Trigger had got her nickname though. 'Just one other thing,' she said. 'Did this row, or disagreement, or whatever you want to call it, between Lauren and Aaron continue after the class, do you know?'

'I wouldn't have thought so. Like I said, Lauren kept herself to herself most of the time. Anyway I think Aaron quit uni not long after that.'

'Quit?'

'Well, I didn't want to say, but he may have been asked to leave in point of fact.'

'Do you know why?'

Trigger looked down at the linoleum floor. 'It may have been something to do with exposing himself.' She sniffed. 'It wasn't to any of us girls. I think he was in the bushes by the car park and someone saw him with his thing out. He was staring at a young girl. She was the daughter of one of the bigwigs here, apparently. Don't know what she was doing on campus, mind. She was only about fifteen.'

All of this was fascinating to Andrea but there was nothing yet she could use for an article on Lauren's past. Nevertheless, it was powerful ammunition to offer DI Reid in exchange for something racy for a front page perhaps. She let the conversation float around for a while as Trigger spoke about student life, the price of canteen food and the shortage of decent boys on campus. Then she apologised for using up so much of her host's time and knotted her scarf to face the cold air outside.

She was thinking about the voice she had listened to on her phone earlier. Was that 'normal'? It had sounded reasonably educated but there was something about some of the extended vowels that definitely made it seem like her caller had a South Wales accent. People in these parts often said 'vairy' instead of a more clipped 'very' and his strange choice of the word 'mangled' had stood out. He had said it as if the word had two 'a's.

She stopped to take out her purse as she was passing the reception

229

building. There was one ten-pound note and a couple of pound coins. She looked up and breathed in hard. No more taxis today, she could walk down Townhill Road and wend her way back into town to the police station. She could even call Gus Reid and ask to meet him in Sketty or Uplands. Once she told him of her suspicion that it was the dubious Aaron Ferie who had asked to meet her the next day she could doubtless persuade him to meet her somewhere not too far away.

But even as she had resolved on this plan the younger of the two men who manned reception popped his head out of the door. 'No need to call for a cab if you're going into town, Miss,' he said. 'I've got to go and pick up the Vice-Chancellor from High Street station. I'm going now. Do you want a lift?'

Andrea smiled winningly. She was good at this she knew. 'That would be most welcome,' she said.

'Name's Peter,' he said as they got into a white Ford Focus with City University livery. 'You're Andrea Linney, aren't you? You write for the newspaper.'

Andrea laughed lightly. '*A* newspaper anyway. Would it be alright if you dropped me in Uplands?' She thought for a moment then decided to be more personable. 'It's big story I'm on. We don't get too many like this, you know.'

Peter gave her a wry look. 'Just as well. The quiet life suits me these days,' he said. 'I used to be in a different line of work. A lot more action.'

'Really. What did you do before?'

The man did not reply immediately. He was clearly considering what would be appropriate to reveal to a total stranger. 'I was in the army. Special Forces actually. Still, I get to wear a uniform in this job too.' He smiled to himself as he negotiated a sharp bend in the road.

42

I've been a bit extravagant. Sometimes it's unbecoming, trying too hard to appear original, but I just had to do it. Not just words but a lovely visual clue. I cut the back off an old blue folder I had. Don't know now what I bought it for, perhaps it was to keep lecture notes in. Nothing in it, of course. Then I invested in a Pritt stick and a packet of Paxo golden breadcrumbs. It's not a packet obviously, it's not a box either. If the place where I got them hadn't had self-serve how would I have asked for them? It'd be too weird to ask 'Might I purchase a cylinder or a tube of your very best golden breadcrumbs, my man.' The gentleman who serves me is from Pakistan, or it might be Sri Lanka – I know he's not Indian anyway. Fellow by the name of Nobil. If he has a brother I'd like to think of them as The Two Nobil Kinsmen. I don't say that to him of course. I don't think he's a great reader of minor Elizabethan dramas.

I went to the local because it's only a few doors away, though I did give regard to the thought that it might be better to be a little more anonymous about it. Those women at the check outs in supermarkets don't even look at what you buy. They just beep it across their little glass screens like traffic police waving cars through, chatting to Doreen or Yvonne on the next till all the while. But I went to the local because I was excited at my new scheme and I already had the Pritt stick. I didn't want to waste time going into town. However, I digress.

I wrote my message in faint pencil so that I could trace the letters in glue, then I poured the whole pack (tube? cylinder?) of breadcrumbs on it and left it for a tantalising ten minutes. Stupidly I did the pouring over the carpet, so if the crumbs hadn't stuck satisfactorily I couldn't possibly have retrieved them and I would have had to go back and repeat my purchase. Now that would have been suspicious! As it was, Nobil looked at me with that expression that says, 'I simply don't believe you are the type of person to make your own fishcakes.' I smiled at him. He dropped the change into my hand to suggest that he couldn't bear even the most fleeting moment of physical contact. If he had been a woman not a man he might have come to regret that slight, I have to say.

But all's well that glues well. A lovely two line message in golden yellow on a pale blue background. Where to deposit it now? I suppose I could take it with me to Townhill tomorrow but I find I am increasingly impatient. Where would the

231

Peelers be certain to find it and know it was meant for their delectation though?

If I'd stumbled upon my ruse a bit quicker I could have sent it by mail, but then I would have had to buy a large envelope and the Post Office person would definitely remember me. Large letter? Small parcel? Registered or special delivery? Shut up and give me a stamp, you feckless imbecile! I thought about stapling it to a telegraph pole, like a lost kitten poster, but it needs to be seen flat on. The trouble is, there's CCTV everywhere so it has to be pretty surreptitious, yet not observably so. Obviously I would love to have delivered it to the Evening Post building but that's not on because of all the people about and doubtless an army of cameras. That's what would have been so good about a message on the whiteboard in the lecture theatre, no cameras, hardly anybody about. Hmmm. I wonder if there's somewhere else up at Townhill that I can easily access but be certain that no one sees me.

If I had the MR5 on the road I could just drop it out of the window, but some do-gooder would only pick it up, tut and drop it in a litter bin. I can't use the car anyway so that's whistling in the wind. If only it was as easy as bribing a little kid to take it to the police station, or the newspaper office. They do that in those gangster movies set in Baltimore or South Central, but I guess you can bribe a kid with a popsicle or a corn dog (whatever that is) in places like that. Here in Swansea they'd demand a spliff or a gram of Charlie.

So here I am, armed with all the breadcrumbs a half decent detective would need if he was going to get it all solved before the ads come on, and I can't think of a way to stop the birds eating the trail. So it goes. 'The big show is in my head,' Vonnegut said. I think it was in Breakfast of Champions but I can't remember now. I want the big show to be on show though. And when am I going to be on TV? They've found Miranda by now but there's been nothing online about it yet. I give them a four piece jigsaw – all corner pieces, for god's sake – and what do they do? Nothing. Enquiries are proceeding. I bet they have to fill out a form to find their own arsehole. Wow! That was inelegant! But probably true. Bureaucracy gone mad, I tell you!

Enough of the exclamation marks, Aaron. We've all had a drink. Actually I haven't, but I like the saying.

***

When I was ejected from the family home I had to stay with an ancient aunt of The Major's. I say 'ejected' but of course it was more a question of self-expulsion

232

because it was me who burned down the whole shebang. Tee hee. The poor old thing was shocked at the loss of her third favourite nephew, naturally. And that dreadful woman he'd mistakenly married. But she was even more shocked that it fell to her to look after their offspring for nearly a year. I told her, the sadness in my voice like treacle on toast, I'd be no trouble and I'd be out of her hair as soon as I received the house insurance money. But we both knew they'd baulk at giving me anything if they could get away with it. Loss adjusters. The clue's in the title, isn't it? You suffered a loss, young sir? Let's see how we can adjust it so that we don't make too much of a loss ourselves, shall we? But they had to pay up in the end. Ha ha!

They stalled for ages though. Said they had to be sure about the cause of the conflagration, as they put it. You'll never pin it on me, guvnor, I wanted to say. I refrained and looked sad and lost instead. Then they wanted to arrange for builders to come in and restore the house to its previous state. What? That hell hole? They said I didn't need to worry about money, they'd use their own reputable tradesmen blah blah. I did actually give it some thought because I was going to get the money for the contents, whatever. Plainly there was nothing in there worth anything but still, you've got to buy furniture and soft furnishings, haven't you? Ooh, and cutlery and crockery. You might even have to re-purchase some of those stupid porcelain shepherdesses and china dogs. O mater! They were NOT tasteful!

To be frank, I was glad the firemen couldn't find any evidence of foul play and the insurance people had to settle. It seemed a small fortune when I was twenty-two. Turns out you need a lot more if you're going to avoid paid employment and you have to pay rent. It's an outrage that I have to pay three hundred quid a month for this poxy little bedsit but the landlord is a right dodgy geezer and willingly accepts cash. I don't even have to see him because I just leave him an envelope. Perfect arrangement for the both of us. You don't get that sort of deal when you go through an agency and I knew I didn't want to be on any sort of credit file, even before I embarked upon my recent adventures. Adventures in the skin trade, you might say. It's an odd coincidence but this place on King Edward Road is only fifty or sixty yards away from the flat where the mater and I were living when she met The Major. She called it Spud Road, which is, as far as I can recall, her only attempt at humour ever. I didn't laugh because I didn't get it then. I was only five. So we remove to the suburban paradise of a house in Killay at The Major's behest and all is hunky-dory. Until they meet their nemesis, that is. A year with the aunt in Tycoch that felt like a life sentence. God, that was awful. Then lo and behold, back in Spud Road. In my end is my beginning!

233

I gave a false address when I enrolled at City. Said I'd lost all my paperwork in a house fire, which would have been true if I hadn't planned the fire, I suppose. I didn't reveal that this domestic misfortune was in Swansea though. People don't check up if they think it involves too much effort and, let's face it, they were getting a few grand in funding for me to be there and that's all that really mattered to them. They did say they would help me sort out a student loan but I told them I was a man of private means. And somewhat private disposition, shall we say. I did even think for a while that I might stick it out for the three years but it was all too facile for me, in truth. Creative Writing, my arse! If they offered a course in Creative Thinking now, I would have aced it.

43

Gus called Jenny Sarka as soon as he thought she might have something to tell him. It was no more than he already knew, though she impatiently told him he'd have to wait for further particulars. Time of death was some time between seven and nine o'clock the previous evening. Cause of death, stabbing with a five-inch blade, non-serrated, probably a kitchen knife rather than a sheath knife. There were four wounds, the fatal one being to the back of the neck. Some clumps of hair had been pulled out but there was no evidence of any sexual assault. Scene of crime officers had already reported that they had found some of Miranda's hair on the kitchen floor. A frenzied attack then, with the perpetrator chasing the girl into the garden before administering the death blow.

This type of attack was invariably personal, despite the commonly held fear of total strangers bursting in and killing you. But if he and Tessa were right and it was Ferie, what was his personal connection to Miranda? On a whim Gus decided to call Josie. He didn't attempt any pleasantries, he merely said, 'Hi, it's Dad. Is there a character called Miranda in Shakespeare?'

Josie told him of course there was. A fifteen-year-old virgin in *The Tempest*.

'Anything special about her?' Gus asked. 'Does she hate men, for instance?'

Josie laughed. 'Well, she's only met two of them when the play opens. Her father and a native of the island they're on. She does meet another one, and she falls for him straight away. Typical fifteen-year-old, if you ask me.'

'His name's not Ferie, is it, by any chance?'

'What? No. It's a bit similar though, I suppose. Ferdinand, he's called.'

'Really.' Gus toyed with the two names out loud. 'Ferie, Ferdie. No, that's mad.'

'The island is a bit of a mad place,' Josie said. 'There's strange

235

noises and disappearing banquets and all sort of unrealistic stuff. Good play though. Why do you ask anyway?'

Gus sighed. 'We've had another murder. A girl called Miranda. She's not fifteen though and I can't speak to the state of her hymen, I'm afraid. No doubt I will be able to when the post- mortem's been done.'

'O my god, that's terrible, Dad. You don't think this is another clue about Aaron Ferie, do you? The islander, his name's Caliban, the only other man Miranda has ever seen, he's tried to rape her in the past. Do you think it's actually Ferie?'

'Well,' Gus said, 'whoever did this was not intent on rape. It was a vicious attack, like the one on Lauren Tracey. Different MO though. He seems to have chased her through her house and stabbed her as she was trying to get out of the back door. There was blood on the bead curtain affair they had hanging in front of it.'

'You're having me on,' Josie gasped. 'He thinks he's Hamlet, not Caliban!'

'What?'

'Hamlet stabs his father-in-law, or his intended father-in-law to be more accurate. He stabs him through a curtain, thinking it's his uncle.'

Gus was taken aback but immediately knew that this was not the same thing. How could the killer have planned to stab Miranda through a bead curtain? He'd tried to grab her before she got to the back door. 'He's no Hamlet, this one,' he said.

Josie almost chuckled again, despite the horror of what they were discussing. 'Are you quoting T. S. Eliot at me now?' she said.

Gus tutted and complained that he didn't know what she was talking about now.

'There's a poem about a guy called Prufrock – I think it's some sort of pun on Pru Frock, as in effeminate type, and/or Proof Rock, as in sturdy, reliable manly type. Like Dwayne 'The Rock' Johnson, you know?'

'Yes yes, never mind the puns. What's that got to do with this?'

'Oh sorry, me being all academic again. There's a line in the poem where he says he is no Hamlet, nor was meant to be. Is any of this making sense?'

'Not really,' Gus said. 'But thanks for the English lesson. Listen,

I've got to get on. But hey, can we get together and talk about something more savoury. How about that dinner we talked about? Any chance you can make it tomorrow night?'

Josie hesitated, but only for a second. 'Yes, of course. That'd be really nice. Where are you thinking?'

'I'll book somewhere,' Gus said. 'I'll be sure to make it somewhere where there's no mention of Shakespeare though, if you don't mind. I'd hate to see a pasta alla Cleopatra or some such on the menu.'

'There's no stabbing in *Antony and Cleopatra*, Dad. And anyway, what restaurant in Swansea- would serve Egyptian food? It just doesn't make any sense.'

'Nothing in my life at the moment does, Josie. Despite your literary theories.'

He ended the call and immediately called Tessa. She was attending the post-mortem and might have further details about the most recent murder. He also intended to tell her something of the literary connections Josie had just made. But he would put it a little less excitedly, and more in the spirit of noting some oddities, rather than claiming to have solved the week's two murders with little more than a copy of *The Complete Works of Shakespeare*.

Tessa told him she was finishing up at the mortuary and she would see him and the rest of the team before she had to go to a meeting with Terry Newlands at four o'clock. Gus texted Ben and Stephanie to tell them to be in the briefing room in half an hour. Then he sat at his desk and took out the spider diagram he had drawn four days previously. Underneath the quotation about lighting a candle he wrote 'To thy law my services are bound'. Then he added 'Sticks and stones' just in case. There was just enough room underneath to write 'I do suspect I have done some offence' but there wasn't room to complete the quotation. It didn't matter: disgracious wasn't a real word anyway.

He was still waiting for responses from Ben and Stephanie when his mobile sounded. It was Andrea Linney again. 'I'm a bit busy at the moment, Andrea,' he said. 'I'll be calling a press conference later on today though.'

'About Lauren? What have you found? Is it about the reconstruction?'

Gus paused before answering. News had not yet leaked about

Miranda's death then. 'Events are rather overtaking us, I'm afraid. You can't write anything till after this afternoon's briefing, but we've had another murder.' He heard a sharp intake of breath from Andrea. 'It's another young woman. Girl, technically. A seventeen-year-old was killed last night and it seems like too much of a coincidence to regard it as a separate case. That's about all I can say right now.'

Andrea interrupted him before he could continue in his officialese. 'Listen, Gus, can we meet right now? I'm in Uplands, in a café called Crumbs Kitchen. Do you know it? It's where a bakery used to be on Uplands Square. I think I may have something very important. Someone phoned me, and I think it might be the killer.'

Gus's first instinct was to be sceptical, but there was an arrogance about their chief suspect that meant he couldn't afford to rule out this possibility. A man who left clues to his crimes might well contact a journalist to offer some tempting titbit. 'I'm supposed to be in a meeting soon. Can it wait?' Then he stopped himself. 'No, cancel that. I'll be there in fifteen minutes. Tell me though, what did he have to say for himself?'

Andrea said he hadn't admitted anything but had said he had important information for her. He wanted to meet tomorrow. Had actually suggested tonight, but she had put him off because he sounded fishy and she was only prepared to meet him in daylight.

Fifteen minutes later he was sitting next to Andrea at one of two tables on the pavement outside the café she'd suggested. There was bitter chill in the air but it was more private than the tables inside. She had already ordered him a coffee. 'I got you an Americano,' she said. 'It's what you had in Costa last time. Safest bet, I thought.'

'Observant of you,' Gus said. 'Now tell me, what makes you think it was the killer who contacted you? And when did he phone?'

'It was about one o'clock. He rang the *Evening Post* office and they gave him my mobile number. It wasn't anything he said, more his tone. I interviewed one of the girls who was in Lauren's class and she said this Aaron Ferie guy had a quiet voice but was well spoken. For some reason that made me think of the voice I'd just heard. I know it's nothing and it was probably a crank caller but I had a spooky feeling, if you know what I mean.'

Gus put his cup down and shifted the annoying spoon from his

238

saucer. 'You say he wants to meet you? Where and when did you arrange?'

'I suggested a bar or a café, you now, somewhere bright and public. He didn't go for that. Then he suggested Lady of Lourdes church in Townhill. I said I wasn't much of a churchgoer but I'd meet him outside the primary school on the other side of the road. We agreed on two o'clock tomorrow.'

'He didn't give you any idea of what sort of information he had?'

'No. He tried a bit of flattery. Said I was a reliable journalist, something like that. But the other spooky thing was he said he knew what I looked like. I was going to suggest I'd be wearing a flower in my buttonhole or, you know, some sort of spy stuff. But he said no need, I'll recognise you. Then after he'd hung up I thought he must have done some research on me because I haven't had a photo with any of my stories lately. As I say, it wasn't so much what he said as the tone of his voice. Creepy. Over-confident, something like that.'

Gus decided this was something to be taken seriously. It could be nothing at all, but it wouldn't harm to have someone in attendance. Ben could keep an eye on Andrea from his car. Actually, there was a police station not far away so he could use a squad car rather than his own vehicle. If the man was simply a nuisance he might simply turn round and decide not to pursue his plan. If he was someone well intentioned and from that area he wouldn't think the car being there was anything unusual. Then Gus resolved that it would be better to have Ben on obo from an unmarked car after all. It could be the murderer. And it would be best to have someone else with Ben in case they walked off and needed following on foot.

'I know you've got misgivings,' he said, 'but we'll be there to oversee what happens. If he's got a car don't get into it. Indicate you need help and we'll be there immediately. We'll be very close by.'

Andrea gave a wincing sort of smile. 'How exactly do I indicate? You don't want me to shout, do you?'

'Wear a hat. Take it off if you feel troubled. Keep it on if everything's alright. A hat is perfectly acceptable in this weather and people take it off and ruffle their hair, don't they? That's what you do anyway. Got it?'

Andrea flushed with excitement but just nodded.

239

'If I'm right and this second killing is down to our man we're still going to have to do a press briefing at six this evening. It would be too suspicious not to. So I'll see you again then, okay?'

Andrea nodded again.

'Now I have to get back and try and stop the bosses panicking. We'll only be telling the press there's been another killing, so no serial killer stuff, understood? You'll ask us if the two murders are connected and we'll say we have not yet made any connections, okay? It'll probably be Tessa Penry doing the briefing anyway and she won't stand for any nonsense. I'm obviously going to be telling her what we've just discussed so she may choose to ignore you, so don't take offence at that. You'll get your big story one way or the other, don't worry. And thanks for this. You could have gone out on a limb and who knows, perhaps come to harm, but I'll make sure you're perfectly safe.'

Andrea smiled, fully this time. 'And all for the price of an Americano!'

Gus made a sort of gulping sound and went to reach in his pocket, but she brushed his hand aside. 'Only joking,' she said.

44

She bit my hand off. After a bit of argy bargy about my choice of venue, of course. Women are so stupid. You say 'I like your hair' and they fall over in a swoon and promise you eternal devotion. You say' You're a great journalist' and they drop everything to meet up and hear you tell them you love their hair. I exaggerate slightly maybe, but it wasn't all that hard. I've still got to persuade her to go for a little stroll with me, but it'll be daylight and there'll be people around. Pity it won't be a school day because there could be kids running round in the yard and no woman can resist the sound of a kid screaming with delight. But she won't be worried. Not till I get her close to my special place anyway. She may need a little persuasion then. Of the brick kind, I mean.

I've been thinking about posting my breadcrumbs on the church door. Nailing it, like Martin Luther. A tad less sermony, of course. There may be too many people around for that though. The other option is to stick it on the door to the storeroom. That would fit the pattern a bit better but I'm not that keen on the obvious. That's actually why I thought of the church in the first place. Less obvious than the Townhill campus. I'm going to say I've got something to show her (no, not a puppy!) and get her to come for a little walk with me. It's only a few hundred yards away, bear with me. When we get to Shinks' sentry post it'll just be a young woman and a bloke with his hood up strolling down to the car park. Nothing to see here. Then the tricky bit, but it's out of sight apart from the side door to the gym, and there'll be no one in there on a Saturday afternoon. All sleeping off Friday night's debaucheries. Then bang bang Maxwell's silver hammer, to quote from the modern bards. Well not modern, but in living memory I suppose.

It'd be nice to do the whole explaining thing. Sit her down, strap her to a chair, stuff a hanky in her mouth and just state clearly what it is in her that disgusts me. Tell her in no uncertain terms and, if I'm honest, in rather eloquent detail how it's all been planned. And that she's just the unfortunate one who got caught up in it because she just wouldn't give me the credit I deserve. Type of thing. But there can't be any undue kerfuffle. I'll have removed the padlock earlier but you can never account for everything. There could be paint cans or stepladders or scaffolding poles. Stuff that goes bang in the day. No noise please, we're trying to work here. I'm imagining it'll be like the garage on The Strand, but I could see

241

what was inside there and I know this place is used a lot more for maintenance gear so there's no telling what we might bump into. Literally!

Then, a letter to the editor, I think. Dear Sir, How is it possible that you could think it appropriate to send a little chit like the ravishing Miss Linney on a mission as perilous as this recent fiasco has turned out to be? Yours truly, and a bit perditiously in point of fact, A Concerned Citizen. P.S. Love the obituary column. Sports coverage? Not so much.

I neglected to do something that I wanted to do when Miss Minors and I had our little altercation last night. I wanted to stab her in the eyes, for looking at me like I was the lowest form of life she'd ever seen. Strangely, she didn't recognise me at the bus station though. She still regarded me with distaste despite that, however, and that's just not nice. I was thinking about the hands for Andrea Linney, because that's what she uses to cast aspersions on people. My first idea was to chop them off, but I can't be carrying an implement that would do that and obviously she has to lie where she falls. Then a brainwave, because I don't need to go overboard with the sadism, just something symbolic is fine. I've just found my suede mittens. They were in a box of stuff I don't want to throw but I don't know what to do with. Now they're going to be perfect. You can't type with big fleece lined mittens, so I've made my point and there's no noisy sawing or chopping to be done. Also, I may well need to make a sharp exit.

All sorted then. But what next? There's that pretty little black policewoman I saw up at college with the defective inspector, but that could be a step too far, even for yours truly. They've got stab-proof vests for one thing. And CS gas and truncheons and whatnot. She would have to be off duty and I don't know how I'd wangle that one. But let's not get too far ahead of ourselves, shall we?

45

Gus told Tessa about his plan to observe Andrea Linney's meeting with her mystery caller as soon as he got back to the station. They summoned Ben and Stephanie to the meeting. Tessa fiddled with a pen. 'What do you think are the chances it'll be Ferie?' she said.

'She just had a feeling that it was someone suspicious,' Gus said. 'Something about his voice too. She couldn't really pin it down though.'

'Wouldn't she be suspicious about anybody who called her out of the blue though?' Ben put in.

Tessa was looking dubious too. 'I suppose we can't afford to take any risks. Are you due to be working tomorrow, Willis?'

'I've got a long weekend off, as it happens, but don't worry about it. I want to catch this feller, ma'am.'

Gus turned to the board behind him and picked up a marker pen. 'She's meeting this guy, whoever he is, outside the school in Townhill. That's here.' He drew a cross in the middle of the board. 'If she's in any danger nothing will happen here, but he may just have chosen a random place and he may want to get her into a car and take her somewhere. I've told her not to let that happen. I know we could follow but it would be very obvious, and he could hurt her in the car and throw her out before we force a stop.'

'We didn't find anything useful on CCTV on the nights of the first murder. Nothing to suggest he had a car. I haven't seen anything emerging from Eaton Crescent at the pertinent time for the other murder either.' This was from Stephanie. 'Do you think it's possible he wants to lure her somewhere on foot? He may have chosen that location because it's so open and there's four directions he could go in. If he's suspicious of any police presence he'd spot us a mile off.'

Ben spoke again: 'And as soon as he does see he's being watched he could just say anything, offer this Miss Linney a useless bit of information and be in the wind again.'

Tessa still looked doubtful. 'What's his motive for harming

Linney? So far the only connection we've established between Lauren Tracey and Miranda Minors is that tenuous City University link. Linney isn't from Swansea, is she? Do we know if she went to City University to study? Check that out. Why would he attack her? And in broad daylight, as far as we can tell.'

Gus was anxious to keep his DCI onside. 'He wanted to meet her tonight, after it was dark, and he didn't want to meet anywhere in public. Andrea was being cautious. But it seems to me like he's anxious to get to her. That could be because he's genuine, of course. A concerned citizen and he's afraid there might be another attack.'

'Perhaps it's not the killer, but someone who knows him. And perhaps knows he's planning to strike again,' Ben said.

'If it was Aaron Ferie who killed Lauren Tracey, we're assuming it was because of some perceived offence, right?' Tessa turned to Gus for ratification. Gus nodded. 'And we're also going with the theory that if it was Ferie who then killed Miranda Minors it was because of something to do with his time at university. Agreed? Maybe it was a grudge against the mother but he found it easier to get to the daughter.'

'Or, Ben said, 'it's more to do with solitary young females. The City University thing is a coincidence.'

Stephanie was looking at the red X that Gus had drawn on the board. 'What if that rendezvous is a distraction? What if he's already calculated that we're likely to be waiting for him there, and he grabs her before she ever gets there?'

'That's a good point,' Gus conceded. 'I want someone watching Andrea all the time.'

'Is anybody watching her now?' Ben asked.

Tessa threw down her pen and leaped up. 'Okay. It's less than twenty four hours. Gus, do you want to put a uniform outside Andrea's house tonight? Stephanie, you'll take over tomorrow and stay with her all the time till she gets to the school. Get there well before time. You can arrange with the headmistress to go inside and keep watch from a window. Gus, what's in the area around the meeting place?'

Gus drew a circle to the right of the X to indicate a roundabout and a cross to show the location of Our Lady of Lourdes catholic

244

church. 'There's a community centre called The Phoenix Centre about here and some open ground here,' he pointed to the sketch, 'and houses down here and here and here. There's a little terrace of shops about a hundred metres down this way.' He thought for a moment 'And another couple of shops down this way.'

'Okay,' Tessa said. 'We'll need to find out if there's anything going on in that community centre. If it's open even. Ben, you and I will be in a car near the roundabout. Gus, what are you thinking?'

'I'm thinking he may want to get her to go with him to the Townhill campus. I just keep coming back to that. I know you said Andrea Linney has no links to the place but, and it is a but I concede, if it is Ferie, I think this whole thing goes back to his time there. I can wait somewhere nearby, if you think that's best, but equally if I wait at the university I can get to wherever else he's headed quickly enough. It's two or three minutes away by car.'

'There's two ways to get into the campus, sir,' Stephanie said. 'You can't watch both
at the same time.'

'Call me if he looks like he's headed towards the university. If he's coming across Townhill and he's intending to enter the campus he'd have to come in through the main entrance. If he sets off back down the hill from the roundabout he could still be going there, but he'd have to go back down to Uplands and walk all the way back up via Penlan Crescent. Either way, let me know what he does and keep in touch all the time.'

'Okay, 'Tessa said decisively. 'We'll all be in place a good hour before time. Stephanie, you'll have to let Andrea go on her own for the very last part, but keep her in sight. Anything else, anybody?'

Gus asked Stephanie to stay for a few minutes as Tessa and Ben left the briefing room. 'I take it you haven't been involved in any operation like this before? No? Right then, a couple of tips. What you wear is up to you, but make it as unremarkable as possible. When you're walking to your observation post in the school have something to hand you can be looking at, or looking for maybe, like a purse or phone, so you can stop for a moment and seem like you're in a world of your own. Obviously wear an earpiece but don't fiddle with it. If you're first to see our suspect, don't go all supercharged. Just report.

Look down as you do it so it's not obvious your lips are moving. You're probably thinking I don't need to say any of this because it's all common sense, but things can happen in a bit of a blur and you have to be completely certain of everything that's going on in circumstances like these. If indeed there is anything going on. Don't get frustrated if nothing happens either. There's usually a next time.'

'Thank you, sir,' Stephanie said. 'I appreciate you including me in this.'

Gus smiled. He hoped she would feel the same way when it was all over.

46

At her meeting with Terry Newlands Tessa had concentrated on relating what information was available from the forensic reports on Miranda Minors' death. She had skirted round the plans the team had for the following day because Newlands, as she had already learned, was not a man for detail. She rang Gus when she was released from the meeting and told him she would handle the press briefing. She also said that Newlands had once again raised the possibility of the Bunn brothers being involved but she had been able to tell him that Jugs and Darren had both been arrested on Thursday afternoon, 'They tried to break into a crisp factory,' she told him. 'It doesn't even make crisps anymore. I guess they fancied a snack, but they got a sandwich at the station in Cockett for their pains anyway.'

Gus had guessed that she would prefer to assert her authority by handling the press but he didn't mind. In fact, he was not sure he could trust himself not to give anything away. An eagle-eyed journalist might spot from body language that he had already conspired with Andrea.

'Newlands always wants an easy life and an easy arrest.' he said. 'Anyway, I need to go home, get some rest. You should too.'

He was not going home immediately, however. He had decided to reconnoitre the university campus. It seemed inconceivable that Ferie, if it was Ferie, would attempt anything nefarious in such a public place, but there was a boldness and conceit displayed in everything the killer had done thus far. Anyone who left cryptic clues for his pursuers was an extreme egotist. The chalked message behind the bin was one thing; the painstaking message in nail varnish another altogether. But to slip a note comprised of letters cut out of a newspaper under someone's windscreen wipers, possibly in full view of any number of lecture room windows, was sheer folly.

Night fell quickly at this time of year and though it was only just gone five o'clock as he entered the grounds there was an almost palpable desolation about the silent scene. He had noted previously that there was a small car park in the centre of the quadrangle between the halls of residence and the new part of the main building, He wanted to check sight lines from here but he decided not to simply turn right and park up because he wanted to make a circuit of the teaching block and see if there were any blind spots away from security cameras. He gave a wave to the man watching him from the Reception building and drove slowly round, looking for whatever might strike him as potentially dangerous. He stopped for a moment as he passed the most obvious place, a grassy bank that dropped away from the main car park. It was dotted with a few trees, denuded now in winter, and some low bushes. It was by no means a perfect killing site, especially as it was illuminated at this time by a yellow glow from the lights left on in the windows of the teaching rooms overlooking the bank. Unsafe now, it would be scarcely viable in the light of day, when anybody could appear. And Andrea would never let herself be led down there, Gus thought. He moved off in first gear. There was a big yellow industrial skip on his right as he turned back up the hill. It was next to what looked like a storeroom. It was made of thick corrugated steel painted a dark shade of green and Gus wondered if it had once served as a ship's container. The heavy bolts suggested that it could not be broken into noiselessly. He carried on past another skip on his left. It looked like it was full of shredded paper. Then he was back at the other end of the top car park. He found a space in the middle and checked what he could see ahead and in his mirrors. Not perfect, but he could see across to the Reception building and, to his left, keep an eye on the doors into the new building. He could also see both entrances to the main hall of residence. He adjusted the interior mirror so that he could more easily detect any movement behind him.

Satisfied that this would be a reasonable observation post, he got out of the car and walked quickly over to Reception. Les Jenkins gave him a querying look and Gus started to fumble for his ID, but there was a buzzing sound and he was ushered into the comparative warmth of the office. Gus showed the man his card and explained that he would need the parking space he was currently occupying to be kept free for him the following morning. Jenkins wiped his hand under his nose and jotted down the registration number of Gus's old

Mercedes. Another man in a blue uniform appeared from a side room and looked over his colleague's shoulder. 'What's up, Inspector?' he said. Gus was surprised at this form of address because he had not announced himself by rank.

'Just a line of enquiry, Mr?'

'Call me Peter. Everyone does. Peter the Porter.' Though he had a slightly worn and lined face there was a remarkable brightness to his eyes.

'Nothing to worry about,' Gus continued, 'but we would like to keep an eye out tomorrow in case someone we're interested in talking to turns up.'

'Is this about the Lauren Tracey enquiry?' Jenkins said.

'Yes, but please don't advertise that there'll be a police presence. That would kind of negate the point.'

'Awful shame for the family, that,' Peter put in. 'Respectful young lady, she was. Well-spoken too.'

'You knew her, did you?' Gus asked, a little surprised.

'Not really. Not to talk to. She sometimes asked me to ring for a cab, if it was raining. I think she did that so she could wait in here in the dry. I didn't mind, of course. She must have thought it would be too cheeky to call on her mobile and then barge in here.'

Jenkins interrupted his friend's reminiscences. 'Is it true that Mrs Minors' daughter has been attacked as well? There was something on the radio just now.'

'I'm afraid so,' Gus sighed. 'It doesn't mean there's a connection of course.'

'So you're looking for someone here?' Peter said. Then, nonchalantly, 'student or member of staff?'

Jenkins looked sideways at his friend. 'Now now, Peter, don't start getting an itchy trigger finger.'

Both men laughed. 'Private joke,' Jenkins said.

'Are you on duty tomorrow?' Gus asked.

'Wouldn't want to miss any excitement,' Peter said. 'You working tomorrow, Shinks?'

'I'll be here,' Jenkins said lugubriously.

Gus thanked both men and then turned again as he was leaving. 'If the man we're interested in comes here tomorrow we're expecting him to be accompanied by a young woman. She'll be wearing a brown mac. I'll be keeping an eye out from my car over there, but could you just pop out and give me a wave if you see them? Discreetly, I mean.'

Peter the Porter raised his hand timidly to the level of his shoulder. 'Like this, you mean?'

Gus smiled. 'Just stick your head out of the door and look in my direction, perhaps.'

Peter and Shinks were still giggling like schoolboys as Gus hurried back to the Mercedes.

47

The weekend promised to be milder than the past few days, with only a light southerly wind. Gus woke at his usual time on Saturday morning and immediately checked the weather from his bedroom window. There was a bank of light grey stratus cloud overhead that gave the world a sense of being locked in. It did not suggest rain, however.

He showered, made himself toast and coffee, and ran through various scenarios. If nobody turned up Tessa would be impatient and want to call off the exercise, but he felt they should give it at least half an hour. Who would wait this long? And out in the January cold? A journalist keen on getting a story. Why would Andrea's caller be late? Any number of reasons, but if it was their suspect, probably because of extreme caution. He might peruse the rendezvous well beforehand. He would see two people chatting in a parked car, a man and woman, but thus shouldn't arouse suspicion. Tessa and Ben wouldn't be able to park too near the school because of its proximity to the roundabout but they would be quite close by. Stephanie was to arrive at the school a few minutes after Andrea but she would be letting herself in with a key provided by the head teacher. Evidently a cleaner then. If he arrived after that and saw someone looking out of a classroom window he would still have to presume it was a cleaner.

If whoever came to meet Andrea was an ordinary member of the public performing what he saw as a public duty Andrea would soon let them know. But why would someone like that want to talk to a journalist in this surreptitious way?

If it was Ferie, they might be able to recognise him from the description George Wright had given. Or if not recognise, have a strong suspicion it was him. Short, ugly, red hair. The hair colouring was the only objective thing though. Unless he was extremely short. Tessa and Ben would be able to gauge his height by comparing it to Andrea's. She was 5'5". He made a mental note to call her and tell her to wear flat shoes.

He took a bite of his toast. It had gone cold.

***

Josie Reid woke up with a splitting headache. She had only drunk a couple of glasses of cabernet sauvignon the previous night so it wasn't a hangover. She tested her forehead to feel if she had a temperature, but that never worked anyway. She found a single paracetamol in a strip in the bathroom cabinet and gargled it down. It wouldn't do the trick, she knew. She would wait a little while anyway, but she sighed as she realised she would have to go out and get more painkillers. And something to eat, she saw, as she opened the fridge for milk. She could get a pizza delivered of course.

She had planned to do some serious work on her research today but her body seemed to be deciding for her that what was on the cards was only some light reading, or maybe daytime television. Also, sitting on the desk in her office were two or three of the important texts she needed to make some headway on her project. Perhaps she had left them there semi-deliberately. The trouble with being in charge of your own workload was you were always looking for excuses not to tackle it. Tomorrow maybe. But procrastination was a thief of your own destiny. As soon as the headache cleared up, she resolved, she would go in and get the books, maybe even spend a couple of hours working at her desk. Then she could come back home and watch television guiltlessly. She made herself some camomile tea and sipped it with a certain distaste. Head still throbbing, she emptied the cup in the sink and made a cup of Yorkshire tea instead. Medicinal, she told herself. Putting the nearly empty milk carton back in the fridge she abandoned her pizza delivery idea. She would ring her father and suggest they have that meal tonight. It would be a lot more nourishing, and of course he would offer to pay. And actually, it would be some company on a Saturday night.

***

Andrea was up and about early. The piece she had written for today's edition was still on her laptop as she opened it. She had

252

offered her own headline: 'Swansea Killer Strikes A Second Time' but the sub-editor might well improve on that. DCI Tessa Penry had refused to acknowledge that it was the same killer in yesterday afternoon's press briefing, but she knew from Gus's concern for her safety today that the police were convinced that they had a serial killer on their hands. She had asked Penry a few questions but elicited nothing she didn't already know. Nevertheless, what she had written was sensational enough without her having to resort to over-dramatic language. At first she'd toyed with the word 'butchered' and the phrase 'repeatedly stabbed' but she settled on 'viciously attacked'. Police were following up on a number of leads, of course, and the public were advised to be vigilant. The one liberty she'd taken was to suggest that the killer might have known his victims and perhaps have borne a grudge against them. She had heeded Gus's warning not to say anything about the cryptic messages. Hopefully that would be the line she could take when they caught the murderer. The Shakespeare Killer. She was dreaming of her piece being syndicated.

She was not apprehensive about her appointment. Perhaps it was foolhardy not to be, but Gus had assured her there would be eyes on her at all times. She was not to get into any vehicle and she couldn't imagine anyone actually attacking her in the street, even if it was a serial killer she was meeting. It would almost certainly be a crazy person of some sort, but more than likely it would turn out to be an attention seeker or conspiracy theorist. Still, it was an adventure, and perhaps something she could write about at some stage.

Long before time she took out the clothes she was going to wear. Jeans and a woollen jumper, flat shoes, the brown mac she had told her caller she'd be wearing and a brown suede cap, this last item as required by her guardians. She wondered about her rape alarm as she put a Dictaphone and pen and pad in her shoulder bag. Should she even arm herself? No. People who carried a knife were people who got stabbed, often with their own weapon. The thought made her wonder about the poor girl who had been murdered two days ago. In her own home! A person's worst nightmare.

It was still only nine o'clock. She turned her radio on, less to listen to a particular programme than to hear the soothing voice of a Radio 4 presenter. It might calm the jitteriness she was suddenly feeling.

***

Gus, Tessa, Ben and Stephanie were in the meeting room at Alexandra Road. It was twelve thirty. Gus had already told them that he had checked out where he intended to be at two o'clock.

'Should we engage as soon as the guy approaches her?' Ben asked.

'And say what?' Tessa snapped. 'You look suspect, sir, would you like to come with us?'

Stephanie was on edge too. 'What if it is our killer and he just walks up and stabs Miss Linney?'

'I've told her to keep an eye on his hands at all times,' Gus said. 'You'll obviously be doing the same. If he keeps them in his pockets and it looks at all suspicious she'll signal and you can engage. If he persuades her to go anywhere with him you'll casually get out of the car, Ben, and follow on foot. That's why I suggested you wear jogging gear. You can trot along the opposite pavement. Stop and do a warm down exercise or something, if necessary. Tessa, I take it you'll turn round at the roundabout and follow at a bit of a distance if he comes my way? If they go back down towards Mount Pleasant or off in either of the other directions just make sure they're always in sight. And let me know.'

'And if he just says a few words and moves off I'd still like us to keep an eye on him,' Tessa said. 'Even if he's a nosey neighbour I'd like to know where he lives and perhaps pay him a surprise visit later on.'

At just before one o'clock Gus drove back into City University's Townhill campus. Les Jenkins saw him and waved, unnecessarily enthusiastically. Gus saw in his rear view mirror that Peter the Porter was exiting Reception and walking across to the car park. As he drove into the quad from the other side he saw the man holding the 'Reserved' sign that he had just removed from the parking space Gus had chosen the previous evening. Gus wondered what he did all day. Like Les Jenkins, he was ex-army. Perhaps a stint in the forces made you regard orders, and a prompt execution of orders, a necessary and almost pleasurable part of your life.

He stayed in the Mercedes but lowered his driver's window to exchange a brief word or two. Yes, it was not so cold today. No, he didn't need a drop of coffee. Brown coat, yes. Also, a hat. No, he didn't know what colour that would be. The man smiled enigmatically and strolled back to his quarters, not with a particularly military bearing, but still with a sort of feline ease. The gait of a man who would instantly leap into action at a barked command, perhaps.

Gus hoped he was right about his theory that it was Ferie who had summoned Andrea and it was here that he intended to do whatever was on his mind. Perhaps make her write some message to the police about the deadly assassin roaming the streets of this seaside town? Perhaps forewarn her of some upcoming dastardly plan he had? He might mean to do Andrea some harm, but Gus could not see why. As Tessa had pointed out, there was no connection between Andrea and either Lauren or Miranda. As long as he did bring her here, however, he could be approached and questioned. And Gus would discover where he was living; his 'lair' as Tessa had put it. Thinking of this word caused him to remember using it himself, only a couple of days ago, with reference to Dotty Hawtrey's office. Funny how words could be ominous or merely jokey or sarcastic.

He considered again the wording of the messages they'd received. They were quotations, of course, but were they meant simply as sarcasm? The one about the candle could be a reference not to Guy Fawkes, or Macbeth, but an ironic remark about how little light the police would throw on the crime. 'Sticks and stones' wasn't a quotation but a childish saying, and the rest of it - 'words can never hurt me'- seemed to run counter to their theory that it was Lauren's verbal attack on Ferie that had been some sort of spark. But Gus was still unsure that this typed phrase was anything to do with the murders. The other two were quotations and had been scrawled using chalk and nail varnish. Wouldn't they all have been simply typed, if it was the message, not the medium, which was important? 'To thy law my services are bound' could clearly be seen as heavy sarcasm. Then, 'I have done some offence'. That was massive understatement.

Gus wished for a moment that he had read more. He'd enjoyed books as a child, but when it came to studying 'literature' his secondary school teachers had made such heavy weather of it all that he had been put off for life. Yet it was an integral part of Josie's life, something that flowed through her. She loved words, relished their slipperiness. She was quick and clever, whereas Gus was thoughtful, but slower moving. What was it that drove this psychotic killer to bandy these phrases culled from literary sources? And did he relish them for their multiple meanings and potential ironies? Or was he a self-taught oaf who regarded himself as clever but would trip himself up in his own tangled web?

***

Stephanie had arrived at Andrea's Mumbles flat at one o'clock, when the officer keeping an eye on the place was going off duty. She went upstairs, noting with some surprise the rich heavy pile of the red stair carpet, to find Andrea waiting for her on the landing. She was shown into a large front room on the first floor. The furnishings here were opulent too. Either journalists were better paid than people realised or the flat came fully furnished and was owned by someone with money and good taste. Stephanie walked over to a bay window overlooking the park, and beyond it the bay. 'This is a great flat,' she said.

'Yes, I was lucky getting it,' Andrea said. 'Do you want a coffee? When d'you think we should set off? Have we got time?'

Stephanie perched herself on a floral chaise longue in the bay window. 'We've got a bit of time,' she replied. 'We'll go in about half an hour. I won't have a drink though. I just have the one coffee a day.'

Andrea looked startled at this new idea. 'Well, I'll make myself one if you don't mind.'

While she was in the kitchen Stephanie examined the bookcases in the alcoves either side of the chimney breast. Lots of chic lit, some books on grammar and guides like 'How to Express Yourself Better'. Some travel guides to various European cities. Stephanie had only ever been to Spain and Greece, and France with her parents when she was too young to remember anything. Andrea was about the same age as her, perhaps a year or two older, but she was very different. Spoke differently obviously, but more than that. More cosmopolitan, perhaps it was. She guessed that was the word you used for people who knew about things you'd never even thought about. She'd certainly been to more European cities than Stephanie. Budapest, Berlin, Barcelona. Perhaps she just liked places beginning with the letter B.

Andrea returned holding a mug with a picture on it of a monkey sitting in front of a typewriter. She noticed Stephanie looking at it. 'Gift from a sarcastic admirer,' she said.

Stephanie laughed. 'My boyfriend only buys me underwear and perfume,' she said. 'I think he's trying to make me more feminine. Probably afraid I'll turn into a lesbian if I stay in the police force!' Her own laughter was a little forced and the two women fell silent, aware that they were only using up time before they had to embark upon a mission that might prove pointless or annoying. Or very dangerous.

**

Ben and Tessa headed out of the station at twenty past one. They used Tessa's car, a nearly new Ford Focus in metallic grey. 'It's perfect for observations,' she said. 'It's so bland and unremarkable I sometimes can't find where I've parked it in Tesco's because I can't remember what it looks like!'

Ben gave a sort of appreciative snort, but he knew his superior was just talking for the sake of it, or perhaps to relax him. He buckled up and stared out of the windscreen.

'Easy, tiger,' Tessa said. 'We're probably not going to see any action today. It's just an obo, keep telling yourself that.'

'I'm just a bit worried about putting someone in danger, if that's what we're doing. I mean, she's a young woman. Be different if it was a man.'

'And do you mean by that that women are not capable of looking after themselves, Sergeant Willis?'

Ben looked hurt. 'Obviously not, but this isn't just a drunk or a junkie lashing out at an innocent bystander is it? We're talking about a man who kills young women for fun.'

'Fun. Hmm. I wonder what sort of pleasure he does take,' Tessa mused. 'There seems to be a certain rage, but there's also this cold calculating side of things. The quotations, for instance. I haven't come across anything quite like this before, I must admit. But let's not get

257

spooked, shall we? We talk to whoever turns up to meet Andrea Linney and we go from there.' She started the car. 'Nice running gear, by the way.'

Ben looked down at his brand-new Nike trainers and blushed for half a second. He'd bought them straight after leaving work yesterday and Evie had at first rebuked him for putting new shoes on the dining table and then looked at him very suspiciously when he removed the tissue wrapping. She still looked dubious when he explained they were for an important assignment at work. He was fit, but he was not a runner. For one thing he was sceptical about the dangers of acquiring the sort of frame that runners had: they were invariably too wiry, too thin. It made a young man look old, he felt. Ben liked to think he had the frame of a central defender or a second row forward. He did not play either football or rugby however.

They drove up to Townhill in silence and parked a hundred yards away from where Andrea was due to meet her mystery man. As they were waiting, Tessa called the station with the instruction that the local sub-station be informed that a police operation was in place, just in case an over-zealous constable turned up and tried to move them on. 'Keep looking forwards,' she told Ben. 'I'll keep an eye on the mirror. I think Gus has been assuming our man will be coming up the hill from town but he could be local and he could come from any direction.'

'You mean local to Townhill, Ma'am?'

Tessa looked at Ben as if he had broken wind or been sick on himself. 'Yes, precisely.' She tutted and looked in her rear-view mirror, adjusting it for a moment to dab at her lipstick then readjusting it to see the road behind them.

Ben looked to placate his superior officer. 'Should I get out now and start jogging, do you think?' he said. 'I could be doing lengths of the road.'

Tessa considered this proposition. 'That's not such a bad idea. Give it ten minutes though. Don't want you too exhausted if we're called into action all of a sudden.'

Ben bent down awkwardly in the passenger seat to tighten the laces on his trainers.

***

At ten to two Stephanie parked her Clio illegally, half on the road, half on the pavement, fifty metres from the roundabout in Townhill. Andrea stepped out of the car a little unsteadily.

Stephanie wound down the passenger window and leaned across to offer some last words of advice. 'I'll park up while you go round the corner,' she said, a note of authority now in her voice that surprised both women. 'DS Willis and DCI Penry will be watching you from across the road. You'll see me walk past you and go into the school. Don't pay any attention to me, but don't look like you're deliberately not paying attention. Okay?' she added.

'What do I do if he's already there?'

'Just go and stand outside the schoolyard entrance. Wait till he comes up to you, then move off a little. I'll just walk past you. I'll look like I'm fumbling with my keys or my cleaning stuff. Keep him talking till I get inside and get to a window. Remember, you're not alone.'

These preparations were making Andrea even more nervous, so Stephanie gestured her away and started the car again. She turned in the road and parked a little further down the hill, in a layby by a cluster of small estate shops. She leaped out of the car and hurried back up the hill, to see Andrea standing rather forlornly by the crossing signal outside the school. There were no pedestrians around, but she saw a dark grey car parked a little way off. Two heads were visible above the dashboard but they were not recognisable at this distance. An image of Ben and Tessa Penry performing a lovers' embrace for the benefit of any onlookers flashed across her mind. No, surely not. Tessa was ancient. And Ben had a steady partner.

She brushed past Andrea, unlocked the school gate and approached the double door entrance. Once there she glanced briefly behind her but there was no one else in sight. She went in, her shoes clacking noisily on the tiled floor, and turned immediately right into the first classroom. Pulling up a stool she positioned herself by a window. She had clear sight of Andrea, who looked smaller and more vulnerable now as she fidgeted on the pavement. It was eight minutes to two.

At two minutes to two she saw Andrea's face change expression. A figure had appeared but was partially obscured by the pillar of the school gates. She willed Andrea to take a step backwards so that the person would step towards her and into better view. Andrea was not smiling but she did not look fearful either. If anything, there was a look of pity on her face.

'He's here,' Ben exclaimed. Tessa was struggling in her bag for a pair of binoculars. She pulled them out but Ben pushed her arm down. 'Not now,' he said, 'he's looking over at us.'

Tessa pinched her nose and blinked, then risked a look at the couple on the opposite pavement. The man was about the same height as Andrea but he was wearing a hooded duffel coat and looking down. She could not see his hair colour or much in the way of his facial features. Andrea was doing the talking and he seemed to be listening passively. After a minute or so they moved off westward. 'I think Gus may be right about the university,' Tessa said quietly. 'Let's give them time to pass then we'll turn round. I don't like this road though. Too open, and too many speed bumps if he suddenly gets into a car further up.'

'I'll get out here,' Ben said. 'I'll jog down to the roundabout and come back up on their side of the road. That should look pretty natural. I can easily catch up with them if I need to and Miss Linney looks like she's fairly comfortable. It's probably just someone reporting his neighbour or something. Don't you think?'

'I don't know,' Tessa said. 'We'll soon see.'

She watched Ben jogging away and adjusted her driving mirror again. Andrea and the man in the dark duffel coat were walking slowly along Townhill Road, apparently in conversation. She started her engine and drove slowly down to the roundabout. Ben was starting to come back, a steely expression on his face. Unaccountably he winked at her.

Andrea had studied the face of the man who approached her as best she could, though he had his head down, as if struggling against the elements. She was unable to determine his age, even when he did look up, despite a scrawny reddish beard which might have suggested someone in his early twenties, or even younger. The eyes were bright blue and expressionless. She saw that he had his hands in his pockets and she took a step backwards before he spoke.

'Andrea Linney? I'm Theo Burgess,' he said. 'We spoke on the phone yesterday.'

260

'What do you want to tell me, Mr Burgess?' Andrea was hoping the man would be intimidated if she came across as professional and impatient.

'You're covering the Tracey case, aren't you?'

'We've already established that, haven't we? What information have you got for me?'

'It's something I need to show you. It'll become clear when you see what I've discovered.' He gave a sort of smile, but it was not a pleasant one.

'I haven't got time for riddles or games, Mr Burgess.'

'Please, call me Theo. I'd like it if you would, you know. If you just walk with me a little way I'll show you something that will change your career. Your whole life, in fact. You can't say no to that now, can you?'

'Where are we going? If what you've got to show me is somewhere else why did you ask to meet me here?'

'I didn't. Townhill School was your idea. But it's just up here. Not far at all.' He walked ahead of her and didn't look back, confident that she would follow. Andrea had no choice but to catch up and try to press him further.

'You're being very mysterious, Mr Burgess ...'

'Theo, I tell you.'

'Theo then. If we're going to go somewhere I need to call my editor and tell him.'

He was unfazed. 'No need. We're five minutes away and you can be back at your newspaper office in twenty minutes. Or didn't you come by car?'

Andrea hadn't expected to be asked this and hesitated for a moment before telling him that she'd had a lift from a friend. Just in case he'd been watching her as she got out of Stephanie's Clio. He shook his head slightly. 'Boyfriend dropped you off, did he? Wasn't he jealous about you meeting another man?'

'It was a friend, not my boyfriend.' She was wondering if he had seen Stephanie and was testing her. He did not respond. Instead he waved airily over to their right, across the playing fields. 'Marvellous view over the whole of Swansea in a minute. You can't see it yet, but there's a bench on a road we're just coming up to, it's called

Pantycelyn Road, and I sometimes sit there to appreciate the panorama, as it were.

'Yes, I know it,' Andrea said, sounding more impatient than she meant.

'You're not from Swansea, are you? From somewhere in the Midlands, am I right?'

Andrea did not feel like going into any personal details so she ignored the question. 'Are you from around here? Townhill, I mean,' she said.

He smiled sadly. 'No, I just come here for the view, as I said.' He paused then decided to elaborate. 'I was brought up on an estate. The only view I ever had was of my neighbours going about their business. Not very edifying, to tell the truth.'

They had reached the end of the flat section of Townhill Road by now and had to cross over a roundabout to descend in the direction of the university campus. This stranger might be intending to head all the way down to Sketty but Andrea felt that Gus had been right in his guess at their likely destination. Just before the entrance gates, however, the man took her arm and steered her onto another street, a narrow curving one banked by council houses on one side but open on the other side.

'Pantycelyn Road,' he said triumphantly. 'And there's the bench I normally sit.'

Andrea disengaged her arm. 'I hope it's not just the sea view you've brought me here for. I'm a busy woman, you know.'

He turned back. 'No, I just thought you'd like a quick glimpse of the bay. Look what you could have won, sort of thing. We need to go over there.' He pointed at the entrance gates to the university.

'Will you please just tell me what you've got to tell me so I can get back to work,' Andrea said, still trying for an assertive tone but just missing.

'It's vital evidence that points to the killer, Miss Linney. I hope you brought your camera. And your little notebook, of course.'

Andrea pushed ahead of him but he quickly fell in step. As they were level with the Reception building he pointed off to his left so that his head was turned away from the windows there. 'You see, observe how Pantycelyn Road sweeps round the hill in an arc like a rope round a sack. A noose even. It's the same sort of contour as the bay. I like to think that these are two brackets within which people in this small town live out their lives.'

Andrea sniffed. 'That's very poetic, but wouldn't they both be opening brackets?'

The man looked at her quizzically. 'You can't have two opening brackets, Andrea. There's got to be a closing one.'

They walked down towards the lower car park,

It wasn't until they were ten or fifteen metres down this path that Peter the Porter threw open a door and waved across the car park to where Gus was sitting. He had been answering the phone and only looked away for a moment but then he saw a couple, a man in a duffel coat and a woman in a dark coat. He slammed down the receiver and burst through the door to give his signal. Gus, who had heard nothing from the rest of the team yet, was fiddling with his radio to try and restore Classic FM when he looked up and saw the man waving at him.

He jumped out and walked briskly over to where Peter was standing.

'That's the girl you were talking about,' Peter said. 'She's with a bloke and they've just ducked into our maintenance shed. It should have been locked but he just swung the door open and they've disappeared inside now.'

Gus ran down the hill and dived at the door, which had been pulled to but not closed properly. 'Andrea!' he cried. 'Are you okay?'

At this moment Ben appeared at the entrance to the campus, breathless but ready for action. He stepped to one side as Tessa's car lurched through the open gates. 'Down here,' Gus called out.

Inside the maintenance shed Andrea was half-sitting, half-crouching against a wheelbarrow. As soon as her companion had opened the door he had pushed her inside. She had spun round but suddenly felt a sharp pain in her stomach that doubled her up and caused her to collapse. She had only managed to utter a breathless 'oof!' She realised he had punched her in the gut and she was almost as shocked by the idea of this piece of savagery as stunned by the actual blow. She heard shouting outside and saw her attacker's face ablaze with fury now.

263

'Brought some friends, have we?' he hissed. Then he grabbed her hand and pulled her back to her feet. Somehow he contrived to hold both her wrists in one hand as he grabbed at something from his inside pocket. He pulled it out and Andrea saw it was a piece of blue cardboard. He threw it on top of a lawnmower leaning against the side of the shed. Only a few seconds had actually passed but Andrea was surprised that only now was she able to get any words out. 'Get your hands off me!' she shouted.

'Ferie! Come out now!' she heard from just outside the shed.

The man's face contorted into a gargoyle grin. 'Just coming,' he said calmly, twisting Andrea round so that she was in front of him now. She felt sharp steel at her throat though she hadn't seen the knife appear in the man's hand. He pushed her forward till she was standing in the doorway, though he was still obscured behind her in the dark of the windowless shed.

'Could you just stand back a little?' he said. 'Miss Linney and I need a few minutes to chat about something. About something she wrote in the newspaper actually.'

Gus took a step backwards to where Ben and Tessa were now hovering. 'Just put the knife down, Aaron,' Gus said, with as much composure as he could muster.

'Oh, I'm not sure I want to do that just yet,' Ferie said. 'But you are good, detective. I've left you a little note. It's just inside there on top of the lawnmower. You won't miss it. I was rather hoping we wouldn't be having this encounter till after you'd read it, but c'est la vie. All's fair. If it looks like a duck, etcetera. Have you got any clichés you'd like to throw in?' he was addressing Tessa and Ben now. They were both eying him intently and wordlessly. 'No? Hmm. Well, I don't see any armed police or helicopters, do you? So, I think Miss Linney and I will retire to somewhere a little more congenial for our little discourse. Move back, please, you're making me feel very claustrophobic.'

Tessa spoke at last. 'Aaron Ferie, I am arresting you for threatening behaviour, carrying an offensive weapon and, unless you drop that knife right now, intent to commit grievous bodily harm. There may be several other charges in due course. You do not have to say anything but it may harm your defence if you do not mention, when

264

questioned, something you later rely on in court.'

She had scarcely finished speaking when he burst out laughing. It was a strange high pitched giggle. 'You cannot be serious,' he said, in a reasonably accurate impersonation of an outraged John McEnroe. He pushed Andrea forward, still with the blade of his knife next to the white flesh of Andrea's throat. 'I hold my life as nought you see, but as it goes, I bear a charmed life anyway.' He raised his voice to a throaty snarl. 'Now will you stand back!'

Ben had been sidling round to his left, preparing to launch himself at Ferie's knife hand, but Ferie adjusted his position. He gave Ben a wicked grin. 'With you, goodman boy, an you please, I'll flesh ye!' He giggled again, then put on a sad face. 'Not a student of the great tragedies, eh? It's Kent. Kent the character, not the county.' Ben's expression was still resolute but there was bemusement on his face too. 'Oh, come on, *King Lear*!'

During this exchange Gus had been assessing the chances of grabbing at Andrea whilst Ben tackled Ferie. He reasoned that the man was high on the excitement of this stand-off and would not easily be talked down. He felt a hand on his back and realised that it was Peter the Porter. 'Allow me, sir,' he whispered.

Gus moved back a pace. 'Don't get involved, sir. We know what we're doing. We don't want this to escalate any further.'

Peter ignored him and stepped forward so that he was only a foot or two away from Andrea and Ferie. 'Let her go,' he said very calmly.

'Ah, the porter at the gates of hell!' Ferie burst out. 'But it seems you don't have your rifle to pick me off! I suspect I may have the upper hand, you whoreson cullionly barbermonger.' He shifted the knife slightly as Andrea tried to draw her head back.

'If you're talking about my air rifle, no, it's safely stowed away, lad.'

'What?' Ferie's face contorted with puzzlement at this calm reaction.

Before Gus or Ben could move Peter suddenly sprang forward and twisted Ferie's hand away from Andrea's throat. There was a yelp of pain and the knife clattered to the ground. Now Peter was behind Ferie, jerking his arm up behind his back in a movement so fast that no one had seen quite how he had done it.

Gus took out the pair of handcuffs he had in his coat pocket and

265

passed them to Ben. 'Do the honours, would you,' he said. Tessa started to repeat the arrest statement but Ferie interrupted her.

'Oh please,' he said. 'It's so crashingly mundane. Stop taking yourselves so seriously. When you look at it, life's a piece of shit; that's not Shakespeare by the way, but it should be. Oh, and the one in the shed is from *The Tempest*. Miranda. Apt, no? And I guess that's all from me, folks. Except perhaps this last one: from this time forth I never will speak word. You people won't know it but it's Iago. And not the one from Aladdin!'

'Barking mad,' Peter said.

Gus was inclined to agree. He turned to Andrea, who was being held round the waist by Tessa. 'Are you alright, Andrea? Sorry it all got a little too close for comfort.'

She pulled herself more upright and passed a hand down the side of her neck. 'No blood, is there? No? Everything's fine, Inspector. It all happened so fast I hardly had time to get worried. You were quick on the scene, thank goodness.' She turned to Peter, who had now handed Ferie over to Ben. 'Thank you. You were very brave then.'

'Not me, Miss. You were the brave one. I served, you see, and disarming insurgents was just part of my training. It's kind of like a taekwondo thing. Oh, and before anybody gets too het up about the rifle Ferie was talking about, that's just an urban myth. A story got round that I'd shot some pigeons in an exam room once. I shooed them out, is what happened.'

Andrea looked at him oddly. 'You just said you had a rifle safely stowed away.'

'Yes, miss. At home. But it's only an air rifle.'

A flashing light appeared at the top of the rise as a patrol car nosed through the entrance to the campus. 'Your lift's here,' Ben said to Ferie with evident satisfaction. 'Nothing to say? Well, there will be a charge, I'm afraid.' He chuckled at his own joke but Gus and Tessa just looked at each other as if he was their awkward teenage son. 'Well. More than one charge, in fact.'

'Don't milk it, Willis,' Tessa admonished, but without rancour.

'Do you think he's going to confess to the murders, or just keep schtum?' Gus asked Tessa as a uniformed officer helped Ben push Ferie into the patrol car.

'He said he's not going to speak,' she replied. 'But when we know where he lives and we've done a search there should be plenty of physical evidence. He may have read a lot of books but I don't think he's all that bright, do you?'

Gus thought about it. 'And I'm pretty certain he won't stay silent for long either. Loves the sound of his own voice too much.'

'Or Shakespeare's voice,' Tessa said. 'He appears to be someone who can only talk in quotations. Weird, that. I can never remember any of the stuff I was supposed to learn at school.'

'I didn't learn enough to fret about remembering it,' Gus said hopelessly. 'But you can get by with knowing something about human nature, can't you?'

'My English teacher told me Shakespeare was the person who invented the idea of human nature. I never quite understood that.'

Gus looked up at the brightening sky. 'My daughter Josie tells me there's a lot of good stuff in his plays. Maybe I'll go and see one or two some day. Can't imagine reading any of them, I must say.' At that, an astonished look came over his face. 'And here she is!'

Josie had suddenly appeared behind him. 'Pat, like the villain of the tragedy,' she said. 'Is that Aaron Ferie you've just bundled into the back of that car? Is that the ogre you've been chasing? He is odd and you are even with him, I see.'

'What?'

'It's a play on words. In a play about words.'

'I hope you're not quoting Shakespeare at me, young lady,' Gus said sternly. 'We've just been subjected to a barrage of that from our suspect over there. He even told us which plays he was referring to, the smug bastard. It's not a good look, Josie.'

'Sorry, dad,' Josie simpered, as if she were eleven again.

'What are you doing here anyway?' Gus asked. 'Don't you academic types have the weekend off, unlike us servants of the law types?'

'I had to come and retrieve some stuff for the project I'm working on. How did you track him down to this place though?'

'Mr Ferie led us here, almost deliberately, it seems,' Tessa said. 'As you say, he's a very odd character. Seems to fancy himself as a villain out of Shakespeare. I gather you helped your father with one of the quotations he teased us with?'

'Hopefully, yes. I'm a servant of the law myself, it seems.'

Gus pulled her gently to one side. 'If you've got your stuff I'll get one of our officers to give you a lift home. This is a crime scene now.'

She smiled. 'Okay. Are we on for dinner this evening though?'

'Why not,' Gus said happily. 'There's got to be something we can discuss in our own words, rather than snippets of sixteenth century iambic whatever it's called. I'll call you as soon as I've done with interviewing Mr Ferie. He's promised to hold his tongue. Maybe he'll give us a break and refuse to speak until tomorrow at least. I can have the evening off then.'

48

That evening Gus and Josie met in a restaurant which he hadn't frequented since he had split up from Adele. The irony was not lost on Josie.

'Wasn't this mum's favourite restaurant?' she said.

'She dragged me here quite a few times, yes. I'm not that fussed about the food but the view is amazing, don't you think?'

They were in The Grape and Olive, a restaurant on the top floor of Swansea's highest tower building. There was a view out across the bay but Gus had asked for a table with a view back over the city.

'Maybe I shouldn't be talking to you like this about her but you know what she was like. One time she complained that she hadn't been given enough prawns and demanded another portion. The waiter brought over a pint glass filled with these giant prawns. He was being sarcastic, you know? She emptied the whole lot into her handbag and gave him back the empty glass. We didn't come back for some time after that, it's safe to say. Also, she had to throw the handbag out because she left the damn things in it overnight and it stank to high heaven. The staff seem to be new now though, so we should be safe from any waiters' wrath.'

'I know mum's pretty erratic. She's even worse these days. but I used to blame you for the divorce, you know,' Josie said.

Gus knew this and knew too that he had been too stubbornly absorbed in his job to pay enough heed to his failing marriage. 'I take my share of the blame,' he said. 'You and your brother kept us together for the last few years. Your mother and I'd seen too much of each other's faults but neither of us was quite prepared to sacrifice you two on the altar of our egos. Until I couldn't stand it anymore, of course. I'm sorry about how you must have felt back then.'

Josie reached over the table and laid her hand on his arm. 'It's a long time ago now. I've got some experience of trying to make it work with the wrong people myself, I'm afraid.'

'Are you talking about George Wright?'

'George? Good heavens, no. He's a married man, dad. Well, sort of anyway. No, I can handle George alright. He's a pussycat really. You know what he said to me the other day about old Dotty Hawtrey, you know, the dragon lady secretary? He said you had to cross your eyes and tease the Dot. Quite clever really, except he's terrified of her in actual fact.'

'That is quite clever. You two wouldn't make a bad couple, I'm thinking, if he weren't married already. You'd have super intelligent kids anyway.' Gus took a gulp of his Barolo.

'Probably best to lay off the relationship advice, I'd suggest,' Josie countered with a laugh. 'But what about you and your boss lady? Tessa, is it? Any prospects there, dad?'

Gus shook his head. 'Too rich for my blood,' he spluttered.

'If she's rich you should make a grab!'

'You know what I'm talking about, Josie.' He knew he was being teased but he was glad to be chatting so pleasantly again with his daughter. Too much time had slipped by with both parties pretending that they didn't need an occasional evening like this.

They looked out at the city and the twin mounds of Townhill and Kilvey Hill. A giantess on her back, Gus thought. Resting now. The streetlights were strung around Townhill like a necklace of yellow diamonds.

'It looks so different from here, doesn't it?' Josie said. 'Almost Mediterranean. It doesn't feel like that when you're walking around.'

'It's a bit safer to walk around now, that's my main concern.'

The waiter arrived with their main course and they fell silent for a while as they ate, Gus picking thoughtfully at a whole sea bass and Josie joyously forking spaghetti with clams. When Josie spoke again it was about the case. Gus knew she would want to know all the details and had already settled on how much he was prepared to tell her.

'What did you find when you searched where he lived?' she asked.

'We may have found the weapon that he used to knock Lauren out before he strangled her. It's been sent for analysis. It was a brick. He hadn't even hidden it. We also found Lauren's keys. No sign of any of her other possessions, but you'd presume he would have disposed of them pretty sharpish. The main thing was a book though. A journal, I suppose you'd call it. It was the diary of a mad man. We think it's fairly certain he killed his parents, though it's possible that was just him fantasising. He's not saying anything yet, but the entries in the journal alone will keep him banged up for pretty much the rest of his life. Broadmoor, rather than prison, we suspect.'

'Did it say why he killed poor Lauren Tracey?'

'There was a rant about how she'd humiliated him and how she got what she deserved. His precise words were "When I laid her to rest", as if he was being thoughtful. We were always of a mind that the killings weren't sexually motivated but he clearly fancied her. But he also plainly knew he'd never stand a chance.' Gus exhaled deeply. 'From his scribblings in this diary thing it seemed as if his beef with Miranda was more to do with her mother, who was apparently implicated in his expulsion from university, but it was almost certainly sexual too. Peter the Porter, the guy who grabbed him when we were trying to arrest him, he was helpful about that. Ferie had flashed her from the bushes a couple of years ago and the poor girl wasn't just terrified. She was horrified. The look of disgust on her face was enough for him to harbour a deep hatred towards her. She was just unlucky she ran into him while he was on this rampage.'

'And what was all the Shakespeare quotation stuff about?' Josie said. 'It sounds to me like he had some fantasy about being a superman, but he was comparing himself to Richard the Third and Caliban. They're two of Shakespeare's more freakish creations.'

'Yes, I gather. Iago too though, though I gather he's supposed to be very clever.'

'What were the Iago references? They were in this journal, were they?'

Gus nodded. 'Something about a motiveless malignity. I'm told that was what a famous critic called Iago. But it makes no sense. Ferie was all about revenge. He was envious, sexually frustrated, and bitter about what he thought people were saying about him. Hence the attack on Andrea Linney. He was going to kill her for calling him a crazed killer with a grudge. I thought that was rather an accurate portrait myself. Then, and this was pathetic, when we found the message he was going to leave for us in the maintenance shed it turned out to be a quote from Miranda in The Tempest. "Make not too rash a trial of him" it said.'

'That sounds like a whimper, not a challenge. Do you think he would have been done after today? Or did he have some kind of blood lust? I wonder who he might have targeted next, if you hadn't caught him.'

Gus winced. 'That's the scary thing. There's a reference in his diary to one of our young constables. Girl called Stephanie Beddall. Actually you met her, didn't you?'

'Yes,' Josie said. 'Pretty little thing.'

'Woah, that's more or less exactly what he called her. I don't know what motive he'd have tried to come up with to justify attacking her, but she might have been next in his twisted list.'

Josie looked thoughtful. 'That's horrific,' she said. 'Will he plead guilty, do you think? He'll have to, won't he, if you've got all this evidence of his planning?'

'He'll plead insanity, I should think. The voices were ordering me blah blah. Shakespeare was telling me, I could hear the iambic ... oh, what is it again?'

'Pentameter, dad.'

'Shakespeare's got a lot to answer for is all I can say.'

'You should get to know him better perhaps. There's a *Macbeth* coming on in The Grand Theatre later this year.'

'That's the one with the murderous wife, right? No thanks. Bit too close to home. You might just about be able to persuade me to see a comedy though. Does he do funny?'

Josie smiled happily. 'Yes, dad, Shakespeare do do funny. Actually I'm going to be running a trip to Stratford soon. You should come along. I'll get hold of tickets for *The Dream* or *As You like It*. You'll like them. No monsters with knives and bricks, just folk larking about in the forest.'

'Forest eh? Now that sounds suspicious. They're not burying bodies, are they?'

Josie laughed at this. And it felt good to be laughing.

Acknowledgements

I would like to thank the people who kindly read early drafts of this novel and made helpful comments and suggestions. These included the inevitable corrections involving authenticity and consistency but also some very interesting ideas which I did my best to incorporate. So, my gratitude to Ben and Janet Kehoe, Mike Neale and Paul Webb and, as ever, Jamie and Pat.

Also by Lloyd Rees

Novels

Don't Stand So Close
The Show-Me State
Voices Without Parts
The Mondegreen Affair

Poetry

To Liu and All Mankind
Swansea Poems
Mangoes on the Moon
Simple Arithmetic
The Two of Us

CPSIA information can be obtained
at www.ICGtesting.com
Printed in the USA
BVHW030302060922
646255BV00015B/436